ARCHER'S GRACE

BOOK ONE DAHLQUIN CHRONICLES

ARCHER'S GRACE

By
Anne M. Beggs

Dedication

This book is dedicated to my family.

To my husband, Russell J. Beggs, DMD

To my daughter, June

To my son, Steven

With love, respect, joy and gratitude.

ACKNOWLEDGEMENTS

This book and these stories would never have been committed to paper or "e" if not for the encouragement of my beloved, devoted family. My husband, Russell J. Beggs, DMD; and children, June and Steven, who listened to the stories on road trips and demanded I write them down.

Next - to my dearest friend, June Nichols; Uncle John and Cousins Michelle, Chris and Bill who endured 700 pages of head-hopping tripe and exposition, and still called me *Author* and encouraged me to keep writing. You guys, dang! It was bad. Hopefully, you won't recognize this book from that doorstop. Thank you.

Thank you to Professional Editor Douglas Childers, who also saw through the rough 700 pages and didn't shame me out of putting fingers to keyboard. Thank you to Historical Editor Jody Allen who provided much guidance, research and encouragement.

To my writer's groups, especially Cathy Cress and Eiko Ceremony who read through two full manuscripts and gave helpful, needed critique. Thank you.

Again, to Cathy Cress who continued to guide and drive me through marketing, social networking and to publish **no matter what**.

Huge, thank you to my daughter, June, for her ardent support as editor and proofreader.

And very special thank you to and gratitude for Editor Thomas A. Simmons, who pushed, prodded, motivated and enlightened. Thank you for enjoying my stories as I wanted to write and helping me to publish. Prosit.

FORWARD

This book is a work of fiction, with most characters and places being imaginary.

I may have researched the Middle Ages into middle age and beyond but have chosen to write my characters and their stories outside the historic framework. I can recommend many textbooks and resources online for hard core history. Because my Medieval fetish runs long and deep, research has been as much fun as writing-however, my characters speak with greater urgency.

I do attempt to recreate everyday details of life, food, dress, and living as much as I can within the fictional world I have built.

PART ONE

DAHLQUIN, CONNACHT, IRELAND, AD 1224, 7th of June

The hunter acknowledged there was always risk leaving the security of the castle with naught but two hounds, a steed, bow and arrows, but mayhap the greater risk lay in missing this glorious ride altogether. Absence of rain was celebration enough. Hounds and horse and red deer devoured the turf in joyous strides in their natural world where heaven and earth were one.

Fatigue and thirst brought the partners to water where the old stag, too, drank. Dismounting, the hunter tethered the wire-haired hounds to a yew. Tails low, heads drooping, the restrained hounds gazed up, their wet, brown eyes enlarged with beckoning as the hunter ordered silence before remounting.

The hunter peered through the coppiced hazel and brambles, attentive to each flare of nostril or blink of the red stag's eyes before slowly drawing the bow, *Cara* by name, which meant friend, companion. And so it was: a short, straight bow of pure mountain yew from Connacht's highest forest, strung for a fast, light pull from ground or horseback. The hunter shot many bows, but *Cara* seemed to sing in the hand, the soul of the ancient tree reborn in this weapon, this guardian of Dahlquin.

Anchor. The hunter sought the feel of this new hand placement, not at the edge of the mouth as before, but past the collarbone, nearly to the shoulder, the mounted archer's stance. *Steady old friend*, the hunter thought as the stag lowered his head to drink, weary from the morning's chase. Only a heart or lung shot would satisfy for there was no honor in a clumsy kill.

Release. The broad head disappeared into the furry chest without a sound. Four cloven hooves sprang from the earth. The tethered hounds yipped then barked. Had they heard the string? Or was it the scent of blood revealing success?

The dappled stallion flinched. Alert, the stallion turned his head to the left, slowly returning his attention to the hunter.

"Easy Garth, good boy," cooed the hunter stroking the sweaty mane and neck of the horse, as much for the sake of the dying stag as the noble steed. Blood spread from the puncture wound in a widening circle on the heaving stag. Now began the wait for the wounded animal to bleed out. A prolonged chase would taint the flavour of the meat and dishonor the spirit.

After a few cautious glances, the stag lowered his head to graze. Scarlet ribbons unfurled from the stag's nostrils; the pools startled him. Lifting his head, he tried to swallow but instead coughed, blood foamed from his mouth. Even his eyes seemed sanguine tinged to the grateful hunter.

With head bowed, the hunter made the sign of the cross and gave praise. "May you have goodness, Blessed Mother and Queen of the Forest." Another voice was reciting the prayer, startling the hunter.

"Nice shot, Eloise. Even with that light bow, you buried the fletch."

"Tommy!" the hunter yelped, her long, amber braid swinging to her side. "How long have you been here? And Nova," she added recognising her pony.

Tommy, a shortened version of his name Tomaltach, Eloise's childhood playmate, was a pigeon-boy-turned-archer and apprentice bowyer. Social standing had made little difference to these two co-conspirators of disguise. Both now in their seventeenth year, it was a new dynamic and not so easy to exchange garments and identities.

"Stable master sent me after you. On your pony, Saint Sebastian be praised, because the old King of the Forest gave you quite a 'harty' chase," Tommy grinned. "Glad I wasn't on foot."

Eloise chuckled at his pun, and the deep register of his voice still gave her pause. Such an odd boy. Not a boy. A man, she remembered.

"As I've said before, you would make a suitable game warden. Your stealth. Some quiet mastiffs instead of those hunting hounds. Taking the thieving poachers down with your arrows," Tommy said, grinning.

"And you," she added, remembering the dreams of youth.

"Your mouth is bleeding," Tommy said, his green eyes wide with concern.

Eloise tasted blood but felt no pain. "Fletch burn," she offered, hoping that would appease.

"Is not, you shot from the chest. I saw you," Tommy corrected.

Curse your attentiveness, Eloise thought, shrugging, looking to the stag as he tottered then collapsed.

"Guilt of the Huntress," Tommy said.

Eloise turned to him, stung by the words. "What?" she asked, wishing her voice had been as sure as his. She wasn't…an anomaly.

"Your father's term," Tommy said gently. "You bleed when you kill."

Tommy dismounted to check the stag for a pulse. "Do you want to carry it back or should I?" he asked.

"I'll loose Beast and Dragon," she said, turning toward her two loyal companions still tethered to the yew, relieved at the change of topic. "You take the deer," she answered. "The Old King," she sighed, crossing herself again. "Tough in life and tougher on the trencher," she smiled.

"I'd wager that. But it won't grant your parents' forgiveness, sneaking off as you did," he answered, now serious.

Her shoulders slumped with the reminder. Then she let her breath out and rolled her eyes at Tommy. "Want to trade costumes so I can sneak back in?" She felt herself sparkle with renewed hope.

"That rustic tunic, I would not," he grinned. "But you know I'd kill for the chemise," he winked.

They shared a quiet gaze. Eloise remembered the beatings he had endured for the love of wearing female apparel, well beyond any childhood disguise.

"With or without me?" she asked, trying for an adult smile. A flush of embarrassment roasted her as she tried to bury the sudden image of herself and Tommy together in the chemise.

"Don't tease," he said. His shoulders went slack, but his face took on an impassive expression she didn't recognise.

It sent a shiver through Eloise. *Why did I say that?* she wondered, feeling guilty. *And why did he look at me like that?*

DAHLQUIN CASTLE, A. D. 1224, 7th of June

Walking toward the kitchen, Eloise inhaled. Her stomach tightened as she savored the aroma of venison broth, leeks and hearty gravy. Smiling, Eloise and her mother entered the kitchen, noisy with the sound of three to ten workers chopping flesh or vegetables, pounding dough, plus the familiar voices barking orders, gossiping or singing-always.

The walls were slate grey stone with two large doorways at either end, with one window. Dahlquin had a stone oven for baking bread in the kitchen as well as a baking silo outside the kitchen. The blackened stone hearth was tall enough for a short man to stand in, and twice as long. Metal hooks hung from the top. Today a large, ebony cauldron and two medium kettles hung in the flames. A large metal rack, with three bars, like ladder rungs, was standing in the hearth with the browning and dripping haunches roasting on the highest bar. Soon cockerels would be added. This was the late spring feast that awaited Dahlquin and the guests.

"Uninvited guests are the scourge of hospitality," old Muireann the head cook muttered. Generally noisy, the castle kitchen buzzed with heightened excitement.

"Remember, if you turn away my brother, so you turn away me," someone recited as a reminder.

"That's true for beggars and the like, not well-fed noblemen," another kitchen worker complained above the noise. Seven hungry strangers, for there was no other kind, had ridden to Dahlquin Castle this very day.

"Could be angels, or even our Lord and Savior Jesus in disguise," Eloise chimed in, not believing it. Not this time anyway.

Eloise and her mother, Lady Aine, concluded the details of the evening's feast with the head cook. A banquet, unplanned and spontaneous, required all workers to task: more bread to bake, soup to be stretched.

"Blessed be you delivered the old hart, Maid," Muireann said, jerking an elbow towards the workers about her. Eloise saw haunches on the spit and stripped bones being dropped into the roiling cauldrons. Muireann with cleaver in hand, continued mincing the toughest cuts. "For surely it saves us that mutton for the next emergency."

"Don't encourage her," Aine said, casting a reproachful green-eyed gaze at Eloise. As always, her mother was grievously displeased by the early morning hunt.

"I wasn't alone," Eloise added, trying again to reassure her. She was far safer astride her Garth, Beast and Dragon at her side riding in the unconquerable beauty of Dahlquin than in any estate or village she could imagine. "Oh, splendid day with sun, and now we've guests," she said, unable to suppress her smile.

"Enough," Aine said sternly, handing a leather-bound ledger to Eloise. "By your will, finish the accounting."

"Where is the Seanascal? It's his job to manage," Eloise whined, more petulantly than her usual seventeen-year old self. A tedious task when they had unexpected guests to dress for, and she with a beautiful new surcoat to wear. She frowned, remembering the unfinished surcoat. *More drudgery…to redo that impossible front seam, and add the trim, and see to the hems.*

"The Seanascal is with your Lord Father, interrogating the seven strangers, not *guests*", her mother emphasized. "We need an accounting of all supplies used and remaining. And, since you need reminding," her mother added, "it is foremost your duty as the daughter of Dahlquin to manage than his."

Eloise sighed. *Couldn't this wait until tomorrow?* Guests were a special treat at Dahlquin, a remote castle in western Connacht that guarded the frontier. Good Christian knights were a rare commodity compared with the merchants, jongleurs or unscrupulous raiders: a time to hear news, gossip and tales. Songs, dances, or games might be shared, and the people of Dahlquin could send word of the events in their lives to the other estates of Ireland and beyond.

"Very good, Muireann," Aine said to the cook. "I'll leave you to it." She turned to her daughter. "Eloise, finish tabulating the barley, onions, flour and suet used then meet me in the garden, unless you prefer to spin." As Aine exited the kitchen, her long, blonde braid hung regally, barely moving although she walked quickly. Even wearing a simple surcoat and apron for gardening, her mother looked like a queen.

"I'll finish and meet you in the herb garden, Mathair," Eloise agreed.

5

Some of the workers giggled. Few things displeased the Maid of Dahlquin more than spinning thread at her distaff.

"Back to work!" Muireann ordered her assistants. "It's a feast we've to prepare and all the more labor for us. Seven hungry strangers, from the north."

Eloise sulked in a corner, bent over the musty ledger.

"Mind your Lady Mother, *princess*," Muireann said addressing Eloise with the title of esteem and endearment. "Don't dawdle lest we both suffer."

The gossip throughout the female ranks of Dahlquin Castle concerned the tall, handsome, mysterious, noble, courageous, gentle knights from afar. The wild imaginings and exaggerations of the evening to come had the womenfolk, old, young, highborn or low, carrying on.

In the kitchens just such a group of workers assembled. Save for the middle of the night, the kitchens were always busy. Dahlquin was a large estate and three meals a day were to be provided. The great hearths smoked and belched, cauldrons simmered and sputtered. Children kept the fuel coming and swept the embers and ash. Quick moving terriers were underfoot and the occasional cat made her way stealthily through the shelves, each chasing the opportunistic vermin or snatching the scraps that might fall to the floor.

"Oh, these strangers," said the second cook. "I saw 'em ride in. Tall as trees, straight in the saddles. I could feel the presence of God upon 'em. Father, bless me," she stated, dropping her eyes and crossing herself.

"Oh, I sorely disagree," a kitchen helper said. "They be trouble, I smell it," and she spat into a corner.

"I hear the stable boy say one of 'em is too pretty to be a man, what with his big brown eyes and fine features," said another dreamily. Quietly, Eloise took all this in listening from her corner, ledger forgotten.

"Pretty is they?" the kitchen helper chimed in. "Trouble comes from a pretty man."

"Hard to please a man when he is prettier than you," Muireann added.

"And you'd know about that, would you now?"

"Me? I know a cooking woman is always beautiful," Muireann said proudly.

"Oh, spirits mock you, covered in flour up to your elbows, and your skirts tied above the knees as you lean over the boards," hooted the second cook. All the women laughed with her.

"Exactly," Muireann clucked.

"She speaks truth. Stuffing his face with a free hand while stuffing the cook with his cock," snorted the assistant. The room howled with laughter.

"I've sharp knives here, Finnouala, watch yourself!" Muireann teased. Her words sounded menacing, but her voice and expression were mild. Like the woman herself, Muireann's attire bespoke durability, practicality and pride. The brown, homespun gown, well-worn from years of use, was meticulously mended. Her apron, too, was patched, reinforced, and washed more often than some people Eloise knew. Aine and Eloise made a new apron for Muireann some two years past. A beautiful thing it was, absorbent and quilted. Muireann wore it only on high feast days when the workers ate in the Great Hall.

"Muireann," called a familiar voice, "up to your old tricks again?" It was Sean, assisting the children bringing peat for the hearth. "I always love working the kitchens. Women and wine."

Several workers acknowledged him through the din of chopping leeks, sizzling fat or the barking of orders.

Sean was an elderly man, married to Eloise's nurse, one of the few people around to remember the kitchens before Muireann.

"Greetings, my Maid Princess," he said tipping his head to Eloise. "You're getting an earful this morning."

Eloise smiled. Her cheeks still felt flushed with merriment.

"Mercy, child," Muireann called, "you still here? Off with you."

"I'm not a child," Eloise said indignantly. "I've seventeen years."

"You're a child until you're married."

"And if I never marry?"

"She refuses to spin and wed," someone muttered.

"Or bed," added another.

Eloise turned her head, seeking the speakers of such rude folly. Seventeen was considered by many to be old for a first-time bride. As she scanned the faces staring at her, she saw a smirk, a tear but primarily incredulity. The heir to Dahlquin, not marry? How absurd. All ladies were to run a household and bear children. Anger and shame pressed upon her. Her chest felt constricted, with the familiar heartache of disappointment. Feeling the weight of an imagined yoke upon her shoulders and shackles of a forced master upon her wrists, Eloise bristled and shook out her arms and hands, standing erect against the penetrating stares.

Everyone returned to work as quietly as possible so as not to miss a word.

"You'll marry," Muireann said flatly, "or the Church. Until then you're a child, my Maid Princess," Muireann scowled. "Now don't keep your mother waiting."

"You'll have us all in trouble," Sean warned. "Nurse too."

Eloise frowned. *Guilt on top of scolding, and she the sole heir to Dahlquin! How dare they?* Shuffling out, her frown turned to a pout. They dared because...because she acted like a child, not a leader. And they cared about her, she reflected as she and her hounds left to join her mother in the herb garden, ledger forgotten.

The growing season was barely upon them, the pantries exhausted from the winter and Easter celebrations. Unlike the pleasure parks and gardens of wealthier estates Eloise heard of in stories, the ladies of Dahlquin retreated to this working herb garden. It was vibrant and green with fresh parsley, mint and thyme. White flowered raspberry bushes fluttered with bees. Eloise's two large hounds lay outside the small garden, waiting patiently in the June sun, while her mother's wee dog Dilis dug for rodents and watched for birds.

"Mathair, do you think our guests have been to France?" Before Aine could answer, Eloise suggested, "Or Rome? Might they have seen the Pope?"

"Mayhap." Her mother started cutting sprigs of parsley.

"Are they fair of face? What do you think?"

"Eloise," Aine said putting down her knife. "They're strangers. We'll feed them and offer shelter, as our Savior Jesus would command. Tonight we shall learn their purpose."

"What fun!" Eloise exclaimed with eyes closed, picturing the banquet.

"There is much work to do between now and then," her mother said.

"Work, work, work," Eloise grumbled, rocking back on her heels to observe the herb garden. "It is bountiful," she added. New pride in accomplishment made her smile. This herb garden was laid out in a small, sunny location. The stone wall was covered at one end by a rose bush, with exquisite pink flowers in late spring and large red hips in fall, so important through the winter months. The other end had a vine, which provided luscious grapes in fall and tender leaves in spring, if the near-continuous rain didn't cause too much rot. Outside the castle the farmers tended orchards, more herbs and the crops that sustained them. Flax, horses, cattle, sheep and valuable green marble were the commodities for trade.

Eloise carefully filled a basket with blue borage flowers. A refreshing treat, the flowers garnished most any dish, or dipped in warm honey were a pretty display on a pudding.

"What benefit, Eloise?" her mother asked, pointing to the borage stalks.

Eloise didn't hear her mother's question about the curative properties of borage. Her mind was elsewhere. She snipped some rosemary sprigs and began to weave a wreath including borage flowers, calendula and violets.

"Mathair, how wonderful it must be to move about like our guests," Eloise contemplated, wishing to travel, see things, and have new experiences. She couldn't put words to the restlessness that stirred her soul. "I've never been anywhere." She placed the wreath upon her mother's head, and her mother patted her hand in a silent gesture of thanks.

"Eloise," her mother repeated, "borage. What curative properties?"

Eloise looked at her mother. *Why such a stern gaze?* she wondered, starting a wreath for her own head.

"Borage porridge," Eloise said, flustered at her mother's insistence that every moment of every hour of every day must consist of lessons and drills and ledgers and spinning. Endless spinning. When she would rather be on a horse. Such blessings: Riding, traveling and exploring.

"That stag you killed is not a replacement or substitute for your lessons and responsibilities."

Could her mother read her mind? Eloise wondered.

Aine tried again. "Eloise, you have many," she paused, "gifts, talents. But you have to practice. Hone your skills."

"But I want-" Eloise tried to interrupt.

"Eloise," Aine said, her voice rising. "You ride well. Exceptionally well. You have become part of the horse, by rote practice and drill."

Eloise felt herself smile with the compliment. *Did her mother finally understand?*

"You have the healing gift, Ellie. Deny it all you wish, but you have been called. You can't look away any more than I can."

Eloise took a deep breath and let out a long, exaggerated sigh.

"But you must study, memorize your botanicals and remedies…" her mother continued.

At times like this, healing felt like a curse. Medicine was a dangerous art. Both men and women might be held accountable if a patient had an undesirable outcome. Their mortal enemy, and neighbor, Scragmuir falsely accused her and her saintly Lady Mother of heresy. Though baptized and indoctrinated in the Church since birth, Eloise couldn't help but question. There were so many inconsistencies, mistruths, infallibility. She cringed, remembering the blood at her mouth. *Guilt of the Huntress.*

What did that mean? Her mother hadn't an answer, other than to say: "You are Dahlquin." *And what did that mean?*

"...managing your own estate, tending your own husband and children."

"Hmmm," Eloise said hesitantly, "but... it won't...I can't...." She stopped. Could she just continue like this? Most girls her age were long since married off. Eloise was not in a hurry to be sold into such domestic slavery - at least not with the prospects her father pursued. Argh! Men as old as or older than he was, with titles and estates far from Dahlquin. The young ones were not better. Weak and simple minded, less educated and easily manipulated, without an original thought or action to their credit. She would be trading paternal confinement for a that of a spouse. Plus, she had a reputation herself: a heretic, sorcerer, an outspoken child, disrespectful, too educated, and skinny. Let's not forget bad luck. She was betrothed at birth, but the young Lord of Leinster had died as a child. Scragmuir and their bonded families called her Lord Father the Brother-Murdering Barbarian. They still accused her father of murdering his own half-brother, as well as mutilating one of his dearest comrades, High Lord FitzGilbert's brother, Elroth.

"Eloise, this is what you were born to," her mother said, indicating their garden and beyond. "You have talent, skill. Would you rather break your back in the fields, or a brothel? God has favored you." Aine stood and moved to tend the rose.

"And I have gratitude," Eloise answered. "Truly I have, but Cambridge or Paris are not so far away. Ireland should have a grand school-"

"Not today, I've too much on my mind with these strangers," her mother interrupted. "University isn't for females. The abbey is not your destiny." This was an old argument between them.

"Dahlquin is my home, not my prison."

"Prison? You go too far," Aine countered. "What convict rides a fine courser to her heart's content or plays with such dogs as you have? With privilege comes duty," Aine said, continuing to pinch back her rose.

Eloise sighed. She was the only daughter and heir to Dahlquin. The esteem and vastness of the lands were nothing to scoff at, strategic, too. Her title alone made her a valuable token. She hated that, being viewed as a piece of flesh to be bartered.

"We have a banquet. You and I are to be hostesses. By your will, Ellie, I need you well-mannered and-," her mother dropped the rest. "By your will," she implored.

The two worked on in silence until Aine declared they were done.

Eloise clapped her hands together to get the dirt off her gloves and tucked them into her apron. "By your will, the banquet," she brightened, travel and education forgotten. "With handsome strangers, singing and dancing. Let's go," she chirped merrily.

Lord Hubert sat back in his chair. One of his hounds dozed behind him, the other at his feet under the meeting table. Today had been a drill day and he had dressed in his brown and grey tunic, hauberk and studded boots. He and his men were practicing at the quintain in the inner bailey when he was advised of the strangers at the gate. Worthy kit for greeting well-armed intruders, he thought, not changing into formal attire.

His brother, Sir Reginald, sat to his right. There was little familial resemblance between the two. At forty-eight, Hubert's greying auburn hair receded well behind his head, not unlike a tonsure, with eyes described as steel blue to match his frigid heart. Two years younger, Reggie had a full head of greying brown hair and hazel eyes. Both were tall, eye to eye, with Reggie barrel-chested like their father. The castle Seanascal sat to his left. Four Dahlquin hearth knights sat two each on either side of Reggie and the Seanascal. Guards stood on both sides of the door of the private meeting chamber. The room was small and spare; the only adornments were the large, black, teardrop shaped soot marks where the heating pots sat, unlit on this day. The sturdy board and benches were dark and the surfaces smooth from years of use.

At the other end of the table sat the seven strangers. They included Sir Davydd and his brother Sir Byron, who shared the same flaming red hair with bushy eyebrows that bobbed dramatically when they spoke; Sir Ioan and Sir Ryan, cousins, and Ryan's half-brother, Sir Arnolf, with two overworked squires shared between them all. Pitchers of ale were available plus some good well water.

"Tell us more of this army," Reginald asked, sitting back in his chair.

"They mean to take revenge on Meath," Sir Davydd said. "Young Tiomoid U'Neill got his nose twitched," he laughed, his thick red eyebrows bobbing above his green eyes.

"How?"

"The usual," Davydd snickered, "horses, whores and honor." His friends laughed as well, but the Dahlquin men remained silent. "He seeks redress, is all we know." He shrugged, glancing first at his brother Byron, then the rest of his men who nodded in agreement.

"Seems extreme," Reginald commented, "to seek out the Danes and Norse Hebridians. That's an army large enough to threaten the peace."

"Expensive, too. Tiomoid U'Neill has naught the resources," the Seanascal added. Nor was Dahlquin the most direct route to Meath in central Ireland.

"Not for revenge. Reeks of war," Reginald said. "Does King Henry know? Is England behind this?"

"Tiomoid acts alone, for revenge on Meath, nothing more," Byron said jovially.

"And the U'Neill's, does Lord Magnus stand behind Tiomu?" Reggie asked. The U'Neill's still considered themselves the monarchy of all Ireland, claiming it was their ancestral right, High Kings of Ancient Tara. But young Tiomoid was one of many landless younger sons of the U'Neills. And out of favour.

"Good Sirs, Lord Dahlquin," Ioan offered, refilling his cup with ale, "we've told you all we know. It's an army of some magnitude. But we are not aligned with the U'Neill's nor Tiomoid."

"Don't kill the messengers," Davydd added, "we only bring you news of what we saw. Surely, we were naught in command to interrogate Tiomoid U'Neill! We spoke with them only briefly."

"Send your own enquiries, Lord," said Byron, revealing some agitation.

"Bears watching, doesn't it?" Ioan added.

Hubert nodded. He had been content to let his men ask the questions. Impassively he watched the strangers before him.

"Who are you aligned with?" Reginald asked pointedly. "Who is your liege lord, then?" Valuable information; most armed men were funded by a lord or baron; thus, did they owe him their allegiance in all things. This was the core of their society: sworn fealty to one's overlord or the patriarch of the family unit.

"We're knights-errant, sir," Byron said. "It's our plan to travel the length and breadth of all Ireland. There are many good works to be done, and in doing, we might find our place and pledge ourselves."

"I'm from Wales, sirs, and would seek new opportunities," Arnolf claimed. "My Lord William de Braose crossed King John; his men were 'excused'. Not wishing to die, I left."

The Dahlquin men shrugged. Ireland had little love of England, and they were all too familiar with that sad tale of years past. William de Braose had told all that England's King John strangled his own nephew, Arthur of Brittany. John in turn left William's wife to starve to death in prison and confiscated all de Braose's lands. His vassals were dispersed.

"My condolences," Hubert said, thinking the man would have been a mere child then.

"Lord Dahlquin, your forebears hail from Wales, eh?" Arnolf asked. "Ireland has been good to the Welsh and English alike, we have much to offer each other," and he held up his cup in tribute.

"Sir Davydd here is leaning towards the monastic life," Ioan said with a shove and wink.

"I may feel the calling, now and again," Davydd conceded, nodding his red head thoughtfully.

Knights-errant, bah. Hubert had little regard for the renegade nobility or men-at-arms who would not or could not make the pledge to one liege. They were dangerous, unpredictable. In some circumstances it did happen, as with de Braose's vassals.

Hubert's men exhausted the possibilities, gaining as much information as the travelers were inclined to divulge.

"Let us send word to Ashbury," Hubert concluded. "Our allies should be forewarned as well. An army the size of which you speak will be a plague upon the countryside."

The guests exchanged subtle glances, but Hubert could detect little. Ashbury was southeast of Dahlquin. These men had come in from the north, was Ashbury their next stop? Or the dreaded Scragmuirs to the south? There was plenty of time to warn these strangers of the devious Scragmuirs.

"Let's clean and rest before dinner," Hubert said as he rose, ushering the men out. "My boys will escort you to freshen up," he said to his guests as well as the attendant pages standing by. "They can refresh at the well or sit in the Great Hall," Hubert said.

"The Norsemen will eat dirt for lack of anything better," said one of the Dahlquin knights. The Hebrides were known for their harsh environment. The men laughed as they left the conference.

Eloise and her mother delivered the borage flowers to the kitchen. It smelled divine: roasting venison, fresh bread and the heartiest meat and leek gravy. The preparations for the feast were well in hand. Eloise hugged Muireann, kissing her in appreciation, talk of travel and confinement forgotten. The cook patted the girl's cheek leaving a flour handprint.

"Come, Mathair, what a night this will be," Eloise held her hands out encouraging her mother to spin and twirl with her. Her two large dogs moved ahead, investigating, as they headed from the kitchen building to pass through the Great Hall up to their residential chambers.

"Eloise, not now," her mother directed. "This is neither the time nor place. Dahlquin will be the able host to these strangers," her mother added, as Eloise continued her invitation, "but this isn't a time for such frivolity. These men and their purpose are yet unknown. That is our concern."

Beast, Dragon and Dilis chuffed greetings, then wagged their tails as her father's hounds came into the Great Hall. He couldn't be far behind, she knew.

"And we their hosts. What entertainment, we could sing…and dance," Eloise said, arms over her head as she pirouetted into one of her father's pages. She bounced off the page in surprise and into the practiced arms of a stranger, a knight.

She stared into his green eyes, topped by prominent red eyebrows. An eager grin spread across his face as he steadied her. *Where had they come from?*

"Eloise!" her father and mother gasped simultaneously. Dilis growled and Aine lifted the small dog. Reginald was in striking range.

Recoiling from the admonishing tones of her parents, Eloise studied the knight. He wasn't the pretty one she had heard about.

"Take my excuse, sir," she said. "Shame upon me, are you hurt?" She began to brush him off and tidy his green and grey surcoat.

He laughed, "Takes more than a fine dance to topple this knight. Are we to see more?"

She flushed pink, further highlighting the white flour handprint, and nodding to the other knights she stepped back. "Mayhap, tonight. Mathair and I love to sing and dance," she added.

Hubert moved in. "I apologize, sir, my daughter has…exuberance." He glared at Eloise before turning his attention back to his guests. Years of hard combat showed on his face and in his lined expression. Still he stood tall and firm and confident. No one would doubt he was a man of action.

"My Lady Aine," Hubert said, extending his fist to her. Aine dipped her head to Hubert, then stepped forward, head up, her floral garland as a crown. She placed her hand over her husband's fist. Eloise noticed her mother's small hand seemed to clutch her father's fist, burying her fingernails into his coarse flesh. Her other hand was twisted in Dilis's fur. "Lady of Dahlquin, daughter of Lord Carirthenn, descendant of our hero, Brian Boru the Viking Slayer, devoted servant of God and Crown," her father said in formal introduction. Perplexed by her mother's clenched hands, Eloise studied Aine's facial expression. Fear was not present. Her

14

mother appeared serene; her complexion glowed with the exertions of the garden and pleasures of the kitchen.

"My daughter, Maiden Eloise," her father said. She looked up at him. His glare was gone, replaced by the impassive warrior. Before she could respond and assume her place beside her mother, her father turned his attention to the men before them.

"I present to you-" her father resumed the introduction. Curious about these strangers, Eloise focused on the men before her as her father continued with the introductions of the five knights, Sirs Davyyd, Byron, Ioan, Ryan and Arnolf. They had only two squires.

"By your will, take your leave, we'll see you at the feast," Hubert said, signaling the pages to escort the knights to the well.

"Ladies, I look forward to this evening," Davydd said. He turned to Eloise and his smile warmed. "Mayhap you could teach me a dance step or two."

"Most assuredly, but watch your toes, he's a bit heavy on his feet," Ioan teased.

Was Ioan the pretty one, Eloise wondered? He did have large brown eyes, but pretty like a woman? None of them fit that description.

"Lord Hubert, you have been blessed," Davydd said. "Tonight, we shall dance like never before. Ladies," he bowed and left with the others.

Eloise blushed and bit her lip. *What fun*. Already she imagined the music in her head, practicing the steps. She reached for her mother's hand to proceed to the residential tower. They, too, needed to freshen up.

Her father gripped her arm, nearly yanking her off her feet.

"Have you gone daft? Flitting about when there are serious matters to consider," Hubert said peering at her, his stern brow knotted.

"I have not," she said, offended. "Mathair and I've been exceedingly busy with-"

"You brought embarrassment upon me," he cut her off, "appearing as two vulgar May Queens with dirty hands and-" He glanced up at the floral crowns upon their heads.

"I would be a gracious hostess, as you and Mathair taught me," she huffed, the wreaths were lovely, and her father was taking this out of proportion.

Rather than express indignation her mother bit her bottom lip, sighing audibly.

Reginald caught Eloise's attention; his face tight with disapproval. Though he barely moved, he shook his head.

"Taught you to prance about as an uncouth…public woman," Hubert's voice was deep and grating. He spoke slowly, careful not to curse.

"Uncouth! Mathair never…I would sing and dance to make you proud," she protested. "Seems my only purpose is-" *Slaving away in domestic servitude.* "Dahlquin is-"

"Ellie," Reginald warned, but she ignored him.

Dragon crouched half prone, her tail scraping the floor submissively, seeking an end to the palpable discord.

"Why shouldn't I sing and dance and read and learn and-"

"Go to your chamber." Hubert's voice was flat, without emotion. Eloise knew not to speak now. No one was that stupid. She glanced sideways at Uncle Reggie.

He shook his head and shrugged at her. The disappointment in his hazel eyes brought tears to hers.

Eloise looked to her mother, who didn't attempt to intercede either.

Aine and Reginald watched Eloise stalk off to the residential tower, one hound on either side of her with heads down.

"She needs a mate. And children. Sons of her own to vent that energy," Reginald said to Aine.

"She does, but not tonight," Aine answered.

"Who will love her and shelter her as Hubert and I do?" Reggie asked.

"Who indeed," Aine said.

Eloise burst into her chamber, tears blurring her vision, her father's voice ringing in her ears, and Uncle Reggie's words, 'she needs sons'. A worthless daughter, the only redemption for her crime of gender was to replace herself with male heirs. *How could he say that?* Beast and Dragon entered behind her then rushed to greet Nurse, the kindly woman who had shared Eloise's bed chamber since her birth.

"Eloise?" Nurse called sweetly. The great hounds' tails thumped the Nurse's legs and each other.

Eloise turned to look. Her beloved Nurse smiled broadly, unashamed of her missing teeth. Clutched to her broad self was the blue and gold surcoat Eloise had yet to complete. Eloise blinked back her tears, thinking her eyes tricked her. The seam she needed to tear out and redo was straight, flawless even. Eloise stretched out a hand to touch the garment. The trim was finished. All the meticulous, tedious hemming was done. And it was beautiful, befitting the Maid of Dahlquin for a glorious banquet she wouldn't be attending.

She fell sobbing into Nurse's arms, the blue and gold surcoat crushed between them. All her good nurse's gracious time wasted, but for her irritable father and her own hasty words.

"What? What?" Nurse crooned, stroking her hair. "Joy upon me to do it for you, child. Not tears."

Eloise shook her head, unable to form the words.

"Come, let's get you clean and dressed. Still smell like a sweaty horse, you do," Nurse said, pushing Eloise from her embrace. "Your father's daughter," she added with a chuckle.

Eloise bit her lip; a whimper escaped her.

"I'm not going to the banquet," Eloise said, looking down at her shaking hands, dirty hands - remembering her mother's clenched hands, trying to hide her dirty fingernails. Fighting back tears, the whole ugly argument poured out of her.

An hour later Eloise sat on a stool while Nurse brushed out her long, amber hair. Should have been for the banquet, but now it was simply a routine before bed.

"So soft it is," the nurse cooed, breaking the brittle silence between them. "Luxurious as silk, dear." Eloise didn't answer. "Always liked this color on you, too," the elderly woman observed regarding the surcoat. "Highlights your blue eyes and pearl white skin."

"They're blue-grey," Eloise corrected. *Who cared, no one would ever see them save a handful of kin in the family tower?*

"So they are. All the more desirable, too."

Eloise didn't respond.

"You have many admirable attributes," Nurse continued. "A little shy of medium height, not a giantess. And you're learning to carry yourself regally, as your Lady Mother. Like her, you're trim and modestly built."

Eloise knew her mother was the quintessential noble lady, quiet, subdued and elegant.

"Not like some gluttonous Scragmuir cow," Nurse continued.

Indeed, Eloise could imagine what those Scragmuirs must look like, or rather what she hoped they looked like.

"What you lack in womanly bosom can always be enhanced or padded. Until your mothering years."

Eloise sighed.

"Your father wants only to protect you, dear," the nurse continued. "To insist on singing may have been overlooked. But dancing, before strangers, is a bit provocative, sweet one, truly."

Eloise rolled her eyes. "Not you too," she sighed. "Dancing and singing are suitable forms of entertainment for guests. Mathair and I sing all the time, it's not a sin."

"By his will, the singing," Nurse offered. "Your father might have agreed to that, later, if he saw fit. But you insisted. You demanded." The nurse wiped a tear from her eye. "Lucky you are not to be beaten beyond recognition. Your father is tolerant, patient as a saint with you."

Eloise frowned, wiping away a tear herself. Why was it always her fault? Surely, she was the patient one, in a world so full of restraint and confinement. Often enough she was compared unfavorably to her saintly mother, but now her father, too. In silence the nurse continued to brush out her hair in long, gentle strokes.

"By your will, go," Eloise said. "Don't miss the banquet." Music, distant but joyous haunted the chamber, reminding Eloise of what she was missing.

"With you here alone? We shall dine together," Nurse answered. Faint laughter joined the music.

"By your will, and the blessings of the saints, you can tell me what I missed. I won't be alone," Eloise pointed to the pair of hounds. Dragon yipped in her sleep, massive paws flicked as the prey fled before her in the dream. Beast stretched out by the bed. "I've some confessing and penance to do," Eloise sighed. "And tell Muireann to wear the new apron."

The nurse frowned and started to disagree.

"Don't add guilt to the disappointment upon me." Eloise never suffered alone, her parents saw to that. Her actions had serious consequences for many people, a burden of responsibility that came with her noble birth. "By your will, go, you and Sean together."

There was a loud bang on the door. The dogs barked, clambering to stand as the door swung open.

"Mercy!" Nurse gasped in alarm, protectively standing before Eloise.

"Eloise!" Hubert bellowed, striding towards her as she stood. Hubert's hounds, and Beast and Dragon barked and exchanged robust greetings in the charged chamber.

Nurse dropped to her knees, tugging at Eloise's sleeve encouraging her to do the same. But Eloise stood rooted to the spot in the noise and canine chaos, unable to take her eyes off her father. "Be still!" Hubert shouted at the hounds. "Quiet."

Eloise managed to motion with her hands for the dogs to settle. "Shush," she finally offered.

Hubert had something in his hand. The Seanascal waited in the doorway, why? Hand shaking with wrath, Hubert thrust the object into her face.

Her heart stopped as her stomach lurched. It couldn't be, by her will let it not be.. She glanced at the Seanascal hoping this was a mistake. Not her fault. But she remembered now. Her heart resumed, pounding with deafening rhythm.

"Do you recognise this?" her father growled, lifting her chin with it. She couldn't mistake it or her father's outrage. She closed her eyes to escape the shame, smelling the damp leather so close to her nose. He hit her chin with it when she didn't answer.

"I do, Da- Father," she corrected. "The ledg-" but he slapped her chin again with the dog-chewed ledger, causing her to bite her tongue.

"Open your eyes."

She did, struggling to keep them so.

"The repository of castle resources," he said, his face fixed and harsh. The bible of our wealth." The torn flax parchment pages were still damp from chewing. "Left for the cur. While you dance!" drawing out the word *dance* in a hiss, vilifying it.

Think. Answer him. She could not.

He grabbed the side of her head with his free hand, pulling her hair as his fingers dug into her scalp. He shook her, then turned her face up to his.

"On the morrow, you will complete your usual penance. Climbing the staircase. On your knees." He thrust the damaged ledger in her hands. "Repair this best you can," he said before turning to leave. He stopped at the door, his hounds already in the hallway. You owe the Seanascal grave apology."

Before she could utter the words, or better yet, throw herself at his feet, he was gone, the door closed.

The banquet provided a grand time for most of the Dahlquin inhabitants. The evening meal had significant courses and morsels, but not the formal structure of some estate functions. This allowed everyone more opportunity to listen and share the festivities. Hubert understood even the lowest chambermaid or stable boy enjoyed a little entertainment. Keeping people alert and active made for more productive workers. It was important to reinforce that everyone had their God-ordained station in life, and it was their God-ordained duty to fulfill that station to the best of their God-ordained ability. The Church and hierarchy governing all their lives set very specific parameters for each life. The system was rigid and unbending, all were taught early who they were and what they were born to. Don't argue with God's plan: fulfill the duty as prescribed by the One above.

As Lord of Dahlquin, Hubert's God-ordained station was to keep his manor safely in the king's hands, to keep this frontier of the kingdom secure for Ireland or England, depending on who was present. After that, to keep his tenants, workers, knights and their families safe and protected. It was his responsibility to anticipate sieges, attacks, famines, pestilence, anything that might affect the crops and livestock so vital to the survival of his military personnel, who in turn protected the realm. They were all interconnected: liege to each other at many levels. All men were not equal in the eyes of God, and most accepted it.

RESIDENTIAL TOWER, LATE NIGHT

Hubert, Aine, Reginald and Hubert's hounds retired to the bed chamber.

From the open door Hubert scanned the welcoming space. Four round, three-legged metal heating pots were lit, and the chamber held the familiar warmth and aroma of peat. Two wall sconces illuminated the stone and wood paneled chamber. A large bed was near one corner. A small square table stood near the head of the bed with a full pitcher of wine upon it. To shield the sleepers from the cold withheld by the stone wall, a woolen and linen covering of Dahlquin gold and blue was hung, decorated with embroidery and crewel work, depicting biblical and mythological images as well as Dahlquin family history. Celtic motifs were added by Connacht family members in recent years. Behind this decorative hanging was a thick felt pad for added insulation against the cold. On this same wall, an arched door opened to Aine's private chamber. Behind the door Aine's dog, Dilis, barked for admittance.

"Let him come," Hubert said, waving a hand toward the closed door, so wife and dog might be reunited. One of the attendants opened the door and Dilis raced across the chamber.

Against the adjacent wall two carved wooden chests stored Hubert's robes, garments, mail and armour. A rectangular table stood against the next wall with an ewer and bowl.

Two chairs and two stools were available, and two small round stumps with the bark removed and the wood polished, for use either as stools or tables. One of the attendants stood ready with three cups of wine. Two more servants waited for Hubert's command.

"May you have goodness," Hubert said to the attendants as he, Aine with dog in arm, and Reginald entered behind the thumping tails of his hounds. Hubert nodded to each of his servants and with the wordless finesse of hunters each saw to his duty of service.

Aine sat on a stool near one of the sconces, with a warming pot at her feet and her joyous dog in her lap. Just as quickly as she sat, her attendant, Daire, rushed in with a large distaff. Aine took it and set to work.

"U'Neill," Reginald sighed, "and the Danes." He fell into a seat, exhausted after the banquet. His wine sat untouched. One massive dog tried to fit under Hubert's chair, the other stretched between the men.

"And mercenaries from the Hebrides. It's civil war," Hubert said. "Tiomoid is disowned. Banished. Following old Dermot of Leinster."

Reggie lifted his wine. "To Dermot MacMurrough of Leinster!" He continued his toast as if MacMurrough were in the chamber. "Ah, Dermot, you begged the second King Henry to send an army to help you regain your land back in 1169, " he continued his toast without drinking, "but Henry, that calculating bastard-" he glanced at Aine, expecting a gasp or reprimand. When she merely shrugged, he proceeded. "Henry refused to send his own soldiers, cunningly indicating he wouldn't stand in the way of any of his barons wishing to assist their Irish neighbor, thus launching our invasion." Hubert and Reginald descended from these original families.

"Old history," Hubert said.

"Your family history," Aine said.

"Instead of Welsh, Tiomoid's dredged up the Vikings," Reginald added.

"Vikings," Hubert said with a chuckle. "That is your family history," he said to Aine.

"Bless my greatest of great grand sires, Brian Boruma," Aine replied. "The High King of all Ireland."

"Tiomoid only wishes to reclaim that crown for himself," Reggie said. "He means to take us, without doubt. We support the king."

"All of them," Hubert said. He and Reggie chuckled: Lord Hubert De Burgh of Connacht, High Lord Gerald FitzGilbert and Henry III of

21

England, depending on who was in attendance. Like he himself, the Irish lords lived independently from English rule as much as possible. Most fighting was done between the Irish themselves in an effort to dominate the island. England was just as content to leave them to it.

Reginald looked tired and stooped a bit. Still a formidable man, Hubert knew. "Does it smell of France or England? With us the pawns?" Reginald asked. Already the army consisted of foreigners: how many more backers were there, hungry for the glories of Ireland? "Tiomu has naught but the promise of land and wealth to offer such an army. It's not revenge he seeks, but title. He would make himself king, and spit on the rest of the U'Neills."

"Aine, my love, what do you think? Are Henry of England or Louis of France behind this?" Hubert asked his ever-patient wife.

Aine set down her distaff, rubbed her brow and smiled at her husband and Reggie. She glowed with warmth and light from the sconces.

"Sorrow upon me, my Lord, who am I to conjecture? It does seem unlikely. Their concerns lie in England and on the mainland. Henry is yet a boy. His deputies struggle with his barons and the disasters his father left. Louis has taken up the cross and plans a return to Outremere. His interests lie well east of us."

"Times like this, I wish you were a sorceress, or seer," Hubert smiled at her. "Eh, give me a little glimpse."

"Ashes are what you would have," Aine answered.

In morbid response, Reggie lifted his roughened sword hand and imitated a sifting motion, as if ashes were filtering through his fingers.

Aine winced.

Far too often she had been accused of just that, Hubert knew. Eloise too. *Ellie.* He suppressed a groan. *God's eyes, why was she so incorrigibly foolish? Always arguing. So much at stake.* He shook his head. Clearing the vision of his daughter.

"She's Irish. We're always squabbling, aren't we?" Aine said. "And she *is* Dahlquin."

Hubert blinked. Mayhap he hadn't suppressed the groan. "Seems you can see into my thoughts. Why not Tiomu's?" Hubert asked.

"What are we to do, in regard to the army?" Aine asked, directing the conversation back to the crisis before them.

Hubert shrugged. "Doubled the watch. Ladders ready, barrels, and arms assembled. Just in case."

Their guests were quite sure the army headed east, intent on taking revenge in Meath. Hubert's latest envoy had not returned and that vexed him. Tiomoid U'Neill was but one more displaced young son seeking to put himself upon a throne.

"We've not a quarrel with Meath, would you allow access?" Aine's question was rhetorical.

Hubert sniffed and tilted his chin.

"Not cordial to let an army march through on the way to make war with one's neighbors and allies," Reginald said with eyes closed, as if envisioning such a folly.

"Was there any mention of the U'Connors?" Aine asked.

"The U'Connors were not mentioned. You should know more than I, your eldest sister is there. Do they still hold a grudge?"

She sighed. "Last she wrote, my sister said all was well, with the true Irish."

"All the nobility is quarreling or feuding with each other without bias or reason," Reginald added.

With a wry smile, Aine stroked Dilis. "My Lord, fatigue overcomes me. Forgive my weakness, but-"

Hubert raised a hand for silence.

"Daire," Hubert called out. "Daire! It's time to attend your lady."

Aine's sleepy attendant, Daire, rushed back into the chamber bowing, yawning, and bowing again.

"Shame upon me, quick as a hare, again, the shame is upon me, Lord," Daire said, her eyes downcast as she scooted past Hubert and Reginald to attend to Aine.

This night Aine would share Hubert's bedchamber, rather than retreat to her own. Reggie tried not to look as the servant brushed out his Lady Sister-in-Law's braids. Married women always had their hair modestly braided, thus only here in the privacy of their chambers might Hubert behold the splendor. So beautiful and blonde it shone in the hearth light, any grey went undetected.

Aine rose and she, Daire and Dilis retreated to her chamber for a change into bed clothes.

"We too, eh, Hubert?" Reginald asked, standing in anticipation of preparing for bed.

"Us too. Dubh!" Hubert called to one of attendants. "Prepare a bed for my brother. I would have him spend this night near to hand. With his grace," he said, turning to Reginald, watching his brother's shoulders slump and jaw fall open.

"Awe, by the saints, I'm to be your esteemed guest, camping on the floor. Alone," Reginald said. His mouth frowned, but his hazel eyes sparked mischief.

"You had other arrangements? Some dalliance I was unaware?" Hubert asked, lifting one side of his mouth in a sly smirk.

"Always," Reginald and Hubert said together.

Dubh and the other attendants helped Reginald and Hubert out of their surcoats and hauberks and into bed clothes, for a good night's slumber Hubert doubted he would enjoy.

Aine returned to the chamber, leaving Dilis behind. Hubert refused to share his bed with the little dog.

Cautiously Eloise eased herself off her bed. Gently her feet slid onto the floor and she moved quietly to straighten her bed covers. All this she did by the light of a single candle. Dragon thumped her tail on the bare stone floor, Beast joined her in their happy greeting. Still Eloise could barely hear the mighty tails over the snoring of her beloved Nurse and her husband Sean, both asleep noisily on a pallet on her chamber floor. Since birth, Eloise had hardly known a night without the devoted Nurse's snores in her chamber.

Next Eloise carefully placed her psalter upon her bed, slightly open, spine up so the book resembled a house with a steep roof, a house of God. This was a sign for Nurse or her mother she was in the family chapel. A full night of prayer was the best way back into her father's good graces. He had an uncanny instinct for how genuine her penitence was, so she was very motivated to show her remorse. She had sorrow for the anger upon him, and heartbreak for the disappointment she brought him.

Eloise folded a blanket over her arm. Taking her other beloved book from the shelf, and her shoes off the floor, she tenderly blew kisses to her sleeping nurse and Sean, leaving the slow burning candle to guide her exit. "Shush," Eloise whispered to the dogs as she closed the door to her chamber, pleased she had made so little noise. The corridor was fair bright at this late hour. More sconces than usual illuminated the stone and wood passage. Beast and Dragon cast long shadows as they stretched their limbs, arched their backs and shook head to tail in anticipation of this nocturnal stroll, then wagged their tails in greetings.

"Evening, Cousin," said a male voice.

Startled, Eloise clutched blanket and book to her breast. Slowly she turned to face Donegal, her mother's sister's third son. He leaned against the wall, blond hair to his shoulders, arms crossed, a smug expression. Next to him stood another cousin, Eoin. Both cousins had fostered in Dahlquin since boyhood. She had grown up with them.

"Evening," she returned to Donegal. "Evening, Eoin." He merely nodded his greeting. "I'm off to the chapel for a night of penance." Pungent male odor and smoke tickled her nose.

"A night of penance for your impertinence, I hear tell," Donegal said. "Now you're adding mischief, Ellie."

"I'll pray extra hard," she said, not lowering her gaze.

"You need a guard," Donegal added. He attempted a stern demeanor, pushing off the wall, hands on his hips, challenging her to move toward the chapel. While he tried to think what to do, she knew.

"You go," Eoin answered. "Doubt anyone's available, Uncle Hubert doubled the watch, remember?"

In her distress, Eloise had forgotten about the heightened security, thus Donegal and Eoin. Everyone was on alert because of Tiomoid U'Neill's army. Donegal and Eoin were capable guards and soldiers. Though not yet knighted, each had a sword and fighting dagger on his girdle. Without bleary eyes or slurred speech as other banquet revelers would possess.

"It's best you stayed put tonight, Cousin," Donegal offered.

Eloise sighed, attempting to wring her hands with woeful penitence, while clutching book and blanket. She needed their sympathy, not antagonism. "Surely Tiomoid U'Neill did not amass an army to storm Saint Anne's Chapel," she offered.

Donegal and Eoin exchanged glances.

"With your will," she continued, "and would do me good to purge my soul before the altar. What if I was to die this very night, without a chance at redemption? I brought grievous anger upon my father," she bowed her head solemnly. That she had. "Humility and subordination, before God." Looking up with a smile Eloise added, "Beast and Dragon are with me, I'll be safe in the chapel."

"I disagree, you need a guard." Donegal's hazel eyes glared at her.

The dogs stretched and yawned. Eyes rolling, Eloise tried to rush her cousins before her parents awoke and forbade her leave. She needed to get this over with tonight. *Patience*, she reminded herself.

"As my father wishes, Donegal," Eloise complied. "Would you escort me to the chapel and bear witness to my vigil? Guarding my body and soul?" she grinned. "By your will, Cousin," she begged. It wasn't her place to countermand her father, but here or the chapel Donegal still fulfilled his duty. She tried not to look impatient, but time was wasting.

"Send up Alsandair," Eoin suggested. "He had far too much fun at the banquet."

"A good suggestion, Alsandair," Eloise agreed, "but-" she remembered, "not so much noise. Father doesn't appreciate raucous dice playing when he is trying to sleep. I've enough trouble upon me."

The three cousins smiled appreciatively with the memory. Alsandair had exuberant sport.

"Mayhap Alsandair should escort me," Eloise added. "Sounds like he may be in need of prayer, himself." She longed to ask her cousins what she missed at the banquet. It seemed the music played on hour upon hour. In the morning she would hear all about it, probably from people who would gloat over what her impertinence had cost, she thought pouting, brow crossed.

"We'll find him, then decide." Donegal offered to hold her blanket, and she accepted. He extended his other hand. Curtsying, Eloise placed her hand upon Donegal's. With Beast and Dragon leading the way, Eloise and Donegal left her family's private chambers and descended the spiral staircase to find Alsandair, then the chapel.

Alsandair emerged from a small chamber and was neither happy nor eloquent when ordered to escort Maid Eloise to the chapel. The blond man stretched and scratched his ribs. "Just got off the gate," he grumbled then yawned.

"The gate is it?" called an irritated female voice inside the chamber.

Donegal scowled at the indiscretion for her sake, Eloise knew.

Alsandair grinned. "There's not a gate compares with yours, Lovey," he called back to the chamber.

"Shut up! Both of you," Donegal reprimanded, tipping his head towards Eloise with embarrassment.

She dismissed it with a shrug, trying to place the woman's voice. *Who was Lovey?*

"It's the chapel with the Maid," Donegal said, tipping his head toward Eloise. "Or the bedchamber with Lord Hubert," he said, tipping his head toward the residential tower. With a teasing grin, he added, "Your choice."

Beast growled at something. Dragon followed his lead. Both dogs faced the residential tower warily. Eloise knelt down between them, arms wrapped around each. *Patience*, she reminded herself again, *and humility*. She stood, tidying her blue surcoat.

After a long, grumbling sigh Alsandair addressed Eloise. "Only the chapel? I don't want back talk." He tried to scowl.

Eloise nodded, pretended to wipe a tear, and clutched her prayer book to her chest once more.

"I don't want to hear about universities or fucking- take my excuse-,"
he glared, "nonsense."

"Curse you, man, watch your tongue," Donegal scolded.

Ducking to reenter the small doorway, Alsandair returned with his
battle axe, leather girdle with dagger and scabbard in hand.

"Come on, then." Alsandair stalked off toward the chapel. Eloise put
a hand over her nose, eyes watering from his reek of sweat and ale. Fresh
as roses were Eoin and Donegal compared to Alsandair. She and her two
hounds followed at a safe distance behind. "Lovey," he called back, "keep
the bedding dry till I return, eh."

"I'll pray for you, too," Eloise offered. For surely his sin before God
was great, but not so great as the smell. "And for a bath," she muttered
under her breath, already thinking of the proper recitations for both of
them.

"You do that," Alsandair grumbled. Then after a moment, "By your
will, you do that my Maiden." Surely her prayers were potent, and who
couldn't use a well-placed word to God from one so favored as a
Dahlquin?

The grounds within Dahlquin Castle were quiet and steady as the
North Star. Silence broke only when the guards called their positions,
walking the ramparts, studying the vast dark beyond the reach of their
torchlight for any sign of movement. Eloise took comfort in the voices
and security within the stone fortress. In places the walls were as thick as
three mens' length, the first line of defense. In daylight archers had good
visibility and excellent range of shots through the crenellations and lancet
windows without exposing themselves to danger. More men were needed
to assault a castle than defend one.

Once inside the chapel Eloise lit a series of devotional candles and
scented incense pots, releasing the ceremonious aromas so pleasing to
God. Beast and Dragon set upon rats and mice. Eloise heard a cat hiss.
"Leave it," she called to the dogs, though she trusted Beast and Dragon
to remember cats were part of the pack, most of the time.

Alsandair closed the door. Sat, then leaning against the door, so none
could enter or exit, he closed his eyes.

Before starting her vigil in earnest, Eloise wrapped her blanket around
Alsandair.

The cat howled and spit.

Opening one eye, he said, "Not necessary, may you have goodness,
Maiden."

27

Eloise thought he tried to shake his head, but she tucked the blanket around his head and shoulders anyway, smiling when he slumped.

Then she knelt before the altar, directing her prayers of remorse to Saint Anne, mother of the most venerated woman of all time, the Virgin Mary. Eloise recited all the virtues of a good daughter to the Saint, beseeching her to intercede and bestow her forgiveness. She begged the benevolent Saint to forgive and bless Alsandair who had given up a warm bed to stand guard for her. Silver lines of smoke rose gracefully from the candles as the penitent thought about the humility and obedience of the Virgin Mary, becoming the Mother of Christ. Did Eloise's own father ask so much of her? Eloise questioned and resisted his bidding when it didn't fit her own plans, her ideas. Eloise didn't have plans, at least none she was at liberty to pursue.

The fragrance of the incense brought her back to her purpose: remorse and forgiveness. How could she trust her parents to know the will of God, when it felt so false in her heart? Shouldn't she know best the will of God for her? She thought on the wisdom of Hildegard of Bingen, Abbess from Rupertsberg. The German mystic had preached the importance of pursuing God's love with intellect and heart, for both were divine gifts from the Creator for humanity's betterment and appreciation. Eloise held open the sacred book, one of her most treasured possessions, a gift from her mother's mother.

Earnestly she prayed yet again for guidance; for a sign she was right, or wrong. For something. She inhaled the spicy aroma of the incense, willing it to clear her mind and open her heart to her purpose. She loved her parents, truly, was blessed with noble birth and all the privilege afforded those favored few. Why couldn't she attend a university? Women went on pilgrimage all the way to Jerusalem, surely Cambridge or Paris were not so far away. Sons could make such a choice. It wasn't a sin to learn, but a betterment of self and more knowledge to understand and do God's good work, surely. Did her own mother seek answers from the Saint: why Eloise wouldn't be a good daughter? Kindness, charity, obedience. She started to rock back and forth thinking. Her knees begged she obey the pain upon them and seek a cushion. Too long had she knelt on the cold stone floor.

Carefully Eloise folded the fabric of her surcoat and chemise several times over to create some comfort. Her prayers continued, as did the fatigues of the day. Slowly she began to slump, then sit. Soon she was wrapped with the warmth of two hounds, her head rising and falling with their breathing. The candles burned on for some time, the incense filling the small chapel with thick sweetness.

28

DAHLQUIN CASTLE, BEFORE DAWN, 8ᵗʰ of June

The seven guests rose early, before the dawn. No one suspected their foul purpose. By design, they had drunk far less than it appeared. While it seemed they slept soundly, in actuality they gauged the pulse of the castle. Before light, they would execute the gatekeeper and guards, then open the gate to Tiomoid U'Neill's army. They were mercenaries. Why not? They could be bought, their reward might be in land grants if the invading force were successful. To take Dahlquin would be a prize indeed. Remote enough that Lord FitzGilbert might not rush to its defense. What a message it would send to the rest of the Irish lords! This could be a stepping-stone to eventually taking the whole kingdom, or merely a good place to start one's own realm. Or work out the details of a truce, keep Dahlquin, and be absorbed back into the old regime. There were many possibilities if the only loyalty was self-interest.

With silence and stealth, three of the mercenaries made their way through the grounds. Approaching the gatehouse was harder than they anticipated. Lord Hubert was a careful and thorough man. More sentries to be silenced than expected; still Hubert protected against an assault from without, not treachery within his very walls.

The other three assassins slunk to the residential tower. Much wine and flattery tricked a foolish laundress into revealing the locations of the bedchambers of the lord, lady and their daughter. With the Dahlquins gone, taking the castle would be much easier. Dare they dream of a smooth takeover?

Invade the castle, declare themselves the lords, and demand allegiance. Give the new subjects a chance to live by swearing their fealty to the new overlord: Tiomoid U'Neill. This plan had so many inherent possibilities.

Returning from the chapel, Donegal's mind was full of doubt. Should he have stayed with Eloise, sending Alsandair to join Eoin? He checked in with all the posts through the castle on his way. All was quiet as it should be. Nonsense, he chided himself, Eloise was secure. When he heard a foot fall behind him, Donegal turned half expecting to see Alsandair, dice in hand, begging to trade duty. Donegal's mouth was covered, his head yanked back. As the assailant behind cut his throat, another held his legs firmly. *Eoin!* his mind screamed: he could picture his alert cousin, feel his own failure to duty, *Uncle…* Donegal struggled in vain as his lifeblood pumped furiously from his body. Panic overrode any pain until weakness, darkness, cold and the final humiliation of evacuation ended his days.

The residential tower was quiet again. Donegal's body was left sitting as if asleep, his padded gambeson absorbing the thick, spent blood, but not the stench of filth. Tiny pairs of eyes watched the body. Rats drawn by the smell inched from the hidden depths, cautious only of the cat's return, or one of the dogs.

"Lord Hubert's grown soft," Davydd whispered, Eoin's murdered body at his feet.

"Overconfident in the Dahlquin image of invincibility," Byron muttered, standing outside Maid Eloise's very door.

"Tenacity," Davydd whispered, smirking.

"Careless. Undeserving," Byron mouthed.

Wordlessly, Davydd nodded to Byron and a flick of his thumb to the next door indicated the squire enter Lady Aine's chamber.

With the two guards dead, Davydd moved to Hubert's bedchamber.

Byron slipped into the heir's bedchamber. It was dark but not silent. Snoring rattled the furnishings. His hair stood on end. Neither guards, nor hounds. Barely enough light glowed from the candle to illuminate two sleeping figures on the floor. Nursemaids, perhaps? The bed was empty, unslept in. Byron quietly felt around anyway, for any form. Only a book.

He scanned the room, making a thorough search. Armed as he was it was impossible to be silent. One of the sleepers roused.

"Princess, dear, is that you? Elo-" Nurse was sliced near in half.

The commotion woke the other sleeper. The red-haired assassin grabbed for the man's head in the dark. Sean felt a large hand cover his mouth and part of his nose. A dagger pressed cold and sharp on his throat. *Was it wet*, Sean wondered? *Blood? His?*

"Where is she?" hissed Byron.

Sean could smell blood. *Whose? His wife's?* They were here together, in the maiden's room, sleeping on a pallet upon the floor waiting for her. "Where is she?" Byron's voice grated in Sean's ear. Sean was bleeding and overwhelmed. The stranger threatening, the oppressing odor, and the unconscious game he played not to believe it was his own wife's death he smelled.

"The Maid," Byron demanded.

"Eloise? Not here?" Sean finally croaked through the pressure of a blade already severing the outer layer of flesh. Sean felt his own death as imminent. His wife and now him.

The knight felt the futility of it too. Byron wouldn't get information from this dredge. Worthless filth. Keeping back of the man to avoid the blood, he slit Sean's throat to the spine. Angered, he kicked the bodies, as if this would somehow reveal where his target was.

"Curse the bitch," he muttered. Little wonder it had been so easy. She and her notorious hounds from Hell weren't even here. What next, assist his partners with the lord and lady? Maybe Eloise was with either of them, or they would know where she was.

A small dog yapped in the adjoining chamber.

The squire was to assassinate Lady Aine while the two knights killed the father and heir. Instead of the sleeping lady, he found only a small hairy dog, biting viciously at his ankles. Kicking at the relentless dog, he rummaged quickly through the empty bed as the dog continued to snarl and bite. The squire heard a deep rumbling growl, but there wasn't a source. The heretic's chamber was haunted, the squire thought.

"No one here, either?' hissed Byron as he slipped into Aine's chamber.

Alerted by the dogs, Hubert and Reginald were up as Davydd entered. The savage dogs got the assassin by hand and throat. The table was overturned, ewer and bowl crashed to the floor. A chair slid across the room, propelled by man and dogs, wedging beneath the bed. Reginald was by the door adjoining Aine's chamber, the carnage of red-headed man and flailing dogs separating him from Hubert on the other side of the chamber. Aine sat petrified on the bed.

As Byron came to assist his brother, Reginald descended upon him with an elbow to the face. Feet swept out from under him, the traitor thudded to the stone floor. This man would be taken alive to answer questions and suffer a proper death later. Seeing this, the squire turned and ran to take his chances with the gatehouse.

By the time Hubert could call off the dogs, Davydd was but a torso, mangled and mauled. He would answer to no one but Satan. Hubert hated a mess in his bedchamber. As a knight and lord, battle was a way of life and he thrived on it - but in his bedchamber where he, his wife and child took their refuge, this was defilement. He rushed to the bedchambers of his women. Aine's room lay undisturbed save for the ranting Dilis. That little excuse for a dog helped saved his life. Hubert didn't appreciate the debt to a dog not bigger than a flea on a real Dahlquin hound. *Later*.

His worst nightmare awaited him in his daughter's chamber. The stench of blood and death hit him as he entered. Foul odor when a body was laid open. Emotion buried, he methodically analyzed the scene. Bed unslept in. The nursemaid, hacked almost in two, lay cruelly strewn across the floor. And who was the other? Definitely not his daughter: a man, before the saints, Sean. *Look again, fool, maybe your mind refuses to see what is truly present*, he scolded himself. There were only two bodies. And Eloise wasn't one of them.

"Hubert," Aine said, a psalter in her hand, "Eloise is in the chapel."

Again, Hubert scanned the chamber.

"Light. We need light," Hubert said, taking the single, inadequate candle.

Reginald entered, dragging Byron bound and gagged behind him. Hubert's hounds snarled, snapping at the captive. Dilis sniffed at the dead bodies on the floor.

"What, how do you know?" Hubert asked his wife, suppressing panic.

"She is in the chapel," Aine continued. "She left her psalter on the bed, a sign to Nurse or me. Before God, oh Hubert," she wailed as the brunt of the shock set in.

"Murder! Guards! The guests are traitors!" Reginald shouted. "Stop the guests. Guards!"

Eoin and Donegal were quickly discovered, dead; others were summoned from their posts. Not a trace of Eloise or her dogs, except the sign she was in the chapel.

THE CHAPEL

The two massive hellhounds lifted their shaggy heads. They would not have been out of place guarding Satan's gates, welcoming sinners to the blazing inferno. Saint Anne's chapel was an unlikely place to find the wire-haired creatures.

Outside other dogs barked, alerting the castle residents. Beast and Dragon stood, shook themselves, and growled low and menacing. Eloise roused with her dogs' movement. The floor was hard. She was stiff and cold without the warmth of her canine companions. Where was she, her sleepy mind puzzled as she drifted back sleep?

Hackles raised, the dogs continued growling like rumbling thunder. Eloise roused slowly from her night in prayer and penance. Her drowsy hand felt the wrinkled, dog-haired condition of her blue surcoat.

Now she heard the disturbance too.

"Close the gate!"

"We are attacked!"

"To arms, to arms!"

"The gatehouse is breached."

"Sound the alarm!"

"Close the gate! Close the gate! Close the gate!"

Men shouted, screamed. The sound of metal against metal and metal to shield chimed through the dark. Shrieks of death and victory howled through the bailey and up over the ramparts.

The Great Bell rang out.

Eloise clutched the wooden cross hanging from her neck. Her mind raced as she moved to a window to peek out. Too early for drill or training, this was battle in earnest: right in their inner bailey. *How did so many soldiers get inside? Who was manning the gatehouse?* Sweet Jesus, Lord and Savior save us, she thought. Beast and Dragon growled, their lips curled back, revealing sharp teeth and pink gums. Eloise pictured *Cara*, her bow and arrows, carefully - uselessly - stored in her chamber. She had never needed them more than this very instance.

"Alsandair!" she called. "What's happening?" she asked, shaking him awake.

Her guard jumped up, axe drawn, looking around. He listened intently, analyzing.

"Stay here!" he commanded. He opened the door, peered out: chaos. As quickly he shut the door, fell against it, eyes closed.

"Maiden!" he called, jumping up, "Secure the door." There wasn't a lock. He slipped out.

Eloise pulled herself away from the window to block the door. Then as quickly it burst open. Beast and Dragon lunged.

Several stunned workers stumbled into the chapel. They were terrified. What was worse: the carnage outside, or the savage beasts in the chapel? They would take their chances with God.

One woman backed out from fear of the canines, but was instantly pushed back in by Alsandair.

"Block this door!" Alsandair snarled, matching the dogs in threat. "Don't let anyone in."

"Quiet," Eloise ordered her hounds. "Help me!" she snapped at the waiting group as she pushed a table in front of the door. Secure, she turned back to them. "Sit down and pray. Quietly." Saints preserve us, she thought. "Are we safe in the Chapel? Surely good Christians would not invade the sanctuary of God's house, despite the size," Eloise asked the frightened group.

They stared at her, speechless, wide-eyed.

"We must be safe here. We'll all stay quiet and pray."

Still not an answer from the trembling group. They were praying the dogs not eat them.

She heard her father's voice in her mind. How often had Hubert instructed his daughter, teaching her to manage, to be a judge of people. There is the honor of tournament and sport, the honor of noble love in story and song, the honor between brethren and kinsmen among their personal dealings with each other. And then there is survival. Honor may not exist in war. If someone is willing to take what isn't his, he is willing to take it however he can. Therefore, she must be willing to defend what is hers anyway she can. Neither rules, nor code, nor honor for thieves or murderers. It went against all her religious lessons, but sinful people existed. She must protect herself and Dahlquin. How to balance God's law and survival? It's in God's hands, her father would say. Hubert would have much to answer for, but accepted full responsibility for it: now, and when his judgment came.

They wouldn't be safe. Eloise felt it with each breath. Where would she be safe? How would she get there? Safe. What of her parents? Were they safe? Did they look for her, mayhap putting themselves at risk to find her? Eoin or Donegal would come for her, she thought. Her dogs barked, as communication with the other canines of Dahlquin and as a steady warning to bodies approaching the chapel.

Pitched battle charged the air with static energy. The clash of swords, battle-axes, and other weaponry rang throughout the keep and ramparts. Shouts of men fighting, shouts of command, of positions and reinforcements, and the agony of injury and dying. Fire and its partner smoke permeated everything, blocking the morning's light.

Mathair and the physician will be in the infirmary, she thought. *They need me.* With that goal in mind, Eloise kept watch on the mayhem outside. No one assaulted the chapel, yet. It wasn't of strategic military use. Years had been spent listening to her father and Uncle Reggie discussing war tactics. The endless strategies for attack and defense, drawings in the dirt, use of a board game, teaching her over and over again how best to defend Dahlquin. *I should have paid more attention*, she scolded herself, searching her memory. What she did know was that this many soldiers in the inner bailey were *not* good, nor part of a sound, defensible plan. Taking her chances beyond the chapel with the darkness or waiting to see if she were flushed out were her immediate choices. The temporary security and sanctity of the chapel pressed her to stay put and pray.

"Heavenly Father," she started. Not time for lesser saints, Dahlquin needed help now. "Lord God of us all, by Your benevolent will, help us. Enemies are upon us. Help the men of Dahlquin vanquish this enemy. Keep our men safe. Protect Dahlquin from this unholy siege. Heavenly Father I beseech you, by Your will, protect all Dahlquin, we have been humble servants always." Howls of pain and fury continued outside. Eyes closed tightly, hands shaking, Eloise chanted, rocking back and forth on her knees before the altar. "By Your will help our men, by Your will help our men, by Your will help our men."

ASHBURY CASTLE, 8th of June

Lord Albert of Ashbury sat in the dark chamber, glowering at the two young women in his bed, their arms wrapped around each other as they slept. Charming they had been at table during the evening meal. Alarming they became between the covers. But in the end, despite all their combined efforts to arouse and entertain, he had been unable to sheath his sword. *God curse them*.

Curse God was mayhap more accurate. His male grandeur had been legendary, his ardor unrivaled. Yet for all the well-pleased lionesses the Lion of Ashbury had mounted in his long years...long...he shook his head, none had born him cubs. And now God, in some perverse trick of hard fate, had withdrawn Albert's ability to be hard. Albert was not amused with his own word wit.

His mouth was stale with old wine, and he wiped at his dry lips. With eyes closed, Albert inhaled, remembering the taste. Like amber barley wine, piquant with a pinch of salt and a trace of bitter for balance, and the slick, heady tang of grey mullet. The flavors of Eve.

Albert fought the petty urge, as he always did, to punish the girls for his failure. And next his wife, Mor, for not choosing more competent, salacious companions. It was two years ago, in his seventieth year, when the problem arose. Arose. Albert's own words mocked his emasculated being. Seemed the whole language revolved around copulation. Every word had nuance. So where would his wrath and revenge end? Was he to punish the language makers as well as the females for his short comings? *Damn it!* Or the physicians and priests for not providing a cure for this debilitating state. Vituperate the saints? Saint Giles, Saint Henry II? Nearly forty-five years he had prayed to Saint Anne, blessed saint of fertility, to grant him the sons he needed. Now he prayed for the gift of the game: to rut like the ram as he once did.

It all came down to God. Merciful, vengeful, petty and self-righteous. *Why?* Why he wondered, would God strike down his ability to perform the sacred act of procreation, an act he had so diligently honored? God had withheld his seed. Now God withheld the tool. Yet Albert lived, strong and vigorous of limb and spirit. For the glory of Ashbury.

Albert called for his attendants. He had hunger, such hunger. Food would be the only satisfaction he would have this morning.

"Starvation is upon me, wake the kitchen staff. I require an early meal," Albert commanded as his attendants rushed in, groggy with sleep.

Behind them, a server brought a pitcher of wine, though wine remained from the previous night.

"Are you to break fast without benefit of mass, Sire? And this, our own Saint Bron's Feast Day?" Eoch asked, ducking as he entered the chamber, then raising an eyebrow as he stood. Eoch was fifty-seven, hoary by most reckoning, and still tall as a giant. His dark complexion had warmed with the greying of hair and eyes. He had been a Knight Hospitaler, now he was Albert's second-in-command. Albert valued a religious man-at-arms for protection and guidance. But at these moments of inconvenient piety, Albert questioned the wisdom. And how was it the man could appear, on a moment's notice, dressed, hair tidy, ready for whatever action Albert required?

"Damn you. And damn the damnable priest," Albert said, for little good they had done him.

"And shall we damn the sun for not yet *rising*?" Eoch asked, eyebrow arching conspiratorially, a comical vision of Satan. "I'm your mercenary, Lord, not God's."

"Rouse the priest," Albert grumbled as his attendants hurried to arrange his garments.

"As you command," Eoch smiled, seeming to swagger out of the bedchamber.

A spontaneous mass was conducted with smooth efficiency since the priest was accustomed to ministering to his lord at all hours of the day or night.

With souls once more intact, and God's good graces upon them, Albert, Eoch, and Albert's personal guard made their way to the Great Hall.

The Hall was still dark at this early hour, though five pages scrambled to stoke the fire pit and torches as well as prepare the table. Barking dogs and the comforting smell of smoke welcomed Albert and his men.

Eoch inhaled deeply. Albert glanced about the dim hall, amused as the pages stumbled, bowed, stumbled, bowed again, confused about whether to kneel in servitude or continue with their chores. One little boy, someone Albert didn't recognise, fought back the tears.

"You, boy," Albert called, pointing to the child. "By my will, you. Come to me."

The frightened page hurried to Albert, then dropped to his knees at Albert's feet. His spindly shoulders stuck out like small hillocks, and he shook with apparent dread.

"Will someone not conduct introductions?" Albert bellowed. "If this sniveling page is to serve at my table, I best know his lineage."

Albert glanced at Eoch, exchanging a mild grin.

"You are most observant, Lord, he's newly come," Eoch said. "I'll do the honor." Eoch turned his attention to the shaking page before him. "Up! Rise good page and meet your Lord," Eoch boomed, drawing everyone's attention anew.

Eoch waited patiently as the small boy stood, obviously unsure what to do, for surely subordinates remained kneeling.

"Lord Albert, Lion of Ashbury, founding Lord and Tenant of Ashbury, Connacht, Ireland, Order of the Cross, loyal vassal of the departed King Richard the Lion-Hearted and departed King Philip of France," Eoch recited with the exaggerated flourish of an assembly crier, barely taking a breath before resuming, "Keeper of the King's Peace and Justice by decree of Lord Gerald FitzGilbert, of Leinster and Ireland, and our fair and good King Henry, I present to you young Ruidori, second son of Sir Gwyffed and his wife, in direct service to Lord Bryan of New Pembrokeshire, Meath. Ruidori is fostering here, as of yesterday, if memory serves." Eoch finished, raising an arched eyebrow to young Ruidori who was still deciphering all the titles dictated.

"Has your tongue gone hiding?" Albert asked the perplexed and silent Ruidori.

Ruidori's round brown eyes stared even harder if that were possible.

"Speak, boy," Eoch said.

One of the dogs barked. As the men laughed, the dog barked again.

"May you have goodness, Sire," Ruidori choked out.

"Welcome to Ashbury," Albert said. "Now go make yourself useful."

Eoch motioned the boy away with a sweeping hand. "Chin up!" he called. As Ruidori ran off, Eoch pretended to kick him.

Albert scanned his dark hall, devoid of frivolity or the merest of glad tidings.

"To Hell with protocol," Albert said grandly, feeling jovial after Eoch's mock formality with the page. "Let us raid the kitchens."

"Saint Marta hear our ravenous prayers," Eoch intoned, retrieving his eating knife and thrusting it aloft as if it were his war sword, "for the glory of Ashbury and all who hunger!"

"We're with you, Lord Lion," the guards answered, also raising their eating knives. Two crouched as if ready to charge.

Albert inhaled, satisfied with the scent of men and embers. This is more like it, Albert thought, raising his eating knife in martial camaraderie.

"Lord Husband, my servants cower in your magnitude," a stately female voice intoned. Cringing, Albert lowered his hand. His eating knife hung dull and limp at his side. He and his men turned in mutual surprise. Lady Mor stepped out of the shadows, with two of her attendants. She was hastily dressed, and her bed-mussed hair was slicked down with watered wine. Mor curtsied low to Albert. "A good morrow to you, Lord," she said before rising, stiffly, but without complaint. The years were wearing hard upon her as well.

Albert watched her sternly. What devilment was she about at this foul hour, he wondered. Had she come to mock his failure? Surely not, Mor was not such a low woman. He scratched his back side in contemplation.

"You're up early," she continued as her gaze moved slowly in the dim light as if taking attendance, "and in want of fair sport. Saint Marta has her hands full."

Albert turned his gaze upon his wife's two yawning, mid-aged attendants. Curse his eyes, they were lively enough entertainment, for Mor, in the female tower. He suddenly felt like wee Ruidori, unable or in this case unwilling to speak.

"My gracious Lady Mor," Eoch said bowing with exaggerated flourish, "are we to have the pleasure of your favors as we break fast this morn? What morsel of nourishment might I bring down for you whenst I plunder the wilds of your kitchen?"

Albert gave Eoch a harsh glance. The betrayer! Was there not enough gloom this morning without Mor and her attendants underfoot? Had Albert not endured the compulsory mass before embarking on the merest hope of a pleasant pass time with his companions?

Mor dipped her head, a sly smile softening her face. Curse her foolish attempt at coquettishness, he thought. Why didn't he bundle her off to some convent, indeed, a distant, sunny convent in Spain?

"May you have goodness for the kind invitation," Mor said, "but regretfully, I must decline. I anticipate it's rough company this morning." She nodded to Albert.

Had he heard correctly, Albert wondered? Eoch, The Betrayer, looked disappointed, but Mor smiled with her overly kind, aging eyes.

"Wise choice, Lady," Albert concurred, again raising his eating knife in relief. "Save yourself!" he bellowed with approval.

"While you ransack the kitchens, I shall speak with the stable master and huntsman."

Huntsman. Albert heard one or perhaps two of his guards murmur.

"And why not? Such a radiant idea, Lady. Why didn't I think of such?" Albert asked, truly wondering why he had not, for hunting was a splendid diversion. Always welcome.

"With a kitchen to pillage? Your mind was elsewhere. I've assurance, once fortified with wine and bread, you would have concocted the grand scheme yourselves," Mor answered.

The men laughed, and Albert smiled.

"With your leave, Lord Husband, we'll attend to the preparations."

As Mor and her attendants retreated, Albert turned with the steady deliberation of a seventy-two-year old knight and walked with his men to raid the kitchens. Convent indeed. Perhaps he would keep her around, at least through the Yule.

After a suitable raid upon the kitchen, Albert and his men converged on the stables. Three huntsmen had three packs of five or six hounds each leashed and straining at their collars while the stable attendants finished tacking the hunting coursers. Albert and his seven knights strung their bows, then drew and flexed and drew again. Ten squires and attendants assembled the gear and helped with seventeen horses.

Great sport, archery, Albert thought as his squires helped him with his hip quiver: a noble pursuit for hunting.

"You've ten broad heads, Lord," one of the squires said, "and I'll have twenty more for you."

Albert glanced at the lad in the dim lamp light, wondering if thirty would be enough.

"I'll pack some more, Lord," the squire said before directing one of the other squires in Albert's attendance to raid the armory for more arrows.

"I've more than enough, Sire," Eoch said. "Do you I could continue shooting in joyous merriment while my Lord's quiver was bare?"

"More like joyous abandon," Albert said, unable to contain his smile.

"I must concur, my shooting skills are lacking, Lord. Gladly I would exchange these hunting tools for my shield in your service," Eoch said, holding his bow up as if it were a shield.

"Its archery practice you need, Eoch," said one of the knights.

"Perhaps you hide behind your shield too much," said another with a chuckle.

"Eoch, hide?" Albert barked then smiled at his companion. "The great battering ram of the Hospitalers was merely hiding?" Albert threw his arm over his eyes as if blocking the vision of this new revelation.

"Fear upon me, my greatest shame is revealed, my Lord," Eoch said, making a half bow, "too cowardly even to grace a bow and arrow."

"Well, so be it," Albert said, seeing the stable master signal that the horses were ready. "Today we're all cowards, eh? For archery it is. Saddle up before the noon sun melts us. We're less than a fortnight from solstice."

"With arrow or lance against the wild beasts of Ashbury, and without armour save light chain mail? Not cowardice, Lord, but game sport," one of his knights said.

"Sounds like an indulgence, sir," Eoch mocked, swinging into the saddle of his tall, red mare. "If you are to blandish our good Lord Albert, then do so with flair."

"Are you suggesting, sir, that I lack sincerity?" the knight asked, as he swung into the saddle, rechecking the bow in its sheath on his horse.

"Not more than I," Eoch said, smiling grandly. "I'm exceedingly glad you didn't suggest we escalate our bravado to some silly Greek escapade."

"Eh?" the knight said.

Albert and all his men were staring at Eoch for an explanation.

"To prove we're not cowards. Perhaps you would suggest we embark, naked as Adam came, and engage a bear in hand-to-hand combat," Eoch said

"Don't you mean sword to paw?" Albert asked, laughing when Eoch's expression dropped in exaggerated dismay.

"Again, Lord, you're too wise for me," Eoch said, dipping his head but never taking his laughing eyes off Albert.

"Enough. Let us depart."

As the hunting party moved farther from Ashbury castle, thick fog was illuminated by the nearly full moon, sinking on the western horizon. Albert pondered once again if this might be how death appeared. Although purgatory was presented as fire, burning the soul of sins to prepare it for admittance to Heaven and the direct friendship with God, Albert couldn't help but observe the solemnity of this dense fog with the gloom of the grave. *Excrement*, he muttered to himself, enough of death: at least not his own mortality, but hopefully death to some worthy stag or boar or bear. If he were to face his death, let it be this noble day, by God's will, pitted against the largest bear in the grand forest of Ashbury estate. And not naked as Adam, he chuckled to himself.

"Forthwith!" he declared, urging his horse to walk faster.

"So be it," Eoch concurred, "seems the hounds acknowledge your enthusiasm. They're extra noisy this morning. My horse seems leery."

"Mine, too, Lord," one of the knights said, his voice raised to be heard over the barking. "Wolves seem unlikely with the hounds at bay."

"Wolves? We're still in the farmlands. There is naught but row upon row of crops," another knight said.

"Well cultivated, perhaps the horses want to graze upon the flax, beans and barley," the first knight answered.

Albert blinked, feeling the weight of accumulated fog in his lashes, his face and hair wet with it. The air was moist and fresh, the aroma of turned soil, horses, and damp leather. The smells of life.

"Fog *spriggans*," Albert said, acknowledging the ancient wisdom of his domain, and the animals' ability to see what he could not.

"They sense something," Eoch agreed, smiling with anticipation, patting his mare's neck.

Eoch's mare lifted her head; muzzle up, she emitted a high-pitched neigh.

Albert and his men were silent, straining to listen, but all anyone could hear was the relentless barking of the hounds. Again, the red mare neighed, a long shrill call through the fog. Two other horses neighed as well, believing there were more horses.

"Silence those hounds!" Albert growled, knowing it was futile. The restrained hounds barked and howled, begging to be loosed, to pursue the mighty prey that he and his men so longed to run down.

"Poachers don't have horses," one of the knights said.

"Too dark yet for priests or merchants to be on the move," another said.

"Herd of ponies, perhaps," Eoch speculated.

One of the hounds yelped.

"Ponies would be a nuisance. Huntsman!" one of the knights called to the man in charge of the men with the tethered hounds. "Will you be able to keep the beasts off the herd?"

"I will, Sir," the Huntsman answered. "We'll hold them back to be sure."

"Down ya cur!" one of the men said, and another hound yelped. "Quiet!"

"Well, we certainly have the advantage of stealth and surprise," Eoch said, his wry smile accented by his arched eyebrow. "Let's hope the hounds don't eat these sleepy travelers in their tents."

"Indeed," Albert said, his voice loud. "We have neither musicians or ladies cackling."

"It's quiet as the grave," one of the knights observed, "by hunting standards."

"We'll hardly instill fear in our prey. Surely the deer are sleeping," Eoch said.

"Forthwith, huntsmen! Take the hounds and find something!" Albert shouted. Men and dogs ran ahead into the damp curtain.

Again, the anxious horses neighed, calling into the fog as it consumed the huntsmen and hounds.

This time Albert heard the answering neigh, distinct and distressingly close.

"Albert," Eoch said, caution in his voice, as his mare stopped.

"I heard it," Albert assured him, also halting his horse which anxiously pranced in place. *Spriggans* were known to distort sound, making familiar things seem foreign and discerning the location impossible. One moment the horse sounds close as if he were to step upon it; the next moment, the beast seems far behind him.

Barking, growling and then a sharp screech pierced the fog.

"Run!" the huntsman shouted his voice an urgent command in the mist.

Another yelp and screech. Something was killing the hounds.

"Run! Run!"

"That's the huntsman," Eoch said.

"Lord!" the huntsman shouted. "Army! Archers!"

Shouting, barking, confusion…Albert could see nothing in the grey mist.

Albert's knights encircled him. At Eoch's direction the squires lined up before them, bows drawn into the blinding fog. The horses continued to paw or skitter. The fog seemed to press back upon Albert with the force of this unseen enemy.

"Back to the castle!" the huntsman shouted. "Go, go-"

Albert thought the man had been silenced. Archers? How many? Who would attack?

"Not a word," Eoch hissed to the knights. "My Lord," Eoch said in a low voice to Albert, "we must get you back to the castle."

Albert's mind was spinning as he tried to assess the situation. Retreat? From who? This was his domain. He and his men were lightly armed for a hunt, not battle. They rode hunting coursers, not destriers. What if it were just a raiding party, stealing horses and livestock? He and his men could easily dispatch such vile perpetrators. Wouldn't that be a grand adventure, far better than a mere hunt? For the glory of Ashbury.

"Lord Albert," Eoch hissed again, maneuvering his red mare close to Albert's horse. "We're too few-"

A rain of arrows pelted them. Two of his knights swayed, arrows stuck in them. All the horses spun, some with arrows protruding.

"To the castle," Eoch called, his voice firm and low. "Now!"

43

"I agree," Albert said, signalling to his men. One of his knights was tottering in the saddle. Albert turned, cueing his horse to gallop home.

As more arrows fell upon them, Albert understood this was not a raiding party. An army. That's what the huntsman said.

"Ride, Lord," Eoch urged close on Albert's left side. Eoch rode with his right arm and sword outstretched, covering Albert's back. "Head down."

Arrows fell upon Albert and his men, but they were not blanketed. Unable to see through the fog and semi-darkness, Albert figured the archers could only shoot in the direction of the castle.

"What?" a knight said.

"Fuck!" cursed Eoch.

Coming up behind Albert, Cerberus appeared. Three heads bent, tongues draped out, flapping like ears. The hounds were still tethered together, their necks and shoulders bearing the weight of their collars like yokes and dragging behind them their unanticipated burden: two dead hounds. It was a rampaging hazard as the frightened team veered toward Albert's horse in an attempt to gain the easiest passage back to the kennel. The dead hounds' bodies bounced and spun, further scaring the live hounds and horses. Hemmed in by Eoch and his mare, Albert's courser kicked at the canine pack nearly under his hooves.

"Ride, I'll try and divert them!" Eoch shouted, pulling well back from Albert and his galloping horse.

"Shoot them!" Eoch shouted back at the knights, as Albert tried to ride wide of the pack.

The hounds were falling back, tiring, he prayed. Never did Albert think his men would be hunting his own damn dogs. Never did he think he would be the damned hunted, Albert reflected. As quickly his mind raced on. Secure the castle. Regroup. Then grind these attacking bastards to dust. Whoever they were.

His horse shortened its stride, and Albert just had time to prepare to jump as his horse leaped over the stone fence just looming into vision. Glancing back, he saw Cerberus nearly split in two as a single hound's body cleared the fence, tail-end first, while the other two hounds were caught up. Next to the hounds Eoch came up out of the fog, and another of his knights. Albert returned his focus to the ride, trusting his horse to feel its way through the mist, because at this speed Albert could see little. Could the horses maintain this pace all the way back to the castle? For the glory of Ashbury, they must.

CONNACHT, 8th of June

"Damn it, Roland!" Sir Guillaume exclaimed as he peered through the dragon's breath of remote western Connacht.

"Face it, man, we're lost!" Sir Sedric added. Seemed this island was always shrouded in fog. Sometimes it was so thick a man could barely see his own mount's ears before him. Other times it was thin, wispy and undulated. Figures seemed to appear and retreat within the misty depths, enigmatic sprites or lost souls trapped in some other plane between earthly life and the spirit world. Dragon's breath indeed.

The fog was unrelenting. Roland, his friends Guillaume and Sedric, and two squires had wandered the wilderness of the western marches for a day and this very morning with nary a sign of humanity. Stories were oft told of travelers lost riding in the mist 'til death or madness overtook them, their bodies often found at the very gates of the castle they sought.

Sitting tall in the saddle, Roland tried to scan the horizon. Seemed they headed northeast, yet Ashbury Castle eluded them. He didn't wish to admit they were lost. The Scragmuirs had been quite clear in their directions to Ashbury: it was half a day's ride between the two estates. Black hair curled by the moisture stuck to his brow, he inhaled the clean scent of dew and pine. *A fine place to be granted a fief.* Only by great feats of bravery and loyalty were such land holdings awarded, an honor to be sure. This felt more like ostracism. Had not the Dahlquins been dispatched to settle this hostile parcel of island three generations back? Surely Roland had done naught to earn the disfavor of High Lord Gerald FitzGilbert of Leinster, deputy of William de Burgh of Connacht who himself represented King Henry of England. Nay, Gerald FitzGilbert was well pleased to send Roland.

"Roland, has the fog clogged your ears? We're lost," Guillaume said.

None of these five men had ever ventured to this far corner of Ireland, and up until now they had navigated the fortnight journey from southeastern Leinster across the Shannon River to Connacht without so much as a missed meal. Hospitality and good intentions greeted them throughout. But western Connacht seemed to be off the map entirely.

"I'm not lost," Roland smiled broadly to his companions. "I'm with you."

"Well, I'm lost," Guillaume responded, unimpressed.

"And us," Sedric said, indicating himself and the two squires.

"Not so, you're with me. So long as we're together we can't be lost," Roland offered. "Let's try this way."

The men followed Roland.

"Any chance we have reached the end of the world?" murmured one of the squires. He could envision a large imaginary dragon in the deepest sleep on some mountaintop. With each exhalation the slumbering beast continued to bathe the island in thick, damp fog.

"Bah," his friend said, "you're a nit." Still both young men crossed themselves as they followed the knights further into the fog of Connacht.

Roland and his men rode on an open stretch of track, orchards on one side and on the other side divided strips of land, some fallow, others with workers weeding. Ahead were two oil cloth covered wagons, pulled by one mule each, family members walking alongside. Merchants, but Roland couldn't see their wares.

The track of road was wide with deep ruts, seemingly in both directions, and a blur of horse and animal prints.

"Plenty of travel and commerce," Guillaume said, his slanted blue eyes looking down briefly, then ahead. His thinning, blond hair hung limp with the weight of the mist.

"I agree, mayhap all roads lead to Ashbury," Sedric added, scanning the misty surroundings of open meadow, grasses bent with accumulated moisture. In contrast to his tall companions, Sedric was stocky, arms like beef haunches and fists to match, with brown eyes and curly brown hair that frizzed in a grizzled tangle in the humidity.

"The only damn road," Guillaume said. "Pray Ashbury isn't in a fucking bog."

The squires chuckled.

Roland cast Guillaume a wary look.

"All the more incentive to collect your rents and return to Leinster. Or Scragmuir," Guillaume said, meeting Roland's wary glance with a wry smile.

Roland felt his horse stiffen. Artoch's head came up, searching. One of the squires' horses whinnied into the damp beyond. All the men came to attention, searching like their horses.

"I see them," Roland said.

"How many?" Sedric asked.

Roland counted again. "Five. Like us."

"Five, at the crossroad. Maybe they've sent a welcoming party, Roland, to escort you home."

One of the mounted knights waved, and Roland returned the salutation. The men wore no familiar colours or identifying emblems Roland could recognise, but they were well armed. As were he and his men. The squire's horse bellowed an inquiry.

"Good day to you," Roland said, nodding. "Are you for Ashbury?"

Guillaume cleared his throat in a mild reprimand that Roland not reveal so much to these unknown men. Then he nodded politely to the mounted strangers at the crossroad.

Roland let his breath out and waited for an answer.

"Good day to you, sirs," one of the knights returned. "Ashbury is it?" he asked. "And you would be?"

Remembering Guillaume's reticence, Roland sat back reassessing, studying the face of the sullen man who had just spoken, moving on to each face in turn.

"Forgive us," another knight said, "courtesy gets lost on the roads. Are you seeking Ashbury?" he asked. "Ah, I see by the lads' eager faces you must."

Roland turned to look at the squires, who in turn immediately looked down. Roland noticed Sedric wore a sly grin.

"Now you've done it, poxy knaves," Guillaume scolded the squires. "Revealed our mooching ways, your wanton, hungry maws flapping in the breeze." Guillaume gave them an exaggerated scowl. "Forgive us, too," he addressed the knights. "We're five hungry men from Leinster, bringing the King's blessings all the way to our Connacht neighbors," he finished with a flourish and a bow from the waist.

"Welcome to Connacht," the second knight said, matching Guillaume's jovial demeanor. "Well, follow this road," the knight said, pointing to the left, "but you've a long bit to traverse."

"Left?" Sedric muttered, scratching his neck.

"Most direct route, 'less of course you want to risk farm and orchard and guarded forest. Far be it from me to command *Leinstermen*," he added with a sarcastic lilt.

"Ah, seems we've wandered off course, caught up in the quietude and contemplation in this rugged corner of God's province," Roland said, thinking as Sedric probably was that left, west, was Dahlquin, not Ashbury. "And you would be?" he asked.

"Us? Travelers like yourselves," the first knight said. "U'Neill."

"You're also a long way from home." The U'Neill's lands were in Ulster, northern Ireland. "I'm Roland, this is Guillaume, Sedric," the knights nodded, and Roland introduced the squires. "We're late of Leinster."

"Fair travel to you," the U'Neill knight said.

"Will you join us?" Roland asked, thinking the new companions would be a pleasant diversion.

"We won't, by your gracious will, though it's a tempting offer," the U'Neill knight said, then hesitated. "We're waiting. Meeting up with some lost or waylaid cousins."

"Fair travel to you as well," Roland said as he and his companions cued their horses left, hopefully to Ashbury.

There were no dependable roads or signs so far out, only vague landmarks. Connacht was a vast wilderness compared with the southeast. The communities were spread farther apart and were more rugged and sparse than those of Leinster. Yet three Welsh invaders had traveled out here, building their Norman-style castles well beyond MacMurrough's lands. They were Ireland's Marcher Lords.

The country was magnificent and held an ephemeral beauty for Roland. He had heard tell one loved it or hated it out here. While the dreaded Norsemen of centuries past were no longer the threat, the area was populated by the tenacious native Irish. The old ways were gone, and most were baptized as Christian, but they still resented the forced rule over them from England across the sea. Roland had traveled much in service to Lord Gerald FitzGilbert, and before that for his Godfather, King John. But there had been no need to travel so far northwest, a testament to the infamous "Pax Dahlquinius" as Lord Gerald FitzGilbert often joked. Dahlquin kept the peace between the native tribesmen. Lord Albert, the Lion of Ashbury, kept the peace between Dahlquin and Scragmuir.

"Do you think Albert still keeps lions at Ashbury?" Sedric asked.

There were no lions on these islands, or anywhere on the mainland. Yet Lord Albert had brought home two lion cubs from his sojourn to Outremer, having taken up the cross in service to King Richard and King Phillip, the same pilgrimage Ruaidri Dahlquin had returned from - only to be murdered, by his half-brother, Lord Dahlquin, according to Scragmuir rumor.

"Lord FitzGilbert has seen them," Roland said.

"So, we have heard, and Lord Albert is known to throw his enemies to them. Like a Caesar," Guillaume added.

"But Lord Humphrey said they're long dead. Claims none outside Ashbury has seen them in years. Scrawny, toothless things he called them," Sedric reminded them.

48

"Mayhap Humphrey is ashamed to admit he is afraid," Roland said. "This might be how the Lion of Ashbury keeps the peace between Dahlquin and Scragmuir."

"Plenty of men say they've heard the roaring deep in the bowels of Ashbury," Guillaume said with a grin. "I'd like to see them. Not in an arena, mind you."

"Not even with an ass's jaw?" Sedric asked, grinning too. "Connacht needs a Samson."

"That's it!" Guillaume exclaimed. "Albert keeps his lions at At-March, Roland, that's why no one has seen them in Ashbury castle. You're to be the new lion warden."

Roland thought about his new Lord. Albert of Ashbury was one of the original Welsh lords who ventured to Ireland to help Dermot MacMurrough restore his Leinster lands. That complete, Albert was granted land in Connacht. Ashbury estate secured, Albert had taken up the cross and joined England's King Richard and France's King Philip as did his neighbor's son Ruaidri Dahlquin, the younger.

"He went all the way to the Holy Land to retrieve lions to subdue his neighbors and cousins," Guillaume said with a chuckle. "Fine neighbors you have, Roland."

"Fine neighbors, the Lion of Ashbury, the brother-murdering Barbarian of Dahlquin with his unholy women, and the pious Stag of Scragmuir," Sedric said.

"Pious, is it?" Guillaume asked. "Penis more like it," he chuckled. "Hope Albert is so generous."

"None but women left in Ashbury. All the men have been killed or assassinated. Do you think the Old Lion will really live forever?" Sedric asked.

"Albert is the oldest man in Connacht," Roland said. "Seventy-two, saints preserve him."

"Oldest man in Ireland, I wager," Guillaume added. "And not a child to his name, cock or cunt."

"Not true, he had children, but they died," Sedric said.

"The bastards of infidelity were slain," Guillaume reminded them.

"My neighbors," Roland said, "a little more respect, with your will. Albert gave the babes his name." Rumor had it Albert was seedless, yet when his wives and concubines conceived, Albert readily claimed the children to prove his manhood. As the years went on, and his relatives continued to kill his heirs and each other, Albert claimed that God wanted him, and him alone, to rule Ashbury: thus his robust old age. His fourth wife, Mor, continued to provide Albert with proven fertile women, praying for a true heir, securing her place as dowager.

"Roland, if Albert perceives you as FitzGilbert's usurper-" Sedric said, bringing the conversation back to Roland's new fief and title.

"Lion bait!" Guillaume interrupted. "Not the warden at all."

The squires sighed.

"Bleeding saints on a cross, lads," Guillaume said, looking back at the wide-eyed squires. "It's a blood bath we've stumbled into. Good thing we're lost!"

Roland sighed, and stroked his black horse's damp neck. "This was not my idea," he murmured to horse. Roland was proud to pledge himself to High Lord FitzGilbert, and earnestly did his Lord's bidding - until now. Through exceptional service and bravery, he had earned the title Lord and been granted a small land holding within Ashbury, with tenants and the responsibilities associated with such a fief. Eventually a new lord would have to be granted in Ashbury. Roland was perhaps being groomed for this position. *If he survived.*

As his men chuckled and reminisced, Roland's mind drifted back to Connacht and what his actions had wrought. He had accepted the hospitality of Scragmuir estate, and knew something of Ashbury, but what of Dahlquin?

Lord Hubert's grandfather had come to Ireland in years past. Richard Dahlquin made his claim outside the conquered English domain, in Connacht, and started building on the original castle in the Norman style. He was an ambitious and vicious man, a good choice to subdue the hordes: and perhaps, to keep him busy and away from being a threat to the English crown.

Richard Dahlquin assimilated to the wilderness. He put aside his first wife and took the daughter of one of the high-ranking Irish kings: a hearty, red-haired maiden, with cunning moss-green eyes and a hauntingly angelic voice when she chose to sing or speak. Music bridged the language gap between husband and wife. Out of respect to his new wife who assumed his name as the Lady Dahlquin, so he honored her people by altering his name, Richard, to the more traditional Ruaidri. Soon it was shortened to Rory, in honor of the King of Connacht. The name change was a well-received gesture and helped establish the continued interactions between the two diverse groups. Yet, their two sons bore English names-Hubert and Reginald, as an appeasement, mayhap.

After two generations it appeared to most that it was the Dahlquins who had truly been subdued, so indoctrinated into the wilderness had they become. Dahlquin had succumbed to the heathen influences of this barbarian wasteland yet maintained enough loyalty to the English crown and Irish nobles that a mutual tolerance existed. The English king left Connacht to Dahlquin, and in turn Dahlquin left the east to the king.

Roland had been sent to Ashbury-at-March as another peacekeeper. Despite arguing he was no diplomat, Lord FitzGilbert insisted he was the optimal candidate. Of course, there was no dissent with FitzGilbert's orders, and honor or not, Roland and his friends departed for Connacht.

Roland sat stiffly in the saddle, rubbing his bearded chin with his gloved hand. He wanted a bath and his hair combed out. His companions looked no better. This was no way to meet his new *seigneur* lord.

"Roland," Guillaume called, "have you decided on a bride?"

"I don't need a wife," Roland frowned.

"If we're to cavort about, you'll need a good wife to run your estate," Sedric said.

"A frugal wife to replenish your purse from the fruit of the land," added Guillaume, "one who can brew and fill a decent cup."

"Bah! If it's such a good plan, why don't *you* marry?" Roland asked his companions.

"I don't have an estate to live off," answered Guillaume, the eldest of the three, friend and mentor as Sedric and Roland had achieved knighthood.

"That's why we're with you," chimed in Sedric, clutching his fists together in a pleading gesture. "Feed us and clothe us, Lord," laughed the stout knight, the mirthful sound incongruous with the frizzy-haired man-beast in the saddle.

Roland scowled at both his friends.

"And you are to push a plow?" Roland asked.

"Me?" Guillaume asked incredulously. "That's why you need a wife."

"To push a plow?" Roland persisted.

"Roland, you know nothing. The lady will manage the estate and workers. We show up now and then to flatter her, sow some seed, fill our purses and go."

"I pray such an opportunity, and Roland will always have a warm bed waiting and fertile furrows-" Guillaume didn't finish.

"Enough!" Roland ordered. "I'm not a farmer, and there are plenty of warm beds." He squinted at his tormentors. *Demons desist*, he had much to decide, greater priorities in estate management than a wife. *Details, responsibility, fucking responsibility - in this wilderness.*

"Roland," Sedric ventured; a change of topic was in order. "You're not a lonely man, what is your secret?" Sedric asked.

Roland considered his friends carefully.

"Guillaume isn't lonely either, ask him," Roland answered. Guillaume straightened up is his saddle. He was as tall as Roland, thicker.

"I have," Sedric replied, "he is a braggart," and he gave Guillaume a scowl. Guillaume smiled at him wickedly, making an obscene gesture.

Roland shrugged. There was the difference.

"Speak, man," Guillaume said. "Would you not share with your *brothers?*"

With a deep breath and a few more strides down the road, Roland relented.

"Treat a lady like a whore, and a whore like a lady, and they will both treat you right every time," he said, riding on.

"Really?" Guillaume and Sedric both said at the same time.

"Take heed of that, boys," Guillaume called back to the squires. Over the years he had lost most of the teeth on the left side of his mouth. Missing teeth never intimidated his wide grin, however.

"So, how will you treat the mysterious heretic of Dahlquin?" Guillaume asked with a hint of mischief in his voice.

"Which heretic?" Roland asked. Both Lady Aine and her daughter were notorious throughout Ireland for heresy and other devilry.

"The daughter, imbecile," Guillaume said, shaking his head.

"Roland, the girl may just be full of heathen blood. Nothing more," offered Sedric.

"A succubus," smiled Guillaume. Roland shot him a dirty look. He had smiled little since heading northwest. He was sulking; his dark features intensified the effect.

"A half-animal demon, that would explain a lot," Sedric chuckled. "She would be beautiful by night."

"Is that so, hovering over poor Roland, lapping his manhood dry," continued Guillaume, blue eyes sparkling with lust and mirth.

"Is that how they do it?" asked Sedric, wide eyed with interest. The squires closed ranks, too, temporarily forgetting they were lost.

"Assume the form of a beautiful woman. Large breasts float down upon you, with the smoothest, most unblemished skin, pale and translucent. Breath as sweet as honey," he said with just a hint of lasciviousness. "Slips into bed like an angelic apparition, soft as a male is hard." The men squirmed in their increasingly snug saddles.

"What's a man to do?" agreed Sedric. A tinge of red highlighted his cheeks, proud to be aroused and worthy of such of gentle attention.

"Enough," scowled Roland. "Arses," he muttered.

"She and her mother both, yet it has not hurt Lord Hubert too much. Save he's ugly as sin," Guillaume commented.

"Why else would she wear boys' clothing and sleep with the livestock?" Sedric continued. One heard many rumors about the Maid of Dahlquin, and this seemed to fit the description.

"It's a good disguise by day," Guillaume said, and he and Sedric laughed at the fate of their good friend.

"Those could be lies," Roland offered. Thoughts of ancient magic scared him more deeply than he cared to admit, to himself or his companions. How could he combat it? Not with sword or dagger, surely. He would risk the lions of Ashbury over black magic any day.

"Oh, lies is it?" added Sedric, "She could be the angel by day, kind and pious."

"And ugly and celibate by night," Guillaume said. Again, all but Roland laughed.

"Good thing she is an heiress," Sedric observed.

"The Scragmuirs are none too fond of the barbarous Dahlquins. Maybe we should take heed. They live out here," Guillaume reminded them.

"If the ladies of Dahlquin are heretics, or worse minions of Satan, why would they seek to establish a cathedral?" asked Sedric.

"Satan or angel, could it be so black and white, good or evil?" asked Roland. "Who are these people really? Gerald FitzGilbert loves them dearly, calls Lord Hubert *brother*."

"*Brother*, after what Hubert did to his true brother? I don't know, Roland."

"And his own half-brother, remember that?"

"Mayhap some evil spirit clouds the High Lord's good judgment."

His friends shrugged but offered no answers.

Roland's traveling companions enjoyed teasing him about his prospective neighbors and future brides. The ribald harassment degenerated further.

"You were wrong about the nineteen-year old widow in Scragmuir, remember?" Roland asked. Guillaume had made some frightening comments about the eligible brides prior to their visit at Scragmuir.

"He was," Sedric agreed, "toothless and haggard after three years of mourning, you claimed."

The nineteen-year old widow was quite lovely, had teeth, and a very pleasant disposition. Her time of mourning was over. Although Roland had no intention of marrying her, at least his companions had less to tease him about. She would make someone a handsome wife, just not him. There was a ten-year old, eligible when she came of age, among the highest born Scragmuirs, and other girls with little property to be gained. Quiet and well-mannered were the Scragmuir women, beautiful and goodly wives all. Or so the Scragmuirs said.

Thoughts soon drifted back to the time spent at Scragmuir: two glorious days followed by a miserable day and half lost and wandering. At least in Scragmuir the sun was visible once or twice. Now all the riders were damp with the mist.

"Very generous, Scragmuir," Guillaume reminisced. "Even the lads got plenty of cunt. Eh Tuath? Thought you'd grown a beard."

Roland laughed with his men.

"He's still got hair in his teeth," Sedric said.

"Val missed all the fun," Roland said, still chuckling, thinking of his own squire, left behind in Leinster to recover from a plague of the lungs.

"Just two days ago," Guillaume sighed.

"So it was, and a day and half with only you four to gaze upon," Roland said. "Look there," he said, pointing to an open, rocky meadow where a small herd of red cattle grazed placidly. "Do you see the bear?" A large dark form was grazing among the cattle.

"I do, with cubs," Guillaume added, with astonishment.

"With the cows?" said Sedric in a mocking tone. "Not a bear," he scoffed, but Roland noticed he too was staring at the sight.

"Ugly damn cows, then," Guillaume said.

"Do you think it's one of Ashbury's lions?" one of the squires asked from behind.

"Lions aren't black," Guillaume said, not taking his gaze from the herd.

"Let's see for ourselves," Roland ventured, looking back at the wide-eyed squire, leading the group off the road toward the mystery beast.

A few wary cattle looked up but didn't turn and walk away. The beast and her cubs, however, did move briskly within the herd, showing more fear of detection than the cows.

"Have you ever?" Sedric exclaimed.

Guillaume whistled, revealing astonishment and appreciation.

"As large as a bear, to be sure," Roland said of the beast and her cloven-hooved brood.

"If the pigs are as big as bear-," Guillaume left his question unasked.

"How large are the bear?" Sedric asked, a large grin brightening his ruddy features.

"And that was but a sow," Roland said, smiling at his grinning men. "Imagine the size of a boar in his prime." Connacht had much promise. Roland led the men back to the road, in search of Ashbury Castle, with a warm welcome and warmer beds.

"Do you think Ashbury will be so hospitable as was old Humphrey of Scragmuir?" Sedric asked with hope in his voice. "Or Dahlquin, when we present ourselves to our neighbors?"

"It would be good to bathe again, by his gracious will, and not sleep on the ground," Guillaume added.

"With naught but your own 'worm' as company," Sedric stated. The men laughed and twitched in the tight saddles.

The five lonely, road-weary travelers had been esteemed guests, feasting and touring the estate at Scragmuir, and fresh blood to game with. The women were indeed quiet and well-mannered. While the legitimate daughters were sequestered away, the illegitimate ones were generously available. Guillaume was eager to make his services available to the Scragmuirs if they were in need of more good men. His wanton behaviour had found a home if they would have him. Roland and Sedric were not lonely either.

Roland knew they were treated lavishly, and it was well appreciated after the long trip. While Ashbury was neutral regards the feud between the neighbors, Scragmuir lobbied very hard indeed to make Roland understand the dangers of Dahlquin, poison his mind: black magic, paganism and murder. Both families had their roots in the 1169 invasion, bringing the ancient feud with them, some claimed. Dahlquin had obviously fallen further from grace as far as Scragmuir was concerned. Lord Humphrey still accused Hubert of murdering his elder brother, Richard Dahlquin II, upon his return from the Holy Land. His horse and cape were found in western Dahlquin. The body was never recovered nor his rings, one a gift from Richard the Lion-Hearted, the other from the Holy Land. Lord FitzGilbert declared there was insufficient evidence to condemn Hubert or his men, and no cause. After all these years, Scragmuir kept the memory of murder and the burning hatred for Dahlquin alive. They would further this bitter feud upon any whom would listen.

Talk and politics were not Roland's strengths. Nor was he eager to start his education in such. What was he doing here? Diplomat, peacekeeper, farmer. What would he find? He wasn't looking for anything, he had been happy in Leinster.

"Roland!" Guillaume shouted. "So gloomy. Pining over someone back at Scragmuir, fair Juliana or the widow?"

Roland scowled at the knight, "I am not."

"Juliana was extraordinary," Sedric said with reverence.

"Fantasizing about the succubus, then?" Guillaume inquired with a glint in his blue eyes.

"Roland," Sedric said, "I'll wager the hills still possess a fur clad bride for you, if you're man enough."

Guillaume laughed.

Their horses ambled on, confident in the road they followed.

"Might Scragmuir have given us bad directions?" queried Sedric.

"What reason?" continued Guillaume. "None."

"There was not a reason, but we missed the entire estate. Where are we if not Ashbury?"

Were the mists really the ethereal forms of ancient sprites or pixies? Dragon's breath, indeed, if one believed in such ancient and unknown beasts. Beautiful, too, despite the haunting feeling it evoked. Roland surveyed the landscape once again: open, vast and serene, no wasteland, this. What little he could see through the dragon's breath this morning wasn't a barren wasteland as some claimed. Flax grew well, and the plentiful rivers and cool temperatures were ideal for the production of linen. Flax and sheep provided abundant clothing for Ireland and abroad.

"Ho, you there!" Roland called to laborers in the field, bent to their tasks, the day early yet. They looked up to the mounted knights before them but said nothing, waiting. "Is this Ashbury?"

"It is not, Sir," they answered, shaking their heads in agreement. "Dahlquin."

Roland slumped in his saddle, his weary horse mimicking the response.

"I knew it," Sedric muttered, "left!"

"And the castle - how far?" asked Roland, ignoring Sedric.

In unison all the men pointed east to the horizon masked by fog.

"East is it? Well, we have been lost," Guillaume said.

"How far?" asked Roland once more.

The men looked to each other, east and at each other again.

Head bowed, one man stepped forward from the field. "Sire, it's 'bout half a day walk from here. "Wait," he thought again, "half day there and back. Not with horses." He shook his head to further emphasize he hadn't an idea how long it would take riding. "There's tracks to follow round the fields, will lead you to the castle."

"By your will," offered another, "wide tracks, so our lordship can bring his carts through to collect his due."

"Values his land he does," the first man said.

Roland thought the men prayed he and his horses would stick to those tracks and not gallop cross-country trampling the crops and scattering the livestock.

"So he does," Guillaume called over his shoulder as the knights and squires rode east. "Seems we've rounded the whole damned island."

"I thought I smelled ocean spray, eh lads? Salty," Sedric teased.

They rode on, careful to stick to the wide, well-worn tracks that promised to lead them to Dahlquin.

CHAPEL, 8th of June

The chapel door rattled, distracting Eloise from her prayers; next a thud and scraping. Swords clanged at impact. Again and again the noise jarred her spine. Grunts and curses filled the void. The great wooden door shook violently but held and Eloise could only imagine the battle Alsandair waged against the unknown assailants.

The chapel door flung open. Beast and Dragon snarled a warning, fangs bared. Slanted brown eyes shone out from their shaggy faces, the brass studs on the thick leather collars caught the candlelight. The workers cried out, fleeing to side walls as armed men pushed the door open, the table skidding along the floor. The hounds lunged and the men retreated, slamming the door behind them. Beast and Dragon tore at the door, snarling, tails wagging in victory. As suddenly it burst open again. Three men struggled in.

Eloise gasped, desperate for her bow and arrows back in her chamber.

"Who?" one of the men yelled over the noise in a strange Gaelic, "who's in here?" he asked the trembling peasants. These horrible hounds must protect someone important.

Eloise watched in horror as the armed men moved forward, Beast and Dragon trying to get them. She had to reach the door to get out.

Dragon made a play for one of the advancing soldiers' legs. Pulling and shaking her head he was pitched to the floor, screaming as the dog tried to dislocate his leg. Sword drawn, the man pummeled Dragon with the pommel end. Then he swung with both hands.

"Not her!" screamed Eloise as Dragon screeched, turning a half circle in shock and agony. Again, the dog lunged at her attacker, blocking the door.

The other two men held Beast at bay with axe and sword.

"Stop this. Stop at once!"

Eloise knew the voice, the priest.

"This is a house of God," he wailed, anger sustaining him as he pushed his way through the door. "Maiden!" the priest called, recognising her dogs.

The two soldiers drew up and surged forward against Beast. Searching the semi-dark chapel, one man's eyes fell on Eloise. "There," he indicated, running towards her.

"Maiden?" the priest called again. He had betrayed her presence. Eloise had to move, to escape. "Stop," the priest commanded, spreading his arms to block the attacker, "in God's name!"

Eloise prayed they listen.

But the man pushed past the priest. Trembling, the priest grabbed the man's arm, holding tight as the attacker tried to pull free. Spinning around, the man threatened to strike down the tenacious priest. His eyes were hard and lined as he glared at the priest.

"Before God, my son, cast down your weapons!"

Using the distraction provided by the priest, Eloise tore her eyes away from the fight before her and bolted. She climbed up the High Altar. "God forgive me," she prayed, grabbing a silver candlestick and tucking it in her girdle before scaling the wall hangings as she continued her escape. Using the candlestick, she broke through the beautiful painted glass window. Meant to let God's light and goodness in, this morning it let

Hell's fury out. "God forgive me," she muttered, whacking all the thick, broken glass away. What sacrilege was she committing to save herself?

Eloise climbed through the broken window and cried out as she slipped through the broken glass. Dropping from the window, surcoat torn, hair flying, Eloise ran for the residential tower. Fighting barred her way as the men from the chapel chased her. She ran to the scaffolding, erected for repairs on the inner wall. Despite the encumbrance of her surcoat, Eloise climbed. She could reach the residential tower from the wall.

Climb, just climb.

Curse these garments, she thought. If there had been time, she would have used her knife to cut them away. Sweating with the exertion of her labors, she felt chilled with fear. A soldier below grabbed her hem and yanked. Eloise slipped and hit her chin on the rung. She fought to keep climbing, but the man's grip was too strong. She kicked wildly. *Think,* she told herself, *wait, wait.* As the man below took a second to change his grip to grab her ankle, she hooked him under the chin with her heel, loosening his grip. He fell to the ground.

"Eloise! Up here," Uncle Reggie shouted. He extended a hand, thick and strong, and hoisted her clear up to his level. More soldiers rushed them.

She couldn't formulate words.

"Take this," he snarled, removing his shield. "Hubert!" Reginald shouted. Then to Eloise, "You see him? On the ground," he was pointing to her father on the ground at the end of the scaffolding; a body lay at his feet.

"Da!" she screamed in horror and relief.

"Go!" her uncle shouted.

Slipping his enormous shield over her left arm, she ran. Behind her Uncle Reggie roared. A terrifying sound, it made many a warrior think twice before challenging him. The clash and twang of sword meeting sword and sword meeting shield rattled Eloise to the bone. The unstable wooden scaffolding creaked and swayed as she fled.

Seeing her father renewed her hope and energy. He'd know what to do. Almost there, the warmth of safety crept into her senses. Heavy footsteps quaked behind. Instinctively she drew the shield up, turning sideways to deflect the blow as best she could, still running. A glancing mace blow pitched her onto the wood and rope binding. She winced with the bruising impact to her ribs.

"Arrr!" she heard the familiar roar of Reggie. "Run, damn you!" Without looking back, she clutched her skirts even higher and ran. Reggie struck the mace-wielding soldier with such force the scaffolding rocked as man and sword hit wood framing. More footsteps and this time the blows of Reginald's sword on a shield. The scaffolding groaned, the footing unsteady.

"Father, Da!" she screamed.

Hubert was waiting for her. Eloise perched at the end of the scaffolding, Reginald's shield in hand. The gangway behind was filled with armed men bearing down on her with only Reginald between them. There was nothing left but to jump. It was a long way, but with her father to break the fall what choice did she have? Eloise dropped the shield on the scaffolding and climbed between the rails. It seemed so much higher on the outside of the railings, her father the size of a mere child.

"Jump!" her father commanded, shaking his hands at her expectantly. Blue-grey eyes bulging, as if that would somehow alter the height, Eloise looked down at her father. The thundering sounds on the gangway startled her into action. She let go of the railings and reached towards her father, still dwarfed by the distance. Her stomach lurched, the pounding of weapons in her ears replaced with wind.

She landed in her father's arms, knocking him down with the impact, too late remembering how to roll or slap the ground as she did when falling from a horse. His grunt resonated with deep ache as he expelled all his breath and more as she crushed him into the ground then bounced from his grip. Landing hard, Eloise shrieked in pain and the terror she had killed her father.

"Da," she whimpered, reaching for him.

Her father sprang up, his face so contorted with wrath she barely recognised him. His expression softened a brief moment, and it was enough to reassure her. Before she could spring to her feet, he gripped her arm, the armored fingers of his gauntlet biting into her, emboldening her. Side by side they ran.

FINDING DAHLQUIN

Roland felt Artoch inhale as the horse's barrel expanded. The mighty animal jigged and strained on the reins. Roland glanced at his companions: their horses, too, had flared nostrils, ears forward in agitation and expectancy.

"What the fuck?" Guillaume said, stroking his horse's neck.

"What indeed?" Roland murmured, also stroking Artoch's neck, trying to settle the horse. He searched the landscape but saw nothing unusual. They proceeded, searching and listening.

Roland turned an ear. *Was that a shout? Or a cry?* Metal to metal. Pounding.

He raised his arm signaling *halt.* He glanced at his men and believed they, too, heard the distant sounds of fighting.

He knew which way to Dahlquin. There was a battle. This was much more exciting than wandering through the mist. Fighting is what he and his men lived for. Helping one of the High Lord's dearest friends would brighten any knight's day.

At a slow canter, Roland and his companions followed the noise. They were witnesses to the massacre and destruction that made a path to the ever-increasing mayhem of a castle under siege. As the sun broke through, mighty Dahlquin Castle was revealed. What should have been a beauteous vision was marred: fields void of life, neither crop nor livestock stirred. A swath of death marched to the fortress. Fires burned inside and out. Smoke rose, blurring the sunlight. Angry voices ripped through the pastoral scene, the surrounding woodlands rang with the foul noise of men and metal.

From the scant protection afforded in an orchard, Roland and his companions assessed the situation.

"Probably twenty or thirty archers and one hundred men spread out. Fuck," Sedric said, counting again. "Who is that?" he asked, not recognising any banners or colors.

"A mangonel being assembled," Guillaume added, "and siege towers under construction. I agree, fuck."

A small encampment by the road - the road these travelers had missed - bustled as men prepared arms and ran messages.

"Who indeed," Roland said. "It's-," he hesitated to say 'brilliant', but it was. "Well executed, seems the castle has already been breached."

"Reinforcements from Ashbury would end this quickly, what do you think?" Sedric asked.

"The drawbridge must be pulled up before a battering ram or siege tower is rolled onto it. We could do that," Roland offered, voice low, still thinking. "Mayhap."

"Ashbury could end this," Sedric said again, "prudent to warn them, Roland."

"Prudent to get that bridge up," Roland said slowly, still calculating, ignoring Sedric's pragmatic suggestion.

"Roland-" Guillaume started.

"I'm not a messenger," Roland growled, fixing his black eyes on his companions, trying not to smirk.

Roland dispatched the two squires to Ashbury to warn and seek assistance. Reinforcements would end this quickly, if the squires could find Ashbury and if they could make it back.

After a brief moment of acceptance from his men, they put on their helms and drew their swords.

With the bravado of youth and invincibility, the three lost knights charged the mass on the drawbridge. Assuming authority they didn't have, they pretended to be in command, ordering everyone off the bridge.

"Who is in charge here?" Guillaume shouted to the men attacking the drawbridge. He drew blank stares. Then they all began yelling in several dialects and languages. The knight tried again in Latin.

"Who are you?" asked one of the men warily, in Latin, not recognising Guillaume.

"It is the Master of the Gate," Sedric said, feigning great authority, indicating Roland.

"Get off, let me handle this," Roland said to the assembled men, waiting to take their turn to storm the bridge.

"Everyone off the bridge," Guillaume and Sedric continued to order. "Stand down!" They ducked, the shields affixed on their backs protecting them but not their horses.

"Why?" was the resounding cry. "Who are you?" the attackers persisted.

Again all the men ducked, shielding themselves as best they could from the bolts and arrows.

Roland turned a malicious smile on the man he thought to be in charge. The sword he wielded was yet unbloodied, a naked state for such a blade. "I've a key," Roland said, cocking his head with evil conviction.

"Bah, there isn't a key," a man scoffed. "Out of our way!" and he made to push past the mounted knight before him.

"Scragmuir says otherwise," Roland roared so all could hear. Guillaume and Sedric nodded their solemn agreement. Roland sensed the man's hesitation. "Trust me," he said, growling. Roland tried to place the language the other men muttered among themselves. Some Norse tongue, he wondered? An odd Gaelic? He thought they were acknowledging Scragmuir's desire to provide a key or true means of defeat.

It was all a bald-faced lie on the part of Roland and his companions. A rush of fear and perverse pleasure pumped through Roland's system as he continued their deception. He and his men were aligned with Dahlquin and help was needed. Outnumbered as they were, a bluff seemed the best offense.

"I wasn't told of a plan," the man in charge challenged again. "Who sent you?"

Who indeed? Roland and his companions had no idea whatsoever who laid siege to Dahlquin or where this enemy was from, let alone who the captain of this particular assault force was. Roland stared at the man, eyes narrowed with anger. His first instinct was to strike the insubordinate down, but that didn't seem wise at the moment. He hadn't expected the men to dispute him and he wasn't accustomed to arguing with lower ranks in Latin.

"You should find your captain and ask him," Guillaume shouted in broken Norman-Latin, "and let us do our job. You have not been able to take the bridge."

"You!" the leader shouted to one of his men at the end of the line. "Go find the captain." The man hurried off, and the leader, sword and shield poised, glared at the three mounted knights.

"Time's wasting," Roland gritted, and turning Artoch, walked his horse straight into the man, until the man was forced off the drawbridge. "Everyone off the bridge!" Roland shouted again.

Reluctantly the men backed down. As another round of bolts and arrows whistled by, three more soldiers fell. It now seemed a good time to the foot soldiers to seek shelter while these knights faced the bolts and arrows and gatehouse.

Roland saw the men retreat from the bridge as an arrow deflected off his shield.

If evacuating the bridge had been hard, now the three knights had to convince someone inside Dahlquin to open the portcullis long enough for them to enter before being crushed when the huge drawbridge was brought up.

Sedric and Guillaume pleaded with the men to open the portcullis.

"We're loyal to Lord FitzGilbert, here at his bidding!" Guillaume shouted.

"We've cleared the bridge! Let us in!" Sedric yelled.

Guillaume grabbed an iron bar of the portcullis, pulled his face close and ordered one of the guards to open it. "I swear we come to help. The bridge is secure."

Still the Dahlquin guards stared as the large, angry face of Sir Guillaume pressed against the metal.

"Your soul will rot in Hell for your lack of faith," Guillaume hissed.

"By order of Lord Roland of Ashbury-at-March, open this gate - now!" Roland called in a thundering boom, startling everyone including himself. He sat erect as Artoch pawed the bridge, and glanced back to see a bolt pierce the cantle and another stick in his horse's tail as it flashed defiance. Steam spewed from his destrier's flared nostrils.

The portcullis began to lift. Roland felt the footing shift. The draw bridge was rising as well.

"Stop them, stop them!" two of the attacking soldiers shouted as they ran back to the assault force at the drawbridge.

"Jesus-Fuck!" Sedric shouted.

Roland saw the portcullis lifting with slow, deliberate measure. He felt the bridge slanting -faster than the portcullis would allow access. Artoch crow hopped. Surely the portcullis appeared as a great fanged maw opening to consume them both.

"Roland!" Guillaume shouted.

Praise God the bridge slanted as it did, for Artoch had the coiled energy to buck him clear over the battlement. Instead, Artoch reared, trying to escape the jaws of death. Roland shared Artoch's fear. The blasphemy, *Jesus Fuck* pounding in his ears.

Sedric and Guillaume dismounted and led their horses under the spiked teeth of the portcullis, as Roland and Artoch slid towards them.

"Easy," Roland called, as he dismounted from his skittering horse. "Down," he called to Artoch as he tugged the reins, forcing Artoch's head down as they slid into the deadly gatehouse of Dahlquin Castle.

Roland, Artoch, his men and their horses stumbled through bodies, dead and alive, over the burning coals that had been dumped through the murder holes. Flames from the hot oil that had been splashed on the trapped men in the gatehouse flared up on all sides of the destriers. The stench of burnt flesh was oppressive and the heat stifling.

"I'm Roland, the Lord of Ashbury-at-March. I must speak with Lord Dahlquin!" Roland called out, mounting his horse once more. It was hard to tell which men fought for Dahlquin, and which were invading. "Where is Lord Dahlquin?" Surely Hubert would want to know what he and his men had seen from the orchard.

Guillaume and Sedric, horses skittering to match his own, guarded him left and right.

"Father, Da!" A woman's screams pierced the din, from high on the scaffolding. Roland looked up to see a young woman chased along the scaffolding, calling down to a man on the ground. Dropping her shield, she jumped into his arms. It must have been three men's height. She hit the ground running and the man and woman disappeared behind stone. Fucking Hell, he thought.

Roland was knocked from his horse, and the girl and her jump were forgotten in the heat of battle in the mighty fortress of Dahlquin.

DAHLQUIN CASTLE, 8th of June

"Water," Alsandair called feebly in the chapel as the battle raged outside. Noise and people surged. Pain of thirst drowned his other senses. "Water," he rasped lifting a hand as if it held a cup. He could hear people, feel movement, but saw nothing in the darkness.

Warm hands clamped round his and guided the cup to his parched lips. "Slowly," someone said, "slowly, don't choke."

Alsandair drained the cup, resisting as the warm hand pulled the empty cup away.

"Give him more, all he wants, but slowly," said the voice.

"By your will," Alsandair whispered, desperate for more. After uncounted cups of wine, the blessed relief from dehydration was replaced with the searing pain of his injuries. He forced his mind to retrace the events leading him...where?

"Alsandair," the priest called, "open your eye. Can you see me?"

Instead of answering, Alsandair reached out to feel the priest, whose voice he recognized. Taking the hand, the priest turned it back to Alsandair's face.

"Open your eye. Look at me if you can."

Frightened, Alsandair jerked. His eye popped open. A little cloudily, Alsandair could identify the shape of a man before him. Cautiously he rubbed his eye with the back of his hand and looked again.

The smiling priest nodded. Alsandair grinned back, relieved to see clearly, but with one eye he soon discovered as his hands examined the binding over his right. The priest held a bloodied cloth to his neck.

"Eloise?" Alsandair asked, was she safe? He searched the interior.

"Safe. Tending the wounded, I have assurance," the priest said.

Amidst the roars outside the chapel walls, the priest and workers recounted for Alsandair the disastrous events thus far; how they had dragged his limp body to safety as Beast fought the soldier. His right eye seemed damaged beyond repair, and he suffered a nasty scalp wound that peeled all the hair and flesh in the shape of an ax blade. Maybe cracked ribs, too.

Several more people sought refuge in the chapel as the siege wore on. The injured were tended with more prayer than technique. No food but spiritual rejuvenation was offered.

"Seems clear," one of workers said late in the afternoon, watching for an opportunity to seek help.

"Come, Alsandair." The priest and workers helped him up.

Alsandair bent double and retched. Strong arms held him up. His head spun, his chest ripped in pain. "My ribs," he croaked.

Together they made their way to the Great Hall. "Let's get you to a healer," the priest said.

Hubert and Reginald sat talking with several other knights and men of the castle. What was left, who was left, what was the prognosis? The air was heavy with the stench of overworked men, spent embers and death. Both Aine and Eloise were safe, laboring with the physician and other ladies of the manor to aid the injured and dying. Water boiled. Calf broth brewed. Prayers and chants resonated through the corridors but could neither silence nor mask the cries and groans.

"They're assembling a mangonel," Sir Uilliam said, caked blood from his right ear to his chest. "Siege towers as well."

"By the morrow?" asked Hubert. Wouldn't be long to assemble the mangonel and thus would Dahlquin be subject to the onslaught and heavy destruction from stone projectiles raining down upon them.

"Easily," Uilliam answered.

"The Asp?" asked Hubert, the name given to the mighty trebuchet. Long it had been since this piece of arsenal was brought to use. Unlike the mangonel Tiomu would employ, the arm of the trebuchet was halted straight up, at a ninety-degree angle, allowing a high, clear shot of projectile over the ramparts of the castle onto the attackers. Seemed it shot venom like the cobras of Pharaoh and would swallow up the enemy, as did the staff of Moses.

"Burned but functional," Uilliam confirmed, "it will go tonight if need be. She is a beautiful piece of work, my Lord, scorch marks and all. She'll shoot all the truer for it, I have assurance," he smiled. Sir Uilliam had been with Hubert for many years.

"Promise?" Hubert attempted to smile back.

"They tried to burn the armory, as you know," the constable reported. "Lucky it was you had most of the arrows and bolts posted. The men had their weapons with them. The losses were minimal, truly Lord."

"And the fletchers?" Hubert asked.

"As we speak, lord. Every able craftsman is to task. The bowmen won't go empty."

"For how long?" Hubert queried, face stern.

"Depends, Lord," offered the constable.

"Depends on what?" Hubert raised his voice. "How long, give me some clue."

"With forty-seven archers and crossbowmen," he tried to calculate in his head. "Ten days steady, more if we scavenge."

Hubert closed his eyes and sighed. The smiths couldn't work day and night for days on end. They would need more materials. The production would be drastically reduced in time.

"What's the prisoner say?" Hubert asked at large, "any word? Is Scragmuir behind this? Reeks of their treachery!" These sentiments ran rampant the daylong. Scragmuir would back any assault on Dahlquin.

"Nothing from Tiomoid U'Neill about Scragmuir", the Seanascal answered, "only that we would be wise to concede and fall in with him. Claims to have support of the Danes, Hebrides Norse and other Irish nobles," he added.

"Concede!" Hubert mocked; his face crimson though covered with the grime of a full day's battle.

"Concede is what he said, says it's the new order. Ireland for the Irish. Foreign rule is over."

"And the Danes would be-" Hubert asked, "New Irish?" The men laughed. "Is France behind this, did he say? And Norway?"

"I think not, not Louis. Norway is uncommitted. Definitely not the English. But he is a liar and a traitor, so…his word is suspect," the Seanascal said.

"There's always a chance the man knows naught. Tiomu could have fed him lies," Reggie offered, his injured arm clutched to his chest.

"But it's Tiomu and the Danes, not the rest of the U'Neills?" Hubert questioned again. That would be a massive lot, armed and spread through the island.

"I think not, not yet," said the Seanascal. "Tiomu believes they will join him when Dahlquin and Ashbury fall."

"Ashbury?" A hush followed Hubert's question.

"Ashbury is under attack even now. Tiomu has amassed quite a force. Believe the bulk of it's here, Lord. But Ashbury will not send help, if the traitor is to be believed."

"Satan's horns!" Hubert fumed. "Is there not an end to his tyranny? He is mad. Munster and Leinster will never support this." His large frame shook with the rage he sought to contain.

"Not if Dahlquin stands," Reggie said. "Would be quite a coup for this upstart were Connacht to fall."

"Mayhap the rest would topple," said Uilliam. "The plan has merit."

"England won't stand for it. The tide will be reversed. The God-cursed English will wash in with naught but death and subjugation in their wake." Hubert could visualize the whole turn of events: a bloody civil war between the fractured Irish kings, an unsteady unification with the promise of peace for Ireland. Then Henry with his longbows and more land hungry barons would flood their emerald shores. Would the Scots side with Ireland? Could both nations plague England enough to win a truce? Of course not, neither the Scots nor Irish could agree to wipe their own noses, let alone stand united against England. "It must stop here. We must get word to High Lord FitzGilbert. That is crucial."

"And Henry? Would we seek aide from England?" the Seanascal asked. "It would bode well for us to show allegiance."

"Never England. Henry and his advisers will see Ireland take care of itself. With his best interests always foremost in our hearts," Hubert added sarcastically.

"Never England, hear, hear! To FitzGilbert and Henry!" the men cheered.

The Great Hall served as infirmary. No other room could accommodate the sheer volume of patients and attendants. Herbs and remedies simmered in assorted pots in the Great Hearth under the direction of the physician and Lady Aine. All the torches were lit; any reflective metal was utilized to maximize the light. Laundresses sought all the cloth they could safely gather. Women with needle and thread applied their craft to a patchwork of flesh, not linen or wool. Dahlquin Castle was a confined and tightly knit community with no strangers among the residents. Obligation and familial ties bound the members, none were immune from the loss and suffering.

Eloise rinsed her hands in a bucket of water as Sir Berach was assisted from her table. Then she brushed the stray hairs from her eyes with the back of her wet hand. She and her mother had insisted on having their long sleeves cut off above the elbow exposing their noble forearms before all: a necessity. Fashion was a nuisance in an emergency and the fabric was immediately utilized to bind wounds and staunch blood. One of the cook's aprons was tied on her, the pockets nearly empty of bandages and sewing kit, and the fragrant aroma of kitchen delights long lost in human waste.

Instead of trays laden with delectable morsels, the tables were piled with torn and burned bodies like some macabre feast of the Underworld. Noise and stench rivaled the foulest slaughterhouse imaginable, yet the hard labors continued: a swamp of blood, fluids and reed flooring oozed underfoot. Another soldier was laid on her table, red hair, freckles, hazel eyes. Hubert, named after her father, though all called him Hughy. Breathing labored, his nose frothed scarlet with each irregular exhalation, as did the lacerations in his chest. Softly she touched his warm cheek. Without response. Turning his head she parted his lips. Blood poured out. She had known him all her life. His was ending.

"Maiden," the priest called, leading an unfamiliar knight; a man she had never met and knew nothing of, other than the murmurings about the strangers who secured her drawbridge.

"You are in gifted hands, truly sir," the priest said to the knight at his side.

"Father, by your holy will," someone cried, "absolution. Hurry!"

The harried priest shrugged to Eloise then ran to the dying patient, leaving her with a complete stranger and without formal introduction.

The stocky knight studied her skeptically then looked down without a word.

Eloise stared back at the injured stranger. Who was he, and why this rude behavior?

"By your will, sit," she said awkwardly, patting the thick chamois mat, a dry place on the blood-soaked oak table. The pale stranger tried to sit and Eloise heard his sharp intake of breath, saw him wince as he froze, perched halfway between sitting and standing, his left arm clutching his chest. No foaming or wheezing: relief to her healer's ear.

"Don't strain," she said, searching for an able body to help him.

"Hmff, I can sit," he garbled, sucking his bloodied lip as he eased up.

"I think you have broken ribs."

"Didn't need you to tell me that," he winced, trying for a wry smile.

"Let's not puncture a lung," she said, first attempting to restrain him then heaving with the effort of helping him, twinging as her own bruised ribs pinched her.

"Eh?" the knight grunted, seeming to read her distress.

"Fighting on the scaffolds," Eloise offered: the unstable footing, weapons to crush her skull or ribs. She focused her eyes, already pushing the memory out of her mind, not a time for fear or tears with so many in need of her care. "Easy," she said, tilting his head back in examination. Eyes clear, equal dilation and focus. Dried blood in both nostrils, no foaming. His right cheek was swollen and his bottom lip was bit clean through. "Broken teeth?" she asked, palpating his jaw for cracks.

"Swallowed 'em," he offered, more color draining from his pale face.

"That will hurt in a day or two," she said, placing the back of her hand on his forehead.

"Hurts now," he reminded her.

"In your mouth, of course," she agreed. "Fever's not upon you," she said continuing her examination.

"Oh, fucking-" he blushed, staring at her, so close, his head in her hands. "You mean, when I-" He grimaced.

Eloise nodded, "Umhum. Sharp edges in the garderobe," she said, placing her ear on his chest.

"I suppose it will," he relented, thinking of the discomfort of the sharp-edged teeth when he relieved himself.

"We can hope for a flux, Saints' good will upon you," she said, ear still on his chest.

The knight snorted then gasped in pain.

After moving her ear to his right side, she straightened. A strand from her hastily braided hair had come loose and hung across her face.

"Too many garments," Eloise said gently tapping the tunic, covering the hauberk, padded gambeson and linen shirt, "I can't hear your breathing or heartbeat. I'll be very careful," she said, unbuckling his girdle then lifting the heavy sword, dagger and leather girdle and placing it all in his lap.

Standing behind him, she slipped her hands under his four layers of clothing and gently ran her fingers along his ribs, front and back. Sticking her bottom lip out, she blew the annoying strand of hair out of her face.

Sedric gasped and winced as her fingers probed his ribs.

"You have at least three breaks. In God's good honesty, Sir, if I can feel them it's severe. One flail - do you understand? The rib is broken clear through, detached. Mayhap here," she said, touching the enlargement so he would know precisely. When the knight nodded, Eloise continued. "A punctured lung or other internal damage is still a very real possibility, Sir."

She felt him shake his head. Someone howled, reminding them both of the suffering all around.

"Fight's not over," he garbled.

"Your injuries are not insignificant."

"Acknowledged," he said.

"Am I to know your name, good Sir? It seems we have extended all manner of rudeness and injury upon you, without the merest courtesy or introduction," she said, her hands still feeling for breaks or further injury.

"Sedric Synnot, from Leinster, bound for Ashbury-At-March."

"Ashbury-At-March?" she asked, not expecting that answer.

"If the place even exists," he added.

"Dead Man's Land does exist, but it's a perilous strip of estate," she added, forgetting herself for a moment.

"So I hear. And well hidden, least from us."

"Us?" her hands stopped, distracted. "How many are you?" Dahlquin was to have new neighbors. For a brief moment Eloise thought what a joyous occasion this should be, new allies to win over lest they become too cozy with the heinous Scragmuirs. She hooked her loose hair behind her ear. But immediately her mind returned to the carnage wrought by the last strangers Dahlquin had welcomed.

"There were five of us, Roland, the new Lord of Ashbury-at-March, Sir Guillaume and our two squires. We sent the squires to Ashbury for help before storming your gatehouse and bludgeoning our way in."

"That was you?" Eloise asked, again pushing the strand of hair back with her wrist. "I've only heard bits and pieces."

"Roland was just here," Sedric said, scanning the Great Hall, "looking for Lord Hubert. I haven't seen Guillaume."

Eloise continued her examination, half listening as Sedric talked. She ran her fingers down Sedric's spine checking for swelling or heat. She heard footsteps.

"Ah, Roland, you found me," Sedric said, lifting his hand but unable to wave.

"A rib out here," she said, ignoring the shadow that fell across her. "I may be able to manipulate it back." Her voice trailed off as she gently palpated the region of his kidneys. "Tender?" she asked, feeling him

71

flinch. He didn't answer. "Sedric? Is there pain?" she asked, pressing slightly.

"Pain's upon me," he grumbled like a guilty child caught in some mischief.

"Would you hold this up, by your will?" she asked the looming figure standing next to her, wanting to check for injury. Obligingly the figure lifted the four layers of clothing, exposing Sedric's furry back.

"May you have goodness," she said without looking up.

"Any blood in your urine?" she asked.

"I don't know," Sedric answered.

"Your kidney is swollen. Bruise, laceration. I can't see under your skin. You were struck fair hard," she commented, noting the abrasion. "And here?" she asked moving her examination to the other side. Silence. "Here?"

"Not there," Sedric said with a shallow sigh.

Eloise ran both hands down the length of his sides. A second time with her eyes closed. "Definitely heat and swelling on your left side. You'll have blood in your urine. If it persists for days, by your will tell me."

He shrugged.

"So be it," she sighed. "Let me try and pop that rib back." After pushing the annoying strand of hair back yet again, Eloise massaged the area once more to be sure there were not sharp edges or other injury she had overlooked. Satisfied, with both thumbs Eloise pressed: pushing, gentle, firm pressure.

"Let your breath out," she coaxed.

"Angel of Mercy," Sedric addressed Eloise, "this is my good friend, Roland, the new Lord of Ashbury-at—ugh," Sedric moaned as Eloise popped the offending rib into place.

Eloise stood, sighing with satisfaction at the completed adjustment, ready to meet her bold new neighbor, this Lord Roland. But the tall, dark stranger standing before her was gawking at her.

"What?" she asked, placing a hand on her hip. Blood in slashes or saturated blotches was spread across her apron, along with mucus, brown matter, ash and other aspects of the internal body never intended for viewing. His deep-set brown eyes moved over her in calculating appraisal. Sedric averted his eyes a moment, rubbing his chin, his eyes tearing. With pain, she wondered? Impatience rising, she tucked her chin slightly.

"*Princess*! I've been looking for you," shouted a knight, limping like a hunchback, dripping wet.

"Cairbre," Eloise implored, as he made his way to her through the chaotic Hall.

Smiling, Sir Cairbre started to kneel, reaching for her hem, his movements so stiff and unnatural as to be humorous.

"Do not," Eloise scolded, assessing from his stoop and the angle of his arm he had dislocated his shoulder and his comic display of servitude and devotion was an unnecessary risk. But the slightest glimmer of a smile at the edge of her mouth, and perhaps the perplexed looks of Roland and Sedric, only seemed to bolster his antics.

"*Princess*, by your will, be merciful," he begged.

"Quiet," she said, reaching for his arm. It was inappropriate to address her as *princess* before these strangers. She encouraged him to take a seat on the bloody table next to Sedric.

"Ashbury," he nodded to Roland, "Sir," to Sedric.

"You were about to say, Lord," she said, turning to Roland again. In the shadow of his long, black hair, his eyes shone like ebony, matching the caked blood on his split brow. Unlike Sedric and Cairbre, both pale with prolonged discomfort, Roland nearly glowed, if one thought of robust men in those terms. Eloise did not.

"Only that my friend's Angel of Mercy looks more like the butcher's daughter," he said.

"Ho, now," Cairbre growled, his deep voice edged in warning, glaring at Roland, sweat beading anew on his stained brow.

Sniffing, Eloise raised a hand, stilling Cairbre. She felt a repressed grin, new and welcome, on her strained face. With a finger she hooked her stubborn lock behind her ear, gave it a tug as if securing it, then straightened.

"My Lord Neighbor is astute as well as heroic," she said, her words gracious and melodic, she thought. "I've been called many things, good Sir, but that is mayhap the most accurate by far." Reaching down she lifted the edge of her slept in, dog haired surcoat, spreading the once blue garment in all its ripped and siege-stained glory, a gory testament to her true identity. "Welcome to my Lord Father's slaughterhouse."

"Oh, pray not," Sedric groaned.

Cairbre chuckled.

Roland and Sedric both stared, jaws dropping as Eloise dipped, genuflecting, her bearing restoring nobility to her abused gown as it billowed around her, settling on the damp reed flooring. The ghastly noise in the Great Hall receded to a pounding din.

"I'm Maiden Eloise Aine Echna, of Dahlquin. I bid you gracious welcome and our humble appreciation for your bravery at our gatehouse this very day. Grievous sorrow is upon me, that we have naught but a treacherous siege to offer as entertainment."

After what seemed an exceedingly adequate length of time, Eloise glanced up at the young Lord of Ashbury-at-March and found him staring down at her. Her own bruised ribs ached from her slip on the scaffolding and standing up would not be as gracefully executed as the curtsy had been. Dahlquin should be strong. Grudgingly, she held out a hand.

Cairbre cleared his throat. Sedric nudged Roland with his boot.

Roland took her offered hand and then her elbow, easing her up as she caught her breath.

"May you have goodness. Again," she said meeting his gaze.

His gaze was intense, but not threatening. With the back of his thumb he gently traced the line of her jaw from her ear to her chin, frowning at the abrasion and angry bruise.

"From your jump?" he asked.

She inhaled slowly, stifling the simmering emotions of the morning's exploits, unable to cope if the fear and pain and fury came to the surface. "You miss nothing, my Lord Neighbor." The trace of his thumb still tingling on her jaw line.

"Roland," he said, the hint of a grin softened the lines of his mouth. Blood and grit covered most of his bearded face. His need tugged at her, but her healer's eye could detect nothing dire.

"It was not from my jump, Lord Roland," she emphasized his name, "The scaffolding-" she paused, almost smiling, nearly crying, "was a struggle." Her free hand went to her ribs, and she was struck by two things. One, disappointment she revealed weakness by placing a hand on her bruised ribs, and two that Lord Roland was still holding her other hand.

He licked his thumb, then rubbed vigorously at a smudge on her cheek, forcing her to close her eye. For a brief moment, Eloise felt she had jumped and was falling again.

Sharp, irregular breaths then loud gurgling chokes roused her, and she turned quickly to Hughy on the table. Blood foamed at his nostrils and the slashes in his chest. His eyes opened and rolled back. She squeezed his hand. "Go with God, Hughy," she cooed. Rather than expire, his body eased back to shallow, infrequent breaths.

"Oh, damn it, Hughy," Cairbre croaked, shaking his head. "The lad's dying hard."

Eloise wiped her fresh tears, smearing more blood on her freshly rubbed cheek. Then she dipped her hands in the bucket of cloudy water, splashing her face. *Pay attention*, she commanded herself. *Heal.*

74

"First the shoulder," she said to Cairbre. "Then your mouth," to Sedric.

Only when Lord Hubert strode by did people stop their tasks to bow solemnly until he passed. Whispers and murmurs followed in his wake: "It's His Lordship, see how strong. What power protects him?"

Urgent business pressed him to be brief. He was a soldier to Ireland and God, but these were his people. Some of his best fighting men lay before him. Bravely he took their offered hands or touched a shoulder and offered a prayer for recovery. Purposefully he made his way amid the pleas to his wife and daughter.

"My lady," he said as he dipped his head formally to his wife. She was bent over Tomaltach the archer and bowyer. "I need you and Eloise."

Stricken and pale the boy on the table looked up.

"Tomaltach," Hubert smiled down at him. The young archer had a deep slice to his left arm and face. "Good man, Tommy."

Bolstered, Tommy tried to sit up, but Aine held him down. "I'm not done, this needs binding. Hubert?" she questioned.

Hubert looked to Tommy. The archer answered, "I'll wait, Lady. Go."

"Wait quietly. Don't move," she ordered as Hubert lead her away.

"Eloise!" her father shouted across the hall.

Startled, Eloise jumped. Cairbre's arm with which she had been unsuccessfully wrestling relocated to the shoulder with a loud pop, much to her and her patient's relief.

She wiped her brow with the back of her hand. Her patient flexed his arm appreciatively.

"May you have goodness, kindly, Maiden," he nodded to Eloise. "My Lord, Lady," he nodded to Hubert and Aine as they approached. "Got shoved down the well," Cairbre said, "couldn't climb with my arm." He rotated it gingerly. "Kids had to pull me up. Kids!" he said with emphasis. "Runny noses and all."

"Lord Roland," Hubert nodded, "just the man I'm looking for."

Roland nodded back.

"My Lady Aine, this is our neighbor, newly granted Lord Roland, Ashbury-at-March. He will surely have some tales of valor and prowess to share with us at some near time."

"My Lord Roland," Aine said taking his offered hand and dipping into a deep, graceful curtsy. "May I welcome you to Dahlquin and extend our deepest gratitude for your assistance today. Sorrow upon me you missed our banquet last night. Today is," she paused, looking up at him as she rose, "siege day."

Hubert continued with the formal introductions to all present before getting down to matters at hand.

"Roland, if you, Sedric, and Guillaume will join me, we have much to discuss."

"We'll come, but now?" Roland asked.

Hubert gave him an impatient nod before turning to Eloise. "You and your mother as well."

"But," Eloise said, "I'm not done. I need to stitch his lip," indicating Sedric.

All faces turned to Eloise, or so it seemed to her as she felt the burden of her words. As quickly, Sedric looked down.

Hubert said to her mother, "The meeting chamber."

Grateful not to be reprimanded, Eloise was still bothered to be called away when she had unfinished injuries before her, her mind and hands poised and ready to help. She followed her mother.

"Maiden," Alsandair called hoarsely as Eloise and her mother passed on their way out, "Maiden, a word?"

"Sit, don't get up," Eloise instructed, moving to the small group with him. "Of course." Eloise scanned the faces, all familiar. One of the cook's assistants restrained Alsandair. Realization: She was "Lovey," the voice Eloise couldn't place last night. Eloise tried to smile at all the worn and blackened faces sitting before her.

Her tears plopped on Alsandair's lap and his nose as Eloise bent and kissed his bandaged forehead. "Goodness upon you, Alsandair," she said as she took his hands. Warm, natural, not a fever she noted with relief. "You saved me."

"Now it's your turn," Alsandair said, as he lifted her hands away. "I've but one good eye, by God," he said, tapping under that eye with his finger, "and I won't know contentment till I see you triumphant, you and your father, with Tiomu's head on a lance." The soldier saluted her, a grimace across his bandaged face. "We'll be waiting," he said, still tapping under his good eye.

"I'll pray for you," the others murmured, almost in unison. "God be with you, Maiden, don't forget us."

Eloise and her mother continued to the physician's chamber to clean up a bit and retrieve some healing remedies. They washed their hands and faces. Eloise squirmed and squealed as her mother scrubbed her hands with ash and sand.

"Think of the suffering you have left," her mother scolded. "It's bad enough you met our new neighbors with your hands so stained and disreputable."

Once again dirty hands were a sin, why? Eloise opened her mouth, to question.

"Fortitude and obedience," Aine said using a wooden pick to scrape under Eloise's fingernails. Eloise turned her attention to the crisis before them.

"*Mathair*, since we're here, I must get a purgative and kidney-ease." Her mother nodded.

"I too must replenish," her mother said, quickly scanning the room.

Eloise had never seen the orderly chamber so unkempt. Drawers left open, cabinet doors ajar to reveal half-empty shelves. And still so many ailing kin waiting for relief.

Next, they applied some soothing lotion; it smelled heavenly and with eyes closed, Eloise held her hands to her nose and inhaled the almond essence. Even with eyes closed, Eloise could not erase the images of battered or gouged flesh, her people, in the Great Hall.

Roland, Sedric and Guillaume were escorted by Reginald into the meeting chamber. Two long tables were arranged end to end, with two benches against the wall. Four men filled one bench and a fifth sat on the other. A haggard squire limped briskly to light all the sconces. The five men stood, saluting Reginald, as Roland and his companions entered. Formal introductions were made between Roland and his men and Sir Uilliam, fourth in the chain of command from Lord Hubert, Aine, and Reginald. Bairre, the Armory Steward, and Sirs Cairbre, Maine, and Faeloch crowded on the one bench, leaving the second for Roland, Reginald, Sedric and Guillaume.

The door opened and a steward came in with two candelabras; behind him the wine steward and two porters entered bearing trays laden with pitchers and cups, and another with a small cask. Behind them, three more porters bore platters of head cheese, cured meat, pickled cabbage, onions and bread.

"Ale only," the wine steward said.

"Bless you, sir," Uilliam said. "Take that over wine any day."

"Finest ale in Connacht," Cairbre said to contented sighs and smiles.

"Long as it lasts," the wine steward reminded them.

Seeing the platters of food arranged on the long tables caused a distant ache in the pit of Roland's stomach. Up until now, he had been too engaged in survival to think about eating. Sedric's stomach gurgled just as the porters were putting full cups of the dark, rich ale in their grateful hands.

"May you have goodness," Roland nodded, lifting the cup to the steward in tribute. Roland inhaled deeply as if the aroma of the ale itself might satisfy his thirst and the desire for the comforts imbibing alone could quench. He took in the hearty aroma, anticipating the mild bitter and the subtly sweet - and the faintest trace of apple, he wondered? He tried to ignore the usual acrid smell of so many overworked bodies occupying the confines of this meeting chamber.

"For you, Sir, with our Lady's special regards," the wine steward said, placing a cup in Reginald's good hand.

Reginald lifted his cup steadily, spilling not a drop. "To the Lady of Dahlquin," he toasted. He looked like a man possessed. His hair was wild and askew; dried and caked blood caused tufts to stand at odd, spiked angles. Dirt, grime, sweat and blood ringed his face and filled in the deep lines making him look grotesque. Even his thick, crenellated ears looked menacing. And that hand - how was it the man could walk with such an injury?

"Lady of Dahlquin," the others responded, lifting their cups. They all drank.

The door swung open. Roland watched two knights enter, followed by Hubert, tall and purposeful.

"The Lord Butcher himself," Guillaume muttered, nudging Roland as they stood, moving his finger under his chin, mimicking a slit throat.

"I still can't believe you called her that," Sedric grumbled, his breath shallow.

Roland shrugged. How was he to know? He was embarrassed enough by his words, but for Sedric to reveal that social blunder to Guillaume was beyond stupid. Roland gripped Sedric's upper arm, helping him stand in the least obvious way.

"He said she was flattered," Guillaume muttered. "Eh, Roland? Flattered and frightening."

"Frightening? How so?" asked Sedric.

Roland snorted. Frightened, so he was, by what he saw, deep in her eyes. Trying to ignore his friends' harassment, Roland returned his attention to Lord Hubert.

Hubert had his fist extended, and Lady Aine rested her hand upon it, appearing to glide into the room at her husband's side, the infamous heretic of Dahlquin. For the second time Roland observed how small she was, especially in contrast to her husband and the armed men around her.

As chatelaine, a large set of keys hung from her sturdy girdle as well as a full leather pouch. Behind them came Eloise, also remarkably small, with maybe an inch or two of height on her mother, dwarfed by three enormous, wire-haired hounds surrounding her. With claws and wings they could have been chimeras. The door closed behind them.

The knights and stewards lined up, then dropped to their knees, heads bowed. The porters fell to their knees where they were.

Setting their half-empty cups on the table, Roland, Sedric and Guillaume followed Reginald to the line.

Guillaume knelt. Sedric collapsed to the floor. Foolish gesture, Roland thought, when Sedric could barely move. Reginald confirmed Roland's inclination to remain standing with a curt nod. Roland was unsure of Connacht etiquette. *Why should his own men kneel to Hubert? He wasn't king. Was this an insult? To Roland? Or FitzGilbert?* Then Reginald seemed to step almost behind him. *Why? What was the hierarchy here? Shouldn't Reginald stand with the Dahlquin men, rather than at the end of the line with him?* Roland wondered, trying to find the pattern of order.

As they walked down the receiving line, each knight thanked and blessed Hubert and Aine, then in turn reached for the bloodstained hem of Aine's surcoat in an effort to kiss it, which she would not allow, instead taking their hands in her free one.

Aine blessed and thanked each by name as they placed their foreheads on the back of her hand before kissing it.

At first Eloise was a reflection of her parents' statures, head up, shoulders back, commanding. But Roland noted her bottom lip quivering. She sucked it in.

"*Princess,*" Cairbre said to Eloise, his shoulders hunching as he grabbed her hem. "Forgive my weakness," he blurted, thin voiced.

"Do not," Eloise said, voice quavering, grasping his hands in her own.

Roland's stomach growled loudly, and he didn't hear whatever else she said. He watched as Cairbre buried his face in their entwined hands and Eloise bent and kissed his bowed head. Cairbre held fast to her hands as she straightened. Slipping one hand free, she patted the stout leather pouch on her girdle.

She turned, teary eyed. Studying her parents' backs, it seemed to Roland. She squared her shoulders before moving to the next knight kneeling before her, who in turn took her offered hands, laying his forehead on the backs before kissing them.

"Lord Roland," Hubert addressed, standing before him as if from nowhere.

Roland snapped his attention to Hubert and Aine. He was more fatigued than he thought or distracted. Two of the hounds sniffed at him, neither snarling nor wagging their tails. Neutral.

"We'll break bread over discussion of Tiomu's treachery," Hubert said, his blue eyes sharp, more so because of their deep lines around them, like claw marks.

"Again, our gracious goodness upon you, Lord Roland, and welcome," Aine said, dipping her head. Roland felt warmly received as he took her offered hand, clean scrubbed. The aroma of almonds and honey was intoxicating. Her green eyes were equal in intensity to her husband's, but without the harshness. Anguish. A casualty of warfare, Roland thought, with so much more to come. Her thick blonde braid hung to her knees. He nodded as she and Hubert moved on.

Guillaume drew his attention; his friend's mischievous blue eyes gleamed. Then Guillaume returned his focus to Lady Aine's regal backside.

The Lady looked over her shoulder with a penetrating gaze first on the kneeling Guillaume, and then to Roland. She tipped her head slightly, but her green eyes held steady on Roland. Then she turned, floating at her husband's side to the table.

Roland felt a tug on his surcoat and glanced down at Guillaume.

"Succubus," Guillaume mouthed silently up to Roland, before his mouth curled into a lascivious grin. Roland scowled; hunger forgotten as his bowels lurched. He looked quickly behind him to be sure Reginald, the living gargoyle, hadn't seen, but before he could ask Guillaume if he were fucking mad.

"Sedric, may you have goodness again, Sir," Eloise said taking Sedric's hands, trying to encourage him to rise. Roland watched her smile turn to a frown. She placed the back of her hand on his cheek, then his forehead. "Fever is upon you, Sir."

Sedric was red-cheeked, but Roland suspected it was fever of a different sort that burned his friend. The big hound at her side licked Sedric's face.

Eloise patted the leather pouch hanging from her girdle. "I've brought you some purgative and wound and kidney heal. We'll tend to that lip, too. By your will, I beg you have a seat and rest."

"Roland," Guillaume whispered, tugging Roland's surcoat. Roland glared down at his intrusive friend, remembering he needed to reprimand this continued rudeness.

"Twin succubi!" Guillaume mouthed, rolling his eyes first at Eloise then towards her mother. Immediately he bowed his head piously as Eloise approached, and before Roland could chastise him.

"Fair and gracious daughter of the abattoir," Guillaume moaned softly, grasping not her hands, but her surcoat at about knee height, pulling the fabric to his face. "I'm but a humble Leinstermen, now of Dead Man's Land. My name is Guillaume of Guillford, and I wish you may have goodness and bless you for the kindness you have bestowed upon my *brother*, Sedric, and my ill spoken Lord Roland."

"May you have goodness, Sir," she said, standing as far back from Guillaume as the fabric of her surcoat would allow. It came to Roland's attention that the ladies had removed their ghastly aprons. Eloise was wearing a light blue surcoat, a pleasant color on her. Her lips were thin, pale pink, lighter than the pink of her tear-swollen eyes. "Lord Roland, we meet again," she said, blue-grey eyes imploring. *Do something. He's your man.*

Beyond her plea, within the blue-grey depths, was the visage. He couldn't blink or breathe. He had seen the same vision in her eyes in the Great Hall. Before he could react, Reginald pushed past him, lips pursed, his hazel eyes slits, as he took Eloise's elbow.

"Off," he directed, in a malice-infused whisper, and Guillaume fell back on his heels.

Eloise glanced at her uncle with appreciation. Horror replaced her gratitude. The binding over his left hand was soaked with blood.

"Uncle Reggie!" she gasped. "What happened?"

"Tiomu's men," he said, leading her to the table where her parents waited.

Eloise took his hand, examining the bindings, the blackened, shriveled fingers, oblivious to the knights joining them around the table, as Uilliam directed the three men from Ashbury-at-March to the end opposite Lord Hubert. Aine stood to his right. Eloise and Reginald stood to the left.

"Your hand must come off," she said, unable to raise her voice above a whisper. "This will poison your body," she continued, studying the binding.

"That's what your mother and the physician claim."

Eloise gave him a questioning look.

"I'll not live as a cripple."

"Not a cripple, it's just your shield arm," she whispered, shaking her head. Tentatively she extended a finger, touching the knuckle of his stiff pointer finger, then traced down its cold, black length to the dead fingernail. Fresh, new tears blistered her cheeks. Her stomach turned

81

inside out. Uncle Reggie had always been there for her. Like her father, Uncle Reggie was invincible. It was not possible for him to be defeated. He was second in command, and besides his brother, he was her father's dearest friend next to Gerald FitzGilbert of Leinster. Eloise had witnessed his prowess in practice many times and heard the tales of his accomplishments…he always recovered.

Her Nurse and Sean murdered in her own bedchamber. Donegal, Eoin, those in the infirmary, now Uncle Reggie. Eloise trembled. This was too much grief. There had never been such a day in all her life. It seemed her loved ones dropped dead around her as did the firstborn of Egypt.

"You're safe, Ellie," he murmured, putting his right arm around her, pulling her close, so strong, even now. Her head rested well under his chin, feeling the circular metal rings of his chain mail under his stained surcoat, pressed against her cheek. Wrapping her arms around his barrel chest, she inhaled the familiar fragrance of sweat and blood and leather. He took slow, easy breaths to calm her down. Eloise didn't give in to the heaving sobs hovering under the surface. She would not. "You're safe. That's all I ever wanted." he said. Grief receded slowly with each deep breath Reggie took. Eloise matched his breathing, slow, steady. Uncle Reggie. Drying her tears. As always.

Beast nudged at her leg with his head, then leaned against her and sat on her foot.

"We are Dahlquin," Reginald started, "Family, God, Crown."

The Dahlquin oath, the pledge of fealty earned and bestowed was as familiar as the Hail Mary prayer or her own name. Reggie squeezed her and she joined him reciting the oath.

"I am your man," she heard her father's voice, solidifying the code, the rest of the men and Aine joining in, words reborn in her soul as she formed them. Eloise pushed out of her uncle's embrace to stand on her own, as her parents, the knights, stewards and porters did, each reciting: "And pledge before all gods to defend your land and kin, against your enemies and Satan until the end of days." The power of the oath filled Eloise's ears as everyone lifted their cups, "Dahlquin!"

No one sat. All waited for Lord Hubert.

Hubert and Reginald shared a long gaze. The corner of Reggie's mouth flinched; her father's eye squinted. It seemed neither man took a breath. So much had passed between the brothers over the years. Eloise recognised her father might have to face the world without his brother. Of course, Reginald knew he left his lord brother, sister-in-law and niece to face the world without him to guard their backs. Could a lifetime of memories pass between them in a single glance? There was naught to say.

They knew it. They also knew what must be done. Death was nothing, duty everything.

Hubert looked over the bandaged wrist. The hand was mangled and deformed from loss of blood and nerves, an impediment to holding a shield. At Reginald's insistence, her mother had not removed his doomed hand, but must have cauterized the wound to staunch the bleeding. *How could he persevere? Such an injury would kill most and leave the rest comatose. Yet Uncle Reggie was here. Why had her mother allowed that useless appendage to remain? This was powerful medicine.* Eloise was learning much.

Reginald laid his left arm out, palm up on the wooden table before Hubert.

Like Eloise, everyone stared in mute absorption.

In a moment of unusual drama Hubert removed his sword, *Custos*, from its scabbard. He examined it. The blade caught the candlelight, twinkling as he tilted it to and fro to examine the metal for dirt or flaws. *Custos*: Latin for guardian, and so it was. Satisfied it was in perfect working order he lifted the sword high over his head and brought it down with the swiftness of an executioner.

"Father!" gasped Eloise, as the chamber boomed with the sound of impact.

The sudden movement and ferocity with which Hubert moved caused the men in the cramped room to jump involuntarily. It appeared Hubert used his sword to cut through Reginald's wrist, bone and all. The legend of Sir Reginald's power and loyalty would be further enhanced by the tales of men who saw Lord Hubert chop his injured hand clean off, then witness Reginald sit at the table, accept his Lord's blessing and dine with the assembly. It made an indelible mark on the minds and souls of those present. Dahlquin was graced by God.

DAHLQUIN CASTLE, 9th of June

Summoned, Eloise stood at her father's side along with her mother and Reggie, all of them looking down from the foremost wall. Archers and crossbow men were in every tower and along the ramparts, waiting for Hubert's order to resume shooting.

Tiomoid U'Neill had called for a cease-fire; he wanted to negotiate.

"Lord Hubert!" Tiomoid U'Neill called out at the gatehouse. "Hubert! Let us talk. You are lost."

Tiomoid U'Neill stood behind a large, long shield. He seemed stout, solid and dark-haired, but not much of him was exposed. Still, how easy to drop him with a bolt or arrow. Was it truly necessary to honor a cease fire called by such a traitor?

"U'Neill, take your men and go! There's naught for you here," Hubert shouted down to him.

"Hubert, listen," Tiomoid called up to him, "lay down your arms and join me. It's not too late."

"Never! You are not king here U'Neill, nor shall you be."

"Hubert, Ashbury falls as we speak. You can't stand alone. United we'll take Meath, Munster, and all else who stand in our way."

That can't be true, Eloise prayed, not Ashbury, for they too were like family. Tiomoid U'Neill had as many cousins in Ashbury as he was killing here. What malice.

"And Leinster? FitzGilbert will never bow to you," Hubert shouted back.

"You're the real power behind Leinster. Everyone knows the truth of it. FitzGilbert grows soft."

"Tiomoid's trying to win you over with flattery," Reggie said. "Connacht is the key."

"Lies, Tiomu!" Hubert shouted back. "We've naught to discuss."

"Look about you, man! This isn't the whole of my army. I have the might of Denmark and Norway. They, too, have a stake in the affairs of Tara. England is through."

Hubert glanced at Aine, Reggie and then Eloise.

"The Hebrides are not to be counted on. But Denmark?" Hubert mused to his assembled family.

"Is the King of Denmark in on this?" Reggie asked.

Aine said nothing but shook her head just slightly.

"Denmark, probably not," Hubert agreed. "Tiomoid U'Neill hasn't the influence to sway Denmark. Even so-," he said, fixing his stern gaze on Eloise.

She studied her father's countenance. The lines on his face had become deep fissures as if reflecting the damage wrought upon the exterior of their castle, but the blue steel in his gaze blazed, handsomely stoked with burning resolve.

"Dahlquin will never capitulate," he finished. She blinked hearing his words. They were so clearly etched on his face she already knew them.

"Hubert, you are a thoughtful lord. Save your kinsmen!" It seemed Tiomoid was trying to manipulate Dahlquin a bit. Maybe petty hatred could be used to Tiomoid's own use. "Hubert, Ashbury falls. Join me now and Scragmuir will be next. With our combined forces Scragmuir will be vanquished. Dust! Then naught will stand in our way!" Tiomoid shouted up to Hubert.

Eloise could hear the murmurs along the ramparts, "Scragmuir vanquished, imagine it." She felt the surge herself, almost transported from her role as besieged to that of attacker, with her mortal enemy pulverized.

Tiomoid looked out, smiled, scanning the castle, as if ready to kindle any sign of complicity.

"Scragmuir vanquished indeed," Hubert muttered, turning again to Eloise. "Tiomu hasn't the might to sway Denmark or the Hebrides."

"Probably not," Reggie agreed, "but he has resource enough below."

Already Dahlquin resorted to using debris from its very own walls and structures for return in the trebuchet. No one spoke of defeat, yet. That pleased her father. Dahlquin would stand firm another day. After that...

"Good luck with Scragmuir!" Hubert shouted back at his adversary. "If you can take them, you're a better man than I." The men of Dahlquin laughed and jeered at the traitors outside their castle. Their resolve held.

"Hubert! Think of it, Scragmuir at your feet!" Tiomoid tried yet again.

"Bah, Scragmuir stands fast for Gerald FitzGilbert and England's boy king. So does Dahlquin. Denmark! Norway, Scotland!" Hubert shouted to the assembled army. "Go home, there's naught for you here but death. Ireland will never submit to this false U'Neill. I suggest you take cover. This truce is over." Hubert turned his back on them and retreated. He would have the last word. "Let fly," he said to Uilliam, indicating the Asp.

Eloise watched the assaulting army go mad with rage and shouts. Tiomoid lost this round, would he have another? Dahlquin was outnumbered and without reinforcement. Tiomu need but sit idly by for Dahlquin to starve. Would Scragmuir join his assault? Would another family come to their aid?

The flaming ball hurled from the heart of Dahlquin drew everyone's attention. Ghastly cries emanated from the projectile as an arc of yellow-orange flames and black smoke tumbled screaming across the sky, a banshee proclaiming death. Dahlquin's trebuchet engineer was but a few feet off from where Tiomoid U'Neill stood. Stinging from Hubert's dismissal, Tiomu was livid and he was almost hit with this fiery missile. He strode in for a closer look as the flames died. His eyes stung. The stench of burnt flesh was unmistakable. Tiomu and his men covered their noses. Eyelids burnt off, red hair singed and smoldering, Tiomu barely recognised the charred mass before him as Sir Byron. The dying man convulsed and shuddered. Tiomoid U'Neill was sick with it and vomited. Hubert was a barbarian.

ASHBURY UNDER SIEGE, 9ᵗʰ of June

Lord Ashbury flinched with each step as he limped down the corridor on his wooden crutches. Eoch flinched with him, sharing the pain in spirit. During the race back to Ashbury castle, and despite Eoch's august efforts to shield him from the attackers, Albert took an arrow to his left buttock, an ignoble injury for the Lion of Ashbury to incur.

"Is this how God rewards his avenging Pilgrims?" Eoch mocked, "You, my esteemed Lord, a surviving veteran of the third attempt to reclaim the Holy Land from the vermin heretics of Saladin."

"It's what I deserve for heeding your sage advice to expose my backside and return to the castle," Albert countered, for that was the sum of it. Shot in the arse for running away.

"And who suffers your pain with each step and breath? On whose command did I take up the cowardly bow, forsaking my shield of servitude? Eh?" Eoch asked.

Albert wasn't looking at Eoch, but he could imagine the arched eyebrow and the deprecating expression of his loyal and flagrant companion. Albert grinned - not with his face, but in his soul.

"Our pain is so great, I need crutches," Eoch said.

The sound of coughing echoed off the stone walls as Albert and Eoch made their way towards the Great Hall. A torch burned from a wall mount. Four men-at-arms sat on the floor together, backs to the wall. One of them, Sir Orin, had a leg bent with both arms wrapped around the knee. His other leg was extended with a thick wrap round this thigh. Next to Orin was a soldier, Cormac. Both his legs were bent, his arms crossed upon his knees, and his head rested upon the lot. His right hand was wrapped in bloody bindings. Next to him was another soldier, Ailbe, who appeared unscathed as he sat with his knees well bent, his head propped against the wall, eyes closed. Last was the archer named Albert after the Lion of Ashbury. The archer never spoke, though he was neither deaf nor dumb.

"Greetings, warriors of Ashbury!" Eoch hailed.

Albert saw all four men, startled to see Sir Eoch and himself approaching, scramble to kneel. Ailbe was quick to assist Orin.

"Hold!" Albert called out. He balanced on his crutches and motioned with his hands that they remain where they were. "Stay seated. I only wish I could join you," he added with a wry smile, then tenderly placed his left hand just above the injury to his back side.

"Cormac," Albert said, "what news, man? Still waiting?" Cormac's wife was the second woman to go into labor during the siege. Ashbury had welcomed one new daughter with the first rays of the fog-shrouded sun. Whether through her cries of release, or her anguished mother's cries of relief, the challenge had been taken up by Cormac's wife. Life was always in the balance, Albert knew.

"We're waiting, my Lord, with yours and God's will." The young man's voice was wary, but Cormac gave a half smile, revealing his bloody mouth and cracked teeth. His left eye was nearly swollen shut. Part of his left ear was missing: an old injury, revealing Cormac still let his left guard down.

Albert studied the young man. From the hoary age of seventy-two, most of his men appeared as mere boys to him. Cormac had anguish streaked across his battle-riddled face.

"And?" asked Albert with a shrug, encouraging Cormac to speak.

"It's a breech," Cormac said, revealing the source of his anguish. "The babe caught fast for hours. But the midwife says he'll be delivered very soon now." He gasped, which started a fit of coughing.

"We're keeping vigil," Orin said, reaching over Ailbe to give Cormac a hearty shove, "can't have Cormac alone when his son arrives feet first. That's a cautious and prudent boy, I am thinking, checking the waters first thing before plunging in headfirst."

"So he is," acknowledged Eoch, "and eager to take up the fight against the traitorous U'Neill as well."

"Ailbe?" Albert asked, shifting the focus to the other father-to-be.

"Confinement, sir," Ailbe answered, "still in confinement. My wife has another fortnight, God willing. May you have goodness for remembering, Lord," he said before a deep cough racked him.

"God willing," Cormac said, crossing himself as his coughing slowed.

"God willing, indeed," Orin called out. "And where be the god-cursed lads with our drink?"

There was a brief pause while all the men waited for the answer no one had. The torch fluttered and a thin line of black smoke coiled toward the center of the corridor.

"My Lord Albert, Sir Eoch," Orin continued, "I would invite you stay and share an imbibement, but alas," and he started to shout, "we're abandoned by our unsuccessful ale-hunters." Raising his voice caused him to cough as well. Now three men coughed, wet and labored, as if by some sympathetic reflex. The ominous sound of lung-plague rattled Albert. It was near summer solstice, yet his men rasped as if winter's disease had infested them. Or siege disease.

"Siege or not, a man must have drink!" agreed Eoch, raising his voice to be heard over the coughing. "My Lord, with your gracious leave, I will once again attend to your needs by pillage and seizure."

Albert nodded his head and Eoch departed. Was it just yesterday morning, he reflected? He, Eoch and his men; such a trivial escapade it now seemed, to raid the kitchens and embark on a fortuitous pre-dawn hunt. Albert looked upon them, two still coughing. Yesterday was a lifetime ago for many. Some had lost their lives in service to Ashbury. He knew each by name, lineage and function. And from yesterday forward, all of Ashbury were forever affected, like a famine or plague, pilgrimage or flood, their lives would forever be marked relative to this siege by the Ulstermen. And for some, lovers, parents, this was a new beginning.

"God's blood," Albert said out loud, "every day." He paused; why limit himself to the dawn? "And again, I say God's blood and the myriad of blood, bowels and boils. Every moment is a new beginning, eh?"

All four men looked up at him, questioning, coughing.

"An opportunity to live, to be the glory," Albert continued. His men stared respectfully, not fully grasping the import, the whims of God and Fate. He sighed, "Orin, your thigh. What misfortune?" Albert asked, saving the philosophical lecture for a more receptive audience.

"Like you, my Lord, an arrow," Orin answered. "And your remedy, Lord," he scowled and shook his head with the memory. "Savior Jesus, I cried out like a branded calf, Sir. I don't lie. How did you devise such a wicked treatment?" Orin grasped his leg as if the pain had returned.

Albert shook his head, too. "Aqua vitae?"

Orin nodded his head.

"Branded calf you say. I howled some blasphemy myself, Orin," Albert said, remembering the searing pain as he lay across the board, clutching the rough wood. First the arrow was removed from his left buttock with torturously slow deliberation - to save the flesh and muscle the physician claimed. *Curse the bastard.* Then the lifesaving water of life was poured into the humiliating wound. *Curse the Maid of Dahlquin, for it was her remedy.* "But it's effective," Albert said, though his eyes teared with the memory.

"What? The blasphemy? I could've screamed that without the waste of whiskey on my leg. Blessed Mother save me," Orin said, and then coughed. "Think of my disappointment, my outstretched hands begging the cup of your finest, Lord. Instead of holding the vessel to my needy lips, the bastard dribbled it on my savaged flesh. Fucking Hell fire, like a branding iron, I swear. Why?" Orin implored.

"Why, Lord, why pour good whiskey upon the wound?" Cormac asked. "That is a blasphemy."

The silent archer, Albert, pointed to Cormac, nodding his head in agreement, then mimicked pouring a cup upon his leg, with a scowling frown of disapproval. Then palms up, he shrugged with a tilt to his head, *why indeed?*

"Fair waste," Ailbe agreed, as he looked down the corridor wishing, as they all did, that some potent drink of health and heaven was soon to be delivered.

"Yule last. The fourth day of Christmas," Albert reminded them all, leaning on his crutches so his hands were again free. "My god-daughter, sweet, gentle Maiden Eloise from Dahlquin and her nurse were visiting." The men nodded.

"I remember," Cormac said, "with the dancing grey stallion."

Orin chuffed, and the archer, silent Albert, blushed with his smile.

"A grand beast, him," Lord Albert concurred.

"I'd be dancing too, were she riding me," Orin added.

"Ha," Ailbe chuckled, "golden spurs, but naught else."

"Dancing or bucking, her choice, that?" Orin answered, his laughter starting him to cough again.

"Quiet, Lord Hubert will hear you from this very spot," Albert counseled. "You may owe my god-daughter your very leg or life."

"So, you were explaining, Lord," Cormac said.

Albert resumed his story. "We had a cook with a severe cut, nearly sliced a finger off," Albert held up a hand to show them the fingers in question. "Maid Eloise treated him right there in the kitchen. Wiped away the blood, assessed the wound and demanded aqua vitae. Like you, the shocked cook thought his thirst was to be sated, but the little-" Albert paused. He was going to say vixen, but revised his description of Eloise, "my beloved, kindly god-daughter dipped his bleeding fingers in the cup." Albert dipped two fingers in an imaginary cup. "The cook fainted clear away." "I believe he would," Orin said, crossing himself. The other men followed his example.

"He survived," Albert said before continuing. "I suffered a minor injury myself, slipped on the steps, ground my knuckles nearly to bone. I tried the Maid's remedy, aqua vitae for hand and gut," Albert flexed his hardened, gnarled hand. He held both hands out and compared them in the flickering, smoky torch light. Not a scar, not a trace of the age-induced fall. "Water of Life is a healing agent, before God."

"But it scalds like Satan's bitch," Eoch said, returning with three porters in tow, two laden with skin bags, sliced cheese and pickled eggs. The third had a thick pad and blanket.

"The best arrangement I could concoct, My Lord. A cushioned dais."

"May you have goodness, Eoch," Mor said, stepping out of the shadowed corridor, "as you said, My Lord Husband and his worthy court." She had a wee child in her arms.

90

Once again, all four men on the floor were startled into action and rushed to kneel in their Lady's presence.

"Da," the child in Mor's arms called. "Da," the child said again, little arms reaching out as Mor set the toddler upon the floor.

"Gerdie," Cormac said, catching his son in his arms and squeezing the boy tight, suppressing the deep coughs.

Mor nodded to each man. Her features were worn, but the dim light masked the deep lines and imperfections. In fact, Albert noticed her features had a softness he had not seen in the days before the siege.

"Cormac," she said, "I've come straight away from the lying-in chamber. You, good sir, are the father of a fine and fit daughter, feet first, with clenched fists and soft downy hair. Your wife sends her apology that it isn't the second son you hoped for. But, Cormac," Mor went on, "she is a treasure, a living treasure of God's love. You have been blessed."

"Prosit, Cormac!" Albert boomed. The other men followed with congratulatory praise, patting and shoving.

"If you wish to see your wife and daughter-," Mor started to say, extending the invitation.

Cormac was already waving his friends farewell. "With your leave, Lord," he said bowing to Albert, Gerdie still clutched to his chest. "I would very much like to be with my family."

"And so you should," Albert agreed.

Eoch pressed himself against the wall, in an exaggerated fashion so all knew Cormac's path was clear and none stood between him and his women.

Cormac's cough echoed off the stone walls as he jogged to wife and infant daughter.

"And prosit to you, Our Lady Mor," Eoch said, lifting one of the skin bags to her. "It seems we may well owe our very lives to you. Without your wise, or even prescient counsel that we remove our obstreperous selves from the confines of the orderly castle, we wouldn't have foiled the surprise attack of our truculent U'Neill cousin."

"Slaughtered in our own beds, mayhap," Ailbe said.

"Or someone's bed," Orin muttered, with a wink.

"My Lady," Albert said, "once again I and all Ashbury salute your sagacity."

"My Lord Husband," Mor said, dipping her head, "I am your humble student, Sir. I learn and live by your exemplary conduct for the glory of Ashbury."

DAHLQUIN CASTLE, DAY THREE OF THE SIEGE,
10th of June

Stone missiles continued to rain upon Dahlquin on a regular basis, eating away at the mighty fortress walls, but the real hazard was to the castle inhabitants. Death and injury hung over the defenders hourly. U'Neill's men launched a diseased carcass into the compound with the hope to contaminate the well or sicken the defenders. The debris not returned by Asp was dispatched to any of the numerous fires kept alight.

Human resources were in abundance. Dahlquin was well garrisoned with archers and crossbowmen. Skilled and deliberate, they manned the embrasures throughout the castle walls night and day, though all knew their bolts and arrows were in limited supply.

Natural resources were the weakness. Food and arms were rationed with brutal efficiency. Each day the siege continued was a day the countryside was raped by the attackers. Crops and livestock were stripped and consumed. Nothing was stored. Fields lay fallow. The growing season was short enough without a complete cessation.

"Here they come again!" shouted Hubert as the sun sank in the western sky, leaving them to fight in summer's long twilight.

"Steady!" called the captains of each station.

Eluding the mighty trebuchet, two large, wooden siege towers were pushed simultaneously against the walls of Dahlquin Castle. Each tower was four stories high, and each story held ten armed men ready to ascend upon their enemy. Permeated with water, the leather-clad structures were near impossible to ignite. Bolstered from below, they were strong and steady.

"Missiles!" ordered Hubert. "Now!"

Oil-soaked projectiles were launched, short-range into the towers. The first simply rolled off the slanted roofs and spilled ineffectively to the moat.

"Again!" Hubert shouted.

With adjustments made, a second volley was lobbed into the siege towers, only to be deflected. No life was exempt from helping repel this nemesis, all able-bodied men and women were utilized in the engagement.

The trebuchet was abandoned as the inhabitants clamored to repel the invaders. Babies and the smallest of children were tucked away in the infirmary. The very elderly, sick and dying were left to keep vigil and pray. Eloise, Aine and her attendants took up crossbowmens' positions.

It was difficult to push away the towers with single poles. Ladders had strength and durability, and the strength of many men could be harnessed, but could as easily be traversed. As the flaming missiles continued, a company of men labored to shove the gargantuan siege towers over with the ladders.

"Push!" shouted the team leaders. "Push, God damn you! Put your backs into it!"

Each man, baker and clerk alike, heaved and pushed, willing themselves to have the strength of twelve oxen. Shirtless, their sweat-soaked torsos glistened in the firelight, their grunts lost in the din of battle.

Children ran the stone stairs and wooden scaffolds with armloads of fuel. They stoked the fires, heating the kettles of oil to be spilled off the walls onto the attackers. Anything spilt inside the castle was cleaned. The youngest labored under skin bags of water and wine for the able defenders.

Women assisted in lobbing the flaming projectiles or pushing against the siege towers as their talent allowed. All were exhausted and spent as Tim'U'Neill launched this late-afternoon assault.

"Push!" the captain shouted again. "The Danes will have you after your wives and daughters! Now push! God knows they will!"

"Now!" Hubert ordered. Another volley of flaming missiles, bolts and arrows was launched upon the ever-encroaching siege towers. Screams and howls emanated from one of them; several men jumped from their positions within the inferno. The defenders cheered wildly, resuming their tasks with renewed vigor.

As enormous grappling hooks were launched from the towers over the castle wall, the defenders wrestled to dislodge them. Too slow to evade the metal claw, one man was pinned to the wall. His blood ran warm and slippery along the metal and stone. His comrades couldn't free him or the dangerous attachment. U'Neill's men climbed out, fighting and anchoring the tower.

Hubert and his soldiers descended upon the armed invaders. With pickaxes and poles they fought to shove the men off as more soldiers continued to ascend the tower and empty in their multitude upon the Dahlquin defenders.

"Push, you Danish whores!" the captain commanded. "Push!" With a long groan, the defenders were shoved back with the momentum of the tower. "Push the bloody wads back to Hell!" They did.

Black smoke billowed from the burning siege tower. Screams and shouts and acrid smoke permeated the senses. Darkness descended with the smoke, defender and attacker alike fought blindly, choked by ash and stench. A huge cracking noise deafened all, then the splintering of wood.

"We've done it boys! Push it off!" the captain called as one mighty siege tower slowly began to slip away from Dahlquin. Tiomu's men scrambled to evacuate the smoldering tower as it broke in two. Below was chaos; men ran like ants from a smoke-infested hill. A mighty cheer went up from Dahlquin. The ramparts rang with their victory. Just as quickly, the defenders now exerted every effort on the siege tower that had breached them.

As Tiomu's siege towers assaulted Dahlquin Castle, his mangonel rained down upon the defenders, pummeling the walls and interior opposite the towers, the blows causing a tremor Eloise could feel through her boots, amplifying the crashing sound. Armed with crossbows, Eloise, her mother and their attendants picked off the enemy below with slow, deliberate accuracy. Bolts were still at a premium, and this wasn't over. Eloise took comfort on the occasions when her Lord Father's commands could be discerned above the pandemonium. Tears streaked her blackened cheeks. Eyes and nose burnt; her ears pounded with the incessant tumult. Her own trusty recurve bow was strung forsakenly over her shoulder, because at this distance it lacked the armour-penetrating power of the executioner's crossbow. Foot in the stirrup, her shoulders cramped as she reloaded the crossbow and fired: one less traitor below.

Beast was barking. Movement caught her attention. Her mother whirled and Eloise turned to look. Her father was confronted by two assailants, a streak of blood between his eyes from brow to jaw, an ax blade arcing to sever her father from this life. Aiming, Eloise worried a bolt at such close range would impale the attacker and her father.

A bolt hit under one of the attacker's arms, penetrating the chain mail, the fletch brushing her father's cheek with the proximity.

"Aine!" Hubert yelled. His blue eyes blazed, highlighted by the scarlet swath across his face as he tried to push the dying man from himself.

"Lacking faith in Cupid, husband?" her mother shouted back as she bent, reloading her crossbow.

"Cupid?" he sputtered, thrusting his dagger up under the other attacker's helm as their sword hands locked together.

"To guide my arrow to the heart of your enemy!" Aine offered, shooting the assailant. Her father cut the wounded man's throat before shoving him away. *Fucking Hell*, he seemed to say, his expression softening. Husband and wife exchanged a glance Eloise couldn't read.

"To your posts!" barked Hubert at her and her mother, amidst the shouts and fighting.

"Not a word," Aine warned Eloise, reloading her crossbow.

Eloise shot an attacker jumping from the rampart and he fell at her father's feet.

Eloise loaded and shot, loaded and shot, tingling as she reconsidered her mother. She was not only a capable defender, but a confident one.

Eloise flinched at a piercing whistle, glancing up as the next missile hurtled over the ramparts. "Curse you!" she gasped as it blasted into one of the two long castle stables, where the finest palfreys and coursers and gear were kept. Crossbow left behind, Eloise and Beast ran towards the screaming as horses fled from the stone and wood shards, a grey cloud hiding the damage as frightened horses sought escape.

"Garth!" she called, pushing her way past the tottering stable as another missile hurtled into the damaged structure. Horses whinnied and blew, hooves skittering and pounding to be free of the projectiles and pain and fear. Chickens tried to fly. Eloise tripped on a cat. A loose red gelding bolted past her, a bloody ear hanging. A liver bay gelding joined him forming a frightened herd of two: Cabba and Sorgha. The animal cacophony and thunder of impact were drowned by the pounding of Eloise's heart as she fought ahead, barely able to see, choking on the dust.

Garth. The dapple-grey stallion's nostrils flared as he circled in the debris-strewn paddock. She stood immobile, relief, disbelief, absorbing the reality; her Garth, sound, unhurt. But the others, for she knew every horse by name, age, breeding and temperament…family.

Scampering back over the felled stones and timber, Eloise pulled her surcoat up to cover her nose and mouth from the cloud of destruction in the stable, distorted light coming in through the gouges in the roof. Splintered timbers, sharp as daggers, hung precariously above stalls as frightened and injured horses fought to escape their crumbling prison.

Beast lunged at a fleeing rat. A pigeon laid at her feet, flapping a useless wing, the rest of its body immobile. Idiotically, Eloise reached down, pinched the primary feathers together and lifted the dying bird from a pool of blood left in the dirt. *"Damn waste of time,"* her father's voice chided in her mind, as she placed the pigeon out of the passageway, crossing herself then grabbing a halter.

Although Eloise had spent many happy hours in the stables with only horses as her companions, at this moment she was desolate with emptiness, knowing every able-bodied person was risking their life repelling Tiomu's siege engines. She had to save the horses.

She struggled to lead the first injured horse out of the rattling stable as Beast barked at the flitting mare. Eloise didn't hear the missile until it hit the corner of the barn with a jolt, bringing more cracking timber and crushed stone raining down on them. The mare lunged past her as Eloise tugged sharply at the lead rope, running behind the exiting mare. Once in the paddock Eloise fought to get the halter off but the mare proved too difficult, wanting to join Garth cantering around the paddock. Eloise let her go.

"Beast!" she yelled as the hound nearly upended her trying to hide underfoot from the last assault.

Mayhap it would be best to let horses be horses and use their herd instinct to guide them to safety. With a clear path to the paddock she could open the barn door. But there wasn't a strong enough barrier to keep them from bolting the wrong way, stampeding into the bailey or kitchens or aviaries. But with Garth to lead them, *of course*, she and Garth could open the door and bring the horses behind. Reaching for Garth's headstall she hesitated; grabbing the soft leather and curb bit, she needed firm communication. She ran to the paddock.

Blocking all the shouts, cries and incessant pounding of battle, Eloise kept Garth and the mare moving away from her, circling the paddock. She studied Garth for injury, letting him settle, drawing him into her. She was the leader; he could trust her. Garth's near ear turned to her. His head dropped as his amble slowed further. Her attention was focused on Garth, as his must be on her. *Great Spirit upon you*, she thought, *look to me, come to me.*

Her five-year old stallion tightened his circles around her, dodging the rocks and splintered boards. "I smell like blood and bone and flesh," she cooed, "but I'm not a wolf," she said shaking her head. "You know me.

Friends." She let him do another lap around her. "Garth," she called gently. "Easy, easy," she said with firm conviction.

"Ho," she said, and Garth stopped, turning to face her, coming to her when she summoned. Eloise stroked his neck, feeling him tremble. "Good boy," she cooed, stroking his face, then massaging at the poll as he dropped his head. The mare halted, watching, seeking security.

Again, the whistle as another projectile smashed into the castle wall with the boom and crash of the stones. Garth turned his head to her, as if hiding from view or seeking protection. Beast cowered under the stallion.

Another missile blasted into the wall. The mare bolted. Eloise tried not to think about the gaping hole in the paddock fence.

"Garth," she said, massaging his poll, burying her own face in his neck. Calm, easy breathing, woman and horse, together against the chaos as a thick cloud of sharp pebbles and dust rained on them. Taking a deep breath, she stood tall, shoulders back, indicating a change. Slowly she lifted the bit to his mouth, touching his lips. He took the metal and she slipped the leather headstall up his face, carefully placing it over his ears. "Thank God," she whispered, picturing the horse with the damaged ear, feeling the tears forming, brusquely pushing them away with the back of her hand. She grabbed his mane and jumped, swinging her right leg over his back, readjusting the bow on her back and quiver on her hip.

Again, the wall shook with impact, more stonework giving way as she and Garth exited the paddock for the tottering stable.

"Maiden, saints be praised!" the stable master howled, exiting the stable with two of the horses in tow.

Before Eloise could acknowledge or thank him, a flaming ball hurtled over the wall, a shooting star of doom as it careened into the battered stable. Timber cracked, stone rattled. *Whoosh.* All noise was absorbed as the stable burst into flames, straw, splintered timber and hay igniting.

Garth spooked, his front legs splayed.

"Ho!" Eloise called, throwing herself back as Garth rocked on his haunches and pivoted. "Ho!" she yelled again as several horses ran through the broken stable wall into the paddock.

"Easy," she said, both hands on the reins as horses jostled by, the acrid smell of burnt hair and worse, flesh. The paddock fencing caught fire.

The wall behind them exploded, showering stone fragments on them. Tiomu's mangonel was being reloaded with unbelievable speed, beating a hole through the wall. Horses screamed, spun, reared, some running as if blind into the falling rocks. Two tried to return to the security of the stable, ignorant the flames of Hell awaited. "Ho!" she screamed futilely as the horses vanished into the inferno. Gulping for air and bracing for the cries of agony she anticipated, Garth continued to spin, unable to find an escape.

Another explosion drowned all animal sound as the castle wall behind her started collapsing. The horses surged away from the avalanche only to be repelled by a wall of flame as the stable fell towards them. Garth reared, extending straight up, as if seeing an escape route into the sky.

"Eloise!"

"Da!" she shouted back. But she couldn't see her father, or anyone through the flames and belching smoke, ash and dust. Her tears were unable to flush away the contaminated air.

Garth trembled and rocked. Eloise planted her butt into his taut back, as if her weight might root them to the firmament. He sprang into the air as if scalded, and when they landed, she understood. The ground was shaking. The wall had been hit again, stone collapsing inside and out, tumbling into the moat and onto the besiegers. Through the grey cloud of destruction crawled Tiomu's men, armed moles, with lances, maces, swords and falchions, clawing through her fortress, to infect the very heart of Dahlquin.

"Da!" she screamed again. He needed to know. The siege towers were toppled, but Tiomu's men had forced entrance, behind the flames.

Another projectile blasted the wall; the breach was larger. Eloise urged Garth forward, believing there was passage through the blaze, praying the loose horses would follow to safety. She could make out a small fire line, buckets full of water dousing the lapping flames. A brief vision of her father, Uncle Reggie, then a wall of smoke, and she trusted Garth to find his way to them, to safety in their guard.

Burning and weakened the stable collapsed, creating a satanic bellows, roaring with the intensity of an angry deity, creating a barrier of flames. Garth and the remaining horses bolted, colliding in blind panic. Singed flesh and hair assaulted the nose and burned the eyes. Garth reared again, the flames forcing him against the obliterated wall. From this height Eloise thought she saw a way out. Straight down was death among the strewn stones, but at an angle, down the steep - vertical - bank, through the moat. To uncertainty. Without a way back into the castle, her home, her people. Tiomu's army before them, separating her from the whole of Ireland.

That or incineration.

"Back, back, back," she commanded Garth, heels tapping. Garth was ready to explode, feeling like a mighty bow, drawn to full, held too long. "Over!" she called, premature, rushing the departure in her own panic of searing flesh and betrayal to her horses for not protecting them. "Over," she said again, legs cueing, upper body leaning, anticipating, encouraging.

Garth lifted. Horses are unable to see clearly what is directly in front of them without turning their head to view with one eye then the other. Garth didn't want to burn, and horses never want their feet in jeopardy, flight is their survival. Garth believed he had to leap, to clear something, and he trusted his leader to guide them to safety. Feeling his leader's urgency, prompted by his own, Garth launched through the breach in the wall, sailing over the broken stones, over the invaders who ducked or fell away from him. There would be ground, he would find purchase, escaping the noise and confusion and heat and fear.

Herd instinct prevailed and the remaining horses turned, following Garth into the unknown, without vision or guidance. Those landing on the rock pile would break or damage legs, those who landed on the slope, as Garth, would have a chance.

Eloise couldn't look back, every fiber focused on balance and staying with Garth, trusting him as he had trusted her. The vertical bank was soft, offering the slightest traction, and Garth lunged down the embankment, no possibility of stopping, only to keep up with the downward momentum, finally leaning back on his hind end, sliding on his rear.

Wishing like never before she was in a saddle with stirrups and support, her pubis bounced painfully against Garth's withers as she leaned further back, squeezing with her legs, unfolding disaster playing out in slow motion, knowing at any moment she might slide forward over his neck, falling ahead of Garth, to be trampled. This slowing down of time gave her clarity to adjust her seat, cling with the desperation of accomplishing the impossible, while uttering a wordless prayer.

"Saddle up!" Hubert shouted, holding the headstall of Reginald's bay stallion as the stable master tightened the girth.

"Faster," Hubert shouted, his daughter trapped between a wall of flames and a collapsing wall. Reginald stood at Hubert's side, instructing the squire tying the shield on his handless left arm. Reggie was sallow colored as death, hazel eyes clear with resolve, his personal battle with mortal pain searing across his features like a solar flare, to be wrestled away, subdued by a grimace, as if an evil presence or foul odor had infiltrated a private interlude.

"You too!" Hubert barked at Roland, as stable boys ran to fetch Roland's black destrier and saddle. "Get her out of there."

Roland nodded, thinking it was suicide. Hubert dumped a bucket of water on himself, as if ready to run into the flames himself.

"Hubert!" Reginald shouted, shaking his head. "Not you."

Roland covered his head as rocks and shards fell from the last blast. In the next instant he helped one-handed Reginald mount up, wondering where the man found the resource to continue. The knight appeared as a corpse in every manner save silence and lack of voluntary motion, a resurrected minion serving Dahlquin beyond the grave.

"Eloise!" Hubert shouted again, over the din, searching for her as Roland did, through the blanketing dust and smoke, the swirling cloud of stampeding horses, as if she and the herd were trapped in some level of purgatory, Hell fire lapping at them, taunting them, and barring them from returning to this brutal level of martial challenge, despite the efforts of the fire line to throw bucket upon bucket of water onto the billowing inferno.

Roland blinked. Movement, men. Climbing, nay oozing through the breached wall.

"Tiomu's men!" he yelled.

Crack, then a creaking boom, and the stable collapsed with a hail of splinters and rocky shards pelleting everything. *Whoosh*. Air, sound and even thought were sucked into the shattered depths of the stable, then a wall of flame blasted from the structure, scorchingly bright and forge hot.

Hubert cried out, defiant in Satan's own wrath. He took hold of the reins of Reginald's skittering stallion. Roland, Hubert, and Reginald searched the blaze, seeking a glimpse of Eloise though no mortal's vision could penetrate the flames or choking smoke.

"Fuck-," Roland muttered, hearing it twice, looking down.

"-ing Hell," the stable boy continued, staring at the unholy visage before them.

"Did you see Tiomu's men?" Roland asked, wanting confirmation.

"I saw them," the boy said, his hand moving to his stomach.

As quickly as it erupted, fuel and air spent, the towering wall of fire withdrew, like a flamboyant red fox retreating into its dark hole, leaving the steady, relentless fire to consume everything in slow, well-chewed portions.

The paddock was empty. Not a single horse or trace of Eloise.

"Where are they?" one of the stable boys asked. The other boy crossed himself. Beast jumped up on the stones, barking, wavering, searching for a way down, snapping at the approaching men. Then he went over the side.

"Go, go!" Hubert shouted, swatting Reginald's great horse on the rump as knight and mount lunged forward.

Reginald and his bay destrier galloped past the burned fence, jouncing through the stone-strewn paddock with increasing speed as the first invaders' heads appeared over the battered ledge. Reginald, sword drawn, shield at the ready, jumped through the breach and disappeared into the smoky unknown as his beloved charge must have done moments before.

"What are you staring at?" Hubert shouted, striding toward Roland, piercing blue eyes drawing closer, withdrawing his sword. "Bring her back!"

As Roland swung into the saddle, Hubert turned, charging into battle against the invading soldiers, his stable hands armed with pitchforks and fiery brands, his knights appearing from everywhere.

Shield in place, Roland and Artoch entered the stone-strewn battlefield, picking their way between debris and men-at-arms below them. No advantage to mounted combat in this pit, he thought. Unlike Reginald before him, Roland wouldn't blindly jump to his doom, in pursuit of a girl who may already be dead by any number of ways: broken neck, crushed skull, punctured lungs, trampled, drowned, impaled - with Reginald to fall upon her crumpled body.

"Bring her back!" was the last thing Roland heard as he too made the leap of faith into oblivion, in pursuit of the girl with blue-grey eyes.

Eloise could barely fathom what was happening. She and Garth escaped a heinous death by fire, only to be careening down a cliff face, like a childhood nightmare of falling, but she wasn't sleeping, it was she and Garth, one mind, one body, unity in motion or...before she could complete the worrisome thought, they plunged into the moat, mud, muck and filth spraying back at them and again she was clinging, praying, wordless.

Free fall forgotten, Garth lunged and dipped, not committed to swimming, seeking a foothold. Eloise slipped and slid, struggling to keep her boots out of the infested moat, the polluted water giving off a putrid, new scent to her siege-beleaguered olfactory senses. Several other horses tumbled or leaped into the water, men and beasts lunging for safety.

The far bank was a swampy, fetid bog, sucking Garth down to his chest as he used all his strength to pull himself forward. Each soggy step risked a crippling injury for Garth. Eloise considered her options as Tiomu's men advanced. She checked her quiver: plenty of arrows. But could she direct Garth out of this mire while shooting?

She slid the bow from her shoulder, reaching for arrows, as she sighted on an approaching soldier. Nock, draw, release. Arrow, nock, draw, willing Garth to lift his mud-leaden hooves as if taking on the weight herself, with no thought to any of it. Instinct. Release. The mail-clad soldiers flinched and slowed.

The soldiers faced the same conditions. Unable to approach, they waited on solid ground.

Around her men cursed and grumbled as the horses churned in the muck before breaking through to solid ground. An eager soldier reached for the reins as Garth slogged out. Eloise shot his face.

"Come on, blighter," another grunted, tugging on the reins as Garth yanked his head back in protest. "Using girls and horses for defense?" he said, looking at Eloise.

The soldier held fast, pulling Garth's head around, forcing Garth to turn sharply. Eloise was unable to take aim on him, shielded behind Garth's neck and head as he was. Too late she thought to draw her dagger, and the soldier grabbed her right wrist, wrenching her down. Some of her arrows clattered to the ground.

More soldiers approached, then dropped to the ground.

The soldier holding her wrist looked first at the men on the ground, then at the castle.

"Crossbows," he muttered.

In that moment, Eloise grabbed one of her spilled arrows and jabbed him above his gauntlet.

"Fucking bitch," he moaned, blood seeping through the padded sleeve, tossing her to the ground.

Eloise tried to land in a defensive crouch, arrow ready.

"Hold!"

She froze, recognising the soul-searing roar of Uncle Reggie.

Eloise twisted to see Reggie, eyes wild, his horse chest deep in the mire as she and Garth had been...and too far away to help. She turned back to her attacker just in time to see a boot coming to her face. She closed her eyes, gut clenched, thinking pain, feeling wind, hearing a growl. Then grunting, rattling, howling curses. Garth blowing. Looking up, Eloise's heart raced as she saw a slick ooze-covered beastie, her own Beast, latched on her attacker's arm, snarling, pulling on the appendage.

"Ho!" she called to Garth as her stallion backed away. His reins were stuck on the attacker's gauntlet, and Garth was pulling the brawling man and dog towards him. Try as Garth might, he couldn't escape the flailing man and hound.

"Go, go!" Reggie commanded her, moving to the bank of the moat, eyes blazing to match his steed's.

Spilled arrows within easy reach, Eloise snatched them up and then stood, returning them to her quiver. Peripherally, she saw a crippled horse, heard shouting. She turned to see two soldiers attacking Beast.

"Ho!" Eloise screamed running at Garth. His reins were loose and she gripped them and a handful of mane, trying to spring up from the ground onto his back. Frightened, Garth skittered sideways as Eloise tried again to climb on the tall horse's back, her panicked movement frightening him more. "Garth," she reprimanded.

Nostrils flared, eyes popping from their sockets, Garth tried to move away from her and the battle.

"Stand still! Ho!"

His massive head bobbed, his moat-filthy tail slashed. The horse was asking for help, drawing Eloise to him.

"Good boy," she tried to coo. *Think*, she commanded herself. Running along with Garth, she vaulted and pulled herself up on Garth's back.

"Beast!" she shouted. "Beast, come!" she called, galloping away.

"Ride, damn you!" yelled Uncle Reggie behind her.

Roland slid down the steep bank. The high pommel and cantle of his saddle, so effective in keeping him firmly centered for battle, forced his body forward and interfered with Artoch's ability to negotiate the descent. Too much weight forward, Artoch pitched headfirst into the moat, humping up his back with the impact of spurs until Roland was able to right himself.

Before them Reginald was bent low, his bay destrier gaining speed, in pursuit of Eloise.

"This is not possible," Roland muttered to himself as Artoch lumbered out of the fetid moat to follow the riders in front of him.

Tiomu's men ignored the last rider and instead scaled the wall to enter Dahlquin castle, the first jewel in Tiomoid U'Neill's crown.

From her sheltered position on the crenellated rampart Aine watched, sighting down the shaft of her loaded crossbow as her only child, beloved brother-in-law, and new neighbor rode out of sight and beyond her reach.

Looking over her shoulder, Eloise checked that Reggie was still behind her. Anyone else, she wondered? Were they pursued? Where should she go? What next? Sitting up, she cued Garth to slow, checking behind her again. Reggie was falling back, and she slowed to an amble. *Another rider*, her heart pounded, *God, with your will*, she pleaded. She looked again. Reggie was also looking back. Her uncle sat up, slowing his horse, but not attacking.

"Walk," she said to Garth, letting her breath out. Her stallion made a rough transition, his barrel heaving for breath as he walked out. His back and her seat were drenched in sweat. They both snorted and she stroked his wet neck.

Hearing the riders approach, she looked back again to see Reggie and, most unexpectedly, Lord Roland of Ashbury-at-March, side by side. She waited, anxious for the company.

"Why the Hell did you slow?" Reginald growled at her, before any salutations could be exchanged. "It's your job to ride, not wait for a dead man."

"To be with you," she snapped. "And ride where?"

"Ashbury. Unless it, too, is under siege as Roland suspects. If there isn't help in Ashbury, then Leinster," Reggie said.

"Leinster?" she questioned; her voice shrill. Is this your idea?" she asked, turning to Roland. Before he could respond, she was back at Reginald.

"You were at counsel," Reginald continued. "If Connacht is under siege, FitzGilbert must be warned. Whether he sends arms or not, he must know."

"What of Meath?" Roland asked. Eloise and Reginald turned on him, looks of incredulity on both their battle stained faces.

The summer sun was sinking toward the horizon, and the evening light was dimming.

"Lord Bryan is as dangerous to Eloise as Tiomoid U'Neill," Reginald scolded, pointing a gnarled finger at Eloise. "Never forget that."

"Bryan FitzGilbert supports Gerald FitzGilbert. He is loyal to Leinster," Roland said. "He won't side with Tiomu."

"He will not," Reginald croaked, staring at Roland, looking ever more like a gargoyle. "But marriage to Eloise would give him Dahlquin. That," Reginald said, closing his eyes tightly as if walking into bright sun, "must never happen. Bryan has reason to take his revenge on Dahlquin, in ways hurtful and damaging."

"We won't go to New Pembrokeshire, Uncle," Eloise murmured. "I remember."

"There isn't a safer place for you than Leinster, as ward to Lord FitzGilbert. Until you can return to Dahlquin," her uncle growled.

"I'll return with you," she countered in a shrill tone. "Don't leave me in Ashbury or Leinster."

"You need a disguise," Reginald said. "We'll look-"

"I'm not staying in Leinster. Cowering like a beaten cur, when my family, my home-" she looked over her shoulder in the direction of Dahlquin Castle, "I will not."

Reginald studied Roland a moment. "Extra clothing?" he questioned. "Me neither," he said, shaking his own head. "Ellie," he looked at the pouch at her waist, his face twitching, more sallow. "I don't suppose you have-?"

Eloise gazed at her uncle's pain worn face then shook her head. "Shame upon me, Uncle."

Roland's mind spun with the increasing burden of implications as the three unlikely riders walked their horses amid the sunset. Maid Eloise, a notorious heretic, alleged succubus and sole heir of Dahlquin. Seventeen, nearly alone, and in greater peril than she could comprehend. Preposterous.

"Flies," Eloise said, noting the buzz.

"Death," Reginald said. How odd the word sounded when spoken by someone who seemed immune, Roland thought, swatting at the swarming flies.

The grasses were flattened and torn. The ground was churned by hoof prints and paw prints. Vultures lurched to the sky from a horse carcass. Some brown hide, bolts, scraps of wool and linen, a well-chewed and discarded leather girdle, the dagger and eating knife still in their scabbards. A saddle, scratched and covered with dirt, saddle bags still attached.

"Tuath," Roland said, crossing himself. "Guillaume's squire." He dismounted, retrieving the girdle and weapons. He searched the ground for any tools or clues to the lad's demise and the other squire. The shadows got longer and darker as the sun continued to set.

"It was quite a battle if they killed a horse," Reginald said.

"Hoof prints through the woods," Eloise said, following them. "Maybe the other squire got away."

"There's not a bone left," Roland muttered, "not even a skull or pelvis."

"Oh, sorrow upon me. Lord, here's more!" Eloise called.

Wolves or bear made quick work of the human bones. Only gear and scraps of clothing remained. And the dead horse.

"I think they took the other horse. I can't find any tack, but more tracks. Sorrow upon me." She was crossing herself, and Roland followed her lead. Both squires killed.

"Let's search," Reginald reminded her, dismounting to help Roland search for anything of use.

Roland lifted Tuath's cap, a silly, grey woolen thing with dangling tassels at both ears and down the back. His sister made it for him and Tuath cherished it, despite all the teasing he received.

"That'll do," Reginald said, snatching the cap from Roland's hand. "Ellie, get over here," he ordered. "God's own blood," Reginald scoffed, examining the dead squire's cap. "Ah, the beasties have taken most everything away. But a hat and a saddle, that's something. Take the reins," Reginald said to Roland, handing him his bay stallion's reins, "and tie him off". Garth and Artoch grazed uneasily at liberty, not choosing to leave the security of their herd of three, but clearly agitated by the horse carcass. "Tired stallions make little trouble," Reginald observed.

Roland nodded, but he wasn't sure he agreed.

"Let's hide the hair," Reginald said to Eloise.

"I'll try the saddle on your horse," Roland said, "and the saddle bags. Hobbles," he muttered, searching the contents of the saddle bags, also finding two blankets and a mending kit with needle, awl and thread, and a skin bag. Any extra linen, wool or coins Tuath might have held for Guillaume were gone.

"His name's Garth. I'll do it," Eloise said.

"Let him!" Reginald barked at her. "And keep your eyes open for Tiomu's men."

"I saddle my own horse-"

"Get your hair up, I'll cut this," Reggie interrupted. But with only one hand, he could not.

"Roland!"

Using his dagger, Roland cut off the extra length of Eloise's surcoat of muted blue and grey, so it hung at the knees, as a youth's garment did. Next the linen chemise.

"Cut it into strips," Reginald said. "Quick, quick, we've killers at our heels."

Roland complied while Reginald continued with his instructions. "Ellie, you ride as Lord Roland's page like you did for your father, you know what must be done? Thinner," he told Roland.

"I know, sir," she answered.

"You ride when he says, stop when he says, and eat *if* he says."

"May you have goodness, Lord," she said taking the first of the thin strips and using it to tie one of the newly plaited strands of hair tightly to her scalp.

"Speak when spoken to. Back talk is forbidden," Reginald continued. Then to Roland, "You are to deliver Eloise to Lord Albert, failing that, High Lord FitzGilbert. No one else. If you touch or harm her in any way," he growled, starting to shake. "Do you understand?"

"I have questions," Roland answered, bristling under the accusation. Did he see a tremor in Reginald's hand? Was this sorcery growing weak?

"Hold the questions," Reginald said to Roland, while handing Eloise a long swath of the chemise. "Bind up, you can't go jiggling down the tracks. Hurry up!"

Roland thought she was blushing as she turned her back, but it was hard to tell under all the dirt and ash. She was slipping her arms out of her sleeves.

"Turn your eyes, Ashbury," Reginald barked, stepping in front of Roland.

Roland did, but felt Reginald glowering at him. Then Reginald grabbed him round the neck. Roland turned. Reginald changed his grip and pulled him close, almost nose to nose. Reginald's hazel eyes glowed with a zealot's unleashed passion.

"You let any harm come to her," Reginald croaked, spittle collecting at the corners of his lined and bleeding mouth, "I'll haunt you from the gates of Hell." Roland felt an icy breeze pass over him, leaves rustled, and the grazing horses lifted their heads. He shivered involuntarily, and Reginald looked a little more satisfied. Then nodding towards Roland, he released his grip.

"It should be me," Reginald said, as much to himself as to Roland. "I've always been there for Ellie. All of them." Reginald's gaze moved from Eloise towards Dahlquin Castle, and with a sideways sneer back at Roland.

Eloise stood transformed before them. She was mayhap the worst dressed, most disheveled page Roland had ever seen. If one didn't look too closely, especially at her soft, oval face and bare neck with hair obviously missing or hidden, she might pass as a youth of twelve or so.

"All grown up," Reginald said softly, "but not taller than a sprout."

"Uncle Reggie," she started, her voice tapering off. "I must check the saddle."

Roland watched her check and shorten the stirrups. He hadn't thought of that.

"Take my shield," Reginald instructed Eloise, "for luck."

It was a large, long, and well-beaten, shield, with a distinctive design, bearing an old-style metal boss, with a patchwork of hide, resembling a protective turtle shell. The blue and gold colors had faded or been battered off.

Eloise was in tears when Reginald hugged her. His appearance gave Roland the shivers, but Eloise wrapped her arms around him in a tight hold. Surely it was a different man she embraced, Roland thought.

"Don't, Ellie. Not the tears, just kiss this old war horse goodbye," he said jovially, taking on a more festive attitude as she let him go. "We ride out together. My last stand, your escape. Dahlquin. Family, God, Crown."

Bearing witness to this intimate exchange stirred something in Roland, but he couldn't place it or name it. Restless. Movement.

"Riders," Roland said. "Tiomu's men. Must be at that speed."

All three studied the approaching group. Eloise checked the girth on Reginald's horse.

"Put that shield on," Reggie commanded.

"I can't shoot like this," Eloise said as she slipped the enormous shield over her back. A great land turtle.

"Just ride."

Then Reginald gave her a boost into the unfamiliar saddle.

Roland was amazed when Reginald swung up into his saddle unassisted. Then Reginald slumped, clutching his handless arm.

Eloise cued Garth and her mighty steed lunged forward.

"Go!" Reggie shouted as she and Roland galloped off. "Stay left. Right is a dead end."

Fwooit. Fwooit. Arrows in flight. *Thunk.* An arrow hit Uncle Reggie's shield.

"Ride!" Reginald roared behind her. "Go, go!"

Fwooit. Shoot or ride, she wondered, her mind briefly visualizing Parthian shoots. Glancing back, she saw Uncle Reggie tall in the saddle, barrel chest thrust forward, arms outstretched. A human shield. His head bobbed. She saw him flinch to the side before righting. Jerking.

"Don't look back!" Roland shouted, riding up next to her, his shield extended toward her.

Thunk. Grunt. Eloise rode hard, but her mind continued to play out Uncle Reggie's demise behind her. Slumping forward, trying to sit, slumping, his back full of arrows. Tiomu U'Neill's treachery.

"Ho there! Halt!" Tiomu U'Neill's men shouted. *Fwooit.*

This had to end. Eloise pointed right and headed Garth in that direction at a full gallop.

"Don't go right!" Roland yelled.

Eloise went right. Roland followed. They tore through low branches, following a creek. Eloise slowed, waiting for Roland to come up alongside.

"This is the wrong way!" he shouted.

"Will your horse jump?" she queried, ignoring his comment.

"He can jump," answered Roland. "How do you think I got here?"

"Good, it'll be easier in the near dark. He won't know what's happening" she replied.

"Your Uncle said this was a dead end, didn't he?" he asked as the horses carefully picked through the middle of the rocky creek.

"We can make it," she said, feeling each step as Garth tensely picked his way through the creek, reminding her he didn't care for this either.

"We've got 'em now," she heard the soldiers following them. "They're trapped!"

"Easy now," she said. Roland and Eloise stood at the mouth of a waterfall. The creek ended within twelve inches of Artoch's hooves.

He raised his shield, anticipating arrows.

"Fuck, nay room to fight," Roland muttered, "it's a dead end! Dead as in us."

"It's all right, now just spur him and hang on," she said.

"What?" Roland asked, turning a hard look on Eloise. "Are you daft?"

"Do it all the time, it's only about three or four men's height," she scolded, "very deep and still. Go now, they're almost here." Her voice rang with desperation. "Do it yourself, or I will," she said, preparing to smack Artoch on the rump.

Roland turned Artoch to face the ledge. "This is asinine," he muttered.

Eloise looked back over his shoulder at their adversaries. Bows were raised. Sword blades reflected the rising moonlight in sharp silver and pewter hues against the solid grey and black tones behind them.

"Together, so we don't fall on each other," she called over the noise. "Hang on tight to his mane," she instructed. "Wrap your legs tightly. Now!"

Roland spurred his mount like never before. The dark horse lunged off the ledge and into thin air, a terrible sensation as man and horse careened downward. Artoch's hooves flailed before him, seeking a foothold. Roland's shield caught the wind and was yanked off arm and shoulder.

The shock of the cold water caused him to forget the fall. He sank. The weight of his chain mail, sword, boots and clothing pulled him into the chill dark. He grabbed something, thrust his hand then his arm through what he prayed was a stirrup. He gripped the stirrup, his life line, with both arms. Out of breath, Roland started to panic. Surely his arms would burst, his chest contracted. Artoch struggled to stay at the surface, sucking Roland under, where he would be pummeled to death and the horse would drown. Instead of fighting, Roland forced his mind to relax, to give in to the cold depths, so black and peaceful.

Eloise and Garth headed for shore. They'd jumped off this waterfall a dozen times, but never with her bow, quivers and a shield. Uncle Reggie's shield banged the back of her head, then floating and banging, pushing her face under water. The quiver floated and tugged at her waist. She coughed and her head was thrust under again. *Saints preserve us*, Eloise entreated.

Nearly submerged, Roland's black horse beat the water with his front hooves as if trying to climb on the surface. Where was Lord Roland? She dare not shout, alerting the soldiers they had survived. Roland had to be here. He must. She got another mouthfull of water and coughed.

Rounding Garth back, she stretched but couldn't find his horse's reins. After several attempts she urged Garth to swim in closer. She reached the bridle. Following the metal, she located a rein strap and wrestled it free. Once over Artoch's head, she and Garth lead him on the swim to shore. Eloise had not seen Roland, but he must be hanging on for something was pulling his mighty destrier underwater. *God keep him safe*, she prayed and coughed.

Panic overcome; the disciplined warrior challenged every belligerent fiber of his charged being to find the strength to be calm. Scraping and gnashing, then a thud on the head roused Roland from his concentrated effort of restraint. Rocks and gravel beneath him. The horse dragged him well up the bank. He dropped to all fours gasping huge gulps of air. Choking and sputtering, breathing in the best air he had ever tasted, he rolled onto his back and rested his oxygen-starved body.

Eloise checked Garth, the saddle and bags. She could spy Tiomu's men, perched at the top of the waterfall, unwilling to follow their prey. She didn't think they could see her, Roland or the horses through the trees. Roland crawled up the bank next to his horse and Eloise crossed herself.

"May You have goodness, Blessed Mother, Jesus our Savior and God in Heaven," she whispered. Garth grazed as she ran her hands down each of his legs, feeling for strain or injury. Finally, Tiomu's men retreated. Seeking a way down or back to Dahlquin Castle, Eloise didn't know.

"If my father captures Tiomu alive," she hissed, venom permeating each of her words, "I pray I'm allowed to peel the skin off his hairless balls, before filleting them and feeding them to the hogs." Crossing herself again, Eloise approached Roland's horse.

"Easy, my friend," she said to the heaving destrier, running her hands along the horse's legs as she had done with Garth. "Good boy!" she cooed. "You're a fine, solid beast. What's your name?"

Assured the destrier was uninjured, and after both horses had a brief rest, it was time to leave.

"Well, you lost your shield and helm but otherwise we're fine. Shall we saddle up?" she said to Roland, swinging into her saddle as she asked.

If Roland hadn't been so glad to be alive, he might have been livid, jumping off a waterfall. 'Will your horse jump?' Absurd!

"Are you coming?" she called over her shoulder, her grey horse vanishing into the night as she rode away.

Water poured out of his clothing and rippled through his chain mail as he swung back into the saddle. Artoch skittered nervously as more water sloshed on him. The destrier hesitated a moment before trusting his rider to keep them upon solid ground. Roland urged him on in pursuit of Eloise.

Moonlight guided Eloise and Garth as they cantered a track skirting an apple orchard, the trees in full summer leaf, shimmering grey and coal in the night. Then a narrow field, with hills lifting, foresting as they grew in elevation. Here she urged Garth to move out, confident in his surefootedness, the passing night air chilling her until she shivered. It's just a little cold, she challenged herself, nothing more. People are dying.

Roland planted his seat firmly, upper body balanced and loose, doing nothing to hinder Artoch as he galloped after the grey stallion, then almost collided with Garth.

Garth spooked, lunged then spun, snorting. Eloise listed, the awkward weight of the unfamiliar shield further unsettling her. "Ho!" she called to Garth as he pivoted to a sudden stop. Head up, nostrils pumping, he bobbed his head once asking Eloise to loosen the reins. Eloise felt his body expand, ready to pop. Head turning left, right, snorting.

Artoch veered immediately, misstepping, as Roland pitched dangerously. "Bleeding saints," he muttered, repositioning, clutching the reins. "What the-"

Both horses stood but feet apart, distant trees casting long, eerie shadows in the moonlight.

"Wolves," said Eloise, her voice as deep and eerie as the shadows.

"Are you sure? I hear nothing," Roland asked, searching the colorless landscape.

"The horses told me," she answered, searching just as intently.

"Wolves?" he questioned again.

"Do you have an ax?" Eloise asked, not remembering. Garth shifted, pivoting his hind end. She shortened the reins, massaging them with her fingers. *Listen to me, don't act on your own.*

"Do not," he replied.

Expecting to hear things, she did. Roland drew his sword, and she knew he heard it too. Whether wind or wolf, something was moving, circling. Twigs snapped. Heavy breathing. *Wait*, that was the horses, she realized.

"Ho," Roland murmured. "Ho, now."

This would never happen if they had hounds with them, Eloise thought. She seldom, if ever, traveled without hounds clearing the way. Wildlife fled before dogs.

"We can't outrun them," she said, thinking out loud. "If we climb-" she scanned the hills. "We missed the trail head," she said looking, checking. It was harder to tell in the luminous twilight. Sheer, rocky and trees. She shivered violently with fear. Garth tugged at the tight reins, pounding the ground to move.

Roland held his breath. Movement. He saw a wolf. *Fuck*. Breathe out. He gauged the comfortable feel of the sword in his hand. Loose arm, wrist; poised. Deep, easy breath.

"This way!" Eloise called, chattering. "It's steep, but we should be able to pick our way through the game paths until we hit the main trail."

"Will not," Roland answered, his voice sounding as if he were about to choke the life out of something. "I followed you over cliffs twice today. Not again."

"We can make it. They can't take us down in the trees." She was fairly sure.

"They will pick us out of the trees easy as squirrels," Roland said.

Movement again. He licked his lips.

Growling, snarling. The horses bunched together then tried to dart. Roland and Eloise held fast, directing their frightened mounts to face the wolves, trying to keep them rump to rump, against their natures for horses are flight animals, depending on speed and safety within the herd, not a standoff.

"We should-" Eloise tried again, like her mount, preferring to evade than confront.

"Not!" Roland barked.

Resigned, Eloise said, "I need my bow."

"Give me the shield," he said. Carefully, and not an easy feat, she passed the enormous shield to Roland. Instead of using it as she thought he would, Roland tossed it at a shadowy figure, darting towards them. Eloise drew an arrow.

Soundlessly the wolves were at the horses' legs. Roland bent and swung the sword, missing. Garth reared as wolves lunged at his muzzle and neck. Artoch spun and tried to kick, but Roland kept him bent and moving, then side passing as a wolf tried for the horse's throat. Roland thrust his sword into the wolf.

"Ahh!" Eloise shrieked, a sharp stab slicing through her shoulder.

A piercing yelp and the wolf fell screaming and thrashing in the grass and leaves. Roland leaned and swerved, blocking and dodging as the snarling beasts returned again and again.

Feeling her mouth full of blood Eloise tried to spit, but her mouth was dry. Pain receding, Eloise struggled to keep her seat as Garth fought to run, to escape the fangs. Pivoting, she drew her bow, but the wolves were too fast, Garth swinging or rearing. She dare not let fly in motion, she might shoot Roland or Artoch. In desperation she committed herself to charging the wolves.

"Get him, get him!" she commanded, wheeling Garth toward a crouching wolf. Ears pinned, Garth lunged forward. The wolf snarled, but when the horse showed teeth, it sprang back. She heard another ghastly yelp that ripped through her spine; in a spasm of near paralysis, she almost dropped her bow. Tasting blood, she knew Roland had found success. What was happening to her? She almost fell on her head when Garth kicked. She clung to his neck, boots gripping offending areas. The horse bucked and spun as Eloise screamed "Ho!" and "Easy!" until she was back in the saddle. "Go," she said, and they chased a retreating tail.

She knew the wolves had fled, their death howls draining the life from her as if she, too, had been mortally wounded. Fear, pain and confusion vibrated within her, death of her loved ones. Garth sighed, bringing her back. She stroked his wet neck, relaxing her seat, watching Roland.

"I think they've gone," Roland said, circling her, sword at the ready. "Christ's sweet blood, I've never in my life," he continued, "big as fucking ponies." He looked at Eloise, "Shame upon me." Wiping his sword clean on his soaked leggings, he replaced it in the scabbard on his girdle. He dismounted to retrieve the shield. "And that screaming, like banshees," he said, looking at her warily.

Had he heard her too? She hoped she had imagined it.

"Chill upon you like a frost," he said. "We'll build a fire and dry our clothes."

"Not here, by your will," Eloise said. "Let's ride," and she did. Her teeth chattered and she shivered with cold, wet exhaustion.

"We must stop, Maid--er-" he started, unsure how to address her.

"El", she answered. "Just call me El, it'll pass and close enough to the real thing."

"Exhaustion must be upon you, let's find a place to rest," he said.

"I would like to rest, Sir, we need dead fall for a fire," she answered. "And woods to mask the blaze. And grazing for the horses."

Roland stared at her. "That would be good," he acknowledged.

After several more miles they found a spot wooded enough to have a fire, with the smoke broken up by the trees and grazing for the horses. Eloise set about collecting firewood with naught but summer moonlight to aid her.

"Saints be praised!" Roland exclaimed when Eloise produced a small flint and iron oxide from her belt pouch.

Even with spark, there is a trick to starting a fire when cold and soaked. But with some maneuvering they got it lit and shared a brief smile of satisfaction in the firelight. Then Eloise returned to the hobbled horses.

Shivering, she unsaddled Garth and rubbed him down, carefully feeling for injury or wolf bite.

"Goddess be praised, such nobility." Eloise rested her head against his side, pressing her cold, stiff fingers on him, relishing the warmth of his body. *Don't cry* she told herself. *Don't cry.*

"What's his name?" she asked, starting the same procedure on Roland's horse.

"By your will, let me," insisted Roland. He seemed embarrassed to have her attending his horse. "Artoch," he added, grabbing the saddle. "He's a destrier, not a pet."

"He is exceptional," Eloise said, stroking Artoch's neck and shoulder. Artoch lifted his head from grazing, waiting. "Genial, brave. You're fair with him," she added.

"He tell you that, did he?" Roland asked.

"He did," she said turning to Roland, ready to resume her chores. "Horses never lie."

They laid the tack out to dry, and as Eloise spread one of the blankets over a furze, she was gripped by the revelation that in order to dry her own clothes, she would have to disrobe. Despite the finger-numbing cold she felt embarrassment and shame nearly drown her. For miles they had sought this ideal location to dry and rest, yet she had neglected to even consider the prospect of undressing, alone, with none but this Lord Roland from Ashbury-at-March. She gently removed *Cara* from her shoulder and clutched the wet, abused bow to her chest. *Cara*, the bow that sang in her grip. Hanging *Cara* on a furze her shivering fingers went to the cold, wet buckle on her strap holding her quiver. The buckle wouldn't loosen. Thank the Virgin she wore this rustic surcoat and simple chemise without all the tedious cords and laces requiring a nurse or attendant to unfasten, she reflected, her eyes unfocused on the ground before her. She fingered the swollen leather and buckle of her quiver.

A shadow darkened what little of the ground she could see.

"Would you help me?" Roland asked.

He had already pulled off his tunic and laid it to dry.

"Do you know how to remove a hauberk?" he asked, already bending over. "Just start easing it up my back," he said, his arms outstretched towards her.

Although Eloise had witnessed many knights having their armour and mail removed, and a laborious chore it was, she hadn't been called upon to assist.

"Satan's horns, this is like dragging lead," he said, his voice muffled in the wet clothing and mail, "caught upon my gambeson." He tried to squirm backwards out of his tunnel of metal and linen, almost pulling the hauberk from her uncooperative fingers. "I know it's heavy but try not to let it fall in the mud."

"I'll try," she sighed, coaxing the links off the padded shirt beneath.

Suddenly it gave way and the hauberk slid off in a clattering ring. Eloise braced to capture the runaway armour. Roland pulled his arms free in time to grab the end, taking most of the weight.

"May you have goodness," he said, pushing his wet hair off his face before turning to lay his hauberk upon another stout furze. His rumpled gambeson was caught under his arms. She watched as he pulled it and the linen undershirt off and laid them closer to the fire. Next, he sat on part of a dead trunk removing his boots. He unfastened the points on his mail chausses and slid them off. Then his linen chausses which he laid near the fire. Standing, he spread the mail chausses near the hauberk, with his back to the fire.

He glanced up at her, his face dark in shadow.

"Do you need help?" he asked, his voice deeper than she remembered.

They stood in silence as Eloise realized she had been stupefied watching him undress. Saints preserve her, her mouth was hanging open. She slapped it shut with her chilled fingers. Before she could find her voice, he was walking over.

"Turn around," he said, making a twirling motion with his finger.

Swallowing hard, Eloise spun around, relieved not to face Roland in naught but his braies.

"Hmmm."

115

Eloise turned to face him. "I can't. It won't," she said, trying to pull the tight-fitting strap and wicked buckle from her waist.

He sighed, before tackling the stubborn buckle. Eloise held her breath until the buckle gave way and she could remove her quiver. She removed her girdle and pouch.

"I'll take all that," he said. "And return with a blanket."

Eloise now faced the prospect of truly undressing, behind a wet blanket Roland held up.

Shivering and wet, a snort escaped her as she struggled to slip her elbow out of her sleeve, her soaked linen chemise wound tight on her arm, further weighed down by the wool surcoat. *Satan's horns indeed* she thought, sighing, and very thankful Roland wasn't complaining, or worse, offering to help. God forbid.

"I didn't realize Tiomu had so many men," Eloise said, returning her thoughts to the plight of her family. "Men in reserve, just waiting for their turn to fight." She envisioned ship upon ship landing on the northern shore with more soldiers unloading to descend upon Dahlquin and all Ireland. She paused with her own words. This went beyond her home, her needs.

"He has many men, but the castle is secure. Dahlquin can hold out for weeks," he said.

"But that hole?" she asked, pulling her elbow through. "Finally," she sighed, slipping the surcoat over her head.

"Easily blocked," Roland offered. "More importantly, it was an outer wall. Best you father abandons the stables and remains behind the greater, fortified wall."

The snug-fitting chemise proved as difficult as the wool surcoat, but eventually it came off. The cold air prickled her exposed skin and she hugged herself and the soggy binding already loosening from her chest. This must remain, and she bent to remove her calf sheath and dagger.

"Do you think Tiomu was lying about Ashbury?" she asked.

"I believe his men misdirected us," his voice trailed off.

Shame and modesty aside, the drenched bindings on her breasts would not be refastened. Exhaling in defeat, she unwound the linen. Only her wooden cross pendant remained hanging from its wet leather thong.

"I've finished," she said, embarrassment weakening her words.

Roland wrapped the wet blanket around her, then held his hand out for her wet clothes.

Eloise hesitated, not wishing him to handle her garments. A chill rattled her and she shook head to toe.

"Sit by the fire," he said, "and hold that blanket tight, will you," his voice again taking on that low register. "I'll lay these out to dry."

Roland sat across the fire from her with only his saddle blanket across his lap, rotating his braies by the fire with prodigious care. Eloise watched the mesmerizing quality of the fire. The coals glowed in vivid red and grey ash, vibrant yellow and muted gold flames rose up, twisting and spiraling. With brilliant elegance and seductive grace did the blaze give way to the darkness. Eloise also took notice of the bronze warrior before her. Muscle and flesh absorbed the firelight and reflected back a tawny glow. A thick mat of dark hair covered his chest. The savage bruises and lacerations he bore, which only last week would have roused her attention, seemed minor now.

"May you have goodness, Lord," she said after Roland added more wood.

He nodded and she was relieved for the quiet between them, for she couldn't fathom a single word. When he yawned, she was compelled to do the same.

Exhausted and numb, Eloise experienced only the fire before her. It warmed her skin and dried her garments. Faintly aware of the satisfying smell, the cracks and pops of the burning wood, she had some momentary respite from the groans and anguish left behind at Dahlquin. Unable or unwilling to acknowledge her naked vulnerability with this stranger, Eloise eventually fell asleep.

CONNACHT, 11th of June

Tiomoid U'Neill paced his tent. He didn't like the report. Careless. Three riders and loose horses had escaped the castle. Sir Reginald had been slain, but two of the riders had been pursued to the waterfall's edge, only to jump off rather than be taken. Drowned, he had been told. Surely no one could survive that.

By daylight he had sent a patrol to retrieve the bodies. He would mock Hubert by staking all three bodies before Dahlquin as a reminder of their fate. Instead of bodies, his men found tracks up the bank and beyond: two riders had escaped. Surely Meath or FitzGilbert was their purpose.

"Fools!" Tiomu shouted. One body would give Dahlquin hope.

"Fools," the captain of the patrol confirmed, "the tracks were headed southeast. Could be they would seek relief at Ashbury. I sent two of my riders after them."

"Good decision," Tiomoid said, "taking the initiative to send two men. Already they're woefully behind." Tiomoid slammed his fist into his other hand. "Damn careless!" he said remembering the failure of his men last night. "Bring the cowardly bastards to me!" he ordered his captain.

"The cowardly bastards will be brought, sir," the captain said, waiting until he was dismissed.

"They will serve as an example of a job incomplete." This would give him a body count of three. Tiomoid would match barbarism with barbarism, and all would know he was meant to be king.

Tiomu's two riders cantered on the trail of the escapees from Dahlquin.

"They ran a good clip," Broccan said. He was an U'Neill cousin, with more ambition than property, easily fueled by Tiomu's vision of U'Neill domination.

"Luck was upon them," Seamus said. "Escaping the castle. The falls." His family served Clan U'Neill, existing on the Ulster march.

"Not that one-handed bastard, though," chuckled Broccan. "Unlucky as Hell, I say."

"Him, some powerful Dahlquin magic, that," Seamus offered.

"Bah," Broccan snorted, "piss-poor magic, I be thinking. To lose hand and life."

"Sir Reginald, someone claimed. Second in command. Why send him?"

"A dying man," Broccan said slowly, "had to be a decoy, slowing us up so the others could escape. Unbelievable ballocks Dahlquin has, to launch such an escape. And luck," he conceded.

Their horses veered. The men corrected as their nervous mounts snorted then tried to spin and flee. Seamus backed his horse.

"Broccan!" he called, fearing an ambush.

The riders tried to settle their horses, listening, searching.

"Vultures," Broccan observed as a black bird soared down, disappearing from view.

"Something was ambushed," Seamus said, urging his reluctant horse forward.

Still the horses balked, refusing to move forward despite the coaxing spurs.

"Fucking stupid beast!" shouted Broccan, spanking his brown horse with the braided end of his reins as the horse tossed his head, spinning in place.

"You're the fucking stupid one," Seamus scolded. "Your red hair masks a black heart. Hold mine, I'll look." Seamus dismounted and handed his reins to Broccan. "Don't lose him," he said as he trotted down the track to explore.

The vultures grudgingly took to the sky, their long black wings pumping, scaring the horses anew. Seamus whistled.

"What is it?" Broccan called impatiently.

"Coo, quite a hunt," Seamus exclaimed. Paw prints. The same two horses' hooves they'd been tracking. He scratched his head, examining the ground before him. Not dogs. Not beaters. Not a mistake, the escapees had been attacked. Seamus scanned the surrounding area.

"Seamus!" Broccan shouted.

"Wolves," Seamus called, trotting back to his companion.

"Dead wolves?"

"Two of them. And our lucky prey has escaped yet again," he said, mounting up. "Best we skirt this track, and go through the orchard."

ON THE ROAD, 11th of June

Although the sun had risen, it remained shyly behind high cloud cover. Having dressed during the night, Roland lay sleeping as Eloise wrapped the linen scrap around her bosom. Next, she pulled her dry linen chemise over her head and slipped her arms into the sleeves. She ignored the fraying hem where only yesterday the garment had been cut away to resemble a youth's length. Her wool surcoat too had been hacked away, butchered, like her family. Her hand went to the wooden cross pendant hanging at her chest. She lifted the worn cross and kissed it, before saying a prayer of thankfulness for surviving another day.

"You're a pilgrim, then?" Roland asked.

"What?" Eloise yelped, spinning in surprise to see Roland awake and studying her. *Had he watched her dress?*

"That wooden cross, it looks like something a pilgrim would wear," he explained. "Is it upside down?"

"My father gave it to me," she said. "It's his design."

An ingenious design, a simple wooden cross with a leather thong around the neck, a small blade hidden within, held by a metal clasp. With one hand Eloise could grab the top, the handle of a small dagger, whose transept served as the hilt: a weapon of last resort. Were Eloise assaulted and all other means of escape thwarted, she could grab this small blade and impale her assailant by eye, temple or throat. Her mother had one just like it. Eloise could never imagine her gentle mother using this blade, though her father and Uncle Reggie assured her Aine was quite capable. After witnessing her mother's confidence with the crossbow, Eloise had much to reevaluate.

"It's a humble design," Roland commented.

"Our Lord and Savior was crucified on a wooden cross," she said. "It's comforting," and it *was*. She crossed herself, and he followed her lead. "It's upside down, until I lift it in prayer." She demonstrated by taking it in her hand, and so it was right side up, facing her. She kissed it and let it hang.

"Very pious," he commented solemnly as he rose and brushed his garments.

"And a thief wouldn't waste his time on such a worthless item," she added. A gold or silver cross would be a target, reducing its value as a weapon in the final moments. Very clever, her father, and she smiled at the thought.

"Pious and practical," Roland chuckled. "Clever man, your father."

Eloise pulled on her boots and attached her calf sheath.

"Let's conduct our own mass, eh, before saddling up," Roland said as he kneeled. She joined him. "Heavenly Father," he began, and she bowed her head clutching her wooden pendant as she made the sign of the cross.

They rode through southern fields undisturbed by U'Neill. Along with the edible crops of wheat, barley, turnips, cabbage, onions and leeks, a crop of flax grew steadily. The farmers busily weeded the vital crop, the source of valuable linen of which there was never enough. Though Connacht had poorer soil, Ireland had the perfect conditions to grow, cultivate and process the flax stalks into the fibrous strands needed to make the linen used for clothing, tableware, bedding and more. Was all this at risk, Eloise wondered? Their very lives and existence was right here, thriving before her, but for how long? The crops that would sustain the manor through the next year lay at her feet, acre upon acre, unprotected, unknowing. Through the open uncultivated lands, she prayed the herdsmen had taken the cattle out to farther pastures, away from Tiomu's thieving hordes.

"Oh, active bears," Eloise commented, for on the same trail they were traversing were three piles of bear skat. "Egg shells, too," she said, seeing the remains in one of the piles.

"Wait," Roland said, "ho!" to his horse.

Eloise watched as he studied the piles. He glanced up at her once before resuming his investigation.

"God's blood!" he exclaimed, riding next to her. "How big do the bear get in Connacht?"

"Well they vary, the cubs start out not bigger than cats. They can grow quite large, nearly as large as a bull."

Roland whistled. "We, my men and I, saw a pig as big as a bear. Last night I witnessed wolves as big as ponies. So, I wondered what size a bear might attain."

"Your comparisons are accurate. Still, bears are the size of bears, pigs the size of pigs and wolves the size of wolves."

"Hmmm, they're larger than I'm accustomed." He rode on a bit. "I like it," he said, and Eloise thought he looked pleased. They rode on.

Eloise contemplated Roland's observations. Were the animals smaller in Leinster? Or had these noble creatures been hunted to such a small stature? Hunted till stunted. The wordplay should have been humorous, but she found it a sad paradox. She hunted as she was taught. Thus taught, she honored the sacred responsibility of predator and prey - and she savored the benefit of the kill for the nourishment provided.

She didn't give voice to her perturbation, but the question was posed in her conscience.

"Is hunger upon you?" she asked some miles later. "These farmers should remember me."

"Oh, hunger consumes me," Roland agreed, "Starvation is upon me." They ambled into a farmyard.

A woman emerged from a small hut, two children clinging to her. Another woman with a crying baby came out of her hut as well to see who approached.

"Remember me?" Eloise called out, waving. "I'm Lord Hubert's page. We came through here a month past." She had not come dressed as a page then, but one was with them. "Aine and Aine," she identified them by their same names. "Like my-" Eloise corrected herself, "Our Lady Mother."

Both women kneeled in their doorways but appeared afraid to speak.

"We've grievous hunger, with many miles ahead of us. Lord Dahlquin would ask you to share whatever we may take with us."

Artoch took that moment to pee in their yard. Roland leaned forward in the saddle as the potent-smelling urine splashed and puddled. As if it were contagious, Garth did the same. Eloise rolled her eyes as she too leaned forward to relieve the pressure on his back and kidneys.

"Take what you will," Aine, the older woman said, head down, her undressed children staring slack-jawed and teary eyed at Eloise and Roland.

"We want some eggs, bread or cheese. We can't wait for something to be prepared. What can we carry away now?" Eloise said more urgently. Did she look such a threat? She glanced at Roland, tall, dark and menacing in the saddle. His hair was windblown and knotted. Beard and clothing unkempt. He looked like he might eat the baby. Eloise glanced down at her legs and boots and touched her face with the back of her hand. Did she look such a fright, too?

"You just had a baby. I remember that," Eloise spoke gently to Aine, the young mother. "A little girl."

The two women exchanged glances, then nodded. Except for the crying baby, the yard had an ill quiet. There were neither chickens nor fowl of any kind and Eloise saw the hog sty was vacant with not a piglet or lamb in sight. Roland, too, was scanning the empty farmyard.

"What happened here?" Eloise asked. "A raid? Scragmuir!" she said, the old hatred coming to the fore. Now she saw the deep ruts in the ground; carts or wagons had been here.

"I think not," Roland said to Eloise, turning his attention back to the women. "Answer the boy!" he commanded.

The women trembled. One of the small children began to wail and his mother clutched him beneath her. "Shush, shush," she said, her face down in submission.

"Is this how you address one of your Lord's men?" Roland asked, his voice matching his harsh appearance. "Speak."

"Soldiers. Knights. Claimed Lord Hubert was dead," Aine whimpered. "Said Tiomoid U'Neill was our new lord."

Eloise gasped.

"They took everything!" the young mother said, crying with her baby. "Everything but crops in the field. They-" she dropped her head and wept into the dirt.

"U'Neill," Roland confirmed, glowering as he surveyed the surrounding land still in cultivation.

"Did they-" Eloise started, afraid to hear the answer. "Did they hurt you?"

She could tell by their sobs they were ill-used. And what was to be done? She remembered the carnage wrought within the castle walls, the gruesome murders in her own bed chamber.

"Did they steal anyone?" Eloise asked, holding her breath hoping none of their own men, boys or girls had been forced into servitude to Tiomoid U'Neill.

Both women shook their heads.

"My-" Eloise caught herself again. "Our Lord Hubert is not dead. He will make Tiomoid U'Neill pay for his foul crimes perpetrated upon Dahlquin. Tiomu's blood and that of his traitors will suckle your swine."

"How many were there?" Roland asked.

"Eight," The elder Aine said, looking to the younger Aine for confirmation. Aine nodded.

"Maybe three knights. And the carts and drivers."

"Where were they going?" Roland asked. "Were they from Dahlquin or Ashbury did they say?"

Good questions. Eloise had been so outraged by this attack on her people she wasn't thinking in the present. *Where indeed?*

Trembling, the elder Aine looked up. "Don't know, Sire." She cringed, expecting reprimand. When none came, she continued. "After taking all the food and stock, they commanded us keep to our labor, lest we wish to fight." She hesitated. "They left us naught to eat. Same with the farms about."

Eloise felt her stomach ache with hunger, hers and theirs. Her bow, *Cara,* was in her hand, humming with potential. Her quiver was armed with broad heads and bodkins for a siege, not blunts or hare tips for a merry hunt. Were Tiomu's men poaching her father's game even now? Greed and lust ravaging the sacred lands entrusted to her family? Curse him!

"We drink boiled grass, fills the gut with warmth, little more," Aine was saying as Eloise still calculated the possibilities of rallying these farmers, setting snares and hunting game. The excess could be smoked and held in reserve for her father's men when they broke free of the castle. Together she and they would wreak such vengeance upon U'Neill...

"Bring us some," Roland was saying.

"Boiled grass?" Eloise asked. Why would he take that when she would have flesh and greens within the hour? Aine and Aine rose and disappeared into their huts.

Garth turned his head and Eloise turned to see the farmers, four men, three youths and five women walking in from the fields, tools in hand. She waved, but they didn't return the gesture.

"You know the leader?" Roland asked her.

"Rori, the Headman," she said, for almost everyone shared a mere handful of the same names, usually after her own family or other relatives, as did Aine and Aine.

"Headman!" Roland called as the group approached. "We're from Dahlquin Castle. Lord Hubert is not murdered. The traitor U'Neill lies. But we are at war."

Eloise watched as the group digested this news. She was disappointed they didn't cheer such good fortune as the castle inhabitants did. Her disappointment turned to momentary anger. They should kiss the very soil they tilled to be servants of her Lord Father, Hubert of Dahlquin, rather than dredges to the traitor U'Neill or the heinous Scragmuirs.

Aine held up a wooden bowl of warm grass broth, but Eloise shook her head. "I can't, may you have goodness," she said, looking at the mud and sweat covered workers. "Let them take their meal. They have earned more." Her stomach growled in protest as Aine quickly handed the bowl to her husband. He gulped it down lest Eloise change her mind.

Eloise listened as the headman shared what he knew, that U'Neill's men were collecting anything edible for the armies at Ashbury and Dahlquin. Snares were set and the streams were netted. They would return every other day and if there wasn't enough food, they would reduce the hungry mouths by taking the children. As she listened, she studied the farmstead. Pitchforks, clubs, brooms, wood, twine, hand plow, saws and axes for chopping: all formidable weapons in trained hands. If she could kill a bullock or deer, sequester the meat so the families wouldn't starve…rather, she thought, and a new idea came to her. Taint the meat, of course, and have it ready for U'Neill's carts.

Roland returned his empty bowl to Aine. "Pray they lied about Ashbury and relief may be at hand," Roland said, looking over the gaunt, bruised faces. "Come," he said to Eloise, cueing his horse away.

"Go?" she said, as Roland left.

Eloise bristled with each stride Garth took away from the farmstead. "You heard what they said, Ashbury is under siege," she reiterated.

"Probably, but I must see for myself. It's only a slight detour from Leinster."

Leinster was a ridiculous idea. Four long days from home and even longer back were High Lord FitzGilbert to send aid. Uncle Reggie would never have proposed such in his right mind.

"Lord, by your will, they haven't any food," she started, keeping her voice low, gentle. "We two could hunt and trap, smoking the excess for Dahlquin castle. Confidence upon me, we could hide out from Tiomu's men-"

"Confidence have you?" Roland huffed.

Was he mocking her? She wasn't sure, but time was wasting.

"I have," she said. Eloise decided not to share her ideas of fortifying the farmers and making more bows and arrows, as well as storing food. "They're unprotected," she offered. "We could hide the children at least. I have the responsibility." This was her role in the social trinity of their society: pray, work or fight, and fighting meant power and protection.

"Protection is your *father*'s responsibility," Roland said, emphasizing the word, "not yours, and not today."

Was he insinuating her father was negligent? Or did he mean to suggest she was insufficient? He was a stranger. Eloise stared, searching for clues, hoping he would clarify his statement. He stared back. She watched his features darken from anger to aggression.

She glared into his deep brown eyes, searching for answers. *Who are you, what do you know of Dahlquin, of our lives?* Roland sat back, sucking in his breath before turning his head, jaw clenched, lips pursed. Was that fear she had seen?

After a long pause Roland turned to her. "You," he said, pointing his gloved finger, "are my responsibility."

"Your burden, you mean," she said, feeling her own frustration.

"Would you dishonor your uncle's memory? It was his command."

Now it was Eloise who sat back so deep in the saddle Garth stopped, pitching her forward. She cued Garth on, the necessity of managing a five-year old stallion overriding the howl of anguish in her gut. "Good boy," she cooed, caressing his withers, encouraging Garth to resume his ground-eating amble. How many miles, how many adventures? So many images and memories of Uncle Reggie and her father came to Eloise in the ambling rhythm. *Sit up. Back straight. Don't let him root like that, you're riding a horse not a pig. You* are *Dahlquin, someday you'll understand.* Eloise knew she was heir to Dahlquin, but it was a place. She was a maiden. And here they were at the familiar stone fence, the boundary between Dahlquin and Ashbury.

"The castle is but one and a half hours riding time," she announced to Roland as they approached. "The fence is easily jumped, but we can pass through." To deter cattle escaping from estate to estate, the opening was disguised by straight line stone barricades. Horses and people could easily traverse, but broad cattle were disinclined to wedge themselves in. Eloise continued, "The main road is open. Cattle easily lost."

Before they passed through, something caught her eye.

"Oh, wait!" she said, dismounting. "Oh, by your will, by your will," she muttered, sneaking along the stone fence line. Garth took a step and a twig snapped. Small birds took wing. Eloise glanced back, pointing an accusatory finger at her stallion, but Garth was nibbling as if nothing had happened. Eloise put her hands together in prayer once more, *Blessed Mother Goddess, if it pleases you.* Eloise stepped carefully, walking on the sides of her feet, the smallest thus quietest surface, her hand moving along the roughhewn stone for balance. *May you have my gratitude upon you, Blessed Mother,* Eloise mouthed when she saw the black eyes of the female grouse unmoving on her nest. If she were stealthy enough…breathe in, breathe out, slowly, she moved her foot then her hand, easing along the fence. Don't stare directly at the bird, she reminded herself. Watch with soft eyes, unfocused. The grouse moved her head then froze again. Eloise knew if she could get closer, closer…. The feathers were such a marvel of camouflage and would make stunning fletching were she going home. Eloise eased forward. The bird moved her head again, then spread her wings. Eloise sprang at the bird, hands reaching for the darting grouse. She felt the silky feathers soft and full against her palm and fingertips as she clamped her hands closed.

Only feathers.

"Oh, damn that!" Roland exclaimed as the mother hen soared away in distress. "Sorrow upon me," Roland added in apology.

Eloise, too, was disappointed. The bird seemed so surely in her grasp. But her hunt wasn't over.

"Look at the gift Ashbury has for you, Lord," Eloise said holding up three warm eggs. "The bird would have been a bonus, but here is your first meal in Ashbury," she said, setting the eggs on the fence while she dug out her eating knife. She chipped the top of one. "Saints blessing upon you," she said, handing it to Roland.

Roland took the egg, held it up and examined it from several angles. Eloise was already chipping another.

"Like this?" he said, putting it to his lips like a chalice. He looked pale.

"Like that, immature, just yolk and white."

Roland gulped it down then hesitated. "Not bad," he smiled. She handed him the second. "Aren't you going to have it?" he asked.

"May I have the last?"

"With your will, and the blessings of the saints," he said, waiting for her to chip the last egg. "Prosit," he said lifting the little egg to his mouth.

"Prosit." Eloise exalted as the warm, thick egg slipped from the fragile shell into her mouth. Was there ever anything so good as fresh found eggs when lost in the wild? Using her tongue to blend the white and yolk on the roof of her mouth, she savored the rich, moist texture. It was a challenge to allow small portions of the viscous egg to slip down her throat. As she swallowed the last, Eloise prayed the mother grouse would lay another clutch soon enough.

She got back in the saddle and they moved on.

"So, this is Ashbury," Roland said looking around.

"This is Ashbury. Not Dead-Man's-" she paused, "not At-March. Your fief is southwest."

"I've never seen it, or any of Ashbury," Roland said.

"You have never been to Ashbury Castle?" Eloise asked. "How? Why did you come to Dahlquin?"

Roland seemed to think long and hard before answering.

Waiting for an answer, Eloise wondered what sort of looby she might be burdened with. Then she smiled, remembering a lost knight five years past. The large roads were marked, but if a traveler got on one of the paths or trails…and hadn't Sir Sedric mentioned being lost? She was born here; even now she led Roland on trails known only to Dahlquin or Ashbury.

"We were sorely misdirected," Roland reminded her, "by Tiomu's men."

"At council," she sighed, remembering his story. Mayhap she was the looby. "Ho," she said, sitting back. Garth stopped.

"What?" Roland asked.

"This isn't right."

In the meadow before them was a large herd of shaggy red cattle and a newly constructed wooden pen. Inside the pen were about 40 calves. Anxious mothers grazed nervously outside the pen, while the rest of the herd hung close.

"This pen is new," Eloise said as she studied the herd of about one hundred.

"Lord," she continued, "have you ever herded?"

Roland gave her a puzzled look but didn't answer.

"It's a small herd, but there are only the two us. If we loose the calves, we could drive the herd to Ashbury, and-"

"Is it market day? Or have you forgotten we're at war?" he said with a sarcastic edge to his voice. "Surely the miles have taken a toll on you," he added with a kinder tone, dipping his head only slightly in patronizing acquiescence.

Eloise ignored his comments, knowing when he heard her plan he would leap into action. It was so obvious. "Dahlquin will help itself," she murmured to more puzzled looks from Roland. "We stampede the herd over Tiomu's army." Isn't that what she had promised the farmers? The blood of Tiomu's traitors would succor the land. But she hadn't imagined it so blatant. How prophetic. She couldn't help smiling.

"Daftness upon you. It would take days to get there," Roland said, no longer puzzled. "And I've never driven a herd to market or slaughter," he added in a low tone, but Eloise suspected he was contemplating the possibilities.

She looked at the sky; was the sun peeking through the gloom? She saw startling blue, highlighted by a black cloud of equal portion. Brief rain. Always.

"It would take longer than an hour and a half," she agreed. "But it would give us time to formulate our plan, mayhap pick up some extra hands along the way, and more cattle."

The cattle grazed on the coarse green forage. One of the cows bawled for her calf in the pen and the calf wailed back to her, his knobby head poking through the wooden slats.

"You believe we can direct that band all the way to Ashbury?" Roland asked.

"Well," she started, assessing the reality. "We are just two, without whips or staffs or dogs to do the hard work." She sighed.

"I've never," Roland said slowly. "I don't know."

"Let's try. And more work for Tiomu's men to capture them again," she added, brightening with that vision. "If I'm not to taint the meat, best disperse it far from Tiomu's use."

"Let's try," Roland agreed. "Loose the beasts," he said with his brown eyes glinting.

They walked their horses toward the pen. Artoch balked, side passing away from the docile creatures.

"Easy," Roland scolded, cueing hard with his legs as Artoch snorted but didn't advance.

"He doesn't think it's such a grand idea," Eloise said, amused by the great war horse showing such alarm at bovines.

"Set him upon a single bull and he's all teeth," Roland said, rolling his spurs up the stalled horse's barrel. "But in a field of cows, he turns coward."

"Horses," Eloise shrugged, letting Garth graze amidst the herd hoping Artoch might settle seeing his companion at ease. "Do you fight with bulls much?" The grisly sport was fraught with unnecessary danger for the vulnerable horse.

"I wish there were more opportunity," Roland said, "there's little enough hunting in Leinster." He grinned as Artoch walked briskly to Garth's side, ears erect, nostrils dilated. "I suppose he is concerned the whole herd will rise up against him."

Eloise was insulted and relieved when Roland didn't ask if she had ever baited a bull. Her first and only episode baiting a boar had been a failure of epic proportion. Six months ago.

"Don't come between the cow and calf," Eloise instructed, smiling.

"You hear that, Artoch?" he asked, patting his horse's neck as Artoch finally put his head down to snatch large clumps of turf which he chewed with his head up, keeping a vigilant eye on the suspicious cows.

Sitting amidst the herd, Eloise began to reconsider the idea. What if the herd was unbiddable? What if the stupid beasts returned to Scragmuir, all one hundred? Unthinkable. Which was worse, to feed Tiomu's traitors or the dreaded Scragmuirs? The consequences were dire indeed, and none but this stranger's counsel. Lifting her cross pendant to her lips, Eloise also lifted her eyes to the heavens. The divisive sky with both sun and rain gave not a clue, nor did the celestial host of helpful saints.

"Well," Roland said, "have you had a turn of mind?"

"I'm weighing the consequences," she admitted. "You are perceptive."

"I'm not convinced about the stampede, but I'm all in favour of liberating the meat from Tiomu's resource," Roland said.

She tucked the pendant under her surcoat. "Release the beasts," she said with renewed commitment, cueing Garth to the gate.

"Halt!" a man cried out.

"Do not!" shouted another.

Eloise saw two men running towards them with staff and pole in hand. Roland drew his sword.

"Open it," Roland commanded her. She did, and the calves sprinted past her to their mothers.

"Do not!" screamed the men waving their arms and tools as they ran.

Unperturbed, the cattle returned to their foraging while the calves butted and suckled their mothers. Eloise pulled her bow over her shoulder, her fingers wrapped around the leather grip, secure in their placement. Thus embraced, *Cara* hummed in her grasp. She pulled an arrow from her quiver, nocked and took aim at the man with the longer, more dangerous staff. The men didn't attack, but quickly spread around the grazing herd. She let down. They were not a threat from that distance.

"Who are you to steal these cattle?" Roland yelled back at them.

"Lord Tiomoid of the U'Neill's," the man with the pole said, almost in tears. "He has laid siege to Ashbury-"

"Siege to all of Connacht," the man with the staff interrupted. "Dahlquin, Scragmuir and Ashbury are his."

"Scragmuir!" Eloise gasped, still trying to get the herd on the move.

"Tiomu's lies grow by the day," Roland said, scowling at Eloise for speaking out of turn. He gave the men a quick glance. "We have come to deliver these beasts to Ashbury Castle directly, now help us get them moving," he said, then turned his attention back to Eloise. "El," he said waving his arms.

"Haw, haw!" she shouted to the cattle, waving her arms, arrow still nocked in her bow. "Go, go, go!" she yelled, cueing Garth into the ambling, shaggy mass.

"By your will, I'm begging," one of the men pleaded.

"Out of our way!" Roland barked at them. "Traitors like you deserve to be trampled." Roland was also waving his arms at the slow-moving cattle.

"Not traitors, not!" the two cattle men shouted. But they continued to keep the herd calm and together, in direct violation of Lord Roland's command.

Roland poked a cow with the tip of his sword, and she leaped out of his way, only to start grazing out of reach of his sword tip. "Horns," Roland growled, kicking at the unmoving cows. "Tails," he snarled, again poking a cow with his sword. Ears back, the cow eyed him. "Cloven hooves. They're Satan, I tell you."

Eloise gulped hearing Roland utter Satan's name. Unable to grab her wooden pendant tucked in her surcoat, she crossed herself three times, praying for protection from any image of Satan.

The cows gave Roland little heed, though he and Artoch were well-armed and fierce.

"Connacht is overrun with God-cursed hellions!" Roland shouted, but the reunited herd shuffled along amiably among themselves, grazing or touching noses.

"These cattle are for Ashbury!" Eloise shouted, still waving her arms and kicking at the cows before her. "The traitor will taste his beef on the hoof!" she yelled; her voice shrill as the cattle finally began to move as one.

"My son and daughter. U'Neill will kill them!" the man with the staff cried out, whacking one of the cows as she trotted past. "He has taken the children."

Eloise sat up, staring at the man as she ambled past. She knew hostages were used to coerce the laborers against their feudal lords or tribal chieftains. Isn't that how Tiomu got her father's men to build his siege engines? It was too horrible, too cruel. But to capitulate was to serve the greater evil. The father was running with the cattle, risking death to turn the herd. Was she willing to accept responsibility for his death and his children's? His children may already be dead, with more to come under such tyranny.

"Haw, haw, haw!" she yelled at the trotting cattle, sweat sticking to her neck and under her arms. "Tim U'Neill must be defeated," she said, hoping this was the right decision.

"El!" Roland shouted. "Run. Tiomu's men. Run!"

Eloise looked up, which way? Roland was galloping towards her, his sword arm waving her southeast, away from the trail to the castle. With *Cara* and arrows in hand, she could easily shoot the riders, but Roland obscured her view. Without time to return her arrow to her quiver or sling her bow over her back, she leaned down and Garth lunged forward with

Reggie's shield banging on her back, and this time the cattle parted like the Red Sea.

"Run!" Roland continued shouting as if she were standing still. Run Garth did, like a Connacht wind, blowing over the land. With each expanded stride forward, Garth sucked in air. With each contraction, he expelled it. It was a divine rhythm, and Eloise felt blessed to share it. *Grisly sport, racing.* She blocked such thoughts from her mind. Never consider falling. Commit to the ride. Fly.

Her eyes teared up with the wind in her face and she held lightly to the reins with one hand, *Cara* and the arrow held carefully by her hip. Garth's four black hooves pounded out a one-two-three, one-two-three, one-two-three beat as they hurtled over the open and uneven terrain.

Garth had ridden hard, and they must slow down. Eloise peeked back under her arm. Roland and Artoch were mere specks behind her.

She sat up and exhaled slowly. Garth plunged on. "Easy," she said, touching the reins, sitting taller, leaning back until she thought the wind might unseat her. "Easy!" she barked, massaging the reins more vigorously, forcing her seat to move in a slower movement to Garth's. "Good boy," she cooed, again slowing her movements. She picked up the reins, *slow down*, she thought. Garth resisted. Eloise blew her breath out, pushed her feet forward and firmly massaged the reins, asking for collection. Finally, Garth transitioned into an easy canter, down to a walk. When he started "talking" in relaxed horse grumble, Eloise knew he had returned to her fully. She stroked his lathered neck as he moaned to release tension. "Was there ever such a partner?" she asked him in a murmur. *Uhugh uhugh uhuhuh* he groaned.

Seamus and Broccan had ridden hard all day in pursuit of the escapees from Dahlquin. The farmers concurred that two hungry riders, identifying themselves as Lord Hubert's men, had come through. Food was not given, the farmers insisted. Seamus had choked the grass broth down, but Broccan spit the brew into the woman's face calling it piss water. That was miles ago, and here they were at some boundary, Ashbury perhaps, but Seamus had never been to Connacht before and wasn't sure. His horse was near collapsing.

"Foul nag you've got there, Seamus," Broccan said, not for the first time.

He wasn't a foul nag yesterday. Seamus valued the gelding and regretted ruining the animal in this chase. Broccan's horse looked not a whit better, but the man cared little. Seamus cared and that made him easy sport for Broccan's malicious humor.

"If this is the frontier between Dahlquin and Ashbury, then we've about two hours 'til we meet up with our force," Seamus said.

Passing through the fence, Broccan sat up.

"Before God!" Seamus exclaimed. "There they are. Stealing the cattle?" It wasn't possible, but there they were, the black and grey, man and boy. After all this time, this ignoble chase was at an end.

"Or playing with them. The poor sons of sows on the ground are making a stand, aren't they?" Broccan said with a chuckle.

"Let's get them," Seamus snarled, sword out.

Broccan drew his sword and the race was on. Both horses were exhausted, and with ears pinned, they cantered rather than galloped towards the cattle.

The man on the black horse looked up.

"He's seen us," Seamus called to Broccan.

"Run you cowardly bastard, run! You're surrounded," Broccan yelled.

Seamus watched as the man and boy fled. The once docile and uncooperative cattle suddenly charged, but instead of moving as one fluid herd the worried red bovines split into three different groups running and circling in a whorl of pounding bodies. Broccan cut left, his curses lost in the thunder of hooves. Seamus nearly ran over one of the cattlemen as his gelding veered sharp right, stride for stride with a wild-eyed calf. Shaggy red cattle pressed in on him from the other side, crushing his feet, oblivious to his spurs. Ahead of him was a wall of cattle fleeing perpendicular to his group. He felt his gelding hesitate as if seeing the red wall, but never losing stride for there was naught the horse could do.

"Fuck!" Seamus murmured, his bowels clenching. In the final moment, the cattle and his gelding veered sharp right again, almost spinning in a full circle. For a brief moment he saw Broccan, whose wide-toothed grin and flushed cheeks appeared almost demonic in mirth. The gelding broke down to an amble and Seamus directed his heaving horse away from the cattle.

"Keep walking, old fellow," he said, patting the gelding's neck. "That's enough."

Miraculously, neither the cattlemen nor he and Broccan were hurt.

"There's a saint for cow men," Broccan said, approaching, indicating the two men still trying to redirect the settling herd.

"But not for your horse," Seamus answered, noticing the horse's limp. "We'll get fresh ones at the castle. And more men, too."

"Fucking lucky, those two," Broccan said, pointing a thumb in the direction of the escapees.

"Lucky," Seamus said. "Lucky bastards indeed," but he was thinking of themselves. "Let's see what they have to say." He waved at the cattlemen.

"Who were those riders?" Eloise asked when Roland caught up with her. Both horses were still puffing from their long run.

"Tiomu's men, of course," Roland answered with a gruff edge to his voice. His cheeks were flushed.

"Of course," she said with exasperation. "But where were they from? Were they with the carts back at the farm?"

Roland gave her a long, dour look. "My gut tells me they followed us from Dahlquin."

"Dahlquin? But- Sorrow," she said bowing her head when she saw the anger on his face. She was sorely out of place.

"Tiomu U'Neill is a thorough man. It's what I would do," he said. "Run us down." His voice sounded gravelly, and Eloise thought of hares gone to ground.

"Any hope we may have held that Ashbury was safe," Roland said, looking in the direction of the forbidden castle, "has been dashed. Nod your head if you agree."

Eloise inhaled, preparing to speak, but thought better of it and nodded her head.

"I know you had some gallant notions to stay and fight, to protect your people."

He was telling her what she didn't wish to hear. The prospect she had been avoiding since...since losing Uncle Reggie. Was her only salvation in Leinster? To sojourn so far from home?

"I made a promise to your Uncle, and so did you. It's the only choice left us."

Eloise swallowed hard before answering. "Ride when he says, stop when says, eat *if* he says. I remember, Lord Roland," she said, bowing her head, fighting back the tears she must not shed, for Dahlquin pages shouldn't cry. Inhaling, she pulled her wooden pendant from under her surcoat, "Holy Christopher, blessed saint of travelers, by your will keep us safe," and she crossed herself. "Blessed Spirit, Abarta performer of feats, by your will help us in our quest," and again she crossed herself. "Holy Saint Nicholas, blessed saint of the poor and needy, by your most gracious and benevolent will, keep the children safe. They are the innocents in this war." Eloise pressed her hands together in prayer. *Blessed Mother, Guardian of the wild,* Eloise prayed in silence, *I didn't wish you goodness for Your grace in protecting Dahlquin or even take time to say goodbye when I left.* She visualized all the glories of her native home, the forests, rainbows, waterfalls and mountains, the red deer and wolf packs, burly bear and armored swine, and the unnumbered flocks of birds. All this was behind her. Meath, the Bog of Allen and Leinster stretched beyond. With this Lord Roland of Ashbury-At-March.

PART TWO

ON THE ROAD, EASTERN ASHBURY, 11th of June

"In retrospect, that stampede strategy deserves further deliberation," Roland said as they stopped at a creek to water the horses. The corner of his mouth lifted in a reluctant grin. They had ridden for miles without talking.

She returned a tight-lipped smile of acknowledgement. Artoch was so lathered he looked as grey as Garth.

"We couldn't get those stubborn cattle to move more than a few feet," Roland continued, "but Satan's horns, when Tiomu's men charged us, those cows broke rank, pooling and eddying like a great bovine river."

"Really?" she asked.

"Those riders couldn't pass." He chuckled. "Did you know they would do that, the cattle?" His voice was startling in its softness.

She gave a gentle snort. "The beefy beasties can be unpredictable. Honestly, I had believed we could stampede them to Ashbury," she admitted. "We needed some dogs and whips and prods."

"We did. I will keep that in my arsenal of ideas," he said tapping his head. "It has merit. But had they moved along for us, we may have been caught unawares and killed."

She and Roland drained the skin bag they had and when the horses finished drinking, she got down to refill it. Once out of the saddle it seemed prudent to check the horses and tack. As Artoch and Garth snatched at the variety of greens, barely chewing before swallowing, Eloise retrieved the hoof knife from the saddle bag of one of the squires. *Go with God*, she thought, for though she never met the lad, she was most grateful for his supplies on this treacherous journey.

After checking the horses' hooves, Eloise raided a few trees of green apples.

Apples, apples hard and green,
Suck the life juice from mother tree,

136

She sang as she picked, thinking they just might come in handy.

Whence come autumn with shorter days
Your juice will flow, and quench my ways

Back on the road Eloise and Garth began to canter at the pace set that morning. Roland urged Artoch to speed up. The destrier took a few eager steps but returned to his slower pace. Again, Roland spurred the horse on. Eloise looked at her escort. Armed and capable, mounted on a fine destrier, but Artoch slowed them up.

She gave them a "hurry up" expression over her shoulder. Having committed to go to Leinster, she wanted to do it fast, at messenger speed. If only Roland were on a courser.

"Excellent time we're making," Roland grumbled. "Riding the horses to death will accomplish naught. It would be much slower on foot," he reminded her.

Eloise ignored him and kept to her pace. How much better the world appeared when viewed between the two dappled ears of her beloved Garth. This she could do, ride for help, on a horse she trained. Not sitting on her arse, *sorrow, Mathair*, she whispered, spinning thread or weaving cloth.

A cloud passed before the lowering sun, and they rode in shadow. At least it wasn't rainy. This was hard enough without inclement weather. Roland said a silent prayer of thanks for the good conditions, remembering the dragon's breath he and his friends had endured.

FitzGilbert would be surprised to see Roland back so soon. What bad tidings he brought with him: civil war, war with Denmark or the Norse. U'Neill had over four hundred men at Dahlquin. How many men did he have at Ashbury? Tiomu led the assault at Dahlquin. Ashbury must be the secondary effort. What ballocks to lay siege upon two castles, Roland thought.

It always came down to fighting. He had earned his fief by fighting, and winning, repelling a brutal attack upon High Lady Brigid's own dower estate. A disgruntled Welsh uncle had descended upon the walled village. Only a handful of armed men stood before the onslaught. Roland was richly rewarded for his brave stand as was Lord Rory the younger. Now, even before he had set eyes on his meagre holdings, he would have to fight to gain it back. At-March, Dead Man's Land, a highly contested strip of land separating Dahlquin from Scragmuir. Would there be anything to fight for? He and his friends had found nothing but mist.

He kept a watchful eye on Eloise and Garth ahead of him. Hunger nagged him, and he pushed his horse to the limit just to keep up. He glanced behind him. Did he see a cloud of dust just behind them? Nay, he was sure the riders had gone to the castle for fresh horses and men.

Roland checked on Eloise again. Garth cantered sideways, almost a skipping step. Was the horse alarmed, did he refuse to go farther? Next the grey stallion pivoted and cantered just as briskly from the other side. Then the horse led with his hindquarters. His long silver tail swished dramatically. It was an awkward step for a horse to try and canter backwards.

"Do it again," he asked.

"I will," she answered with a shadow of a smile. It was contagious and he smiled back without realizing it.

"Why are you teaching him to canter backwards?"

"Good boy," Eloise rubbed Garth's thick neck then stroked the crest. "Oh, it gives us a challenge to work on. My good boy," she cooed, as she cued him to again do a leg yield, backwards.

"Dahlquin is renowned for horses," Eloise said, in case Roland didn't know, "surely as far back as my great grandfather and beyond, they all had an eye for good horses."

"FitzGilbert treasures his," Roland acknowledged.

Eloise smiled, thinking in particular about the Royal Whites her father had supplied to FitzGilbert. Of course, they were truly grey, gone full white.

"My Lady Mother doesn't care much for horses. She recognizes their value, but she has fear."

"By your antics, I believe," Roland said with a slanted grin. "Poor woman."

"Hmmm," Eloise said, letting his comment slide by. "My father had me in the saddle as a wee babe. Of course I don't remember it, but I have heard it told oft times, it feels like a true memory. I was in *Mathair's* arms when Da rode up on a big red stallion, with a white blaze and two white feet, hind. I squealed and laughed and Da took me up in the saddle with him, much to *Mathair's* distress. I took hold of the leather reins and we strode around the inner keep. *Mathair* and Uncle Reggie said my eyes were large as platters, pudgy arms and legs flailing, me shrieking with joy as if my movements were responsible for that most magnificent event. After a few laps, Da attempted to return me to *Mathair*."

"Let me see if I might guess the rest," Roland said. "You kicked and screamed and cried."

Eloise was still smiling with the memories of horses and the familiar movement of Garth beneath her.

"Marish even then," Roland added.

Eloise shrugged her shoulders; how often she was compared to a mare. "I rode nearly every day after that, with Da or Uncle."

"I believe that."

"Good boy," she called to Garth, stroking his neck. "Lord?" She paused, looking at Roland, then sighed, unsure if she should proceed.

"You were going to ask me something?"

"What do you think is happening?" she looked over her shoulder, west towards Dahlquin. "Is the castle breached?"

"It is not. With hot oil, the crossbowmen."

"But that hole? Tiomu's men were clambering in."

"An outer wall and a loss. Your father will fall back behind the stouter rampart. He has only to hold up behind the walls until FitzGilbert arrives. The advantage is with the castle."

"So it should be," she sighed again. "I should be there. I can shoot and tend wounds." She swiped at her eyes. "I should be in the paddocks training horses. If not riding, there is little I would rather do than work with the horses."

Other images came to her, nauseating memories of her failures: carelessly dancing into the arms of one of the traitors, longing for more and fighting with her father about it. Uncle Reggie's unwelcome reminder she was not a son. The chewed ledger. She heard in her mind the agony of the horses at the siege, burnt hide and fear. Their need and pain stabbed at her as she rode. And her human patients.

But Garth was here, and he was safe.

"You spend a lot of time in the stables?" Roland asked.

"I do," she shook her head, clearing her senses of the suffering, blocking the faces and the stench. There was nothing to be done for them now. *Don't dwell on it, just ride.* "It's where the horses are," she added. Was he such a nit, she wondered? "When Garth was born," she stroked his neck repeatedly as she spoke, "my father let me spend the night in the stable."

"You do that often?" he asked. "Sleep with the livestock?"

"Well, I wouldn't call it that!" Eloise exclaimed. "But my mother and I have oft spent a night in the stables when a valuable animal was in peril."

139

"And with Garth?"

"And with Garth. He would know me as surely as he knew his dam," she said, remembering the thrill. "And my father wouldn't permit me to bring him to my bedchamber," she added.

"You must have been like a second, gawky filly to that mare. Which of you had the longer legs?"

She tried to look indignant, but it was funny. She sniffed. He did have a sense of humor to match that infrequent smile. The traumatic events of the past nights and days had forced her to detach, stepping outside herself, enduring the events but not allowing herself to be absorbed by the emotions. Today she rode with changed clarity and purpose, but she was still female, still seventeen.

At this pace they would be through Meath in a day. Dangerous as Scragmuir? She wondered. Then Leinster, Lord FitzGilbert would send help, and she would be back in the saddle with her father, and her mother, Alsandair and all Dahlquin's children would be safe.

How urgently she longed to get to FitzGilbert and seek help, and still it frightened her to be going there now. She worried how Dahlquin would make up the lost planting season, and all the cattle stolen and butchered. Already the stores had dwindled from last year's harvest. Locked within the castle walls, none could hunt nor pick. If not murdered one by one, they would soon starve. How would the farmers manage with their children held hostage? Artoch was falling behind. The mighty horse was spent. Nothing to be done for it, they would have to stop and let him eat and rest.

Coming upon a stream, they stopped. With building anxiety, Eloise refilled the skin bag and watched the horses drink. "Hurry up," she scolded them. "Day light is wasting." Not their concern, she knew. Eloise shared some of the green apples with them. Garth was reluctant, but Artoch eagerly took the small orbs.

Roland scanned the distance behind them. Unsatisfied, he climbed a tree for a better view.

"See anything?" She called up to him. She longed to believe the riders were not after them, that it was just a coincidence.

"I can't see much, nothing troublesome, at least. But I've not a doubt we're pursued. They probably stopped at Ashbury for food and drink, fresh horses and more men," he said, dropping out of the tree.

Saddling up, she rode with her bow at the ready. They would need something to eat or trade, so it was best to be prepared.

"Of course, who could ever overtake you?" he muttered, riding behind her on the narrow track. "Surely your butt is forged of steel."

"Easy prey, the way you slow us down," she retorted, but his compliments stung her in ways she didn't understand. Confused, she rode in silence. After two miles she spoke.

"My Lord," she ventured, "I know nothing about you or your family?"

"Hmm," he grunted, glancing at her impassively.

"You have borne witness to much of my family. In our darkest hours. It would be a comfort to stop thinking of you as a stranger," she added, giving him what she hoped was an imploring and appreciative grin.

"Stranger? After all this?" he said, waving his arm behind him to include all the mayhem they had endured. Drying their garments by the open fire, she remembered, feeling her cheeks flush.

"Exactly," she countered, moving past her embarrassment. "You know much about my family and our histories. But you, Lord, are an enigma." She continued to grin, unwavering as he seemed to consider the opportunity before him.

"Enigma. Ha," he laughed. "Knowledge is power, thus I keep my advantage." He gave her a superior half grin.

And so it was: the Forbidden Fruit of knowledge. Eloise longed for more knowledge, for education she believed existed beyond Dahlquin. Here was this stranger, from beyond Dahlquin, and just like her parents, he would deny her answers. Suppress knowledge, suppress your opponent.

"Wise is the master," she said, giving him a half-nod of disapproval before adding, "I suppose this ignorant page will just have to ride faster to ease the boredom of the miles."

"Ow, would you be so heartless to cause the death of my-" Roland paused, "noble steed?" he countered, but his smug expression had waned.

"I would not, my Lord, as you say, the power is yours. To entice me with tales of your illustrious family," she said, unable to suppress a grin, "or to eat my mud."

Roland's eyebrows rose and his dark eyes glinted with ebony mischief. His lips were pressed tightly but bowed up at the edges. Eloise suspected he was accepting her challenge with a caveat of his own. *Don't reveal your feelings*, she counseled herself, but the grin remained.

"Let me propose," he said slowly, "first tell me what you know of me. Mayhap I will embellish the history."

Disappointed, Eloise pondered that a moment. She knew little. More importantly she didn't want exaggerations. That would only make him a mythical mystery, while remaining a very real stranger.

"Not up to the challenge?" he goaded.

"My Lord, I will speak what I know, first." Eloise hoped she tipped her head with an adequate amount of regard and reservation, before tilting her head with an arched eyebrow. "Lest I shame you into revealing a lineage best kept secret."

Roland's expression tightened only slightly, and the corner of his left eye twitched. He scratched his temple with a gloved finger then rubbed his chin, the half-smile returning. "My secrets become more powerful by the moment."

"I'll start with that," Eloise said bemused. "My Lord Roland of Ashbury-At-March, comes from Leinster, has two brave and glorious brother knights, Guillaume and Sedric."

"I'm brave and glorious," he added with a friendly smirk.

"Your brave and glorious squires were murdered on the route to Ashbury," she continued. Eloise crossed herself with their memory. This was true history, not folly.

"Two brave and glorious lads were murdered as we discovered," Roland said. "But my squire, Val, remains in Leinster, recovering from a plague of the lungs, poor lad. Poor but alive, I trust."

"I hope he is well recovered," Eloise said, almost singing her delight to hear something uplifting.

"Val will be sorely displeased with you, if your rigorous pace kills my horse. Isn't that right, Artoch?" Roland said stroking the black stallion's sweating neck. "Val is wickedly fond of horses, especially this one," Roland said, giving Eloise a warning look as he continued to stroke Artoch's neck. "He can converse day and night with unending enthusiasm about anything equine. He'll love Connacht."

"So, he will," Eloise agreed, a bit surprised by Roland's sudden burst of warmth. "Hmmm hm hm hm hmmm hmmm hmmm" she hummed merrily, her voice rising and dipping. "It will be a pleasure to meet this exemplary young man. I have fondness of him already, strange as his name is. Dahlquin has been blessed by our new neighbors."

"That is most gracious of you to say," Roland nodded to her. "It's an honor and a blessing upon us - me, as well."

"And that is the extent and breadth of my knowledge of my brave and glorious Lord Roland of At-March. Sir, your family tree is sadly bleak, and begs some foliage. Might we start with the distaff side?" She continued to let her voice rise and fall. Already she was forming a song of Lord Roland's history as they had shared; an enjoyable task to ease the miles and aid her memory.

"My Lady Mother's name was Ariana."

Eloise sighed. "Ariana," she repeated the name slowly, with a lilt. "That is one of the most beautiful names I've ever heard. *Ariana*," she nearly moaned in admiration. "Was?" Eloise asked as she caught the past tense.

"Was," he paused. "She died during the winter of my seventh year."

"A thousand shames upon me for your suffering and loss." Eloise crossed herself and said a prayer for Roland's mother.

"Like your mother, she was pious and gentle. I pray for her spirit always."

"My Lord, it grieves me to have brought up such a painful memory. I didn't know." Aching with Roland's loss, and wishing she could hold her *Mathair*, Eloise wrapped her arms about herself.

He paused before speaking again. "She had thick black hair that hung past her waist. Sad brown eyes." Roland sighed, and Eloise worried she had pried too much. But Roland seemed to brighten, his lips softening into an almost smile. "She was from southern Spain. Andalucia."

Eloise gasped, almost squealing with this news.

Smiling, Roland continued. "I've never been to Spain, nor met any of my Lady Mother's family. One day I would very much enjoy a progression to my mother's homeland."

"Oh, a family progression," Eloise sighed, imagining such a pilgrimage and adventure. "Santiago di Compostella, down to Andalucia." She clapped her hands with momentary glee.

"An extensive journey to be sure," Roland said. His brown eyes glowed and his gaze felt like a summer caress upon her.

"You must favor her, you're very dark," Eloise continued, feeling both warmed and startled. Mayhap he was descended from Rodrigo Diaz, El Cid, and his mother a former Infidel, blessedly converted to the true faith. Oh, that was exciting to think on. How exotic! "By your will, tell me more," she asked. This was precisely what she longed to hear.

Such a wonder he was so tall, and broad shouldered. Very muscular, not unlike her father. But where Hubert was fair, Roland was dark, with well-chiseled features. His hair was a thick mane that didn't get enough regular grooming, his dark brown eyes smoldered with emotion. My, she was spending some time thinking about this striking young lord...and she was staring. Was her mouth gaping? She closed it. Did he notice? She snapped her attention back to the road. Peering out of the corner of her eye, she thought Roland was grinning. She was embarrassed and felt her cheeks burn.

Eloise closed her mouth and turned away. Her cheeks were rosy and when she glanced back at him, he knew she was embarrassed as well as intrigued. It seeped through him with the delicacy of fruit wine, *bonum vinum*. Roland felt he was fast becoming intoxicated. If ever there were an enigma, it was the girl next to him.

His mind turned back to his mother. He'd almost always known her to have sad eyes, Roland reflected. Life wasn't easy for her either. Perhaps harder. It would be difficult for a mother to watch her children unfairly used and be helpless to do anything about it. As a child, he had been furious with his mother for allowing his father to be so cruel. Roland remembered crying, cursing, sometimes striking out at her in frustration. Instead of retaliation, his mother would hold him, rocking and singing until he settled - as she did with all her children in the seven short years he had with her. Now he understood his mother had done as much as she could to intercede for her children. It wasn't a woman's place to disagree with her husband. A man wasn't restricted by law as to how he dealt with his family. Beyond his father's hall, Roland discovered a martial world, governed by laws and a code of conduct that did not condone such behaviour. Tyrants abounded, but they were the sinners.

His life without her warmth and love became untenable. To this day he thanked God that his father had fostered him. Roland had never been back, and never intended to return - or did he?

"And your Lord Father?" Eloise asked. "Am I to hear of him?" Eloise smiled up at him expectantly. How different her existence had been. Her blue-grey eyes were eager and hopeful, waiting to hear more good of him.

"My father," Roland hesitated. Eloise had been exceedingly pleased with his mother's Spanish lineage, though he provided little of substance. His father's title, wealth and power were much to be commended. "Lord Guy of Charnley, Earl of Cardiffshire, in southern-" He didn't finish.

"You're English," she interrupted, eyes wide with astonishment, her hand over her mouth. "Does my father know?" she asked in a hushed whisper, removing her hand from her mouth. The glee in her eyes was replaced by something more disdainful.

"He does," Roland said, offended by her reaction. This was an unpleasant revelation to her, when she should have been impressed.

Eloise stared at him anew. "I wasn't told. Spain is neutral enough, but England." Her voice was low, secreted, as if the very words were distasteful.

"I'm not an abomination." Her derogatory tone irritated him. "Your overlords," he added.

"Shame upon me, it's just…the Earl of Cardiffshire. You're from Leinster. Such shame not to have known," she stammered. Her blue-grey eyes poured over him as if he needed washing. She studied every part of him, careful not to make eye contact. Clearly, she didn't appreciate the Earl of Cardiffshire's status, especially in relation to her humble Connacht standing. His father, whom he despised, corresponded directly with King Henry. Her own Welsh grandfather sailed to Ireland under the direction of the former King Henry. Had she forgotten her own English heritage and servitude?

"Such shame because you were rude? Or because I'm English?" He glared at her sternly.

The edges of her mouth started to turn up and she looked down, in an attempt to hide her amusement. "Both," she shrugged, her answer short, blunt and English, without apology.

Roland had no reply. Connacht abounded in insubordination at every level. He remembered the challenge in the farmer's presence with their implements of toil held as weapons. And Eloise, not only willing to hunt to feed them, laborer's, but encouraging them to rise above their station to fight.

They rode on in silence. Roland's back ached from all the long miles in the saddle. When Sir Reginald had instructed his niece that Roland would dictate if they would stop, if they would eat, and if they would rest, Roland believed Eloise would be the burden, unused to the harsh rigors of life on the road without comfort of wagon, beds or tents. However, it was he who was tired, he who needed sorely to rest and he who was hungry. Yet he couldn't bring himself to reveal his human weakness to this Maiden of Dahlquin. Up one hill, down another, through fields of wheat, barley and flax. Farmers, shirtless and bent to their endless tasks. Would these fields soon be stripped and wasted as the ones they had passed? Should he risk telling these poor workers? Would they desert, or join U'Neill? Saints preserve him, he was thinking like her. Again, Roland looked back over his shoulder. They were coming, he felt it. While these men pursued him and Eloise from behind, what were they riding into? Would Lord Bryan be waiting for them?

Lord Bryan of New Pembrokeshire should be warned. He wouldn't support Tiomoid U'Neill and his mercenaries against Connacht. But, aye, Eloise was a risk. God's blood she complicated things.

How straight and regal she sat in the saddle. No mere page, her. Her presence exuded through the trappings of a servant. And her slender legs. No wonder women always wore gowns. Legs were a huge distraction and led to a very shapely behind.

"You ride well," he broke the silence, hoping to renew the companionship they had shared.

"May you have goodness, Lord," she acknowledged. After a pause, "So do you."

Roland was unable to detect if her reply was sarcasm, an obscure compliment or masked insult.

Either way, he enjoyed seeing her at ease after the long, grueling ordeal of the days and nights before. In this moment, the lines of worry and anguish were replaced with gentle eyes, at least for her horse, and the glimmer of a smile, at his expense, mayhap. How much prettier she would be if not hidden behind the garments of a page, and her hair hidden under that silly cap of Tuath's. How long was her hair? He had only seen it braided and mussed, at Dahlquin Castle. How might it look lying across her shoulders, or his pillow, well mussed indeed? Rosy lips from the shared chalice of fruit wine, left unfinished upon a table. He suppressed a groan.

Her boy's clothing, what a relief to know that was all gossip. He snorted. What a fool he had been to give heed to such malicious rumour. He could hear Guillaume's words even now: "Don't content yourselves with the idle gossip of the stable hands and kitchen wenches. The High Lord counts on strong, intelligent and educated knights to support him." Roland breathed a silent curse to his friend. Was it not Guillaume who suggested Lady Aine and Eloise were twin succubi? Were they? Frowning, Roland rubbed the back of neck. What was Guillaume doing now? And how did Sedric fare? He was poorly when they left. How quickly things changed. Roland continued frowning.

"What's amiss, my Lord? You look angry." *I'd be angry if I were English*, she thought. Then she crossed herself and asked forgiveness; it was mean to make folly of her guard and escort. Besides, his lineage wasn't his choice. She watched him. Mayhap he had hunger. Mayhap he had anger to be stuck as nursemaid to her while the fighting was back at Ashbury. *You are my responsibility*. His words echoed in her mind. She didn't ask him to come, and she resented his intrusion, his assumption of responsibility. It was not Uncle Reggie's right to assign her over to this English…usurper! What did he know of her or Dahlquin or Connacht or Ireland for that matter? Her kinsmen were dying back at Dahlquin, depending on her to seek aide, and she would do it, surly *English* knight or not. *She* was responsible. If they were followed, all the more reason to keep a steady pace.

"Would you like to stop and eat?" Roland asked again, ignoring her question. "It's a week's ride to High Lord FitzGilbert's castle. Surely you don't intend to do it without stopping."

"May you have goodness for your concern, but I would not." There was insufficient need to stop again. "It's four days to Leinster, messengers' pace."

"Artoch isn't a messenger. Neither am I," Roland chuffed. "Seems I just said this. Bah. The horses need to rest. And it's a week to Leinster," Roland corrected.

"If you wish to stop, let's find a place. You can take a week or a month or a year to get to Leinster, my Lord."

Roland studied her. Scrawny, she and her mother. *I'd never let my family go hungry. Your family?* a bemused voice asked in his head. *You have no family, who are you to judge? She's in your care now,* he thought, *feed her for Heaven's sake.*

"You look near starved, we should stop and eat," he announced.

"My Lord," she huffed. Or was she sighing? "Great hunger upon me." She placed a hand on her belly. "But we haven't anything to eat, yet. So, with your will, don't stop on my unworthy needs," she countered. "As you, my Lord, anxiety is upon me, like a bristly mantle with the weight of iron to reach High Lord FitzGilbert. There are miles ahead of us and plenty of daylight. Every person we pass on this road is suspect. Are they in league with U'Neill? Are traitors stealthily making their way to slit the throats of the unsuspecting?"

"I decide."

"You decide, my lord," she answered with a page's crispness.

The day *was* young. By the time they got something to eat, built a fire and cooked it, precious daylight hours would have passed. There wasn't time. Not to cook and not to eat if they were being chased.

"You know this area better than I. Are there any villages, lodges, farms around?" he asked, an edge of hope in his voice.

"There are villages and farms in the next dozen miles or so," she offered.

Their first evening's ride had been a solitary one. More people shared the roads with them. Late spring, early summer was a busy time in this agrarian-based society. They passed acres of fields in various stages of plowing, planting, weeding and tending. The hours were long, tedious and backbreaking for the villeins and freemen who worked the earth. Most of what they produced went directly to their lord. The lord in turn paid handsomely to his king. All this he knew. But now he felt it. *I am such a lord, I must do this.*

Crossing a stream provided an opportunity to water and rest the horses. Garth and Eloise seemed able to ride without stopping. Artoch and Roland were used to travelling at a realistic pace, or at an army's slow progress. Roland laid out upon the dry bank, gulped water, dunked his face in the cool stream and drank some more, as muscles stretched and loosened. Eloise held the reins as both horses drank deeply.

"Not thirsty?" he asked between slurps.

"I have thirst," she said, waiting. When Roland and the horses were sated, she crouched down, upstream from where the horses had muddied it, and used the skin bag, filling, drinking and refilling. Standing again, she stretched her back, arching as a cat might do if it could stand on two legs. She curled her hands around each other and bent at the knees, making a very satisfied noise, between a squeal and a sigh.

Warmed by the sight and sound, Roland smiled. She shook out her legs, touched her toes a few times. Roland had to look away because her short tunic revealed entirely too much leg. He thought of Sir Reginald's last words: 'I'll haunt you from the gates of Hell!' were Eloise hurt. Roland felt that cold breeze blow over him again. Could that foul spectre read minds from the grave?

"What was that all about?" Roland asked, nodding his head in the direction of the stream.

"Sire, what did I do?" she asked.

"Afraid to get wet?" he asked, knowing she wasn't, having witnessed her jump off a waterfall.

"Ah, my father had a way with one-time lessons," she answered, rolling her eyes at the memory.

"Well?" he asked.

"I was ten years old," Eloise started. "Father, Uncle Reggie and I stopped to water the horses, my pony and ourselves. Hot and sunny." She closed her eyes a moment as if remembering the warmth. "I had such thirst. I just jumped off my pony and started drinking alongside the hounds. Just as you did. So good and cool." She sighed. "I even remember the song birds, such a joyous day. Then a huge, painful weight was on my neck, shoulders. Pinned me face down in the water. I was drowning for sure. The more I struggled, the greater the pressure. Rocks scraping me," she said, rubbing her cheeks expressively. "I panicked."

"Where was your father or Uncle?" Roland asked

"Where indeed, I wondered? Couldn't open my mouth to scream. I thought I was dying. I heard a familiar voice. 'Enough already, Hubert, she'll die. Christ's Blood let her up.'"

"Your father?" Roland asked. "Why?"

148

"I couldn't breathe. I flailed uselessly. Even now, I still remember hearing the birds. I was dying, but they continued singing. Or was it angels in heaven?"

"What happened?" Roland asked, extending his hands, palms up in quandary.

"Flipped me over with his boot. I was choking, gasping. Da glaring at me. Uncle Reggie looking stricken. 'Never leave yourself vulnerable like that,' my father said in a low voice. 'Never be a slave to your comforts. Use the tools you have to warn you of danger.'"

"Then I said something rude, like 'go thirsty?' and Uncle Reggie thumped my head." Eloise demonstrated flicking her middle finger with her thumb. "Hurt plenty with his massive fingers," she added, rubbing her head as if just thumped. "Da said 'Use your tools. One, the horses.'" She held up a finger as her father had. "'When they have thirst, they drink. All their effort is on satisfying their thirst. That's where predators congregate, to catch the careless. Two, the dogs.'" She held up a second finger. "'You keep guard while they drink.' Uncle threw a rock in the bushes and the hounds took off. The horses looked up, alerting me. 'After, you can kneel down like this.' He knelt and used his hands to bring the water to his mouth. Thus, he could turn his head around and survey his surroundings."

Eloise paused, rubbing the back of her neck, remembering her injured pride, sore face and the pain her father's boot had left on her neck.

"That was a bit brutal," Roland said as they prepared to leave. Eloise led Garth over to a rock and climbed into the saddle, revealing her fatigue. She exhaled, and nodded she was ready.

"That's what Uncle Reggie and I thought," she said continuing the story. "He tried to make excuses for me. 'She's but a little girl,' things like that." She reflected. "But I have gratitude my father didn't hold back because I *was* a little girl. I want my father to have pride in me, pride in the things I can do. He is hard and demanding. He causes such anger upon me, seems so unfair, part of the world that's so unfair." She wanted to scream at the injustice of it. "Enough of me. What about your father?" Eloise asked. "The Earl of Cardiffshire."

Roland was silent a good long time. "I haven't seen my Lord Father the Earl in years. He remains in high standing with the King and has good health last I heard," Roland said, giving no further elaboration about his father. "I have two elder brothers, William and Gilbert. Two elder sisters, Arabella and Diana. One younger brother, Alexander," he added.

"Arabella," she moaned. "Another beautiful name. And Diana, the Huntress. Pleasure upon me. Fortune upon you, God has goodness to favour you with brothers and sisters," said Eloise. Roland could hear her longing for siblings, and new warmth for his English kin.

"Fortunate, you say? Fortunate, with two big sisters trying to dress you up and play doll with you when you're a child! And with two big brothers who are always bigger and stronger and faster than you? Finally, a little brother comes along and you think you'll have someone to be bigger, stronger and faster than, but I can't, he's the baby. 'Help your baby brother, look out for your baby brother'" he imitated a high-pitched woman's voice, grinning at the memory.

"I haven't the gift of brothers or sisters. Longing upon me for someone to share secrets with and complain about *Mathair* and Da with, someone with understanding," she spurted out. "Cousins are not the same. Nor the numerous children fostered at Dahlquin."

"There's a lot of fighting and squabbling goes on," he offered.

"There is great pressure being the only heir," she said.

"True, but if you're not the eldest son, there's naught but to leave and seek your own fortune, as they say. Daughters can be married off. It's a great way to build strong allegiances," he countered.

"Married off? It's not my wish to be married off. Dahlquin is my home. It's a problem. Father has his ideas and-," she cut herself short. "Then what about you?" she asked, changing the subject. "You ran away from home to avoid being a nursemaid?"

"At seven years of age, after my mother died, my father sent me to my godfather, King John, to advance the family's name at his court," Roland answered, "thinking that would be the hardest training grounds of all," he added with a tinge of sarcasm.

"What?" Eloise exclaimed, nearly choking. "Your godfather was the King? Did you live in the White Tower?"

"King John had many godchildren. All the nobility would seek the favour. Truly it's not such an unusual distinction."

"Did you meet Queen Eleanor? Would she be your great godmother?" Before Roland could answer, Eloise went on.

"The magnificent Eleanor of the rich and fertile Aquitaine, mother to King Richard the Lion-Hearted, King John, as well as the illustrious Marie of Champagne, kings and queens all of her children. Well, most of them." Eleanor was a legend to many, and apparently her image loomed large for Eloise. Her words were lyrical. "A woman who led, a woman who planned her own destiny and still influenced thought years after her death." Eloise glanced at him in wonderment, as if he had a hand in such a rich history. "And a contemporary of the blessed Hildegard of Bingen. "Oh, to have had an opportunity to converse with such knowledgeable and witty women," Eloise said with a deep sigh, closing her eyes in reverence.

At that moment he could envision her clean-scrubbed and well dressed, kneeling in adoration at the feet of a queen in a lavishly appointed chamber, with musicians and bards - or to be a queen herself.

"Nay to all that. How old do you think I am?" he teased her, allowing some English to slip in.

Disappointment faded, she chuckled. "How old are you?"

"Three and twenty."

"You have earned much success!" she exclaimed. "So much to tell. What of King John? Were you his squire? What brought you to Ireland?"

"So many questions," Roland muttered, "where to start?"

"Shall I ride faster to conjure your memory?" she asked, stroking Garth, acknowledging his efforts to keep moving.

"King John had many pressing responsibilities. Imprudent of him to waste his time training his numerous godchildren with barons in revolt and a financial crisis, wouldn't you agree?"

"History tells us those were difficult times," she agreed.

"Truly, I longed to be a knight. And my father was correct. It was the most difficult training possible. So many boys and young men, all wishing to achieve greatness before the King. So many distractions, temptations. Martial life is strict and rigorous. Disciplined."

Eloise nodded at him, indicating she well knew that word.

"I met Val in the barns. I was mucking out stables as penance for some-" he hesitated, searching for a word.

"Because you were brave and glorious?" she offered, her blue-grey eyes sparkling in complicity.

"If you wish to embellish it so, I won't dispute," he chuckled, accepting her version. He squinted, his gaze resting on her a moment. "With your fair complexion, few freckles and amber hair, you could be Val's sister." Then he smirked and continued with his story. "Val, being immune to the stench of muck, volunteered, offering his services," Roland emphasized, "in exchange for additional time with the horses."

"The brother I should have had," she smiled broadly, looking all the more like Val. "Was this in England or Ireland? And how is it Ireland came to be graced by your brave gloriousness?"

What to tell, he didn't know his feisty charge so well. King John was difficult, unpopular, and far too busy to deal with yet one more of his numerous godsons. Still young Roland dreamed that eventually he would become a knight, and travel and do good deeds, and serve his king loyally and live happily ever after, or something like that.

"I was twelve when I became a knight in training, a squire to Sir John from Exeter. At fourteen I was forfeit as ransom in a tournament," he admitted despite the residual pain. "As a squire I came to High Lord FitzGilbert, of Leinster." At first heart-broken and disillusioned to be abandoned by his godfather to Ireland, life in the Irish court proved much better than what he endured in England. "I was surprised by my acceptance at the Irish court. It was there I met Sedric and Guillaume, Val too, and our friendship formed."

"I see," Eloise considered.

Roland thought a sarcastic expression crossed her face as she studied him.

"His own godson," she murmured, her brow crossing. "Shame on King John!" she snapped. "And your father. That isn't common practice."

Roland expected her to say something disparaging, but was warmed by her genuine concern, and outrage.

"Happily, I've served Gerald FitzGilbert. He's a strong and wise Lord," Roland continued. "He's been fair with me." More so than his own family, he remembered. A year after coming to Ireland in 1216, nine-year old Henry III ascended the English throne. Uneasy about the politics of the Irish Kingdoms and their lack of regard towards England, Roland oft times found himself biting his English tongue, and rather than reprimand the treasonous, he listened and remembered.

Eloise looked relieved to hear good of High Lord FitzGilbert, for this was a worry almost as great as the one she left behind.

"I achieved knighthood by FitzGilbert's own hand in my twentieth year. Now a small fief at Ashbury." But he had never gotten there. "Enough of me, does your father ever seem disappointed that you were not a son?"

"That is a rather...private question," Eloise answered. They overtook some folks with a cart being pulled by a plodding ox. Roland and Eloise ceased all conversation until well out of hearing. Then glanced back for any sign of Tiomu's men pursuing them. Eloise continued the conversation.

"Well, of course. Everyone wants sons, to carry on the name, so much easier than one daughter," she sighed, hating to be reminded of her disappointing status. "Still, my father has always been loving, and let me play with horses," she brightened. Her shoulders slumped. "Fear upon me, I'm not a good daughter either," she trailed off.

"You're a good daughter," Roland countered.

"I'm a terrible daughter. I've never wished to be a boy. But I don't like all the restrictions, the confinement, the unfairness. I don't believe that is what God intended. Oh, why am I telling you this?"

Lay people were not to interpret God's word, but he was curious what more she might have to share. "What do you believe God intended?" he asked, hoping she would continue.

"Not for women to be chattel. We're not cows!" she blurted, discretion overcome.

"That's blasphemy, you know," Roland stated, taking this reasoning to the next level. She wasn't a cow...but that was the way of it. No scholar, Roland did have some recollection of theology and logic. She was easily provoked, eager to talk, with a passion that begged aqua vitae to match the strength.

"Didn't Jesus question the need for so many laws?" she asked. "What of the Good Samaritan? Shouldn't kindness prevail over rhetoric? Argh!"

"What?" asked Roland, perplexed. What had the Good Samaritan to do with whiskey, passion or blasphemy? Cattle, or was it chattel? Rhetoric? "Wait!"

"I read the scriptures. I study and think but when I ask questions-" Her face was tight and her thin lips had lost the rosy blush of previously imagined fruit wine or the glow of whiskey. "There is much inconsistency in the scriptures. *Infallible* I'm told. Vague passages open to interpretation. *Don't question* I'm told."

Roland closed his eyes and rubbed his temples. Where had all this come from? Aye, the Church, the Word of God was infallible. It was God speaking after all.

"The Good Samaritan," she said, looking exasperated. "Surely you know this."

Roland couldn't nod his understanding fast enough, so she continued the lesson.

"Though the Samaritans were enemies to God's people, infidels laboring on the Sabbath-"

"Aye," Roland said fanning his hands to indicate he knew the story. *Had he ever heard anyone converse so fast, every word articulated so he couldn't not hear even if wanted to?* His weary head ached with the weight of thinking so hard under these grueling circumstances. He stroked his sweaty horse, seeking some commiseration.

"Mean spirited people, men of the infallible Church, make a mockery of God's words and the sacred teachings of our Savior Jesus Christ. Such kindness and wisdom from the Son of God."

She paused and Roland saw she had tears in her eyes. Was he hearing her correctly? Disputing the Church? These could be interpreted as the words of a heretic. Is that why his head throbbed so? As punishment?

Roland waited for her to finish. At the least he expected an apology. Instead she continued to stare at him, as he did her.

"Are you quite finished?" he ventured to ask. His head ached, his mind spun and he couldn't fathom what she meant or why she had come to be so angry. She pulled her wooden cross out from under her surcoat and slowly crossed herself.

"Jesus was crucified for breaking laws that men created," she continued, "laws that went against God. This very day-" Eloise looked around, taking in the partial clouds and masked sun of the Irish sky, the soft ground and verdant land before them. She was born of this glorious and contradictory land; which Roland was just learning to appreciate. "This day is a gift from God," she said with a dewy-eyed warmth that belied their terrible circumstance and that of Connacht. "Yet we're unable-" She inhaled with a gasp, cross still in her hand.

Eloise didn't want to talk anymore. Blasphemy was an act against God, not the false interpreters of the church. God's laws were simple: Ten Commandments of honorable living. Do to others as you would have them do to you. Once again, the anger over the injustices burned her soul. *Not now*, she told herself. Her parents, kinsfolk and home were in peril and she had miles to go to accomplish her goal. Garth lunged forward as she urged him to pick up the pace. She was leaving Connacht, for the first time in many years.

MEATH, 11th of June

Athlone Castle was a daunting obstacle, with its decagonal tower standing guard. Under different circumstances, it might have been a delightful opportunity to visit and rest and feast with these eastern Connacht cousins. Eloise hadn't been to Athlone in ages, not since she was five years old, returning home from the ill-fated tournament and the disastrous confrontation with Lord Elroth FitzGilbert, High Lord FitzGilbert's brother. She and Roland would pay a toll to cross the bridge over the Shannon River, in this case Tuath's knife, and then Eloise would be in Meath, the home of Lord Bryan FitzGilbert, the aggrieved son of Lord Elroth, nephew of High Lord Gerald FitzGilbert. She was the aggrieved innocent victim, but none seemed to recall that part of the heinous saga.

Eloise would depend on Roland not only for protection, but to know where they were going. Everything from this point forward was unfamiliar and of greater threat because she was lost.

The mighty Shannon River, which the Vikings had used to raid and devastate Ireland centuries past, served as a natural demarcation between Connacht and the subdued east. She looked over the side at the grey water flowing rapidly to Munster, and farther south out to sea mingling with the salt water and mayhap washing up on the shore of Santiago, Spain. Or falling off the world entirely, for there was naught but the end of the world to the west.

"Well," she said, as the horses noisily exited the busy bridge, "a relief there isn't an armed guard patrolling Meath."

"Of course not, Lord Bryan is lord of New Pembrokeshire, not all Meath. We'll pass through soon enough. My men and I were guests of the Lord some three weeks past." He seemed to be calculating how long it had been. "He's loyal to Ireland."

"Loyal to Ireland, but not to me," she said curtly. "Our fathers disagreed."

"Disagreement, is that what you call it in Connacht?" Roland snorted. All Ireland knew of the scandalous event.

"Ho!" Eloise called out. She pulled an arrow and nocked. Uncle Reggie's shield on her back was awkward, but she adjusted her draw and tracked a rabbit as it scampered across the road. The rabbit was gone in a moment, and she let down.

"You have much skill with that?" Roland asked, hope rising in his voice. Rabbits were usually caught by snares or traps or blunts, not the broad head she had drawn.

"With the Goddess's blessing, I don't believe we'll starve," she answered.

"Don't like rabbit?" he questioned.

"I do, but it wasn't a clean shot."

"This isn't a tournament! Just slow the vermin down."

Eloise looked at him aghast.

"Is there such hunger upon you that you could ignore the squeals of agony? It would ruin my appetite."

"It was a rabbit. And our dinner," Roland responded, equally aghast. "Nothing more."

"Even a rabbit deserves a quick death. Is it not one of God's own humble creatures?"

"God's humble offering for our meal. Would you turn down what God has set before you?" Roland could play this religious game of piety and devotion.

"I would strike down a reasonable beast for our dinner, but only by a clean shot."

Strange thinking, he mused. Animals were simple creatures. They felt no pain, surely. They had no immortal soul and lacked the intelligent thought of men who were made in God's image. God gave us the animals to eat or work. Why should we feel remorse in that use? Roland wondered. Man struggled to maintain separation from the animals. The similarities could not be denied, but the Bible dictated that man held dominion, a standard was set. What a strange girl, to empathize with animals.

"Do you hunt much?" Roland asked.

"Oh, indeed, I hunt often," she sighed. "I do love to ride, and the chase is exhilarating, truly. But the killing, when it's cruel or wasteful, too much shame to bare. I hunt to eat, not for sport. Mayhap if the prey were silent. It's the terror and agony I hate."

"They're simple creatures, El, nothing more. It's God's plan."

"Then why don't they just die on the table?" she huffed. *Theologians argued that humanity must maintain the dominion that God bestowed. Only a heretic would disagree. At a university learned scholars discussed just such topics,* Eloise thought. *Aristotle would be read at length, Abelard and Bernard of Clairveaux analyzed, Anselm, Hildegard,* so many questions. "I know, because God helps those who help themselves. Sloth is a sin."

"Good examples," Roland said, apparently conceding she did know the scriptures. "It's our place to be strong and well-practiced. And it's good fun."

Eloise dipped her head to Roland, feeling acknowledged.

"You like bird, then?" she asked slowing her pace.

"I like bird. Not more raw eggs, by your will."

Philosophy set aside, Eloise dismounted and handed him the reins. "Wait here. By your will."

Walking on the sides of her feet, she eased to the waterway. The fresh scent of clean water and delicate vegetation caused her empty stomach to ache. Bow pointed down, Eloise nocked a bodkin, holding the nock between her pointing and middle finger. Even now she sensed *Cara's* soul, resonating within her palm, sealing their purpose: survival. Tall reeds lined both sides of the stream and small birds darted in between, feasting on the gnats and flies. Crows cawed in the trees above, warning all that she approached. In the distance a friendly bell tinkled announcing the presence of a flock of sheep. Bleating followed on the breeze.

Eloise crouched and peered through the reeds at a large heron, with its shimmering silver and grey body, a white head and a mantle of long white feathers down his elegant serpentine shaped neck and across his back. Stalking fish just as she stalked him. Or was he? Grey herons were amazing birds, and it seemed they would eat anything only slightly smaller than themselves. With a pang of guilt, she recalled the heron she had witnessed catch a rat, and after a considerable time of dunking, shaking and maneuvering, the heroic wading bird swallowed the squirming rat as if it were a furry fish. Hating rats as she did, she felt remorse in killing such a talented exterminator. But she was hungry, and more importantly, Roland was hungry. On other occasions, Eloise remembered herons that had swallowed ducklings as well as large fish and eels, an added bonus to a fine meal, if extracted soon enough. Never taking her eyes off the bird, she drew her bow, fingers anchoring at the edge of her mouth. The unsuspecting bird focused down the long shaft of his yellow beak just as Eloise poised with her ochre colored arrow. A blunt would be better, not mutilating the flesh and whatever bounty lay within, she thought, aiming at the narrow body of the stately waterfowl. Bodkins and broad heads were all she had. She aimed instead at his round, yellow eye. We too, have hunger, she thought in communal prayer with God's beloved fowl. Letting her breath out she released the arrow. The familiar *ping*, and a splash. Black birds took to the sky, the crows cawed their distress. Dragonflies caught the scant sun on their iridescent wings and darted about the confusion.

Her eye twitching, Eloise rubbed it with the back of her hand. Blood. She rubbed again, but it was gone. *You bleed when you kill.* Relieved, Eloise plucked the bird from the water as it floated by and she located her arrow stuck in the opposite bank. It was too far for her to jump, so she figured she would mount up and retrieve it. She blessed the heron and thanked the Great Mother for the offering. Emerging from the tall reeds, she held the dripping bird high for Roland to see. Clear of the foliage, she saw Roland smile and salute. The warm glow of pride spread over her like a cloak, and she couldn't help beaming back at him: pride, another deadly sin.

Roland leaned over, staring at her, as she approached. "Is your eye bleeding?"

Her hand went to her eye. "Probably from the fowl," she said, hoping that would settle it. Eloise didn't wish to reveal her anomaly, Guilt of the Huntress.

"Oh, you've smeared it. Use your sleeve," Roland suggested, lifting his own arm pretending to wipe his eye.

"I'll gut this," Eloise said, indicating the heron. If we're lucky, maybe there's some hidden game in his gullet. Then I'll braid some of the reeds as a thong to tie the bird with."

Roland seemed to study her.

"In fact," she said, as her mind returned to the reeds, "the tubers are not bad eating. I'll dig a few. Some mint and watercress, if I can find-," she let the sentence trail off.

"You're a right capable poacher," Roland said with a smirk, swinging out of the saddle.

"Poa-ching," Eloise responded, emphasizing the first syllable. "Oh, that's such a low term," she continued, deepening her voice. Then with a grin, "I prefer to think of it as larceny," she said, feeling *Cara* ring with mirth at their complicity as she put the bow over her shoulder.

"Larceny, is it?" Roland laughed. "I'll gut the bird, you take care of the vegetation," he said, searching her saddle bags for hobbles. "Seems I've been corrupted." He hobbled Artoch. They both knew Garth wouldn't leave the herd.

"Corrupted? Not my Lord," Eloise said, handing him the heron.

As if on cue, they both pulled their daggers.

Roland raised his dagger in salute, and Eloise returned the gesture.

"Partners in crime," he said, touching the side of her blade with his, making an X.

Though Roland's touch was light, her dagger resonated in her palm. A soul? Then it was gone. He had withdrawn his dagger and returned to the bird as if nothing had happened. *Partners. He called us partners.* Eloise stared at the dagger in her hand. She tried to recall the sensation, had she imagined it? There wasn't a hint of the vibration now.

"My Lord," she said, swallowing hard before continuing. "Surely it isn't poaching. We're part of the nobility, and in service to High Lord FitzGilbert," Eloise said, walking to the stream to cut the reed stems to braid and tie the bird to the saddle bags. And a stick to dig the tubers, she reminded herself.

"It's a meagre exchange for service rendered," Roland agreed as he cut the bird's head off. "And the 'poached', poaching the King's fish," Roland called out to her.

"Oh, it is!" she chirped, standing to look at Roland to see what type of game the heron had eaten. "Hidden fish indeed. Is it whole?"

"Whole," he said.

"What bounty."

"You would eat this?" Roland asked.

"Of course," she answered. "Do you see a stick up there? My arrow," she muttered.

"Regurgitated fish?" he questioned, his voice sounding squeamish. "Not a stick," to her other query.

Eloise walked up the bank with the reeds. Garth looked up from grazing and she strode over to stroke his forehead. "Good boy," she cooed. Artoch looked up and both horses eyed the reeds. "Not for you," she murmured, shaking her finger.

Hearing a plop, she looked to see Roland tossing the entrails. Silver caught her eye.

"You tossed our fish," she said.

"As you see," he said, pulling more entrails. "Want to rinse this out, as your boots are already damp?" he said, finally looking up.

With large wings tied to its feet, the headless, gutted heron hung from Eloise's saddlebags, tubers and greens tucked inside.

"You have stowed away hearty provisions," Roland said as they mounted up.

"May you have goodness, Lord," she said, glancing again at the bulging saddle bags. This she could do. Provide nourishment. She smiled at Roland, then rode across the stream to retrieve her arrow.

After a while Roland broke the silence.

"Still mad about the fish?" he asked.

"Not mad," she answered. "Curious, I suppose."

"Curious about what?"

Eloise thought a moment longer. It was such a common custom, truly a boon to find such bonus. Roland was an unusual man. "You are, or at least you were a soldier, true?"

Roland nodded, "Even as Lord of Ashbury-at-March, I'm a soldier for FitzGilbert and King Henry."

"You're a soldier, yet you have never felt great hunger upon you."

"Never had hunger?" he asked his voice rising dramatically. "Starvation upon me this whole trip."

She waited for him to finish.

"You're a Lord's daughter, yet you have had such hunger upon you, you'd eat a raw fish?"

She had great hunger upon her, whether as punishment or to hone her hunting and foraging skills. Hungry people were resourceful. Lessons never more appreciated than now. She smiled. "I would have cooked it," she said with a sniff. "Some raw fish is most excellent. And the roe," she added.

"That is different entirely. And you know it," he said.

New Pembrokeshire was all the sign read, but it said so much more; a clear delineation, a warning, not welcome, all these things Eloise felt as she willfully crossed the boundary. The estate of Lord Bryan FitzGilbert, nephew to High Lord Gerald FitzGilbert, was perhaps the most dangerous aspect of the journey after the escape. She could not fall into the lord's hands. He had good reasons to take her hostage: revenge and marriage. Her skin tingled in the hostile air, each breath labored. Was the sky greyer? It was late-twilight-and darkening. Her eyes strained to see things that were not there.

Roland, too, seemed agitated. He hadn't a quarrel with Lord Bryan, and probably wouldn't wish a confrontation while awkwardly guiding her through the manor, she reasoned. They left the main road in hopes of skirting the edges of New Pembrokeshire. All was blessedly quiet as they cantered through this corner of the estate.

Roland had given little care to the devious politics of the feuding Irish nobility. His loyalty was to FitzGilbert and ultimately King Henry. Bryan had some cause for vengeance: Hubert had destroyed his father. Complicated issue, fathers and sons; Roland closed his eyes and willed the images out of his mind. Tiomu's men behind them, Lord Bryan's men lurking anywhere - and why not, it was his estate.

A good night's sleep, beyond New Pembrokeshire, preferably not out in the woods, would be a welcome luxury. Some place with few other travelers.

Eloise pressed her stallion on, cantering down the trail in semi-darkness, anxious to put New Pembrokeshire behind her. The moon wouldn't be so full as the nights past, making it imprudent to proceed in the dark.

"We're almost out," Roland said, relief and fatigue coloring his speech.

Eloise nodded and bit her lip, joy building to be free of this place.

"Wait-"

Eloise followed his gaze. "I see them," she said, deflated.

"And they us." He waved at the mounted figures. "We can't go around now."

"They could be travelers, like us," Eloise said hoping, wishing, praying.

"Could be," he looked at her, "probably not." His eyes were hard and dark, fear and fatigue masked.

"I'm your page, and we're off to Leinster," she started, feeling it necessary to recount their strategy, practice the ruse.

"Don't talk," he said as they continued up to the riders. "If they're just soldiers, fine. Knights might-," he paused, "remember me. Damn," he muttered.

Four knights dressed in the purple and white colors of Lord FitzGilbert of New Pembrokeshire hailed them. Eloise's heart pounded. She tried to smile as if she had nothing to hide.

"Ho, you're in a hurry so late," one of the knights said.

"We are, and you?" Roland asked, trying to change the subject. "Lord Bryan works you hard."

Eloise marveled how pleasantly Roland looked each man squarely in the eye, as if he had nothing to hide.

"Who're you?"

"Lord Roland," he said.

"Going to Ashbury, right?" a knight with a friendly voice acknowledged.

"I passed through on my way to Ashbury, some weeks past. I'm returning to Leinster."

"Thought you looked familiar. Where's the rest? Your companions?" the third knight asked, searching for additional riders.

"Ashbury-at-March, you have a fief. Back so soon?" queried the first knight. Eloise felt his suspicious gaze studying her. He lowered his head trying to see her downturned face more clearly. Why, she worried, would he be so interested in a mere page?

"My companions remain in Ashbury. I've returned to Leinster."

"Connacht not to your liking? A fighting man as you should feel right at home, stuck between Scragmuir and Dahlquin." The knights laughed.

"Who's the boy?" the first knight asked. "Catch him poaching, did you?" Eloise wished they had hidden the bird for just this reason, but Roland countered it was better to present the bird shamelessly than hide it. Reckless it now seemed as the headless evidence hung in shameful display.

"El," Roland sighed, nodding curtly towards her, "delivering him to High Lord FitzGilbert, as page. Then I'm back to Ashbury." He made no offer of a proper introduction.

Eloise nodded her head, keeping her eyes down. She was impressed that Roland didn't even address the accusation of poaching. It's not poaching while in the king's service, something they had both agreed on.

"How old are you, boy?" asked the knight with the friendly voice.

"Twelve, sir," she stammered.

"Twelve? You're a tall whelp," said the friendly one.

"That's old to start as a page," said the first.

"I served Lord Albert," she continued haltingly, lying as she went, "but he's decided to foster me elsewhere."

"So, he has."

The men chuckled.

"Roland, take a lesson, it isn't safe to be a man in Ashbury with all the in-fighting. That right, boy?"

Eyes still lowered, she nodded her head in agreement.

"Especially for Albert's bastards," the first knight added. "Wants you safe does old Albert?"

"Cuckhold," another knight said with a snort.

Eloise hung her head. This was terrible, to be part of such a foul and false accusation.

"So it is," said Roland, with a chuckle as well. "If you'll excuse us, we're off to Leinster. Come, El." Roland prepared to salute in leaving.

"Bah," said the first knight. "Come stay with the Lord. You can't make Leinster tonight."

As Eloise, and probably Roland, feared: an invitation. Lying came easily in battle with an enemy. This bordered on dishonorable. Eloise felt the sweat on her back.

"True," Roland said, "but we can get a few more miles. And may you have goodness for the generous offer." He urged Artoch forward.

"Nonsense to sleep out, when you have the hospitality of New Pembrokeshire," the knight with the friendly voice said, his voice turning stern. Eloise looked around gauging the terrain, in case they had to run. "And so long as you have helped yourself to the Lord's game, the least you could do is have the courtesy to bestow proper appreciation and gratitude."

Roland turned his eyes to glare at the knight, his head following. Eloise thought he gave a wry smile, or perhaps a smirk. Was he mad provoking Lord Bryan's men? She tried not to stare but needed to know when to react. Garth moved his feet nervously, sensing the distress Eloise was sending, to flee. Roland's expression seemed to soften, mayhap it wasn't a smirk after all, or mayhap she was wishing so hard that she tricked herself.

"The bird isn't from New Pembrokeshire, Sir," Roland said, dipping his head graciously. "But I would be lying if I said we brought it from Connacht."

"Oh, hang the bird," said one of the knights. "I'd like another chance at dice. You walked off with a pocket full of my hard-earned coins."

"Not me," Roland countered.

"Eh? Skinned him alive, I did. Want a chance to lose some more?" one of the other knights piped up.

"Play each other," Eloise blurted. "Obviously you don't need Lord Roland." Relieved to have the tempest regards the heron over, she was anxious to get out of New Pembrokeshire.

The men laughed again.

"I've lucky dice with me," the knight said, shaking his hand as if holding the dice.

"Let's play," urged the friendly one.

"Getting too dark. Come let's retire to the castle, Roland, El?" said the first knight, swinging his arm in grand invitation.

"Good sirs," Roland said, chuckling, rubbing his bristly cheek, "I can't afford to stay, dice isn't my game. It was Sedric who had the luck. With your will, on the way back, mayhap? Tonight, we must press on."

Nervously, Eloise cued Garth forward, as if following Roland's command.

"Good evening to you," Roland said, following her.

163

"I think lost love tugs at your heart. Leave someone behind in Leinster?" the knight with the friendly voice asked.

"Too many to count," Roland called back to raucous laughter.

"Or is it an angry man you flee?"

"Or woman?" one of knights shouted to them. "Maybe Connacht was too much to his liking."

Eloise could hear kissing noises: smooching, slurping and slapping noises, making her cheeks burn with embarrassment.

"Don't look back," Roland said to Eloise.

"And turn to salt? Let's ride," she answered. Every stride Garth executed took her farther away from Lord Bryan's clutches and closer to High Lord FitzGilbert, if that were indeed safer. She massaged her face feeling fear, fatigue and filth. Her heart still pounded from sidestepping disaster yet ached to know if Roland had a lady love waiting for him in Leinster. "Any of that true, back there?" she finally asked.

Roland took a long time before answering. Was he counting them up? How many were there? "Only the dice," he said.

She was quiet, unable to sort out her roiling emotions, as if all seven of the deadly sins had risen up within her. Certainly wrath, envy, pride and a hint of vanity. "How much farther?" she asked, returning to the urgency before her.

"When they're out of sight."

"How will I know if I don't look back?"

"I'll know."

She believed him.

FARM

Confusion, fright and fatigue plagued Eloise as she rode, further aggravating her weary Garth.

She glanced at Roland. Tall, commanding. He had acted smug back in New Pembrokeshire with Lord Bryan's men. But it was merely confident posturing. Fear had muddled her thinking. She had fear, and she acted with fear. *Never reveal your feelings*, her father's voice reprimanded her. And why had she not considered Roland might have any number of female attachments? She stole another glance at him, to find him impassively watching her. Their relationship had been so insular, existing first within the forced incarceration of the siege, then as two people, alone on the road, with a single mission: to warn High Lord FitzGilbert. Roland was from a world outside Connacht. Of course, he would have lady loves, wasn't that the term? She couldn't remember the words, only the idea, and she tensed again with confusion.

Garth pinned his ears and Eloise felt his back tense under her seat as he transitioned to a walk, jarring her to the present and the road before them. *Pay attention*, she commanded herself, stroking Garth's neck. Uncle Reggie's shield felt heavy as lead. Garth's ears were still back and he took a few more stiff strides before settling down as she continued to stroke his thick neck. Such a magnificent fellow, she thought, how had she let her mind wander so?

Garth lifted his head, ears fixed on the road before them.

"Horses sense something," Roland said. "Let's hope it's a friendly lodging."

"May such a blessing be upon us," she said, but it sounded like a sigh. Garth emitted a similar sound, only longer and louder, causing her and Roland to laugh.

Artoch bobbed his head in what could only be construed as adamant agreement.

Both horses seemed to pick up the pace, sensing shelter and food and rest. Soon Eloise could make out structures.

"Well, this looks promising," Roland said, approaching a stone hut with wood and thatched roof. She doubted Roland could stand up inside the small structure.

"God be with you!" he called to the man rushing towards them. Two boys joined the man and all three approached Roland warily.

"God be with you, sirs," the farmer said, bowing his head. Eloise noticed the older boy dragged his left foot.

"Good evening," Roland said. "I know the hour is late, past sundown. We're in need of lodging. And cooking." He looked at Eloise, and she held up the heron.

It was near dark, and the family was already settled in for the night. Eloise knew she, Roland and the horses were an intrusion to the regularity of this family's lives. They could ill afford the luxury of lamp light or candles for any length of time.

"If there's room in the barn," Roland continued, "that's satisfactory for the horses and us."

Eloise sighed, slumping in the saddle, for that was exactly what she hoped for. It seemed the farmer slumped as well, but his mouth gaped open.

"Barn? For horses?" the farmer asked. He shook his head. "Pig sty, chicken roost."

She and Roland both searched the grounds in the dim light, seeing only small stone and wood structures, huts, compost and the farmer's stone and thatch hut. Outside the hut were a fire circle, tripod and cauldron.

"Cook the bird," Roland said, voice rising slightly, "while we see to the horses."

With a nod from their father, the boys ran over to take the heron from Eloise, and she passed them the roots and greens from her saddle bag as well. Their eyes glowed in the summer twilight. The younger boy was missing all four front teeth, as children his age did.

"If you would, by your will," Eloise addressed the farmer.

Roland and the farmer stared at her. This wasn't Dahlquin. Still both men waited for her to finish.

"Would you have an extra pot to heat water?" she asked, watching the farmer shrivel. "If you have one," she added, unsure why this was such a burden. "I only need a hand full," and she held up her two hands, side by side to make a bowl.

"Heat some water," the farmer called to the boys.

Both boys turned and answered, "Heat water, Da."

"My Lord," she addressed Roland. His shoulders tightened, and he glared at her. "Might I inquire who our host is, and his lord?"

Roland sat back in the saddle. She waited for him to agree. So tired, all she wanted to do was get out of the saddle and prepare for sleep. *Still so much to do.* He nodded.

"Your name, by your will," she asked the farmer.

"Eoin," the farmer said.

"Who is your lord? Is the castle close?" As soon as she asked about the castle, she regretted it. They didn't wish to present themselves to any noblemen. Fatigue dulled her mind.

"Our Lord Bryan FitzGilbert. Castle is west as you came," he pointed, "Not too close." It was an amusing comment. *Not too close.*

"You are very helpful, and this is a tidy farm. Your lord should be well pleased with you," she added.

"My Lord," she addressed Roland, "this is Eoin of New Pembrokeshire." Then to Eoin, "I'm El, and this is Lord Roland," she said, holding her hand out, palm up towards Roland. She concluded with a tip of her head. If Roland wished to say more, he could.

"May you have goodness," Roland said. His voice was gruff, but he nodded his head to Eoin and her.

"Let's untack the horses and stow the gear here, then hobble them near the green," Roland said, dismounting.

Riding all day was one thing, but when Eloise dismounted, her legs were stiff and weak. As Roland spoke with Eoin about sleeping arrangements, she unfastened Artoch's saddle.

"Good boy," she murmured. "Goodness upon you for your hard service this day." Garth crowded in. "Back," she said firmly, shaking an elbow at him as she reached up for the heavy saddle. "Back."

"Step," Roland said.

Artoch swung his hip at Roland's touch and the heavy saddle slid from his back. Eloise collapsed under the shifting weight. Her arrows clattered and she fell, awkwardly cradled in the shield on her back.

"What happened?" Roland growled, lifting the saddle.

Eloise rolled out of the shield and touched her lip with the back of her hand. It bled slightly. Besides a cut lip, she felt tightness in her chest and such longing for her mother. Roland was scowling at her.

"Shame upon me, my Lord, seems great fatigue is upon me." Eloise had embarrassment on top of everything else. Dahlquin should be strong, she remembered as she clambered to her feet.

"Let me, from now on," he said irritably as he laid the saddle down.

"Take his head, I'll get the saddle," Roland instructed as they moved to Garth.

"I always do Garth," she protested.

"Arguing with me?" he barked.

Eloise looked at him, startled by his anger. His eyes were bloodshot, with dark crescents beneath emphasizing his irritability. He had removed his armored gauntlets and they were tucked in his stout leather girdle. Though his hands were unclenched, she knew they would make tremendous fists. Mayhap he was as tired of this facade as she. Eloise shook her head. She didn't wish to argue with him.

"Eh?" he asked, glaring at her as he lifted her saddle off.

"I am not, Sire."

"Good," he said, laying her saddle next to his. Roland started rubbing his horse down before checking the hooves. She did the same to Garth. "I was a squire once, myself," he reminded her. This time he grimaced, but his eyes softened, and the right side of his mouth twitched up. An attempted smile, she wondered? Eloise sighed, finding it difficult to smile herself. They walked the horses to a cistern, hobbled them, then removed their bridles.

Garth and Artoch will benefit from a good rest, Eloise thought. She missed the company of Beast and Dragon. She had never travelled far without dogs, and once again realized how much she underestimated the security they provided her. Better company than hounds hardly existed. And hers were dead. Garth sighed, pulling Eloise from her grief. He followed Artoch's lead. dropping to his front knees then to his side to roll. She was thankful for Artoch's company, too. Some destriers were dangerous; a timid war-horse would never do. But Artoch was respectful and responsive and she was fond of him. As if reading her mind, Artoch ambled over to her, lowering his dirt-strewn head. Grateful for his approach, she scratched around his ears. Not to be left out, Garth poked his big grey muzzle in as well and Eloise stroked and scratched each horse around the eyes, the base of the ears and under their throats, cooing kindnesses to each.

"Back to cooking," Roland said, inclining his head toward the dwelling.

Eloise went to the cistern, dunked her hands and scooped a handful of water towards her filthy face.

"Leave it," Roland said.

Still bent over the cistern, water escaping through her clasped hands, Eloise looked up at Roland, who only shook his head. She glanced down at her wet, empty hands. *Was it too much to expect? To splash away the dirt and sweat from the day's travails, the blood on her lip, to revive herself before a meal and a night's slumber?* Her hands were trembling. *With indecision? Frustration? Pride?* Too tired to sort out her feelings, she dipped her hands again, rubbed them vigorously, stood and shook them dry as she went with Roland.

She glowered at Roland, but he didn't look at her as they walked in silence to the dwelling. Not silence; they didn't speak, but Roland's spurs *chinked* with each large step.

The boys had made quick work of plucking the heron and already the bird was sectioned and stewing. A woman stood over the cauldron stirring. A hut this size in Dahlquin would support a much larger family or community. Where were the rest? Tending a flock? Farmers didn't serve scutage. Roland scanned the surrounds intently. Mayhap he was thinking as she - where was everyone?

There was something very suspicious about these people. Betraying her might bring a tidy benefit for them, and it roused her from the grinding fatigue she felt leaving the horses. At a distance she could pass for a youth, but not in such tight proximity around the fire, so she kept her head down, hoping no one looked too closely in the dim light. The filth of the miles aided her disguise. *Leave it.* Grudgingly she had to admit Roland was right.

The farmer jumped up and indicated Roland take his stool by the fire. Roland nodded.

The aroma of the cooking bird invaded Eloise's senses. As if to honor the upcoming feast her stomach squeaked and gurgled. Embarrassed to have all eyes upon her, she clamped one hand to her mouth and the other on her offending belly.

"I agree," Roland quipped, taking the farmer's stool by the cooking fire. He inhaled deeply, momentarily closing his eyes, also savoring the hearty aroma.

"Let me start again," Roland said, looking at Eoin, then to the family. "My name is Roland, from Ashbury-at-March. That is Connacht, well west of here. This is El. We're weary travelers bound for Leinster. We'll be gone with morning's light. I wish goodness upon you for this hospitality. We have much gratitude."

The farmer, his wife and the boys all stared at Roland a good long moment. The wife was first to turn away, back to the steaming cauldron and pot before her.

"Eoin," the farmer said. "Small Eoin, Red," indicating the boys. "Duckling," nodding towards his wife.

Eloise was still blushing as Duckling put a cup of steaming broth into Roland's hands, then hers. Duckling was a metaphor in song and poetry for a woman's most intimate anatomy. Was that her real name, Eloise wondered?

"May you have goodness," she said holding the cup to her mouth, letting the steam bathe her filthy face, the moist aroma filling her nostrils, expanding her lungs. Her mouth watered with anticipated nourishment.

"Eoin," Roland said, "By your will and mine, join us."

Wide eyed, Eoin stared.

"Share," Roland said holding his cup up to the stunned farmer. Then he nodded at the confused wife, Duckling. "We haven't money," Roland added shaking his head. "I can't pay for the lodging or peat. But I can share."

The boys giggled and squirmed, unbelievable joy written on their grubby faces.

Once the heron chunks were tender, Duckling ladled the stew into Roland's and Eloise's empty cups, and then into cups for her family.

When she brought out stale bread, Roland soaked his in the broth. Eloise set hers in her lap.

Eoin shook his head, declining for him and the boys. "Morning will bring hungry bellies, save it," he muttered, mouth full of heron stew.

Just what Eloise was thinking: this dry bread would go a long way come morning, unless the rats got to it while she slept. Oh how good it would be soaked in the broth as Roland was doing. Hot and soggy and delicious, the bread was better than she imagined. Let the rats wake to hunger.

Done eating, Eloise went to the hearth.

"Water's nice and hot," Eloise commented, standing to move it from the embers. "I need a towel, or rag, wool or linen scraps. About this big," she said, holding her hands up and about shoulder width.

Duckling jumped up, eyes blinking, thinking hard.

"Just to wet, I won't keep it," she said. "A tunic, scarf? It may be dry by morning. And a spot of grease," she added, knowing lotion was an unlikely luxury here.

Duckling hesitantly produced another apron, stained and holey, but not entirely filthy.

"Blessings upon us both!" Eloise said, removing her dagger from her calf sheath. "Two aprons! Good fortune."

Duckling nearly choked, sucking in her breath, hands nervously wiping down the front of her own stained, wet apron.

Squatting, Eloise dunked half the apron in the steaming water. using a corner to wipe down her dagger, wondering why her compliment caused such distress. Was the apron stolen? Had its owner recently died? She looked up and realized that everyone was studying her. Roland too. She set her dagger down. Then she wrapped the steaming wet apron in the dry half, equilibrating the heat and damp in rapid movement so she didn't scald her hands.

"Lord Roland," she started, "the days have been hard fought, and the miles long." She walked to him with the steaming apron. "Put your head back," she said.

Roland gave her a wary look.

"You, Sir, are in need of a shave."

"You're too young to shave, what do you know of it?" Roland asked with jest and concern in his voice.

170

"I shave my father all the time," she answered.

"I've seen your father, he's bald," said Roland covering his hair with his hands, mimicking a look of fear.

The family members giggled sheepishly, then more fully when Roland joined in with them. It seemed the family had begun to relax a little more, finally accepting that she and Roland were not a threat to them. "Honesty, I have skill," she said encouragingly.

"And pleasure is upon me bearded. Boyhood behind me."

"Comfort upon you," she said. "Just this once, I've never seen your face," she whispered.

Again, Roland stared, but she thought he was relenting. "Head back," she said, gently applying the steaming apron to his face, patting it to his skin and his bristly beard.

Roland stiffened in anticipation of being burned. His worry lines eased; gratitude was upon Eloise when she felt him relax in her hands. She continued to massage his face under the hot apron. Once cool, she removed the apron.

At first Roland kept his eyes tightly shut. Eloise was uncomfortably close and had a dagger in her hand. Shaving was never particularly fun or comfortable, but she did have a steady hand, gentle, too. He peered through the slits of his eyelids to watch her. With a mere trace of grease from the tub near the hearth, her sharp dagger moved firmly along his left cheek. Without hesitation, she started right in front of his left ear and systematically took strokes one after the other to remove his black beard.

"Relax," she said without taking her eyes off his cheek. She wiped the blade on a corner of the apron and continued. Smoothly over the contour of his cheekbone then slowly down to his chin, stopping just above the jawbone. Roland kept his left eye shut tight as she inched mercilessly close under it. From his vantage point the blade seemed rather long for the task at hand.

"Stick your tongue under your lip, here," she instructed, delicately dabbing the upper corner between his lip and nose. This created a much flatter surface for safety and thoroughness.

"May goodness be upon you, my Lord." She continued ever so carefully around his lips, under the bridge of his nose. This was getting more intimate than Roland expected and involuntarily he stiffened again. With a confident grip, she gently moved his head slightly up or down, right or left, enhancing her view in the limited hearth light.

So close. He felt her breath on the sensitive areas of his face. The flesh on his ears tingled. Next his eyelids. The cold of the blade scraping against his flesh was unsettling. He felt vulnerable. The warm, titillating sensation of her breath caressing his head confused his senses. A tingle started at the base of his skull and shot down his spine. Without warning he shuddered like a dog shaking off water.

"That was close," his barber replied, still intent on her work. "Move your tongue here. With your gracious will," she added.

Her features were tight with concentration as she carefully started on his jaw. This was always difficult, little matter who did the shaving. A nick and a pinch. Roland tried not to flinch. A little more, just a little more. He let out a sigh of relief when she finished. But then she repeated the procedure, getting the places showing stubborn stubble.

Eloise looked at him, his cheeks, his nose, and his lips. Under the nose and around the side of the mouth were always difficult. The skin was pliable and soft. The cheeks were easy, and under the chin.

Negotiating the Adam's apple was also treacherous territory. "Try not to swallow," Eloise said, before taking a deep breath and renewing her task.

Roland held his breath without realizing it. He shut his eyes so tightly they formed tears. His chest was pounding to match the surge in his groin. Then it was too much. He grabbed her wrist pulling her hand and the blade away.

"Did I hurt you?" Eloise asked in alarm, turning her attention back to his throat, looking for blood. Nothing. Still he held her wrist, so she continued to search.

"You didn't cut me, *yet,*" he commented. "Sorry," he said, falling back on English. "Take my excuse, and blessing upon you," She hadn't cut him, and he was embarrassed he had lost his nerve. What happened, he wondered? She was no threat, the shave had been going well. Brewing emotions inside him needed an outlet. He had to break the physical bond between them, if only for a moment. He needed to breathe.

"I'm almost done, I promise," she said looking him in the eye. She smiled broadly, and then touched her fat lip. *It must hurt,* Roland smiled back as best he could with a blade about to return to his throat. They shared the smile for a few seconds.

Roland watched as Eloise seemed to wilt. Her smile quavered as her trembling lips came together. No amount of dirt could mask the brilliant flush that erupted from her cheeks and spread across her face. She swallowed then looked away. Lowering her hand with the dagger, she took a deep breath. Eyes closed she took another deep breath. He watched her press her hand and the dagger hard to her heart, as if suppressing a flutter. Or a pounding. She sucked in her bottom lip, opened her eyes and with a determined breath lifted her hands to continue the shave but her hands were shaking.

"I don't understand," she murmured, wiping the dagger on the cloth before putting it in her teeth, then wiping her sweaty palms repeatedly on her surcoat. "I've had much practice," she mumbled before removing the dagger from her teeth. "Easy work, under the chin," she added, her attention turned to his neck.

Tilting his head back, Roland tried to convey ease and trust, allowing Eloise to come close again.

With only a few nicks and cuts, she was finished. It was a shave like no other, and he felt renewed. He sensed everyone watching, waiting for his verdict. Enjoying the suspense, he continued to examine his skin, feeling the tension build. Peeking out of the corner of his eye, he watched to see if Eloise was anxious. She had started to clean her dagger, but now stood as transfixed as the farmer's family, staring as he gently massaged his face in utter absorption. It pleased him to see her concern, to think her heart might flutter to match his own. *What is she doing to me? God's blood, I sound like a fucking troubadour. By your will, take my excuse,* he thought, apologizing in Irish for his profanity in his fluttering heart. Tension suitably built, he lowered his hands with great care and looked around at all the faces of the farmer's family and finally at his page.

"You missed a spot, start over," he said.

"By your command, my Lord," Eloise said with a quaver in her voice. He observed her tentative steps, waiting as she bent over his face. Again, she was close, met his eyes and he surprised her with a wink and large smile.

Eloise grinned, sucked in her fat lip then narrowed her eyes, realizing she was being teased.

"It's quite satisfactory, mayhap the best shave I've ever had outside a-" he caught himself before he said something inappropriate.

"Outside a where?" Eloise asked, her voice a bit shrill.

Roland shook his head, saying nothing. The dying fire glowed.

Eloise shook a reprimanding finger at him.

Duckling spread the damp apron to dry by the hearth. Eoin ordered the yawning boys to bed.

"With your will, take my excuse, my Lord," Eloise said, dipping her head. "Might I take a moment, the need is upon me," she paused. "To check the horses."

"Indeed," Roland acknowledged, knowing she needed to relieve herself, but would check the horses as well.

She nodded and strode off, vanishing silently into the gloaming.

"Oh! Must tell Branagan, our guests are sleeping here and there will be horses about," Eoin said, clambering up from the bench the family had shared.

Eoin startled, stood still in his tracks. Roland turned expecting to see Eloise. Instead he saw dark figures, armed with pitch forks, clubs and scythes encircling them. Roland stood slowly, straining to see the men, count their numbers. Rather than hard-working farmers, bent by generations of labor and servitude, Roland faced a bulwark of well-armed belligerence. He let his breath out slowly, his taut fingers yearning to reach for *El Muerte Rojo,* his sword. That would be too aggressive. Hostile.

"Eoin, the hour is late. Are you safe?" a man asked. He was short, and slightly built, but his voice was a croaking, deep bass. As with Eoin's speech, Roland found their dialect difficult to understand.

"Branagan," Eoin said, "I was just coming to you."

"Who is this? What goes on?"

"Didn't my children tell you?" Eoin asked. "A knight and servant, two horses," Eoin added quickly.

"Smells like cooking," another man grumbled.

Roland waited for the conversation to resume. He couldn't see the farmers' faces but could read their posture and their arms. Farm implements turned to weapons. He had been trained to see the use of such tools as weapons. He was a warrior. They were farmers. *Focus.* There was movement, shifting of weight. Some of the farmers were impatient too. *Fuck. Where was Eloise?*

"We were cooking," Eoin said, "they brought a heron, some greens to cook."

"I only see one man," the short man said. He was scant enough, and the scythe he held gave him the appearance of death come to reap. Eloise was still out there, somewhere.

"The boy is checking-"

"Roland! Lord Roland," Eloise shrieked.

"Mother of God," someone called.

The farmers' circle of menace broke with howls and grunts as a pale horse and rider cantered in.

"Ah, may you all have goodness," she said, looking around as the farmers gave her, or rather Garth, a wide passage. The horse was naked. Rather, Garth had no bridle or saddle, only an agitated rider. "Someone is out there," she continued. "Maybe to steal the horses. Or your-" she glanced about the assembled farmers. "I heard someone," she said directly to Roland.

Roland drew his sword and dagger.

"What?" someone asked.

"Here?" another questioned.

"I heard someone," Eloise said over the questioning.

Artoch whinnied for his friend. Roland could hear him moving as quickly as his hobbles would allow. Then quiet, apparently, Artoch decided Garth wasn't so far and the eating was too good to leave.

"Where?"

"I hear nothing."

"Quiet," Roland said, hearing the deep bass of the short farmer along with his own.

"Out there," she said pointing in the direction she had just come.

"Shh," Roland said, walking up to her and Garth, placing the hand with the dagger on her thigh. "Ho," he murmured to both, scanning the dim horizon.

"God be with you," the short man called, "who is there?"

Garth shook his head and snorted. Eloise stroked his neck. "Ho, good boy," she murmured, encouraging the horse to stand quietly. He lifted his tail and dropped a few stud poops.

"Who is there?" the farmer called again. "Answer me."

Roland didn't think Eloise was one to spook easily.

"If the boy says he heard someone, I believe him," Roland said, calculating the situation. New horses might call out. Artoch and Garth were not presenting as if horses were approaching. Someone afoot; were it a raid, there was nothing to be gained in that field, the stock was in roost or sty. Must be a family member.

"Come forward," the farmer demanded. "Without harm."

"Probably one of the children, wanting to see the horses," another farmer added, to chuckles and grumbles.

"A child," Eoin said with a groan. "Gerroc," he sighed. Then, "Gerroc!" he shouted.

Duckling protested, then shook her head, wringing her hands.

Weak, crying voices stirred from the summer twilight.

"Come forward, girls. Sooner the better. We ache with tired," the short farmer said.

Roland let his breath out as the rest of the men exhaled and lowered their tools. Three girls came trembling forward, maybe fourteen to ten years of age.

Despite the rough dialect, Roland heard a slew of profanity, shocking and humorous at once. He glanced at Eloise, hoping she couldn't understand it. She was watching Duckling, weeping and running to her girls.

Roland felt all eyes on him.

Once again, he and Eloise were the source of threat. *Curse these farmers and their prying daughters. Farmer's daughters.* Those girls were children. *Did he appear such a letch? Did Eloise?* Bleeding saints, he was heart-pounding, blood-rushing tired. Fatigue and anger permeated his senses.

"My page and I are," *no profanity* he reminded himself, "tired from long miles and little food. Too f-frighteningly tried to raise a hand or cock against any of your children." He was starting to shake as the battle-ready episode fell away. "Eoin, by your will, with your leave, and yours, Master Farmer," Roland growled, for surely this short man was in charge. "El and I would like to rest - though sleep may elude me some time now. Does that sound good?"

Given the pause before answering, Roland assumed the farmers were struggling with his dialect as well. He still had his weapons drawn; he placed sword to scabbard and sheathed the dagger. Surely it was over.

"My Lord?" Eloise asked.

"Shh," he said, power was in silence - although he longed to order these insolent farmers to their beds. *God's blood.*

"That is good," the Master Farmer said. "All of us, to our beds."

Some of the men hurried, others walked and mumbled among themselves.

"Eoin, your girls should be safe enough, eh," and the Master Farmer, too turned and walked away with an escort of three.

The family retreated together to their hut; Roland and Eloise to their places in the dirt, under an oil-cloth canopy.

Before Christ and the Virgin Mary he was exhausted. The encounter had charged his system. The fear, his vulnerability, the lesson learned: farmers were dangerous, and he would never be so arrogant again. It was hard to relax and find sleep. Chain mail wasn't designed for pleasant slumber; it was cold and rough and unforgiving.

That, and the proximity of the sleeping Maid Eloise. *You are a lustful dog,* he reminded himself. *Don't think about her, she's just a page, remember, a young boy of twelve.* It was useless. Despite that terribly unflattering costume, he could picture her without any of it. The blood surged effortlessly to his groin. His cock strained against his braises, engorged and pleading with his conscience for relief. It had been some time, at Scragmuir, since he'd lain with a woman, and thoughts of Eloise scorched his mind. Masturbation, so close to a pious, Christian maid such as Eloise? It was sinful enough to take one's pleasure alone, but in the sleeping maid's presence...nay. He groaned painfully and rolled on his side. This was all her fault.

Fitful sleep eventually came to Roland. Dreams of lust and unfulfilled sex haunted him. Visions of farmers' daughters, sometimes dressed as pages, wove through his mind. Would he have sex with all of them? Perhaps in a stable, a loft, in a garden? Nay, not with any of them, although in his dream they were willing. Eloise was naked and inviting him into a bathhouse to shave him, but she really didn't plan to shave him he knew. Her father was there, and he got a shave. Roland was waiting behind a curtain, feeling guilty as sin, watching Eloise shave her father. Only she wasn't naked now, only Roland with his sinful vision could see her naked. And it wasn't a public bathhouse where people engaged in prostitution. Somewhere else, somewhere clean and pure.

DAY FIVE OF THE SIEGE, 12th of June

He woke painfully from his nonsense dream, with the warmth of Eloise curled up next to him. It was cold, and she must have been drawn to his warmth despite the chain mail. She twitched once, then twice and he felt the slump of her body weight as she returned to deep sleep next to him. Roland lay there, motionless. The agony and the ecstasy: the ecstasy of having Eloise so close, to feel her sleeping soundly in the security he provided her. Trusting, loving, soft and gentle. Surely, she felt something for him. He had found it in her eyes this evening. And then the agony. It seemed as if every fiber in his body was longing to embrace Eloise and make love to her without end. How at odds they were, his cock and his conscience. Think of something else, think of Sir Reginald's haggard, ghostly countenance haunting you from the burning depths of Hell. Now there was a sobering thought. He tried to conjure his most nightmarish visions of the suffering and punishments bestowed in Hell: perpetual flames, plagues, blistering flesh, which grew back only to burn off again, anything to distract his mind from the relentless demands of his cock. He was hot. Hot with lust, passion and love. Was this the same heat that would await him in Hell?

As the night sky slowly went from dark to subtle pink on the horizon, a new day promised to begin. Roland got up gently, so as not to wake Eloise. Maybe the new day would give him some relief from his hellish night. The air was still. As the horizon brightened, birds raised their joyous praise to the sun. Rabbits were barely visible at the edges of the cultivated fields. Their time was ending, and the next shift would resume their daily rituals and activities.

The family in the farmhouse began to stir. The fire was stoked in preparation to break fast. The farmer hastily exited the door and Roland nodded in his direction. Roland went for the horses.

Eloise slept dreamlessly on the ground. Garth bent his great head next to her sleeping form, smelled and blew out a large whiff of air. He nudged her with his muzzle. His whiskers tickled her nose and cheek and she brushed at her face. Not getting the response he wanted, he nudged her more aggressively and she waved her arm trying to send him away.

"Stop" she murmured, barely audible.

That was enough, Garth nickered into her face. Without opening her eyes, she grabbed at her horse.

"Quiet, you great looby, it's the middle of night," she said in a loud whisper. Garth was playfully dodging her hands with his muzzle and blowing out his nostrils.

"Quiet, you'll wake the master," and she looked around to make sure Roland had not yet been disturbed. She could see fairly well, and he wasn't anywhere to be found. Garth lifted his head and shook himself from head to tail.

Eloise was disoriented for a moment. Instead of darkness, she found light. Artoch was tacked up and Roland was smiling down at her.

"Good morn to you, sleepy one," he said.

Was that a devilish grin he had, she wondered?

Eloise scrambled to her feet, rubbing her eyes. Her head throbbed with the sudden change from sound sleep to standing.

"Shame upon me," she stammered. "By your will, I must do that," she continued, still rubbing her eyes and staggering in the morning light. "Sorrow upon me, my Lord. I will tack Garth."

178

"Relax," he said, imitating her instructions to him while shaving last evening. That seemed a long time ago after the events of the night. "Lameness isn't upon me, you know." He gave Artoch some long strokes along his thick neck. The black destrier stood with one hind leg cocked, eyes half closed. Artoch wasn't a pet, but he was a valued partner.

Time to start another long day on the road to Gerald FitzGilbert. With dawn's first light the siege would rage on. If it still raged at all. *Don't think of that.* If Dahlquin fell, she would know.

DAHLQUIN CASTLE, DAY FIVE OF THE SIEGE, 12ᵗʰ of June

Aine and Hubert took a few moments to connect in her bedchamber. Her chamber alone had gone unmolested the nights before. Lord and Lady were infinitely busy with the endless and horrific demands of their castle under siege. Aine longed to re-establish some sense of normalcy and routine. All rhythms of castle life were dictated by military need. The great kitchens and ovens were again working. Old Muireann rose to the occasion, directing the bakers and oven stokers. It was by her orders that poultry was slaughtered, or salted beef or fish served. Thus, Aine was free to minister to the injured and direct the caregivers. Clearing the cinders or sweeping the floors now fell to cooks and bakers. Gone were the apprentices and child labor forces. Boys and girls alike were charged with supporting the military lines of defense. They ran to deliver fresh arrows and bolts to the bowmen. Bags and pitchers of water, ale and wine were carried to the thirsty defenders along the ramparts and in the towers. Fuel was in constant demand to maintain the fires and the hazardous cauldrons of hot oil or boiling water, which were kept ready to pour upon the invaders.

Hubert held his wife tightly. She sobbed quietly in his arms. Dilis danced at their feet, vying for his mistress' attention, while Hubert's great hounds investigated the chamber, sniffing and probing.

"Terrible thing, Love, such sorrow upon me," he said to her gently.

"Five children," she sighed, "and a good man."

U'Neill's mangonel had a successful hit upon the castle. A large stone crashed through one of the fire stations. It was such hazardous work, keeping the fires and oil. The cauldron cracked and tipped, spewing the boiling contents all over the children and man with them. As the oil splashed out, the fire spread wildly with it. Water was useless against such a blaze. It was contained with dirt and left to burn itself out on the stone walk. Fortune upon them, it didn't spread to the wooden scaffolding or buildings below.

"Tragic what happened to the children." She wept.

"Terrible," he comforted her again. "Nothing to be done, it happened. Tiomu will pay. I promise you that." Tiomoid U'Neill and his men would pay dearly for this treasonous attack, in this life and the next. Whether by Hubert's hand or God's, justice would be done. "I bring news, horrific and hopeful."

"News, by your will," Aine said. She struggled to stifle the sobs. Time to be strong, time to move on.

Hubert paused, unable to speak, his mouth was paralyzed by the sorrowful words he could not yet form. The image of his beloved brother, staked out like a martyred saint turned to carrion.

"By your will, try and be strong - for me," he asked, his eyes filling with tears. Tears of biblical proportion would one day be shed, when Tiomu was terminated.

Aine nodded, her own red eyes again filling with a flood of tears.

"As we suspected, Reggie is dead. Tiomu has committed another act of unforgivable-" he paused, there wasn't a word. "His and two other bodies are staked out. War trophies. "Eloise and Roland have escaped, confidence upon me, it's true," he said.

"Oh, Hubert!" she exclaimed. He read such hope in her green eyes. Still she ignored the little dog dancing on his hind legs at her hem.

"Tiomu claims all three of our men were killed. Three *men*," he emphasized again. Aine looked puzzled. "He's lying. If he'd taken or killed Ellie, he'd be bragging. They got away. He hasn't an idea what he's lost," Hubert said.

"I see," Aine agreed. Eloise would be a prize indeed, alive or dead. If they had her, he would flaunt it before all. Aine crossed herself twice and gave a prayer of thanks. She cried anew, but with tears of gratitude. Worry over Eloise was foremost on both their minds. Without their daughter…without question, they still had purpose. They were Dahlquin. Dahlquin would stand. This was their duty. *Eloise.*

"FitzGilbert will know. How are the food stores?" he changed the topic back to their current dilemma.

"Lean, it's the growing season now." How far did Tiomu's assault extend? All depended on the livestock and game in this impoverished time. Pantries were near empty after the long winter, crops were not yet mature nor harvested. Fields lay fallow and untended. Hunting couldn't be done, and all the while, Tiomoid and his men devoured the countryside. "Muireann, Uilliam and I have reviewed the pantries. It's noted below." Everything was documented in ledgers and kept by the Seanascal and stewards. "By memory, with starvation rations, four or five months."

"Barring accidents or contamination," he added.

"Things change. But now, we can manage. It's herbs and medicines we lack." They had already depleted most of their stores of such necessary items. "Each day I strip what leaves and shoots I find in the garden. But little remains. Prayers we have in abundance. I think God will understand that we offer prayers and devotions through the assorted fires we keep ablaze and save the candles for the sick and dying."

Hubert hugged his wife again. "So pious and practical you are. Such patience, for me and-," he didn't finish. His eyes teared. He squeezed them shut and kissed the top of Aine's head. She hugged him all the tighter. Dilis jumped on her bed, hoping to get her attention by elevating himself. His little pink tongue dangled.

"I miss her too," she consoled. Aine would have said more, but to utter the words, even Eloise's name would untether her fear and dread for their daughter's unknown fate. Aine knew she would be overcome and unable to fulfill her duty. She must not falter. She dare not mention Eloise or Reggie. *Hubert must be sheltered from these feelings or he would be unable to protect and serve Dahlquin.*

"How do you know?" Hubert murmured. "Oft seems you read my mind."

"And you mine," Aine murmured back as Hubert scooped up the little dog and handed it over to Aine. Aine took Dilis in one arm. She continued to hold Hubert with the other. Dilis tried to lick both faces while held in the embrace.

181

Hubert kissed Aine on her forehead, her nose and then so tenderly on her lips. They lingered there together, eyes closed, enjoying the bond. Maybe tonight they could be together, mayhap.

Hand on hand they returned below stairs. Hubert with hounds in tow, was off to the Great Hall to check on the status of his men, Aine to the infirmary. He kissed the back of her hand in farewell as they separated. In turn, she took his calloused sword hand, with finger joints thick and gnarled. How many times had she relocated or set his mighty fingers? She lifted the beloved hand to her lips and open-mouthed, kissed his palm. *Custos*. Familiar fingers closed gently on her face. Aine could barely draw breath.

She wiped grateful tears from her eyes as she left for the infirmary. Again and again she thanked God for granting her such a noble husband, and prayed for his renewed strength and vigor to see them through this terrible trial. Dahlquin would prevail, God would be their witness.

Hubert watched his wife's retreating figure. Lifting his hand to wave, instead he pressed his palm, the palm his good wife had just kissed, to his own face, inhaling deeply, praying he might yet retain her presence.

"My Lord," Ulliam said, stroking the hounds. "My apologies to intrude, Sire."

"What news?" Hubert called to Ulliam. It was time for an update.

"News has not changed. One mangonel, and lucky they are," Ulliam conceded. All of Dahlquin suffered the endless battering to castle and flesh, from a wood and sinew beast that hurled rocks and flaming carrion upon the defenders with wicked precision hour after hour. "They continue with the siege towers."

"Any more men? Or supplies?" Hubert asked pointedly, as he directed them to the armory.

"None, Sire, Ashbury stands," Ulliam added. Had Ashbury fallen, Tiomoid would have all his resources stacked against Dahlquin.

"Good man, Albert!" Hubert shouted in the direction of his neighbor a half day away in Ashbury. "And Scragmuir? Do they show their faces?"

"They do not. Mayhap they assist Ashbury. Mayhap they're holed up and hiding," Ulliam scoffed. "Scragmuir does not stand with Tiomoid U'Neill. Not yet."

"Nor does Tiomu fly the flag of Denmark or Norway. Speaks only for himself and his men. Thieving bastards!" Hubert exclaimed.

"Aren't we all," Ulliam concluded. "Aren't we all."

MEATH, ON THE ROAD TO FITZGILBERT, 12ᵗʰ of June

The second morning and again Roland and Eloise would conduct their own compulsory mass without benefit of priest or chapel. Unlike the previous day, they would break fast before breaking camp. Eloise knelt, held her wooden cross pendant and bowed her head. Roland kneeled close before her, startling her with his proximity.

"Heavenly Father," Roland started, bowing his head so it nearly rested on hers. *Good Lord she was short.* Her cap tickled his nose. "Jesus the Redeemer." He took both her hands in his, the cross pendant cradled within. Her breath came short and quick, but she didn't pull her hands away. Rather, she seemed to ease into him, and he clasped his fingers together encasing her hands with only the leather thong visible.

"We raise our voice in prayer and give thanks for another morning in service to you, Ireland and your people. I'm especially grateful for the meal we're about to receive." He gave Eloise's hands a squeeze. "Blessing and gratitude for the entertaining turn of events whereby the hungry farm boy's snared rabbit, stolen by the crafty fox, was outwitted by the sure-shot of my travel companion who would do a Welsh long bowman proud. Blessed be the Father, the Son and the Holy Ghost. Amen."

He lifted her hands to his lips, kissed them and then used them to make the sign of the cross. One time. Two times. Three times at which point he was holding Eloise up. Though she never took her gaze from his, she appeared to be melting into a heap at his knees.

"I must confess to my gluttony," he continued speaking directly to Eloise, not God. "I'm not easily sated. By flesh or wine." Her blue-grey eyes widened, but her gaze didn't waver. *God's eyes, what am I doing? Teasing her in the guise of a mass?* He exhaled and grinned. "Six boiled eggs, an onion and stale bread does not seem an equitable trade for a rabbit and fox."

He rested back on his heels, still holding firm to her hands, pulling her slightly towards him.

"If you wish to wait for the rabbit to be cooked, my Lord-" she spoke softly, swallowing hard.

With deliberate ease, he released his grip on her hands, and she, too, rested on her heels. "Same with the fox pelt. It will take hours we don't have."

"Let's break fast," he said reaching for the food and dividing it between them.

Eloise drew her eating knife and cut the onion in quarters. He watched her cringe as she scraped the rat-chewed edges off the bread. He divided the food in half.

"Sire, that is too much," she said as she placed an egg, most of her onion and half her biscuit back with his.

"It would please me more to see you eat. Now take it," he said, peeling his first egg. Eloise waited as he peeled a slice of onion and bit into his egg and the onion.

Eloise did the same. "Oh, it's still warm," she squealed, her eyes closed in delight as she enjoyed her first of the three eggs.

"If only someone had coughed up some ale," he said, "to wash this all down. Ah well," he added, not wanting to seem ungrateful. He felt a shudder, remembering the ferocity of the farmers the previous night, and his and Eloise's vulnerability. *Fucking helpless.*

"We're making incredible time to Leinster. I believe we'll cross the Bog of Allen this very day. Long, and open, without cover. And only the one bow between us," he commented.

"You think Tiomu's men will catch us on the Bog?" she asked. "That's terrifying."

"Well, I can't believe we've come so far, in what, two days? But if we can do it, so can they. Trading out for fresh mounts, maybe."

With every crumb ingested, they began their third day of riding. *Usually, it took a week or more to get from FitzGilbert's castle in Leinster to Dahlquin. They were easily more than halfway*, Roland calculated to himself. Eloise set a grueling pace, and only pride forced him to keep up without complaint. A taskmistress, that one, he thought watching her in the saddle. *What power did she wield upon the horses? They did not perish from exhaustion but continued on stronger every day.*

Dear sweet God in heaven, had it only been four days? His aching muscles told him it had been at least that long. Fighting his way into the castle, only to be engaged in a pitched battle well past sundown. A ridiculous escape. Jumping off a waterfall and nearly drowning or being crushed under the hooves of his horse. Riding throughout the night, cold, wet. Biggest fucking wolves in the world. What a turn of events this had been.

"Ho," she murmured, signaling with her arm. Roland saw fields in cultivation, workers in the distance.

"Treasure," she whispered, taking her bow and a handful of arrows.

He heard a ding, a squeal, another ding, a scud. He saw mud, fur and arrows. Eloise stroked Garth, cooing to her horse. Then she smiled at him, dismounted and collected three hares and her arrows. She blessed each hare, kissed all four arrows before returning them to her quiver.

Roland dismounted to help her gut the hares. *Bleeding Saints, who shoots hares with arrows?* Once again, they mounted and continued with another meal or barter on her saddle bags.

Eloise and Roland passed through some townships and villages, and large acres in cultivation. More travelers were on the roads; Eloise tried to remember when she had seen so much traffic. The jangle and clang of pots and kettles preceded the iron merchant. A richly dressed cleric on a fine white palfrey strode past, with his entourage, their heads held high, as if fearing they might behold a commoner, or, worse inhale the malodourous air surrounding the lesser beings of God's creation. Later five monks clad in their rough, brown robes walked by. One led a well-laden donkey. An elderly monk had a staff and limped briskly with the others. A fabric merchant sat on the bench of his wagon. Three children sat in the back, their bare feet dangling. "How much longer, Da?" one called out.

"Last year I saw my sister, Lady Arabella and her husband, Lord Reynald of South Cross," Roland said. ,

His comment brought her out of her observations.

"Another beautiful name," Eloise commented. "That and Ariana," she sighed.

"It is," he agreed. "And four nephews and nieces," he continued.

Nieces and nephews, wouldn't that be grand, Eloise reflected and her mind drifted to her family. She thought she heard Roland say something about wooden swords and she pictured herself with her father and Uncle Reggie teaching her swordplay and weaponry. This was vital knowledge for the lady of a manor during the frequent absences of her lord (whether father or husband). Knife play, however, is what they taught her in earnest. Hubert and Reginald drilled her in hand-to-hand combat with a dagger. From a young age, Eloise learned the vulnerable points to target, the same vital points her mother taught her to repair.

"Da," she had complained, "it's useless use against mail or tough leather."

"It's not a tournament you train for," her father said, thumping her head. "A man does not wear mail or leather over his eyes. If he does, he's little threat to you. Now pay attention." And another drill would commence.

"Da, you're too close."

"Close is when you're dangerous. You won't get a second chance, Ellie."

He shoved and tossed her around, getting her riled. She hated this game most of all. It seemed hopeless.

Instinctively she touched *Cara*, pressing the bow against her chest, knowing the security archery afforded her from a safer distance. This lesson had been twofold. She would always be smaller and weaker. But she had resources, she had weapons. Never stop looking for opportunities, her father and uncle instructed. *Think.* Eyes, nose, "cut his ballocks off, Ellie," Reggie had cheered once. "If he is man enough to show them, take them."

Startled from her memory, she glanced over at Roland. *Was he such a man? Would she be called upon to use a dagger on him?* Up until now, she had worried only about the perils behind her, and the dangers ahead. Roland had been neither of those. *Last night, that had been special, hadn't it? And at mass -* had she imagined that too? She tried to study him, without detection.

"Is hunger upon you?" he asked. "Wish to rest?"

"I have hunger, but," she stammered. "I don't wish to rest, God's goodness upon you, Lord. With God's and Mary's goodness, let's ride. Every minute is precious to me." Eloise pushed Garth on without looking back.

"The horses will need water and rest soon enough."

Each moment that passed was vital to the safety of Ireland. Eloise knew and believed Roland, too, felt it, like a black cloud that blocked all light and joy. For every mile they put behind them, more loomed ahead without end. Roland squeezed his shoulders back as if willing his tired muscles to relax, she thought, doing the same, but the oppressive burden remained. Neither this day nor their journey was over. The vast, unforgiving Bog of Allen, without protection or cover, still loomed.

"How is it you're not married at seventeen?" he asked.

She had to blink and clear her mind. Where had this question come from? "You know I was betrothed?" she asked, surely he knew that being from Leinster. "As if being married off at the moment of my birth, can you imagine such a thing?"

"It was a great honor. The firstborn of FitzGilbert of Leinster," Roland offered.

"We were babes," she tried to explain.

"You weren't thrown into the cradle with him!" Roland exclaimed. "It's unusual, though, and sounds as if the King wasn't consulted," he added, looking at her more pointedly. "Your parents entered a contract of marriage and title without the King's consent?"

"My Lord-," she said, wondering how he could be so uninformed. Well, he was from England after all, and Leinster was...not Connacht. Old Irish law prescribed that neither man nor woman be forced to marry against their will. This was a civilized and Christian view, crudely overlooked by avaricious kingdoms. "Estate and title," she said with a dismissive shrug. "What if I didn't want to marry him, what if he was awful?" she asked with a frown. Didn't Roland see the damage in this? She sighed. "How cruel of me to talk so of the deceased," she added, for surely it would bring bad fortune. She crossed herself and so did Roland. "Tragically, he died. Oh, my Lord, were you here then, in Ireland?" She couldn't do the math fast enough. He arrived at fourteen, but when was that?

"I was still in England."

"I was four years old when Sebastian died in the Year of Our Lord 1211," she added to help with a timeline. "I hadn't the maturity or concept to grasp what had happened, only that a playmate had died. We were betrothed and then he was dead. Four years old and a widow. Rumours of heresy and Satan ran rampant. The Lady Aine and her devil spawn were to blame. God would not suffer a heretic on the throne." Eloise put a hand over her mouth. She had revealed too much, surely, such painful history, and her own internal fears. Still she felt compelled to say more. "Can you imagine how damaging that is?"

"I knew of the young Lord's death, of course. But I never considered-" Roland shook his head. "Such contracts at birth are damaging for many reasons."

"And of course, there was the unfortunate incident with Lord Elroth of New Pembrokeshire when I was five," she reminded him. Was there an end to the tragedy associated with Dahlquin, she wondered? Now this siege, this war. Why?

"Well, Lord Elroth. He has no one to blame but himself," Roland commented, "deceitful bastard," then remembering his company, "Shame upon me. I have such fucking fatigue." He sighed, rubbing his eyes. "Shame again. Damn it," he muttered, shaking his head. "I apologize. Fuck."

Eloise sniffed, suppressing laughter at Roland's tired rant. It seemed neither one of them could keep quiet.

His head fell back, eyes closed. "I'm just a foul-mouthed monkey's arse," he stammered, "when fatigue is upon me." He shook his head apologetically. "Forgive me, Maid- El," he corrected.

"May you have goodness, gratitude is upon me, Sir," Eloise smiled. "That's the kindest sentiment I've heard in days," she added, charmed by his effort to be courteous, like a knight in one of the Welsh tales she had heard in the nursery. Something Eleanor of Aquitaine would have expected. Not the tears, she commanded herself, a Dahlquin was above that. But she was not, and a tear or two needed brushing away.

"So, back to you, golden-tongued one," he shrugged. "After a harrowing childhood, what happened to the rest of your suitors? Surely your parents have given some thought to the future?" He pinched his lips shut with his gloved fingers, indicating he would remain silent.

"Oh, after about ten years of grieving, the living had to be dealt with." Eloise recounted for Roland some of the prospective spouses: "A pompous young U'Connor knight, a pompous hoary De Clare knight, a hoary widowed knight who had lost his estate, a striking young lord who stank of drink, a drinking lord who liked to strike, men from Wales even."

Roland laughed. "Give your father more credit than that," he added.

"I have fatigue myself," she sighed, realizing she was about to recite an unflattering incident. "I can't believe I'm sharing this with you," she said, leading into one of many arguments she'd had with her father. "After being presented to Lord Echri of Gwynedd, I found him *soft,* even effeminate. Do you know him?" she asked.

Roland pursed his lips, trying not to laugh. "Not sure."

"You would have me marry a eunuch!" I argued with my father. Uncle Reggie laughed uproariously at the truth of it.

She remembered her father's anger at her language and the tone. "*'Impertinent brat!'* he scolded. I was resistant to consider any of the prospects he had screened for possible marriage. I was fifteen and not interested." She paused before continuing. *"'He won't throw any colts.'* That's all anyone cares about, I whined. *'Eloise, watch your tongue,'* Uncle Reggie reprimanded, not laughing any more. So, I pulled my tongue with my fingers and tried to look at it." She winced, remembering Uncle Reggie's disapproving look. "Da grabbed my ear and twisted it. Pain upon me, I bit my tongue," she added.

Roland laughed at this revelation. "You told your father to his face you wouldn't marry a eunuch? You are impertinent. If he can't find a suitable eunuch, will he make one for you?"

"Haven't you been listening? Didn't I tell you the kinds of men my father was entertaining? Gelded or imbeciles, all of them."

"Your father wants a man he can control. You're the blood heir to Dahlquin. His *kingdom*," Roland said, studying her. His use of the word *kingdom* alarmed her, and his face was stern in concentration. Then his head tilted. "You need a husband to throw a colt or two," Roland said, his smirk returning. "And your complaint is?"

"Why am I wrong in this, why can't I have a choice? My father educates me, brings me up with love and happiness and then treats me like one of his brood mares." Tears welled in her eyes, but she wouldn't give in to them. "He has little care for me."

"Little care? He raised you to be *queen*," Roland rebuked, revealing his respect for her father and her father's noble efforts on behalf of an impertinent daughter.

The rebuke wasn't lost on Eloise. Nor his inflections. With a deep sigh of resignation, she cast her eyes around the surrounding horizon. Then she shot Roland a sideways glance. A reluctant smirk grew into a grin on his face. This was only half the story, why she was unmarried. Suspicion over her missing half-uncle, Lord Ruaidri, of years past hung over her head, as well as heresy and sorcery, of course.

"You're fortunate your father loves you as much as he loves his mares," Roland added, smiling.

"You are correct," she admitted, pondering the comment. "Most men don't love their wives or their mares." Tears continued to well in her eyes.

"Some do," he offered.

"Some," she answered, "my parents." She loved them so much, yet in this moment she felt such a surge of jealously. That is what she wanted: love, respect, tenderness. Yet they would deny her all they enjoyed in marriage to secure the estate. Frustration rose in her, and she tasted the bile of anger. She glanced at Roland, who was glaring at her. Why? What did he have to disapprove of?

"You have distress," Roland said, "grieving your parents. Sorrow upon me. Let's speak of something else," he offered, his voice gentle with concern.

"That's all there is, then," she contemplated. "Well. Queen of the herd," she concluded, snorting, then sighing. "So, what do *you* want?" she asked.

Roland looked at her, puzzled.

"You seem displeased."

Indeed. He was displeased. He was in a period of adjustment, and now peril. He was obligated to her safety, and the realm of his liege, High Lord Gerald FitzGilbert. It was an onerous responsibility, and none but his.

"Shame upon me. Rude of me," she said apologetically. Yet she watched him, hoping he would open up. *What would life hold for this fortunate lord? Surely he could make his own choices and decisions.* "I was just curious," she prompted again.

Roland looked at her. She gave a weak and hopeful grin. Talking did ease the long miles. They rode faster and felt the fatigue less.

"You are most unusual," he said. She was tired, dirty and relentless as she propelled her horse across the countryside.

"Unusual, well, I think I prefer impertinent," she said. With that she stepped up the pace. Garth swished his long silver tail with agitation. He had been ambling steadily for quite some time and resented the request for more.

"That too," he added, catching up to her.

Eloise let her fat lip protrude. She took a deep breath. "Well, we're both honest." She didn't apologize.

Roland laughed. She smiled, wryly, watching him laugh. He didn't laugh much. And that smile. She thought she would turn to pudding.

"How do you know I'm so honest?" he asked.

"You telling me you're not?"

"I guess we'll see," he answered.

"Hold me for ransom, then?" She maintained a calm voice, but her head stirred. She watched him intently. *Could she have been so wrong?* She touched her wooden cross feeling it under her tunic, and pictured the dagger on her calf.

"Impertinence upon you," he said for lack of anything better, ambling next to her again.

"Says you," she responded. Maybe he wasn't different from the rest, arrogant, domineering, entitled. Male.

"Did I say it was a bad thing?" he smiled, his dark brown eyes challenging her. "I've been called that myself more than once."

"Not recently."

"How do you know?"

"Who would dare say that to your face, Lord?"

"You would."

She smiled and her fat lip stung. She looked away, licking her lip with her tongue to ease the burn.

"God's blood, look at you," he teased, "trying to hide that smile."

Eloise could feel herself blushing.

"Curse it," he muttered. "I believe there are a lot of things you would tell me to my face," he said, then muttering low, "probably things I don't want to hear."

They stared at each other, ambling along, not speaking.

"We're honest enough," he said, breaking the silence, a gentle grin on his travel-worn face. The expression seemed so open. There was much she wanted to know, much she longed to share, but was unsure how. She was drawn him, desperately it seemed. *What to do?*

"So as one impertinent to another," she proceeded, "why such unhappiness?"

"Unhappiness?" he said, glancing over his shoulder warily.

She raised her eyebrows.

"Aside from Tiomu's men pursuing us," she said, watching him scan the route before them. "Or cutting cross country to cut us off," she added.

"Do you think that's possible?" he asked, looking all the harder with his hand above his brow to block the light. Eloise suspected he was worried and mocking her at the same time.

"Not practical to go around the Bog of Allen. It lays before us, vast, open, unprotected," he said, looking all the harder with his hand above his brow to block the light. "Nay," he muttered, "they must cut us down before we reach Leinster." There wasn't mockery in that.

"If not unhappy, you have displeasure, forlornness, imposition, mayhap?" she asked.

"Do I look any of those things?"

"You do," she admitted, "you reveal displeasure often enough. I wonder what a man as you have to plague his thoughts."

Roland looked at her as if bewildered.

"You have so much opportunity, so many choices," she elaborated.

"Choices, me?" he laughed.

"You don't? Truly, you can come and go as you choose. My Lord, you have a fief bestowed by Lord FitzGilbert, Ashbury-at-March. You'll have a steady income and a home." Still Roland stared at her; he didn't seem to see those choices. So, she continued, "You travel and move about as you desire, with no one to say 'stay home and behave.'"

Roland tried to conceal his laughter. "And you would appropriate armour and travel thus?"

"Not the armour." How she wished she could wear her new blue and gold surcoat now. She felt unusually unattractive. "But the desire to travel."

"You are traveling."

"You're not listening, or do you purposefully miss my meaning?" she sighed. "I wish I hadn't said anything." She urged Garth forward and upped the pace, and again Roland was in her dust.

"Wait, hold, I was impertinent," he offered, catching up, "it's just that maybe travel isn't what you thought. It's work and harsh conditions, such as these. We ride without rest, go without food."

"I would save my home," she glared at him. "We don't have the luxury to visit distant kinsfolk nor the far-off cathedral or sacred sites that would beckon me. That is the difference."

"Ah, a leisurely progression," he said. "There *is* a difference."

Eloise gave a nod.

"So, what are these choices and opportunities I have?" he asked. "What do you see that I don't?"

"What indeed," she frowned, but started again. "You're a titled lord with a fief and holdings. You're young, healthy," she paused a moment in embarrassment, "and handsome. Beautiful women probably throw themselves at your feet. You'll have your choice of a wife. Your father will not dictate to you."

Roland laughed. "You lead a rich fantasy life, El. Where do you get such ideas?"

She didn't laugh but studied him. He was a most fortunate man, confident, capable *and* humble. Would his virtues never end? Rich fantasy life, indeed: he was the making of fantasies. Now she smiled; a small huff of mirth escaped her.

"What a world!" Eloise observed as Roland again glanced behind them. She looked too. Did he see anyone?

"I might say the same for you," Roland said. "You're an heiress to a vast estate, you hold Dahlquin in your hand, King willing," holding his cupped hand out to demonstrate. "Handsome men don't throw themselves at your feet?"

"Never."

"Thankful you should be to your parents. The road to Dahlquin is paved with the remains of ignoble suitors." He smiled at her then looked over his shoulder once more.

"Do you see anyone?" she asked.

"I don't, but I know they're back there. Can't you feel it?" Roland asked, his voice raw and deep.

"Are we riding into a trap? Could the Danes be ahead of us as well?" she asked. There were many Danish communities along the coast. Had they risen up in support of Tiomu?

"Doubt that," Roland answered. "Tiomu starts in Connacht. We didn't see flags or banners, or Danish royalty. He would subdue Dahlquin, Connacht and move east."

"What of England? Will King Henry intercede?"

"Your father thinks not. I agree. What of Henry? He is your king," Roland asked. Seemed most in Ireland forgot that.

"Henry," she said warily. "He is king, of England."

"And Ireland," Roland reminded her.

"As you claim, *he* is our *overlord, aye*," she conceded, mocking Roland's language from their earlier dialogue.

"Blasphemy and sedition," Roland commented, raising his eyebrows. "He is king. By the Synod of Cashel."

Eloise gave him a smug look. "Citing such foreign treaties, blurring church and castle. And we pay handsomely to FitzGilbert and Henry. And for what? Ireland produces all the goods." Eloise thought of all Dahlquin and Connacht provided, the stunning green marble that made up much of Connacht's currency, the flax and exported linen. "If ever I should meet King Henry face to face, I will bow and call him Your Grace. Until then, he takes our hard-earned living and leaves us in peace. Fair enough?" she asked.

"El," Roland said, "I believe you understand better than that. Your Lord Father holds Dahlquin in King Henry's name. You are the heiress by Henry's generosity alone."

"And you, Lord, must surely understand the complexity of our hierarchy. There is great conflict between Pope, King and your liege. How do you reconcile your duty?" She emphasized 'your' addressing his conflicted position.

"Are you implying Lord Albert of Ashbury or even High Lord FitzGilbert are disloyal? Treasonous to King Henry?" Roland asked. Eloise could hear the stirrings of outrage and wanted to reassure him, but he went on. "I know many of the Irish tribes still don't recognise England as their sovereign, but you, your Lord Father, Ashbury and Scragmuir are Welsh and hold Connacht in the name of King Henry. Are you saying it's otherwise?"

"You miss my point. First let me clarify," she said keeping her voice even. "Lord Albert, Lord FitzGilbert and my Lord Father are indeed loyal to King Henry and treason is not afoot." She left Scragmuir out entirely, because she believed Scragmuir was most assuredly capable of sedition and more heinous acts against Connacht, England and God. "My question to you, Lord At-March, is how to reconcile these loyalties. There are rules and a code of conduct. Yet Church and crowns are continually warring. Don't roll your eyes at me, you're not stupid. You are, Sir, quite observant." She was increasingly aware of Roland's astuteness and ability to intuit much from her. "Thus, you must surely contemplate the complexity of your circumstance? Your family, your godfather, Sir John of Exeter, your knighting and oath to High Lord FitzGilbert, now as a subordinate to Lord Ashbury. Our allegiances are as tenuous as vellum and as volatile as a Roman god."

Roland stared.

"What if Denmark is involved? Suppose we have to sign a treaty with that king, eh?" she asked. "What would we call him? Your Grace to all? As you say, Ireland has enough petty kings as it is without others butting in their great royal noses." She thought of the U'Neill's, her own mother's U'Brien's, the U'Connors, and the rest of her tribal blood cousins. Even her own father was, within Dahlquin, considered a king. Family, God, and Crown, *I am your Man*....the Dahlquin oath, a pledge of allegiance to the tribal familial king first and foremost.

"God's blood, exhaustion consumes me," Roland said rubbing his eyes. "And a Dahlquin headache is brewing," he growled, massaging his temples.

"Dahlquin headache?" she asked. Was she being insulted?

"It is. Big as a fu-" he paused, his face contorted. "God-cursed pony. No one should think this much and ride so hard all at once. You talk entirely too much, and about things inappropriate."

"Inappropriate?" she asked, wanting him to clarify such a comment. This was the politics of their existence. "I have yet to bring up the Order of Three. It appears balanced enough, but-"

Roland raised a gloved hand and held up one finger.

"I pray that you be still," he said, squinting at her. He added another finger. "Labor on that, will you?" He put up a third finger. "Lest we fight. Order of Three," he said, massaging his forehead.

It was hard to be mad at him when he was in pain, and she watched him with a discerning eye. Lavender and rose petals would help soothe a headache. A nice, cool mask laid upon his eyes with rosemary as well. And someone to comb out his hair and massage his temples for him. And sing a soothing song of healing. Singing could be done here and now.

She started soft and low, first to warm up her voice and second to ease him into it. His head hurt already, to explode it with a cacophony of ill notes would be rude.

"Feel My Gentle Healing Gift,
As I Would Sing You A Wellness Wish,
Lavender Scent, is Comforting and Cool,
Rosemary is Strong, a Helpful Tool,
Forget Not the Rose Petals, moist as Dew,
This Herbal Bouquet Will Bring Calm to You."

"I wish I had a balm to lay across your eyes. We'll have to pretend," she said softly.

She sang it again and this time he hinted at a smile.

Eloise sang three more soothing songs intended to ease patients and quicken their healing, with verse after verse offering remedies and spiritual comfort. Of course, it was more effective if she could rub in a curative balm or massage out the bad blood. Unable to lay her hands upon him, she infused her voice with warmth and softness and sang with her head tilted to Roland attuned to any change in his demeanor.

> *"When your head doth pound with Thor's relentless Hammer*
> *Your brain is in a vise and you beg release from Mjölnir's clammer*
> *Let a gentle breeze of healing power, cleanse the blood and purge*
> *the bile*
> *May the spirit of Martyred Saint Stephan on his steed unreviled*
> *Balance the humors and add salix your humors unriled."*

Singing was equally therapeutic for the songstress as Eloise concentrated on her breathing, lungs, core and pitch. The words and melodies were trusted friends, a vocal talisman to the soul. Her mind eased, as her body continued to move with the familial rhythm of Garth beneath her. She also sang to Garth, thinking how little grooming and healing balms he had received since leaving Dahlquin. *Yet he continued without complaint, as if he understood the importance of their journey for Dahlquin.*

Roland sat straighter, rotating his head and neck. Eloise thought she heard his spine crack. Clasping his hands behind his back he pinched his shoulder blades together. She stopped singing when he turned to her.

He watched her in silence for some time as the horses walked on side by side. She thought he had been enjoying her singing, mayhap she had misjudged again.

"Goodness upon you," he finally said. "I had no idea." His lips were parted, and he shook his head slowly. You sing like-"

She hoped he would say something complimentary. Her voice wasn't ill, but compared with her Lady Mother, her father oft said she sounded like a wolf howling.

"An angel," he finished, his brows lifted, brown eyes wide. "My headache is improved. And I have entertainment. Prosit," he said lifting an imaginary cup in tribute.

"May you have goodness, Lord Roland," she gulped, smiling, relieved to hear such a compliment. "Pleasure upon me to help you," she added, thinking what high praise she had received.

"If it pleases you, it pleases me," he said, his close-lipped smile broadening. "Pray continue."

Eloise thought a moment. "Shall we try something different?" she asked, searching her memory. Religious chants, carols, *Summer is Coming, Song of my Heart*, she thought with joy.

Eloise started singing *Summer is Coming*. She was thrilled when Roland joined her in the second chorus, *Sing little bird, sing little bird,* until she started the next verse. "Shall we sing it in round?" she asked, her clenched hands shaking with hope. She hadn't sung in days. How had that happened? She always sang, to the horses, her dogs. And with *Mathair*, singing in the gardens, the corridors, up and down the stairs. Often, they sang instead of talked, creatively making the words fit into a melody to converse. A game that must have started in the cradle. Nurse tried, but it wasn't the same. "By your will, by your magnificent will," she begged.

"El, El," Roland said with a chuckle, his palms up indicating she settle.

Did she sound like she was pleading? She was. Music was its own purgative. Roland was healed and she felt…giddy. And she wanted more. "By your gracious will," she asked softly, looking up from her tipped brows.

"I'll try," Roland said, "but it has been a long time. Don't laugh," he said, giving her a stern look that was all bluff.

Eloise pulled her lips over her teeth, trying not to giggle and shook her head, she wouldn't laugh - at him. But she may well laugh out of sheer relief.

"You want to start, and I'll join in?" she asked. "That is easiest. Just sing your own verse, don't think about me."

Roland took a deep breath, looked ahead and started *Summer is Coming, and the land it is a quivering*. She started her verse as he continued his, but within the second line he was singing with her. Eloise stopped singing, but waved at him indicating he keep on, then she kept his beat with her hand before she started her verse. Once again, he fell into her verse and they sang the chorus together.

"My Lord, you surprise me as well, you have a rich voice," Eloise said in encouragement.

Roland nodded his thanks, then frowned and scratched the back of his head. He compressed the right side of his mouth.

"Close your eyes and visualize the lyrics," she said.

He gave her a sideways glance, *humphed* and started singing.

Eloise clapped her hands after completing the third effort to sing in round successfully.

When they finished, Roland asked, "Do you grace any instruments with your talents?"

All ladies had musical instruction; they were expected to entertain their families and each other.

"I love to sing, *Mathair* and I both," Eloise said. "And willingly I studied voice."

"But?" Roland asked.

"Alas, sir, I do lack the patience for instruments. The music is beautiful and truly I enjoy listening. Sitting indoors, practicing? It's rather like embroidery or spinning," she said with drooping shoulders and a dreary voice. "However," she started singing the words as she talked,

"I can sing almost anywhere. It's a gift I can readily share. Without transporting a bulky, fragile instrument, here or there."

She couldn't contain her glee.

"Mercifully my parents let the vielles and recorders pass. Oh, I can whistle too. Clever lass."

"Oops!" she said, having referred to herself as a lass rather than a lad.

"Your impertinence has a charming side," Roland said. "A bow for a distaff, arrows for pipes. Diana with the voice of the heavens. And the heavens must be pleased, behold a spot of sun!" he said, reaching his hand out to catch the rays of sun which glinted off his studded gauntlets.

"I'm still working this one out," Eloise said, "it's not nearly finished, nor have I had any opportunity to hear it sung for myself." She stroked Garth's neck, as if for reassurance. "It's amazing how different a piece sounds when sung out loud, rather than just recited in my head."

"You compose songs?" he asked, intrigued.

"Well," she said, dragging the word out. "Melodies are quite difficult, requiring a truly creative and open mind, I think. But the word play comes a bit easier. Singing made up much of my instruction. Things are easier to remember set to music."

"Let's hear it then," Roland said.

"By your will, don't laugh," she asked, concern etched across her grubby face.

"I will refrain," he said.

Her smile of relief was so dazzling, he couldn't remember a trace of road grime on her glowing cheeks.

She stroked Garth's neck with both hands repeatedly. "This will be new to us both," she said, biting her lower lip, her trepidation returning. She inhaled, gave him a tight smile, exhaled and started singing.

"Brave and Glorious, Lord Roland of Ashbury At-March to Connacht Came,
With two brother knights and their squires, Sirs Guillaume and Sedric by name,
The splendors of Ashbury were hidden from view, for the Dragon's breath had settled,
His brothers did squabble and pester and bother, the wildlife tested their glorious mettle"

Roland could hardly believe his ears. He recognised aspects of the melody, but others were new to him. Her song had the cadence of a hoary epic poem, his own *Chanson de Roland.* Pray this one has a more glorious conclusion, he thought.

"Undaunted, Lord Roland did rally his forces, leading his men to the world's end,
The end of the world as Saint John did portray it was a treasonous siege upon Ireland,
Dahlquin was facing it darkest dawn, from Tiomoid U'Neill's traitorous spawn"

Eyes closed, her face was set in concentration and occasionally she would frown, or her brow knotted, as if she was unhappy with a passage or note. Yet she continued, occasionally stumbling on a word, pausing before resuming, her voice rising and falling with the drama of her tale.

"With courage and wit and power unbridled, Lord Roland the Hero descended upon,
The drawbridge of Dahlquin in dastardly peril, the gate house in squalor so grim,
Three knights and their horses, breathed fire and sword fall, and bludgeoned their way in"

"There are a few more lines," she sang, her voice still trilling. "About the waterfall and wolves. But those are still fairly rough, and I would not wish to share such yet."

Blue-grey eyes implored him. He watched her hopeful expression cloud as she waited for his response. His approval.

Aye, he loved it, was honored. In his own pride or drunken vanity, he or his comrades had never concocted such an heroic song. What could he say? He opened his mouth to utter his gratitude, but her crestfallen expression paralyzed him. He was speechless.

She turned away, exhaled, and started stroking her horse.

"Mayhap Lord Roland," she started softly, "has displeasure." She appeared to be talking to Garth, but he believed her question was meant for him.

Speak, he ordered himself.

"Nay," he blurted, startling her with his English outburst. "I'm well pleased. Truly." She gave a hopeful smile. "I, I'm humbled into speechlessness."

Her eyes narrowed and she studied him briefly before snorting. "Humbled into speechlessness, you?" she said, giving him a sarcastic look. "*Hmph,*" she snorted, glancing at him anew. "Mayhap I could use that." She gazed off, deep in thought, it appeared. "Brave and glorious as he may be, speechless in his humility."

Roland put a hand over his face. Guillaume and Sedric would laugh themselves out of the saddle over that line.

"Oh," she sighed, "it was my desire to sing a noble song of your exploits. But now, fear upon me, it plays like a tavern tune. It wasn't my intention," she said, "to mock you."

"You have not mocked me," he said, "by your song. But I will be if you use that last line. It's the way of it."

She inhaled, a soft grin returned. She vigorously rubbed on her horse's neck, with the hand not holding the bow.

"Then I will continue my endeavour. May you have goodness," she said.

"And goodness to you," he said, tipping his head.

Songs and melodies filled the air. Singing was a lively diversion from fatigue and Roland did feel he had exhausted his conversational skills. He had received some meagre musical training at court. A great waste of time, he thought. There was enough hard work to be done in the day of a page or squire. In the Great Hall he served the knights and visiting nobility, cleaned the weapons and tack of the High Lord and various knights, mucked stalls, fed, exercised and worked with horses. Plus, learning to read, write, add and subtract, religion, philosophy, history. Roland learned young that the king and especially Lord FitzGilbert valued knights with some learning. Did it truly facilitate strategic thinking? Logic, order, discipline? The martial drills, weapons and horse play were the regular highlights to his day, but all left him exhausted and frequently limping to his pallet for a night's sleep, always too brief. To attend lessons in singing and etiquette were a pure waste. Oh, he had done it, Maid Eloise wasn't the only one who could be impertinent. He had a decent voice and that was easier than learning an instrument. The only instrument he needed was his sword, *El Muerte Rojo*. And his manhood. Involuntarily, he shifted in the saddle, assuring himself yet again it was still there.

Eloise was singing a love song, a haunting melody of a lady whose lover had taken up the cross and followed King Philip to Outremer.

There was some beautiful music to be made. Lovemaking could be compared to singing. There was the act itself. Lovemaking could be deep and moving, the way a Gregorian chant filled your soul with awe and reverence, a religious experience if ever there was one. Lovemaking could also be a quick and private secret between two admirers, a passionate little tune that fills the air like the melodies of songbirds. Or the lustful desperation between man and woman when all that exists between them are the raucous choruses of a bawdy drinking song that speeds through the veins until the next fashionable tune comes along. Deep in thought now, Roland realized how much he had missed in music theory. And not just the splendid act of engaging in sexual intercourse with a woman, how about the many musical vibrations associated with the body itself?

The saddle became uncomfortably restrictive and Roland squirmed to relieve the pressure on his engorging instrument. With all this music, his instrument of manhood wanted to play loud and hard. Any song, any melody: he longed to make music with Eloise. He released a subdued groan as he unsuccessfully tried to make himself comfortable yet again. This wasn't healthy. He looked over at the cause of his constricted malady and was startled to find she had begun what was best described as a bawdy tavern song, though her lyrics were those of a child's ballad.

"Ah, excuse me," he interrupted as politely as possible, coughing to clear his throat. Her blue-grey eyes looked up with imploring innocence. It was hard to fathom she was the same pious blasphemer of miles past. Her cheeks were rosy, and her teeth were light and aligned. He dare not look too deeply into her eyes, still alarmed of the visage he had seen. "You know there is another version of that little ditty."

"Sir, I believe there are several variations," Eloise acknowledged, trying not to blush.

"And which variations do you suppose came first? Eh, the proverbial chicken or the egg?" he asked, mischief in his penetrating eyes and teasing in his deep voice.

Eloise hated being caught out in her ignorance, a proverbial dilemma indeed. Roland was toying with her, and she was at the disadvantage. Everyone had seen the indiscriminate mating of fowl, cats and other beasts. She had handpicked sires and dams, dogs and bitches, witnessing the successful breeding and births. She had assisted her mother and the midwife with the miracle of life or death. Again, she found herself enduring intense pressure from Roland's direction as well as an equally intense yearning from within. *Blessed Saint Mary,* she was whining. Dahlquin should be strong and capable.

"Come now, El, you have a penchant for philosophy. What say you, my route scholar?" His upper lip was thin and firm, but his bottom lip was full and well formed. The proximity of his being engulfed her. Had he ridden closer? If she reached in any direction, she would feel him there.

"I'm willing to risk another Dahlquin headache," he assured her.

"There isn't an answer to your riddle, Lord," she replied, keeping her voice even, to display confidence she lacked. "But I'll venture the gift of Sucellus may be responsible."

Roland looked puzzled.

"Bacchus, if you prefer, was responsible for at least two versions of the song in question."

"I prefer the Ballad of Medb," he said, indicating a lewd song of the Celtic Goddess Medb and her Roman slaves. There was nothing philosophical or scholarly about that, Eloise thought, trying not to shrivel under his vehement gaze. Medb, the goddess of war and fertility, Dahlquin could use a bit of her conquering spirit, though Tiomu's men deserved far worse than serving her insatiable lust. Consorts to Satan was mayhap a suitable punishment for Tiomu's lot.

Eloise sang the first two verses of Medb's triumphs and virtues. Roland listened, but didn't join in. The chorus presented a greater challenge.

"Hail, Queen Medb, slayer of armies,
Not hmm *nor tongue her lust can be granted,*
Bearded Salmon-rose lips that bite like a shark,
La la la-ing *her slaves till their* hmms *fell off"*

"Hmms?" Roland questioned. "You can't say *cock?*" He chuckled. "And la la la-ing?"

201

She knew she was blushing, and his scrutiny only caused her more discomfiture. The entire lewd chorus was disconcerting. Did he honestly believe she would say *fucking*?

"You have your limits of impudence, I see," he conceded. "Such sweet lips shouldn't be uttering such vulgarities." His firm lips were curved up in a seductive smile.

"Ah, may you have goodness, I-" stammering, she looked down. Then she tried to sneak a sideways glance to see if he was still looking at her. He winked. Out of her depth in this engagement, without resource for instruction, Eloise took a deep breath and sat up tall in the saddle. The tingling in her groin only emphasized her moist seat. Salmon-rose lips at both ends, indeed. She blushed anew, worried she might slide out of the saddle.

She emitted a weak chortle, not a groan, not a laugh. Not only did she ride in a very damp saddle of her own excitement, it was wet everywhere she looked.

"Blessed Virgin Mary, protect me," she whispered, fishing for the wooden cross pendant under her surcoat. Feeling the warm wood in her palm, she crossed herself six times.

"Six times sinful?" Roland asked.

"Hail Mary, Full of Grace," Eloise started reciting. He joined her.

"Agreed, mayhap it's time we take up the cross," Roland said when they finished the Hail Mary Prayer.

Prayers of penance recited; they took turns singing an inspired song of pilgrimage to Palestine. Roland would sing one verse, Eloise the next. Both voices shared the chorus:

"Good Christian Knights come boldly
To liberate Jerusalem for God and all that's Holy
Our cause is just
Paradise is promised to those who in God do trust."

They scanned the vast, open expanse of the Bog of Allen surrounding them north, south and west. Inspired by the bravado of the Pilgrims of legend, they pushed their horses on. Indeed, it seemed they were on pilgrimage: for Connacht and Ireland. And even England. Past the halfway point, the eternal Bog became less threatening, and more conciliatory as the mounted minstrels ambled overboard or bog as the road provided.

"Come on," she encouraged Roland to join her improvising percussion as she beat out a lively rhythm with her hands on her thigh or the saddle.

"Be thankful I'll sing," he said, without smiling. "No one could travel this fast. It's not possible. Tiomu's men could never keep up this pace," he muttered. He shook his head. "Surely we're but two days from the Leinster castle." He looked at her. "No one would ever suspect our severe duty to hear us sing. It's a good disguise all told."

Garth tensed and she felt his head pop up in alarm. Roland stopped; she and Garth stopped, and Eloise followed their gaze. Across the flat expanse were two riders and a mule-driven cart, mayhap casks in the back.

"Are those women driving the cart?" Roland asked. "Are they waving at us?"

"I believe so," she acknowledged, though she and Roland looked about as if someone else must be about. Then he lifted a hand and waved back.

As if drawn by magnetism, both parties moved forward at a rapid pace.

"Oh, sorrow upon us, you stopped singing," hailed a man, waving as he approached.

"Pray continue," another man's voiced called out. "Been enjoying the music for miles."

She and Roland had grown careless singing across the open bog. One of the men had a child behind him. Their arrival could not have been more ill-timed, and Eloise's startle turned to resentment at this intrusion upon her musical joy with Roland. She noticed the men were dressed in rough homespun travelling tunics and hose with large daggers on their belts in lieu of war swords. Merchants of wine, ale or some other imbibement from the casks in the wagon. One of the women appeared to be about six or seven months pregnant. Tight red curls circled her face as the rest tried in vain to escape her matronly braid. Eloise was reminded of her own unkempt hair tickling her cheeks and neck. The other woman was a black-haired vixen. Her large brown eyes devoured Roland as she smiled in warm hospitality. Surely her lips were vainly painted that unnatural sanguine. She turned and gave Eloise a big wink and a pouty smile of promise. Eloise near swallowed her tongue.

"You're quite a songbird," the man with the boy behind him said, hesitating as he studied Eloise a moment longer, "lad." His brown hair and beard were greying, with dark stains at the corners of his mouth.

"Eh?" his partner said with a grunt, looking Eloise up and down. "Fooled me," he said acknowledging she was a lad. His ruddy brown hair and beard curled tightly and seemed recently trimmed and combed. "Seems a shame to lose that voice. Ever consider harvesting his *noisettes?*" he asked Roland, in a voice deep and gravelly from drinking, gesturing with two fingers together to imitate shears. "Snip, snip. Before his voice goes harsh as a whore's cat."

"What? If I understand your meaning," Roland said with a laugh, obviously caught off guard by the remark. "I never once considered it," he added, shaking his head with mirth.

Eloise felt her cheeks flaming. On top of her embarrassment, she felt long strands of wayward hair down her neck, which had come loose from the tied braids under her cap. It was all she could do to keep her hands from tidying the revealing locks. Her nervousness wore on Garth, and he lifted his head, demonstrating his size and potential to the strangers' horses and mules.

"You should - fair waste that," the first man agreed, chuckling. "Don't worry yourself, Danny, you already sound like a cat," he said to the boy behind. Eloise estimated he was about ten years of age.

"If I might introduce ourselves to you, noble sirs," the second man said, "I'm Lugdach. This is my partner, Brendan and his eldest son, Wee Brendan, though we call him Danny." Roland and Eloise exchanged nods with each and Eloise noticed the men had red noses, though the weather was mild. "And there be my charming wife, Flann." The redheaded woman bowed her head. Her nose, too, was slightly red. "Her half-sister, Medb, the generous."

Eloise coughed. Medb. The vixen was giving Roland a plump-cheeked grin, her chin tilted just slightly to the left as if she were asking and answering a question at the same time.

"The queen of generosity," Roland was saying, his brown-eyed gaze covering her like a wool blanket. He bowed deeply from the waist as if she were indeed the Queen of Connacht, which she most certainly was not.

"I'm Roland, Lord of Ashbury-at-March, Connacht," he added. "This is El, the Angel's Voice of Connacht."

"Thirsty work, singing," Lugdach said with a sly smile. "Fortuna's Wheel has blessed us all, sirs, for we're brew merchants and tavern workers."

Eloise watched as Roland sat up, squaring his shoulders just slightly. The longing in his deep brown eyes and parted lips was unmistakable.

"With a bit of quality beer for purchase by such noble travelers as yourselves, sirs," Lugdach added.

She watched Roland slump and sigh. "You're most observant, for I've a powerful thirst. But alas I've a powerfully empty purse as well," Roland said. Eloise watched the brew merchant slump in return.

"Powerful thirsty, I believe that," Brendan said with a sigh, rolling his eyes. "Brothers in travel, eh. Lending a hand." This time his sigh sounded more like a groan. "Pass that bag," he said to Flann, pointing to a skin bag on the cart seat between her and Medb. She passed the bag to Lugdach, who in turn passed it to Brendan who held it out to Roland. "Have a good swallow."

"So, you know what you're missing," Lugdach added with a scowling grin.

"You and the lad," Brendan said, when Roland didn't take the offered skin bag.

Roland wouldn't take the charity, but his thirst was palpable as he licked his parched lips, not taking his woeful brown eyes from the bag suspended within easy reach of his gauntleted hand.

"If it pleases my Lord Roland," Eloise interjected, keeping her gaze low, ignoring the pesky loose strands of long hair escaping her cap. "Mayhap I could sing a song in trade for your sip."

"Eh? How so, you've been singing free as a bird for miles, why charge us poor merchants now?" Lugdach said, surprised.

"Thirsty work," Eloise reminded them.

"What say you, Lord? Lugdach?" Brendan asked looking from one to the other. "Sounds a fair bargain to me."

"It's better than begging, brother travelers or not," Lugdach grudgingly agreed. Flann said nothing. Medb was all swollen smiles and chest, and Danny had a toothy grin. Roland sat tall on Artoch, his large gloved hand rubbing his jaw. He hadn't spared the vixen a single glance upon discovering the brew merchant's hidden ware. As at the farm, Roland had everyone staring at him, waiting for his decision.

"One song, one bag," Roland queried. "Two songs, two bags?" he asked with a tilt of his head, his gloved hand still on his jaw.

"Robbery, that be," Lugdach scoffed. "One song, one sip."

"Robbery God's beard!" Roland said. "One song, one long pull," he countered.

"Now," Lugdach said, "that depends on the songs. This isn't a tavern with paying customers."

"And not some dreary, guilt ridden dirge," Flann said, speaking for the first time.

"I once met five brewers while crossing the bog," Eloise began to sing slowly, letting the simple words and story form in her mind: simple, everyday rhymes.

"Though graced not with sun, we did not have fog," she sang,
raising her arms to the glorious day.
"Their wares it was heavy, their poor mules looked to die,"

Eloise looked at their mules with an exaggerated look of woe.

"Our travels and singing had left us parched dry,"
"Forthwith, forthwith their spirits so lightened,"

She continued fanning her hands and smiling at the men, boy and women who in turn looked to each other shaking their heads, suppressing a hint of mirth, Eloise hoped. Well, Danny smiled broadly, probably happy to be included in the fraternity of brewers.

"They eagerly sought to quench thirst and thus brighten,"

She sang it again, for it seemed an appropriate chorus, though out of place.

Roland and Danny clapped their hands in boisterous approval. Then Roland took the proffered skin bag, eyes glowing, cradling it as if it were his first born.

Eloise watched Roland take a decent drink of the brew. Shoulders slackening, eyes closed the hearty drink remained in his mouth for a long savour before his Adam's apple marked its passing. He inhaled, eyes still closed, prolonging the flavour. He held up one finger, one pull, and then offered the bag to her. Eloise shook her head only slightly. Her parched throat begged a taste, but she would not deny Roland.

"Know any more drinking songs, lad?" Brendan asked her.

"I do, sir," Eloise conceded, "several." She paused, remembering the numerous and lewd variations of such songs, before singing the Cleric's Cat, about a saucy grey feline who dropped his captured mice into the cleric's brew or wine then ate the morsel well basted.

Danny laughed and squealed with delight while Medb and Flann chuckled with approval.

"Well done, lad," Brendan congratulated.

Lugdach held up two fingers to Roland, indicating the second drink, then changed his meaning by snapping them together again, snip, snip. "It's not too late," he mouthed.

Roland enjoyed another long swig on the skin bag, hugging it to his chest in the hope Eloise would be permitted to sing yet another song. Gladly, for his contentment was intoxicating. Surely the brew had done something to his mouth, for his lips curved in the most inviting way when he smiled at her. Not Medb.

"Sorry Medb, looks like he only has eyes for the bag and the boy," Lugbach said.

"Hmmm," Medb cooed, smoothing her thick black hair, then bringing it full round so it hung over her shoulder and across her full bosom, gleaming like a raven's breast. Her traveling garments were tidy and well fitting, her round face was unblemished with hardly a trace of dirt. Eloise's own filthy cheeks itched, and the caked dirt on the back of her neck prickled as her stringy, unravelling hair nagged at her. Eloise wished she could flaunt her amber locks, cascading down her back and over the shoulder of her new blue and gold surcoat, a bleached linen chemise snugly tied at her rose-scented wrists. She inhaled, imagining her chest, her bosom filling out. The comparison ended there, even without the tight bindings her breasts would never ooze with the crude excess of Medb's.

Again, Medb smiled at Roland with a sanguine pout that made Eloise bristle like a barn cat. Garth too. Roland inhaled deeply; his nostrils flared like a stallion's. The vixen was naught but a rutting sow. A clean, raven haired, buxom sow. Eloise glanced at Roland and found him glancing quizzically back at her.

"If the boy is that satisfying, mayhap I could take his front," Medb murmured, running her tongue over her bottom lip, "and his lord keep the backside." She paused, glancing up from lowered eyes from Eloise then to Roland. "The King and Queen of generosity," she added almost blowing a kiss. "Of course, you may lose that golden voice, lad," she purred to Eloise, "but you'll thank me with proper husk. You both will."

Flann burst out laughing and slapped her leg.

Eloise tried to close her gaping mouth, only to have her lip twitch in astonishment. Embarrassment surged up, replacing her jealously of moments before.

"Medb," Brendan snapped, "remember wee Danny here." His cheeks matched his red nose, while Danny looked about confused.

"I do apologize, sirs," Lugdach said. "My sister-in-law is the epitome of Irish hospitality, eh?" he said, trying to suppress his laughter.

"That she is," Roland said, looking directly at Medb. Even in profile, Roland was smouldering. As he narrowed his eyes, Eloise could feel the radiated heat, heat she coveted for herself. Medb held his gaze with uncowed intensity. The edges of her mouth seemed to hover, almost smiling. Her brows knitted, almost imperceptible, her expression appeared questioning. Nearly as imperceptibly, Roland shook his head, the edges of his mouth hinted up. Medb's pout hinted at a frown. Roland smiled in earnest, then raised his hands and shrugged. Medb did the same.

"Shall we have one more song?" Medb asked, studying Eloise with new scrutiny, her gaze moving slowly over Eloise's face until their eyes met. Eloise didn't expect to favour her, nor had she the desire, but Medb had a kindness to her eyes, wise, playful and non-threatening. Qualities Eloise would seek in a horse and a friend. "A parting gift between friends and rivals, eh Little Sister?" Medb said in a conciliatory voice, nodding to Eloise.

"You don't need to insult the lad," Lugdach said, "though taking the wee songbird from behind, who is the wiser? He is looking better and better."

Everyone laughed except Medb, Roland and Eloise. Roland glanced between her and Medb.

"Might our Lord Roland have another pull?" Medb asked, pointing to the skin bag still in Roland's lap. Lugdach glared at her, and she waved a dismissive hand at him. "Take it out of my share," she said, "I'm the Queen of Generosity. Only wish I had mead, to soften the journey."

"Mead?" Flann said, "ach, the bog is affecting your head, Medbie Love."

"So it is, best be moving on," Brendan said. "One more pull," he said to Roland, "and one more song as we part ways," he directed to Eloise. "Best bog crossing I remember in years, eh Danny?"

"It is, sir," Danny agreed. "Do you know any songs with knights or dragons?" Danny asked as Roland tipped the bag for the last time.

Eloise was about to answer when Medb spoke.

"Drink deep, Lord," Medb said in a throaty gurgle. "And remember well what we *might* have shared. You, yon companion and me," she said with a nod of her head to each of them.

Roland coughed the valuable brew in an aromatic rain upon Artoch's neck.

Danny howled with laughter, and the others chortled at Roland's expense.

"Waste of my fine brew," Lugdach said, passing the skin bag back to Flann, "and the lad's voice."

Roland wiped his mouth and chin with his sleeve, giving Medb a wicked grin. "El," he said turning to her, "let us flee before we lose our virtue and reason. Fair travel to you, Brendan, Danny and Lugdach." He rode over to the cart. "Safe travel to you, Flann, the fair and steady." He kissed the back of her hand and Flann blushed to match her hair but made no effort to extricate her hand. "And Queen Medb." A tug of war ensued as he tried to kiss her hand and she tried to place his hand upon her breast.

"You need a husband," Roland said with a chuckle, finally yanking his hand free.

"I have one," she said beaming, patting her stomach. "He is older than counting, and after four years has finally gifted me with child."

Roland sat back, eyes wide, a 'what' forming on his lips. Medb's hair wasn't braided as a married woman's should be, nor had she been introduced as anyone's wife. What indeed.

"What harm?" she said, "his babe, and I have entertainment."

"Ah, Lord, looks like you lost some virtue after all," Lugdach said, waving farewell.

"Fair travel," Brendan called back.

"Knights," Danny called. "And dragons."

Eloise and Roland rode on some distance. Roland had a fist to his bottom lip.

"My Lord?" Eloise queried, concerned.

He didn't answer but extended his fist briefly. Then he sat up, rested his fist on his chest and belched. A belch that echoed across the bog with its own harmonic cadence. When the noise stopped rebounding, Eloise heard the distant laughter from their former companions.

Roland smacked his lips in satisfaction. "That almost makes up for the ale I spit out. Almost."

Songs of knights and dragons carried Roland and Eloise off the Bog of Allen, and back to firm footing and greater vegetation and trees. Eloise tried to tidy her loose hair, tucking the dangling ends into the braids still tied to her itchy scalp. *Miserable mess, this*, thinking of the tedious process to wash and comb it all out.

Roland sighed. "Good to be rid of that," he added, waving behind him.

"It is," Eloise commented, "So exposed back there."

"Exposed, agreed," he commented, then almost chuckling, "God's eyes, that was close. Medb certainly had a soft spot for you."

"And you, My Lord," Eloise added, remembering the flirtatious exchange, wondering if she had understood it. There was no mistaking Roland's interest, she knew a breeding stallion when she saw one. Jealousy: a deadly sin, she told herself, though Roland didn't act on his lust.

Eloise felt the weight of the shield slip away.

"What?" Eloise gasped.

Reginald's shield clattered on the ground as both horses turned to study the noisy object.

Roland dismounted and examined the shield.

"The back strap has broken," he said, tugging at the enarmes. "These are sound."

"I'll carry it," Eloise said as Roland started to put the shield on his arm. "It's my shield," she said, meaning it was her burden to bear, and not Roland's. Was this a sign? Uncle Reggie's shield bringing her back to her purpose? Had her own envy and lust distracted her?

Roland glared at her then returned to his task.

"No," he said, falling back on blunt English, "it's too unwieldy for-"

"A girl?" she finished for him, confused and suddenly wary. Her posture changed. She met his glare. Dahlquin was strong, and if Uncle Reggie wanted her to have his shield then she would bear up under the *unwieldy* responsibility.

"Aye," he said, his brown eyes narrowing on her, his mouth a hard line.

Anger and spite flared in her. Why? She had had such happiness a moment before. Joyous with singing. And hadn't he?

He studied her, and she returned the scrutiny. Something was making him exceedingly mad. Again. She reflected, tracing back. Isn't that why they started singing in the first place, because he was a surly English knight? But it hurt, stabbed at her to think of him so. That was equally confusing. It was confounding.

"Here," he said, handing the shield up to her.

"May you have goodness," she said, still confounded. Uncle Reggie's shield - a formidable shell of protection, and how often had she witnessed him use it as a battering ram. Was it a betrayal to her or Uncle Reggie to render the shield to Roland? Uncle. Nurse. The unbidden images of her beloved family. She could not cope. This wasn't the time - not in front of Roland, not on the road.

"For luck," he added, swinging back into the saddle.

Trembling, Eloise put her arm through the oversized enarmes. If it had been heavy and awkward on her back, it was heavier and more awkward on her arm. How would she shoot? Wearing the shield, holding *Cara* in her left hand, Eloise nodded, indicating she was ready to continue.

Roland stared at Eloise, studying her. Again, she bristled.

"One moment you're demure, pleasing even, the next we're both ready to strike." He continued to study her features, then his expression softened, his eyes brightened, his mouth formed a half grin. "Now I see what it is," he said. "You take on a fighter's stance."

"Fighter's stance?" she asked shrilly, picturing a warrior, feet planted on the ground, sword drawn or fists protectively up before the face. She wasn't doing that, and she didn't wish to fight, surely.

"Aye," he said, drawing the word out slowly as if still contemplating. "You tuck your chin defensively, as if you're preparing to throw a punch. Oh, it's subtle enough. And your glare."

Eloise thought about her chin. Was she glaring? She was, because he tried to intimidate her.

"It's a challenge. Naturally I get defensive. Suddenly we're both making fists, grabbing our daggers," he said.

Eloise looked at her hands. Her right hand, on the side of Garth's withers, held the reins lightly, her left held Reggie's shield and *Cara*. "I've always been counseled to keep my chin down, lest I appear haughty and foolhardy," she said.

"You have traded arrogance for belligerence."

"Belligerence? I will not cower like a beaten cur and you accuse me of belligerence."

"I do," he said, his grin turning smug. Your own horse feels your hostility. Look at his ears."

She did and Garth's ears were pinned. Feeling her eyes upon him, Garth turned his head slightly towards her.

"Horses never lie," he was saying as she tried to let her breath out. "You told me that yourself."

Was there not an end to his haughtiness? Of course Garth's ears were pinned, hers would be too. She was annoyed, not belligerent. "Easy," she said, though it lacked her usual coo. After stroking Garth's neck, she sat tall, shoulders back, wondering what to do with her chin as it seemed her neck only had one position when she was thus irritated. Leaning slightly forward she clucked, urging Garth into an extended, ground eating amble.

"El, I don't wish to fight with you. And you shouldn't be provoking one with me," he said, cantering next to her.

"I'm not," she interrupted. "I-"

"If you would listen to me," he said interrupting her with a louder voice, "I'm trying to help you. Pages, squires and most especially ladies of noble birth should not assume a fighter's stance, lest they wish to come to blows."

"I-"

"El!" he barked, reminding her she was at least posing as his page. She glanced around to be sure there weren't strangers or spies about to discover her poorly kept secret.

"I think you've never known the back of a hand," he said, his voice low, his expression stern. "And a disservice your parents have done you. And Ireland."

She stared at him a moment. His painful assault on her parents stung like a slap to her face. Brutality was not the way to instill courtesy. Still his words, his accusation reverberated in her. Oft times she had wished her parents would hit her and be done with it. Oh, bother those long hours of penance, or worse the guilt when her own Nurse or attendants had to suffer her confinements. But thankful she was to be spared the beatings poured on other Dahlquin residents.

"That is a *handy* answer, when you have none," she sneered. "Violence is not a substitute for education."

"And this is what comes of educating women. Back talk instead of the back of a hand."

Eloise glared over her shoulder at him as he ambled alongside her.

"Nay fighter's stance," he said, wagging a finger at her.

Eloise sat up asking Garth for a slower amble. *Where was her chin?* She didn't care.

"You claim to desire education. But you're unwilling to learn, all you do is argue," Roland said. The smug grin was replaced by a neutral expression as he, too, slowed.

"That's not true!" she snapped, as the horses ambled on.

"Arguing," he said, without looking at her as she and Garth shuffled down the road.

She suppressed a rising scream. Of course she was arguing. How could she not in the face of such nonsense? Roland was an idiot: a small-minded, pugnacious English idiot. Unwilling to learn? She could read and write. Add and subtract. But there were so many unanswered questions. Was she to accept every answer given her, when she knew it to be false? Did he? How she longed for his speechless humility now. Eloise turned her attention to Garth's ears. The once-black colt was now a stunning dark dapple, and his ears bore the spider web pattern. Eventually his hair would be pure white, but he would always have black skin and black features. Today his sweaty coat glowed rare and coveted purple in this brief sunshine.

Education is power. *Forbidden.* Knowledge is power. *Fruit.* Whose power does that threaten? If the farmers could read, would they be unwilling to farm? Not all knights could read, but they still fought. Would *Mathair* love Da anymore if she couldn't read? How would she manage Dahlquin if she were unable to comprehend a ledger? Does she not tend the sick and wounded with knowledge acquired through learning? If someone died in her care, would the back of Da's hand revive the departed? Had *Mathair* been born with this innate knowledge, might she not have passed it down to me? That didn't happen, I must study and practice... Eloise's internal dialogue stopped as she reflected on the dichotomy of the healing arts. *Healers are chosen*, her mother told her, yet healers must study and practice in order to do what they were *chosen* to do. And how many times did Eloise squander her education daydreaming about less pragmatic forbidden fruit?

"El?"

Drawn from her reverie, Eloise glanced at him. "My Lord," she responded. The sky had darkened, and she could see rain coming. She didn't think they would be able to outrun this shower as they had done running from Tiomu's men and the uncooperative cattle.

"We'll put under those trees and wait it out," Roland said as the first drops hit them.

There was a dense copse of pine, oak and willow with barely enough space for two large horses and their riders. Eloise backed Garth into the leafy shelter, taking care to stand on the treed side away from Roland. The summer shower spattered the road they had just exited, and Garth turned his head to the noisy canopy above him, but little rain penetrated the convenient arbor. Artoch dropped his head to graze, but Garth sampled the pine needles chewing with an inquisitive expression that made Eloise smile.

"How is it your mother, or at least your Nurse or an aunt, never taught you a modicum of fear?" Roland asked.

Eloise stared, wondering what possessed him to ask such.

"You prance through life as if no harm will befall you."

"Prance through life? I'm not prancing. I'm running for my life, and the life of my family. I've never had such fear." She paused, remembering all the death at the siege. Her beloved Nurse, bravely placing herself between Eloise and danger.

"Do you have fear now?" he asked.

What manner of interrogation was this? Why would he ask such a thing? "Of the back of your hand, mayhap?" she asked. The words sounded terrible when she heard them, words spoken in frustration.

Garth shifted his weight. If Roland made a sound, she couldn't hear it. Eloise felt trapped in the leafy shelter by her own sarcastic comment. She could envision Nurse cringing and her Lady Mother equally aghast. The rain on the leaves was a melodious, life-giving song. Why couldn't she have said something as gracious?

"My Lord," she said, but it came out in a weak whisper. "Lord Roland," she spoke again, grateful she couldn't see him. "I apologize. My words were cruel and spoken in-" There wasn't an excuse, why give one. "There's such shame upon me. You didn't deserve that."

Garth rubbed his face in the tangle of willow branches and brush causing the trapped rainwater to fall on them.

"May you have goodness. I accept." Roland's voice was soft and deep. After a pause, "I asked you a question."

Eloise had purposefully stood away from Roland. Avoiding him. She knew she needed more time to think, to process her conflicts. But even out of sight, she couldn't escape his presence, his breathing and the clink and rustle of his garments. *And why was his voice so gentle, when he had every right to have anger and provocation upon him?*

Not a modicum of fear.

He was waiting for an answer.

"Rats," she offered, for it was the truth and even the word was fearful.

His continued silence indicated he was unsatisfied with her answer. She dare not speak now. She started to tremble and pinched her cheek to stop the tumult. He was waiting for another answer. His quiet presence wore on her in the claustrophobic copse. There wasn't room for her defensiveness. Eloise felt helpless against it.

"I live in fear," she said, trying not to wail. "Every day I wake, I have fear. Fear I will be caught in my ignorance. Fear of my unworthiness. That I disappoint my parents, family, all Dahlquin." The words tumbled out, leaning forward she buried her face into Garth's neck. *I live in fear someone will discover I'm a freak and condemn me unholy.* That was mayhap her most frightening secret, one she had only shared with Tommy, the pigeon-boy turned apprentice bowyer, and only because she shared his secret. She lifted her head, commanding herself not to cry. "Oh, I have brought such disappointment. I'm not a son."

Roland said nothing. The summer shower was passing and already the birds sang their gratitude, finding worms and loosened seed heads until the next rain sent them to cover. Eloise exhaled, wiping damp horsehair from her eyes. She sniffed, feeling somewhat amused that part of her burden had washed away with the rain, like some simplistic poem.

"El," Roland said, "that isn't fear. It's shame. They're not the same."

Roland and Eloise returned to the road. Eloise felt chilled from the brief shower and pulled her arms close, the large shield awkward but comforting. Wanting to make up the lost time, Eloise urged Garth into a canter.

Before her on the right stood an enormous oak. On the left stood an equally enormous chestnut. Boughs from each tree had spread across the road, entwining, creating a shady lane. Next to the trees large shrubs had grown thick and expansive, tall grasses filled in the surrounding meadows. Trees and woods skirted a stream and extended farther back. A large field extended left and went back some length until hills could be seen blue in the distance. Ahead, the woods filled into forest.

"Stop!" Roland shouted behind her. "Eloise, no! Stop!"

Garth and Eloise slowed to a walk. Eloise pitched forward in the saddle as Garth balked. His front legs splayed, then he tucked his hindquarters down engaging his hind legs to spin and flee. As Roland shouted, Eloise tipped back in reaction to pitching forward. Before regaining her upright posture, a figure fell upon them from the tree. She almost toppled out of the saddle with him, then more men jumped down on her and Garth. One man slid past Garth's neck, landing in front of the startled horse, grasping for his reins and bridle. The third man took Eloise down hard on her right side.

Eloise curled up under Reginald's large shield. A wooden club beat down on the shield. Over and over he struck, denting it. Her left ankle took a blow and she yelped. The pain struck like lightning and ran up her leg and through her body like the recoil of thunder. She tucked her injured leg more closely toward her body. She took blows near her head and face. She could taste blood, her left nostril filled, and her sinuses swelled. Eloise tried to breathe through her mouth. She strained to suck in enough air through clenched teeth. Her left ear was ablaze and the noise under the shield was sickening. The knuckles on her left hand lacerated, rubbing against the inside of the shield, but she held on tightly like a turtle in desperation.

Roland detected the trap too late. Drawing his sword, he spun Artoch, knocking men down as he sliced through them. There were enough men to overwhelm a single knight, drag him from his horse and kill him. Roland wielded his sword from one side to the next. Artoch pivoted on his front feet, his rear end knocking men down if they didn't dodge away. His sharp, shoed hooves were a constant threat. Spinning around again, Roland thrust back with the blade aiming for a man's eyes, hitting the man's face diagonally. Both eyes would have been better, but Roland moved on to the next.

A man with a huge wooden club struck Roland on his left thigh. The pain was bone deep and Roland braced in the saddle. A large rock struck Artoch. He kicked out his hind legs twice, and Roland leaned back to compensate, luckily missing another large rock which whistled past his head. Twisting at the waist, Roland pulled his sword full around to the left side to defend against the next blow from the man with the club, already held high ready to strike Roland from his horse.

Roland sliced the attacker's bicep. The man roared but kept the momentum of his swing. The club took a glancing blow down Roland's back, and he felt the club drop on the other side of Artoch. With his good arm, the attacker tried to grab Roland. The injured arm was hanging, and Roland had a clean opening to thrust his blade down into the man, following the cheek through the collarbone and into the chest and abdomen. The body dropped straight down, and the sword was free.

Some of the kills were clean and direct, but most were mayhem of nightmarish proportion. No one to cover his back, no assistance to hope for. Fear nagged at the borders of his thought: where was Eloise? Was her body below him even now, being trampled? Had they killed her? All his energy was focused in stopping these men. Let the energy of man and sword unite and commit to the fight. *El Muerte Rojo* and Roland were one, with each breath and each heartbeat. As one they bludgeoned one marauder in the teeth, another the skull, with blade or pommel in turn.

Frustrated beating on the shield, the man put down the club and with both hands lifted the shield and Eloise with it. Without fighting the bigger man for the shield, she let it rotate and brought herself with it, reaching for the dagger on her leg. Dagger drawn, she ground the blade into his chest. Bone and cartilage were tough, protecting the heart and lungs from assault by sharp objects or crushing impact. Fortune shone upon Eloise as her blade slid easily between the ribs. He was dead without seeing her face. His limp body fell. Eloise balanced on her good leg, the end of the shield as a crutch.

From behind, someone grabbed the dagger, trying to wrest it from her grip. Spinning in the direction he pulled, they pivoted round and round. Losing balance, with her blade zinging wildly around, the thief let go as she rotated a little more. She launched herself at his back. Unable to support her weight on her injured ankle, she caught him around the waist instead of his neck with her shield arm. Gripping him tight she stabbed him in the kidney again and again. He arched back, his right hand reaching for the blade. The momentum of his death arch pushed them backwards, Eloise clinging to him so he couldn't possibly reach her. They fell together, Eloise cradled in the shield, his body across her left arm and knee.

She tried to spring up but was firmly restrained. If she could roll to her right, she could use her right hand and right leg to shove the body enough for her to wriggle free. The dying man's thick warm blood seeped onto her. Her dagger hand was flung back, and someone stepped on her upturned wrist.

She kicked with her right leg. The pressure increased on her wrist and the man easily pried her blade free.

Eloise watched in pain as the man examined her dagger. He palmed it, seeming to appreciate the weight and balance. She tried to struggle free and the man ground her wrist with his foot until she was still.

He stared down at Eloise and the dead man across her. Then his calculating eyes rested upon her chest. He reached down, lifting the wooden cross pendant, then dropped it as if unimpressed, squeezing the handle of her valuable dagger.

"Fucking Hell," he murmured, looking closer, his cold eyes studying her face, chin. "Who?" he muttered, then he yanked back her tunic and pulled at her chemise.

Eloise gulped, but was unable to command herself to move.

Unsatisfied he stuck his grubby hand down her clothing and felt the tight bindings wrapped around her breasts to conceal them. Eloise screamed and wriggled against his touch.

"Well," he smirked. "You'll be worth somethin' to someun," he said, grinning down at her.

The left side of her face was swelling up. Her eye was almost closed. A blood clot filled her left nostril and she was breathing through her mouth. "Ugly squirrel," he muttered.

A few smaller stones hit Roland in the head and chest. He wasn't unhorsed and continued to confound the marauders. Bodies lay beneath him, some dead, some wounded. Three men were still attempting to catch Garth. Eloise was nowhere to be seen. With no other men attacking, Roland went to dispatch the horse thieves. Riding up behind one of them, it was fast work to cleave at his head when the man turned. The next man was easy slaughter. The third man turned to face the mounted knight. Not easily deterred, he dodged and circled Roland until he could secure a branch big enough to work as a spear or lance or possibly a large stone to launch. Roland calculated this match. One on one, this man was still a dangerous adversary. On horseback, Roland had the advantage. But anything could happen when two determined men confronted each other.

Horses, like most animals, sense fear. Garth wasn't an exception. From the day he was born, Eloise had been there. As his mother licked the slimy film of the birth sack off him, Eloise was stroking him, mingling her scent with his. And from this early age, Eloise asserted her dominance over him, simple gestures she observed other horses doing with each other. And ones she adapted herself. Her position as the leader of his herd was undisputed, and so he accepted it. Others, however, had to be tried and tested.

These marauders were not experienced horsemen and no match for a spirited stallion. Garth sensed something he didn't like. A stench of smelly men he didn't recognise. Two of the men had fallen out of trees and hurt him. The weight of them and their weapons caused him pain. This pain and surprise cut a deep memory: he would remember the smell, the pain and this place. Others were raining from the tree and jumping out of the bushes.

Frightened, he reared up. He wanted his face away from this man grabbing at it. After a safe distance he stopped and turned to look. Riderless and without direction, he waited and watched. A herd animal, he didn't want to be out alone. There was safety in numbers. Three men approached him. Garth read by the stooped body posture and outstretched arms they were afraid. They displayed submissive behavior. These were smelly men, causers-of-pain. He moved away from them.

To be absolutely sure, the man checked one more time. With Eloise's right wrist pinned under his knee, he reached across her and ran his hand along the inside of her legs. Not a caress, but a thorough search to be sure there wasn't a male scrotum.

Eloise gasped at the violation, trying to squeeze her legs together as his fingers poked and probed. She had never been so misused in her life, and thought she would be sick.

"All right," he said, pulling the dead man off her before yanking her up by her arm. "Up ya go." As she winced and staggered in pain, he removed the shield. He wrenched her right arm behind her back and wedged her hand between her shoulder blades.

He held her against his left side and started towards the woods as Eloise struggled to resist his abduction. Unable to put weight on her left ankle, she took large jump-steps with her right foot. Her left arm ached. Her cross pendant banged against her chest as they ran. It was still there. If she could reach it, mayhap she could retrieve the hidden dagger within and save herself. The terrain was uneven and she stumbled, hitting her foot on high spots. The toe of her boot tangled in a clump of matted grass. Her abductor merely yanked her forward and stabbing pain seized her as though someone still beat her ankle. She tried to grab her ankle, to protect herself from the pain.

Roland caught the movement of a figure running across the meadow towards the woods. No, two figures. Reining forward on Artoch, Roland pursued Eloise and the marauder.

Roland's adversary, the man with the branch, hesitated briefly before running into the woods to hide.

Artoch lengthened his stride and horse and rider caught up with the unsuspecting people on foot. Leaning forward from his charging horse, Roland envisioned his left hand with the talons of a bird of prey. With an iron grip he grabbed the fleeing man behind his neck, willing his fingertips to penetrate the flesh. Penetration or not, it was a painful grip and propelled the man forward with the speed of the knight on horseback. Eloise was dropped as the marauder ran helplessly alongside Roland. Rounding back in an easy turn, Roland cantered up to a large tree stump. Charging in fast Roland rammed the man into the stump. The robber took the full impact face and chest in equal force, then rebounded from the impact and fell on his back in the high meadow grasses.

Eloise crumpled and skidded in the tall grasses. Finally, able to hold her ankle, she curled into a ball cradling herself in the tall grass hiding like a frightened fawn. The pain returned in ever increasing waves.

Roland walked back to make sure the robber was dead. Eyes staring in different directions, blood foaming from the corner of his mouth, it appeared he was trying to talk. His arms twitched. Hearing splashing, Roland watched two young men run across the stream in their bid for escape. Let them go, Roland calculated to himself.

Now for the slaughter. None of these men would be left alive. So, the warrior purged his system of the last remaining need for death. This kind of slaughter was unfit for knights. Squires and others usually completed this dirty work. Still, it satisfied Roland as he stabbed the beating heart of each surviving robber beneath his feet.

Eloise, Eloise!"

She continued to cradle herself.

"Eloise! Eloise?" Roland called again. She took a few deep breaths, rousing herself. His voice, her name. He was searching for her, not sounding an alarm. Her breath heaved, but words wouldn't form as she sought to hail him. She crawled to her knees, then concentrating all her efforts she stood, balanced on her right foot. All she saw was a dark silhouette on horseback with the brighter daylight a halo behind him. She lifted her shaking arms, hands outstretched.

Roland dismounted and embraced her. Eloise squeezed her right side deep into his arms and held tight, tight as she'd gripped her uncles's shield. They stood there together, safe for the moment.

Flies already swarmed and the buzz carried through the still June air. The crows noisily regaled each other from the trees. These large scavengers were working up the courage to come closer, still not sure it was all quiet and safe. The smell of fresh blood permeated the senses of wildlife. Those whose existence depended on such readily available nutrition would anticipate when and where to proceed. The herbivores would stay clear. This was a smell of danger: men and blood. Unaware of nature's janitors coming in to feast on the carnage of their triumph, Roland and Eloise clung to each other.

"My Maiden strikes quick and true," he stated complimenting her on killing two men herself. "I took a moment to examine the men for wounds. Two lethal blows." Taking a deep breath, he rested his cheek on her head. That silly cap had fallen off, and he could feel her soft amber hair. "It's alright now, all safe," he tried to be calm and soothing.

Eloise tried to laugh at his compliment, but instead started to cry. The pent-up anxiety harbored these four days liberated itself: the siege on the castle, her grief for the death of Uncle Reggie, her Nurse and the grief for all the other men she had doctored. Some had survived with her care, for others she could only ease death. For them she sobbed with cataclysmic waves. Beaten and vulnerable, Eloise wasn't strong enough to block the horrific images of Hughy, Alsandair or the others, the vacant eyes of loved ones, the taste of blood and stench of burned flesh. She cried for the fright and uncertainty of her escape from her ancestral home. "Garth," she whined. Remembering her horse, his peril then and now, how had she forgotten her horse in all this?

"Garth is here, well and good," Roland said.

Eloise accepted his words as true, but it wasn't enough to bring her back to the present, as the unbidden memories reclaimed her. She sobbed and wailed in anguish for her parents. Eloise feared for her mother, so sweet and kind. Her body shook, trembling like a stone rampart on impact.

"Eloise," Roland said, squeezing her. Trying to comfort her, she knew, but she was beyond comfort. Lost in pain and worry.

Wolves. The long, grueling journey with little rest, food or comfort, and now this. She let it out. She had been beaten and almost murdered. She had stabbed two men. She didn't weep for them, but she wept for another piece of innocence lost. Nausea overcame her as she remembered the horrible man who stuck his filthy paws down her chest. Even with the bindings tightly in place, he had cupped the mounds of her breasts; he had run his hand between her legs, her most private places. Jerking violently from Roland's embrace she vomited and choked.

Roland lifted the corner of his tunic and wiped her mouth. She flinched and he saw the splits to her upper and lower lips. They bled again. Huge, fierce bruises were already forming. Her left eye, once so full of sparkle and intensity, was completely hidden from view behind swollen flesh. Drops of blood dotted her ear and her nose bled freely.

"Bastards! God cursed bastards," he muttered, wishing he could kill them again. "Are you cut? Bleeding?" he asked, holding her out at arm's length to see for himself.

Sniffing, Eloise shook her head, and the sobbing overtook her.

"Let it out. I'm here," he soothed, taking her back in his arms. He felt an innate need to rock her, and he swayed gently left, right, left, right. "You're safe now. They're gone."

Christ almighty, he reprimanded himself again. *Stupid! Careless!* He went through an entire repertoire of vulgarities, begging forgiveness each time, then starting again. *Your fault*, he scolded, *almost got her killed, and yourself as well. Stupid fucking careless. Let your guard down, let her ride into a trap.* His rocking helped him to stay calm, and soon Eloise was breathing in rhythm with him.

He kissed the top of her head. Then he left his lips there, gently resting on the crown. He took in the full scent of her. Long gone were the traces of bath, flower scented soaps and other spicy perfumes. Just the smell of her, and a week's worth of sweat and grime, and her. She filled his arms and his senses. As the focus of battle wore off, a feeling of success replaced it. Victory. There had been ten marauders. Eloise had killed two, two had run off, and he had killed six. Not bad, all carelessness aside.

A warrior's need to declare victory, to boast, or gloat, or simply celebrate survival were well accepted throughout history. In the extreme, it was the rape and pillage of a conquered enemy's camp. It may be parading joyfully home, or just the robust celebration of men in a tavern. Roland had a need to release his victory tension, just as Eloise was releasing her grief and fear.

To the victor go the spoils and Roland felt possessive, of Eloise.

Shit! Roland thought. *Fucking, bleeding, Saints on the Cross* flashed in his brain. He groaned. The feel of the maiden's body swaying seductively in rhythm with his, the urge to take her and claim her as his own was making him desperately uncomfortable. It seemed his manhood was saluting the victory: it was hard, damp and erect, trapped in his braises. So long since he'd been with a woman, and how he pained to be with this one. Wanted her more than he had ever wanted a woman before, he thought.

It should be. There were conventions that would support his claim. It could be argued her father had abandoned her to his care. He had risked his life ten to one to win her back. She wasn't an unfair fee to exact. And, there was no one to stop him. Surely not the maid herself, she would willingly give herself up to him, he figured, swept up in the same emotion to celebrate their triumph.

He needed to step away, disengage.

Garth made his way to the stream; after drinking, he started to graze. His herd instinct kept him close. Artoch, too, longed to drink. He had suffered some minor cuts and abrasions from the club and stones thrown in an effort to unseat the knight. He fidgeted and shook to dislodge the flies already pestering his injuries.

"Horses are fine," Roland said, "let's get to the stream." They could all use some water. A week's worth of road dirt, sweat and grime covered him. Stale blood and more sweat and grime on top of that from his efforts at Dahlquin Castle. Fresh spatters of blood, filth, more sweat were piled on that. The abattoir himself, he thought.

The movement stopped. Eloise ceased crying. The waves of emotion and sobbing left her exhausted, drained. Too long she had been holding it in. Roland helped her limp to the stream.

Once kneeling, Eloise struggled unsuccessfully to drink. The water seemed to drip everywhere but into her parched mouth.

"Let me help," Roland said, dipping his hand into the cool water and holding it steadily to her split lips. Eloise held his hand with her two.

"May you have goodness," she whispered, slowly getting the water past her bleeding lips into her mouth.

After several handfuls of water, she touched her chin trying to wipe away the rest. She felt her mouth, and lips. Next, her cheek, and with very cautious fingers probed the swollen flesh to feel if her eye was injured. Would she be blind in one eye like Alsandair? Next her ear: it still burned but wasn't lacerated as badly as she feared. The sound of ripping roused her from her examination. Roland had cut a piece of his tunic and dipped it in the water. As he lifted the wrung-out piece of cloth, she caught his hand in hers.

She held it there a moment before whispering, "Shame upon me, you must be hurt too." Regaining her sense of duty, she searched his face, ears, neck for injury. She studied his chest and arms, spattered in fresh blood on top of the old. "Any of this yours?" she asked, reaching out to palpate, then seeing her own hand still shaking far too much to be of any help.

"I'm unharmed," he answered, lifting the cloth to her face. "It's you who is hurt."

Eloise reached for his hand again, but he kept it moving to clean the blood and dirt from her face as she held on to his wrist. *I should be the healer*, she thought, forcing herself to sit still.

"Am I hurting you?" he questioned, when she grimaced.

"You are not, shame upon me, it's just that-" she said.

"Then let go my arm and let me do this for you," he said softly.

She obeyed and let him continue. The cool cloth felt good on her tender ear. She put her hand on his to hold it there a moment longer.

Last night in the farmyard, she had longed to be this close to Roland, to feel his large hands stroke her cheek, exalt in the touch of his fingers through her hair. Now, she wanted to hide from his close gaze. Her appearance must be hideous. *He is so handsome*, she thought. *And I'm an ugly squirrel in boy's clothing*. New tears formed in her eyes. Only a week ago, she was a princess within Dahlquin. Estate, status and a name: today all that was stripped away from her, she had naught but pain and worry.

"Sorrow upon me," Roland said as he brought his hand away from her ear. "I'm not accustomed to ministering to someone as delicate as you."

You're not hurting me, I have embarrassment, she thought. She wanted to hide, put distance between them so he wouldn't see her so. Get back in the saddle, get away from this place, help her parents. That was what she wanted to do.

What she needed to do was take care of her wounds. Where to start? It was hard to doctor yourself. Roland looked at her enquiringly. What next? Indeed, she thought reading his expression, what next? Everything hurt. It was hard to concentrate. *Think*, she ordered herself.

"What is wrong with your leg? Your foot, ankle?" he asked.

How bad were her injuries? Would she be able to ride, should they make camp here? She had to get away from this field of death. There wouldn't be healing with the scavengers, flies and memories of this foul place. They must leave. How could she move?

"My ankle," she said, remembering the stabbing pain. Taking a deep breath, eye closed, she moved her toes, a good sign. She attempted to rotate her ankle and was met with throbbing pain. After two deep breaths, she tried to flex her ankle. Sharp pain stabbed her. She grabbed her ankle with her hands, waiting for the pounding pain to recede. She looked at her booted foot and began to unbuckle it, starting at the top, just below the knee. The knuckles on her left hand were scraped and her fingers were stiff and clumsy. "Would you help me get my boot off?"

"Pull it off? Are you sure?" he asked. "It's swollen like a melon. We'll never get it back on."

"I need to see, to feel," she said, trying to unfasten the next buckle.

"See or feel what? It's injured. Leave the boot for support. That's the remedy."

"What if I'm bleeding? Maybe I can-" She had to turn her head to use her right eye. Her nose was running, and she had to cough. If she could just see her foot, lay her hand upon it. "Mayhap the swelling is the cause of the pain."

"I disagree." He sighed, then, "But, I will try and get it off." He unfastened the last of the three buckles and tried to ease the boot off. "This will hurt," he said, looking directly into her one open eye, "a lot."

Eloise tried to suppress a shriek as Roland struggled to pry the boot off her foot. She dug her fingers into the turf as he pulled. "Damn," escaped her lips.

"Damn is right," he said. "And hmmm, hmmmm, and what else was it you couldn't bring yourself to sing? La la la," he ribbed her, distracting her from the pain.

Eloise snorted then chuckled at the absurdity of her present situation. Unable to grin or laugh, mirth did ease the pain a wee bit and it did wonders for the soul. Humor, despite its blackness, relieved stress.

"What's so funny?" he smirked, pulling his dagger. "Let me see if I can cut this off."

"Wonder upon me, how the bloody hmmm Hell I ended up here," she answered. Four days ago she was comfortably working in the garden of Dahlquin, surrounded by Beast and Dragon, or grooming Garth in the stable. How had she sunk so low? Beaten, lost, with one of late King John's godsons?

"Hmmm? How the bloody, fucking Hell you got here?" he corrected, still working at her boot. "God's boots," he lamented, glancing up at her. "This is ox-hide," he sighed, "only the toughest leather for our High Maid Epona."

"Ox-hide," she concurred, wondering at the compliment 'Epona'. "Ow!" she howled as he tried once more to remove the boot. Her dirty hands went to her bloody, mucous covered mouth trying to press her split lips together.

"Large pliers are what we need. A smith would have such implements," he added, looking up at her.

Eloise watched his expression cloud over. His gaze moved across her face, he could see what she could only feel and guess at. Pain, fear and embarrassment engulfed her. She needed to leave. She wasn't sure she could.

With fingers whisper-soft Roland pulled her nose, drawing her attention to his fingertips and his attempted grin.

"The boot remains," he said, "unless you want me to remove your entire leg from about here?" Using his dagger he traced a line above the top of her boot, just below her knee.

Eloise shook her head.

"Let's wash your face again," he said, sheathing his dagger. "Then see if you can ride."

Red foxes that had been hanging back at the woods edge pressed closer. A pair of foxes from the other meadow had been attracted. A badger drawn by the smell of blood emerged as well. The crows and flies had beaten them to it, but there was plenty of carrion for all. Vultures jostled for position amongst the crows.

As Roland collected her bow, spilled arrows, dagger and Reggie's shield, Eloise balanced on her right foot, stroking Garth, feeling his legs for heat or swelling. He had an abrasion on his face, and she wondered if he had been struck by a club or punched by an evil fist. Plaintain, willow bark and spider's web would ease both their suffering. They were not suffering, she told herself, Dahlquin and Ashbury suffered.

"Here is your dagger," Roland said, handing it to her.

Eloise wobbled, losing her balance. Roland took her elbow.

"May you have goodness," she said.

Eloise took the dagger, held it in both hands, prayer fashion, feeling reverential and thankful. She had killed two men with this dagger. *We'll never be the same.* She put her dagger in her calf sheath.

"And your bow and spilled arrows."

Taking the arrows, she counted all fifteen, then reached out for *Cara*. Her bow hand was swollen and thick as she tried to grip her friend. Unable to feel the soothing hum of connection, she hugged the bow to her chest. *Cara.*

"He saved your life," Roland said, lifting Reggie's shield.

"Once again, Uncle's blessings upon me," she sighed, crossing herself in contemplation of such a miracle.

"Is there strength upon you to carry it now?"

Was she forsaking Reggie's memory, Reggie's gift? She was on a mission, and Uncle would understand.

"Would you, by your will?" she asked, wiping her nose.

"An honor," Roland said. "Now, we need to go," Roland prompted. "Oft side, aye, so I can boost you with your good foot."

After putting *Cara* over her shoulder, Eloise took hold of the reins and Garth's mane in her right hand and the pommel in the injured left. Roland took hold of her lower leg and lifted her up. She balanced a moment, easing her injured ankle over Garth's back. In the first moments of pain, nothing felt secure.

"Wait here," Roland said, jogging off.

What is he about? she wondered as she settled into the saddle, stroking Garth's neck.

"Good boy," she cooed. "My good Garth."

Roland jogged back.

"Will this do?" he asked, looking squeamish, a wad of spider web on his extended fingertips, "with the spider's compliments."

"It will," Eloise said, leaning over so he could apply the medicinal to her ear.

"Ah, mayhap," he stammered, "so I don't hurt you further," he added, taking her hand and smearing the sticky web to her finger.

"May you have goodness, Lord," she said, dabbing the spider's gift to her abraded ear. *If only I had leeches for this eye*, she thought.

Roland secured her damaged foot in the stirrup, but the pain was too great. He removed the stirrups from the saddle, placed them in her saddle bags before putting Reginald's shield on and mounting himself.

All this Torcan observed from his hiding place deep in the trees. The robbery had been thwarted, with devastating results. Eight men killed, most of them family, and he might have been one of them if not for his cousin's flight drawing the knight away. Surely his cousin had made the same discovery: the boy was not as he appeared. The knight's regard for the beaten spindle before him indicated a well-disguised female. Torcan was too far away to hear their conversation, but the tenderness displayed was revealing enough. Who were these two, and what was their secret? Elopement? It didn't matter. The disasters of this foul day might be salvaged, with the girl. The boy, he minded himself as he watched them ride away.

There was another member of the gang who wasn't killed and who hadn't run away. He still clung to the tree. A lad of seven, this had been his first raid, his indoctrination to the family profession of road robbery. Small and frightened, he had been unable to jump from the tree. He held on and watched. Not part of the actual attack, he would have slid down from the tree and helped undress and rob the corpses. Things had not gone as planned. The boy had watched his father, uncle, older brother and cousins butchered. Another cousin escaped into the woods. And now no one was there for the boy. Even as nighttime fell, he wouldn't come out of the tree. He clung doggedly. When his mother came to the field looking for him, he wouldn't come down. His mother was seven months pregnant with yet another child, her tenth. Ten children, and now a third husband dead, a brother-in-law, son and cousin also dead. She held her apron over her face as she checked the bodies. The smell was terrible, and the crows and flies were a noisy swarm. Not a little boy among them. She scanned the scene and then slowly approached the tree. She looked up and he looked down. He wouldn't speak, but he did climb down at her bidding. His career as a marauder was undetermined.

ASHBURY CASTLE, 12ᵗʰ of June

Lord Albert called a meeting in his private chambers. The arrow wound to his arse was inflamed, though the healer didn't recommend maggots - yet. Pain and stiffness spread up his hip to his lower back, as if his 72-year old back didn't suffer enough discomfort. Both legs were swollen and lamented the abuse by hindering his lively gait. In attendance were Eoch, the Captain of the Armory, his Marshal responsible for knights and men-at-arms, the Seanascal, and of course his Lady Wife, Mor.

"We're here to discuss where we stand regarding this heinous siege. We've had much speculation and rumor regards Tiomoid U'Neill and our Ulster cousins. Tiomoid's messenger claims Tiomoid has the might of Ulster, Denmark and the Scots Hebrides."

Albert gave his assembled group a chance to digest this and offer any dissent or further information. There was little grumbling or gossip, as Albert expected from this disciplined group. He continued.

"We haven't seen flags, banners or colors from Magnus U'Neill or our Ulster cousins. We're in agreement that Tiomoid U'Neill does not represent the U'Neill tribe, yet he has somehow with great debt upon himself amassed an avaricious mercenary army. At our very gate and Dahlquin's, we're told." Again, Albert waited for any comment or dissent. All his men and wife nodded their agreement.

"We're cut off. Not a word in or out except what bias Tiomoid's army feeds us. Are we sure of Dahlquin's siege? Have we any way to verify the truth?"

"If I may speak, Lord?" the Marshal said, then he coughed.

"By your will, it's why we're here," Albert encouraged, noting the wet, phlegmy cough that was becoming endemic in the encapsulated castle.

"We're trapped. Besieged within our secure castle, as is our purpose currently," the Marshal started. "Tiomoid's men don't appear to be under pressure from the outside. We see not a whit of support from Dahlquin, which may confirm their siege. But what of Scragmuir? Tiomoid's messenger claims Scragmuir has joined him and even now lays siege upon Dahlquin, thus allowing Tiomoid the luxury of destroying us. Do you think that is possible?"

"Anything is possible, God or Satan willing," Albert said, and he and all in attendance crossed themselves for protection against the naming of Satan. "He claims Scragmuir has joined Tiomoid U'Neill. But what evidence, hard evidence, is there that Lord Humphrey of Scragmuir would turn against De Burgh, FitzGilbert, Ireland? He would obliterate Dahlquin without doubt, but civil war against all Ireland and King Henry? I think not. Am I remiss in my judgment?"

The chamber was quiet save for the coughing of his Marshal and now the Captain of the Armory. Mor reached over and placed her hand upon his, then squeezed it. He glanced first at her hand, their hands, then he looked up to her face. Her expression appeared kindly. Did she wish to say something? Was there some hidden meaning? God-curse it, why were women so hard to understand? Why couldn't they say what they meant? If she had some insight to impart, speak it.

She took a deep breath.

He wanted to shout – divulge it woman!

As if reading the frustration in his expression, she squeezed his hand again, and once more offered a kind, or wan look. It only increased his anxiety.

"My Lady Mor," Eoch said, "it seems you would offer some comfort and encouragement for the trials we're enduring. Your presence here is most welcome, and we all acknowledge that Ashbury Castle could not endure without the stalwart efforts of you as our most noble and gracious chatelaine, and those of our Seanascal.

God's blood, is that what Mor was seeking? Her own self-aggrandisement in this most harrowing hour? Mor blanched. That was not the expression of a woman flattered.

"Goodness upon you, Sir Eoch, for always bestowing your gracious appreciation for my humble efforts in support of my Lord Husband and all Ashbury," she said, head bowed, and Albert noted she brushed a tear away. "It is only my wish to bolster and support our Lord Albert in this most trying hour. Our Lion of Ashbury," she said.

"We're assembled here for the support of our liege Lord," the Marshall said. He added, "There's not a word or sign of Dahlquin or Scragmuir. If Scragmuir isn't in allegiance with Tiomoid, why haven't they ridden to our aid? If Connacht is under attack from Ulster, Scragmuir should support its own."

"Scragmuir is pledged to support Connacht, De Burgh, FitzGilbert and Ireland. We would ride to their defense," the Captain of the Armory said. "Wouldn't we?" he asked for confirmation.

"We would. Scragmuir should come to our aid. But it has only been four days. They might only now be getting word of the attacks. Lord Humphrey is as cautious and thorough as I would be," Albert said. "What would be a prudent decision for Humphrey?"

"A scouting party, mayhap, to discover the size and might of the army. A day out and back. Then a counsel, as we're doing," Eoch offered.

"Same with Dahlquin, if they're not under attack," the Marshal said.

"You're correct, relief would be a week or more away," Eoch commented, as the rest murmured. "And what if Lord Humphrey is gone, on progression or a hunting escapade? He may be gone a fortnight. His men would await his return before embarking on such a grand assault as our siege."

Albert listened as each of his men had a chance to voice his opinion of whether Dahlquin was under siege and when Scragmuir would offer the mandatory relief force to defend Ashbury and, ultimately, all Connacht. For defend they must.

After consultation with Mor and the Seanascal about the available stores to sustain Ashbury through this treasonous siege which could last for months, Ashbury committed to settling in and defending the castle until Tiomoid got bored or was defeated from outside. Or until Lord Albert became bored and decided to lead the attack.

"We agree, the wells are good, the pantries adequate. Even with the lost planting season, we will survive behind these walls of stone," Eoch confirmed, lifting his chalice.

The others lifted their cups and chalices in tribute to the Lord and Lady. Albert and Mor did the same.

"For the Glory of Ashbury!" they all shouted.

LEINSTER, 12th of June

The ride was uncomfortable, and the miles seemed endless to Eloise.

"Roland," she said, her voice unfamiliar and nasal. Her face had such pain she could barely speak. "Artoch limps. Garth is off." She remembered the abrasion on Garth's face. One of the marauders had injured him. Idiots!

"We're in Leinster, a day from FitzGilbert's castle. Half a day if we ride all night," Roland said, watching Garth a moment. Glowering, he studied her head to toe, then flexed his sword hand, grimacing.

"As you command," she said, remembering Reginald's words, *'When he says, if he says.'*

"Starvation is upon me. My hand feels broken, my thigh aches. With so much fatigue upon me it's hard to imagine how you fare. One hundred shames upon me," he sighed, rubbing his eyes with the butts of his gloved hands. "What should we do?"

Garth and Artoch both seemed to rally, lifting their weary heads, nostrils pumping, as if the question had been posed to them.

Artoch nickered.

"Saints preserve us, that smells good," Roland said, inhaling.

"What?" Eloise asked, trying to inhale through her blocked sinuses.

"Burned sausage and fried fish," he answered. "Market Day!"

As Eloise and Roland entered the village, the booths and stands were already being disassembled, and the unsold goods put away. But the aroma of cooking and brew lured Roland on.

"We're grievously hungry and in want of drink," Roland said, approaching a wool merchant who was helping his wife pack their cart. "Any recommendations? I know it's late."

The merchant turned. His wife gasped.

A frightful sight they were. Roland's dark garments were stained with blood and filth. Eloise thought she probably appeared as the recipient of some fretful punishment. She and Roland were in sharp contrast to the merriment of the villagers on market day.

"Finest pasties in Leinster," the merchant said, "if there's any left. Around that way," he pointed. "Follow your nose."

Roland thanked him then dismounted and walked his horse through the emptying stalls, carts and the startled onlookers.

"'Tis a foul wind blows to the north, and dragons," Roland replied to the on-lookers. Eloise nodded solemnly.

Finding a merchant, Eloise crossed herself when discovering he still had food. Roland offered to trade in lieu of payment.

"What do you have, Dragon Slayer?" the merchant asked.

Roland's grin was tired and lopsided, but he seemed well pleased with the title.

"Fresh hares," he said, and Eloise lifted the headless bodies.

"Not in need of those now," the merchant said, shaking his head.

Oh, if only she had her voice. Surely, she might sing an epic tale or two for their supper. What a chanson that would have been…if. But she could barely whistle for the swelling of her face. What else did she have?

"Lord," Eloise beckoned, whispering in his ear when he got close. "I've an eating knife. Trade that," she offered.

"Aye," he said slowly, "Let's see."

She nearly wept for joy as Roland negotiated the knife for five pasties: three suet and onion, two egg and leek, as well as a skin bag of cider. The merchant's wife threw in some wilted cabbages.

On market day every room, bed and pallet were full with traders. Gratefully Roland and Eloise traded the three hares for crowded space in the barn and feed for the horses.

Just as the inn was full, so too, the stable. Each stall held a horse or mule, but the stable corridor had just enough space for Garth and Artoch, hobbled. Eloise watched as one of the laborers from the inn cleared a space for Roland and her to bed down, only slightly beyond the horses' hooves. He left an oil skin canopy for them to lay out when they were ready to sleep.

"May you have goodness," she said to him. "And by your will, may your master have goodness, again." She crossed herself again.

Eloise lovingly stroked around the base of Garth's itchy ears as Roland removed her saddle. "May you have goodness and blessing, Sire," she said, trying to make her voice warm, showing her gratitude.

Horses tended, Roland and Eloise settled in to eat and drink.

"Not a room at the inn," Eloise mused as a big orange striped cat rubbed against her, purring. "Like Joseph and the Virgin Mary."

"At least we aren't being taxed," Roland mumbled, his mouth full of pastie.

"Stables are not so bad. Warm, cozy, fresh straw and horses. And cats," she added, as the orange feline continued his courtship. The cat would surely keep them safe from the cursed rats whose foul existence plagued human and animal alike.

Still chewing, Roland looked at her, then the persistent cat. With a finger he pushed the remaining half of his egg and leek pastie into his mouth. After swallowing hard, he said, "Full of muck, vermin and stench."

"Hmm," she sighed, chewing herself. "But not in the Bible and not in my father's stables." She took another bite of the suet and onion pie. Juice ran down her chin and between her fingers. If Beast and Dragon were here, they would lick her clean, but the orange cat did his best, his purrs becoming a chortle. She wished she could taste more, but aroma and flavor were muted by her battered sinuses.

She held her hand out and Roland passed the skin bag with cider and willow bark added. She gulped it down, willing herself to feel better, to heal.

"Wish I had some assassin's brew," she muttered, thinking of the mystic effects.

"What?" Roland said, choking on his food, bits of crust on his lips. He coughed, pounding his chest. The cat scooted away and stared at him from a safer distance.

"Assassin's brew. Powerful medicine from the Holy Land," Eloise said.

"Powerful indeed," Roland said, still coughing. "You brew it?"

"Well, we grow the plant. Dry the buds and leaves. It's possible to get the medicine from rubbing the plants, but a nuisance to scrape the resin from your hands. Easier to grind the vegetation and add to brew or spirits. Potent smoke, too." She closed her eyes, trying to imagine the effect - without a care of the pain. First the oblivion and then a night's undisturbed sleep, what a blessing that would be.

"You grow it? In Dahlquin?"

"We grow it," she said, wondering why he was so surprised. Originally from Moorish traders, the plant had a vigorous habit. "There's nothing better for massive injury, pain, it soothes *and* emboldens."

"Makes men feel invincible. Assassins," Roland said as the cat approached him then returned to Eloise, purring as if receiving a long-lost friend.

"Defying death, feeling immortal. It enslaves," she murmured. Belly full, exhaustion was taking the edge off her pain and she was talking with both eyes closed.

"Your Uncle Reggie!" Roland said. "Bleeding Saints." He snorted, causing him to cough again. "That explains it."

Eloise glanced at him through half closed eyes - well, one eye was swollen shut.

He lifted the skin bag containing the cider and finished it. "Assassin's Brew, of course, how else could he have carried on?" Roland paused. "Heroic. Cheating death."

Roland seemed almost giddy with the revelation.

"Heroic. But he was so without the brew," she said, tears welling, even in her swollen eye. Would things have been different if she had had some Assassin's brew in her pouch? Would he have had the strength to carry on, be here now? "May you have the blessings of one thousand saints and more, Uncle," she whispered, crossing herself over and over until the tears stopped. His death, his sacrifice. How could she atone? Duty, devotion. And love.

"Now I wish we had some," said Roland, his tone warm. "A few hours relief would be grand."

Eloise was drifting off, but after a few moments she felt disquiet. She forced her weary eye open to find Roland's stern gaze upon her.

"I'm wondering. Mayhap…it would be best, if we boarded you here," he said.

Eloise had to force her mind to process the words, as if translating a foreign language.

"I will not be left behind," she said, indignant, feeling betrayed.

"You can't walk, you can barely ride. I'll be back in a few days-"

"I will not." She tried to shake her head. "You won't find me here." What was he proposing? To leave her here? Helpless? Did he find her a burden?

"A chamber with the apothecary or the constable. I've a dagger to leave as collateral or payment," he continued, ignoring her protests, not even looking at her as he calculated. "Your shield," he hesitated, brow knit.

"You need your dagger, and I must keep Reggie's shield." Roland was mad with fatigue to suggest such.

"Garth?"

"Garth? Never!" she growled, her heart racing as she turned to watch her beautiful horse grazing with Artoch. "He would be stolen faster than-"

Eloise stopped, not finishing her sentence, for Roland was saying the same thing. He also stopped talking, his expression softening when their eyes met. Eloise remained silent, waiting, wondering how he would complete the sentence. His gaze never wavered. His brown eyes seemed to enter her, touching her very soul. Then he fell back, looking away, distressed.

"Roland?" she asked.

Roland shook his head then reached for the last pastie. "One left." He broke it in half before she could decline, holding one half towards her.

"You eat it, with your will, Lord," she said, watching.

Seeing Roland eat both, she cradled the orange cat, wondering what had happened. What had he seen in her eyes, well one eye?

Eloise was asleep, one of the blankets wrapped around her and the cat.

Roland laid out the oil skin canopy the inn keeper offered them in the way of bedding. It was better than lying on their damp saddle blankets as they had done the night before. God's blood, that had been miserable, and tonight wasn't looking any better. Succubus indeed. "Huh," he huffed. Despite her injuries, she was desirable. Why? Was she unattainable? Her injured ankle and face surely added to her forbidden status. Like some maiden of legend. A Princess. "Bah," he muttered, unable to deny what he saw in her eyes, well her right eye. It must be befuddlement of the mind. Exhaustion. The Maid of Dahlquin.

In her nightmare Eloise was lost. Garth was lost. Rather, he was back at Dahlquin, dying. Everyone was dying, and she couldn't get there without Garth. How had she become disengorged? Outcast. She had the dog-chewed ledger and armed with that, she must find her way back to Dahlquin to her dying family. When she opened the ledger, the pages were corrupted, wolf blood saturated the pages, and others were singed, where she had left it too close to the hearth. Useless. She wandered through brambles avoiding the roads for they were dangerous. She heard a whinny. Garth. She fought her way to him, calling, whistling. He was running to her yet did not progress. He was in a bog with only his body showing. When she finally got to him, she realized that he was well and healed, but his legs were gone, only stumps with cloven hooves. He was glad of her presence, she knew, but he was useless, helpless, and completely unaware as he tried to nuzzle her. *Mathair, mathair*, what is happening. *Mathair*, by your will, help me, I need you. Her mouth was full of blood. And her nose. Guilt of the Huntress, for she had killed. She was choking, unable to breathe. Eloise realized that her legs were gone too, she was a stump herself. Uncle Reggie saved her. But she neglected to save him. He lost his hand and now she must sacrifice her limbs. Yet her legs hurt so, legs not there were aching and tormenting, as if they were roots being crushed by the firmament. And she couldn't breathe. Useless. "*Mathair*," she called, the blood pouring from her mouth and   nose. "*Mathair*," she tried to scream, her arms grabbing for her mother.

"El."

That wasn't her mother, but Eloise clung to the hope of the familiar voice, feeling hands clutch her. Da? Uncle Reggie? She still couldn't breathe, she was suffocating.

"El, wake up."

Wake up.

"I have you. El, by your will open your eyes! Breathe! Eloise!"

She was pitched forward; her face felt heavy as a stone, and someone was pounding between her shoulder blades.

"Breathe!"

Much later Eloise sat in the darkness of the stable. She was unable to breathe if she lay down too long, so Roland overturned a manger and propped her against it, but she remained awake, unable to sleep after her nightmare. Pain and exhaustion took a toll on her body, but her mind wouldn't rest. Garth and Artoch took turns lying and standing, shuffling in the confined barn with the other stalled horses. Cats and owls gave them little grief.

Roland lay next to her and she could easily take his head in her lap were it not for the big orange cat already there. She was glad for Roland's sleep. He needed the rest.

Why did he pull back when he looked into her eyes? Fear, disgust? He was distressed by what he saw. That she was a freak, an anomaly.

Yet he saved her life, numerous times. She felt such failure. Strength upon him, smart and capable. Of course, he would have many lady loves.

She had almost kissed him in the farmyard, wanted to kiss him, even now. She imagined how it might feel to hold him, be held by him. Not in fear and anguish, as after the marauders. But to simply hold his hand or stroke his thick, wavy locks, she thought, sighing. Although she could barely make out his form in the darkness, she could visualize his hair; imagine combing out the tangles, liberating the black locks to wind luxuriously around her fingers. Not only to touch his glorious mane, but to massage the strife and tension away from his scalp, the way her mother taught her. That she could do. Even without benefit of lavender or rose petals, without ale or whiskey to loosen the strain. Her hand hovered above his head. Desire, need and…she dare not. Yet her hand remained, poised, his mussed hairs tickling her palm and fingertips.

MEATH, 13th of June

Faster than scared rabbits did those Dahlquin cowards run, Seamus thought. He, Broccan, Donal, Ercc and Maiu rode hard all day, yet they were not closer to catching their quarry. One horse was lame under the grueling pace. The others were exhausted and looked to collapse soon. *Should have brought more horses,* he thought, *and funds for supplies.* Only he, his four men or some act of fate could prevent the messengers from delivering word of the siege to High Lord Gerald FitzGilbert.

Tiomoid U'Neill would prefer to issue the challenge to FitzGilbert himself, with the might of the vanquished Connacht kingdoms behind him. This warning was premature and must be thwarted. As the pursuers fell farther and farther behind, they all prayed mightily for an act of God or Satan to suspend their prey.

Seamus and his men rode into the small, unwalled village. Seamus surveyed the rustic dwellings and shops, thinking it was but a muddy, rural byway off the main route to Leinster. He saw a man sweeping the mud before his door and wondered at the stupidity of such a futile effort, as everywhere a man could presume to set foot was more mud.

"You there," Broccan called, and the sweeping man looked up, smiling, narrow eyes, child-like in their open expression. "Fucking simpleton," Broccan muttered to Seamus.

And so he was. Seamus could tell by the eyes, and the stoop of shoulder. Still the man smiled amiably, simply.

"We need fresh horses," Seamus said. It should have been obvious, as all five horses were covered in sweat, their weary heads bent low. Broccan's horse had lost a shoe, the poor beast. The simple man tipped his head as if sympathising with the exhausted horses. "Is there a horse trader or farrier?" Seamus asked.

"Your master!" Broccan shouted. "Fetch him to us."

The simple man blinked, stared between Seamus and Broccan. Movement caught Seamus' attention and he noticed a man with a pitchfork, another with a long towel in his hands. Before he could address these men he heard a child's voice.

"Mathair, there is men outside."

Seamus heard several children's voices inside before the door opened. At the same time a man came briskly around the corner of the building.

"Shame upon me, the delay," the man said, "may I help you?"

The door opened and a woman spoke to the simpleton. "Very good, Callum, just wait quietly."

"How may I help you good sirs?" the man asked again.

The men with pitchfork and towel remained, watching.

"We're in need of fresh horses. Is there a trader or farrier to be found?" Seamus asked.

The man studied them a moment before answering. "Five horses," he murmured. "Not here, but in the next town, not far. Not far at all. The smith will know more, see the smoke?" The man pointed; Seamus followed his direction and saw a black line of smoke.

"Did any of you see a knight on a black horse and a boy on a grey pass this way?" Seamus asked.

Seamus looked at all the faces assembling around him and his men, but all the people shook their heads. He didn't think so either, the prints didn't come this way. But he and his men needed new mounts. How was it the black and grey rode day and night, seeming to put more distance between them?

Down the path the smith told them the same thing, not a horse in this small village.

"If you go down the route, follow the big road and keep left, you'll come to Saint Brigid's, a town, it is. Two horse traders at least, more come market day. And farriers."

"Left," Seamus muttered. He didn't wish to veer so far off course from his prey. "Did you mayhap see two riders pass this way? Knight on a black horse and a boy on a grey?"

"I did not, sirs," the smith said. "But I'll draw some water for your horses."

"I can't afford to pay you," Seamus said.

"Sorrow upon me," the smith said with mild disappointment. "But the poor beasts," he paused, "say a favorable word about me in Saint Brigid's." He brought two full buckets and refilled them as the horses sated themselves.

There were two horse traders, with a bounty of horses available for prices higher than what Seamus and Broccan had between them. They could trade straight across, but for what appeared to be lesser quality horses. It didn't matter, they needed fresh mounts. In the end they traded two for two with each trader, but one horse, the finest of the lot, was in want of shoes which they also couldn't afford. They bartered a dagger and had the shoes removed, with some additional coins in the bargain.

Waiting for the farrier, the five men sat outside a tavern, sharing a watered-down tankard of ale between them.

They asked anyone passing by about the elusive knight and the boy.

A stout man roughly dressed approached. Seamus and Broccan exchanged brief looks.

The man's hair was dirty and matted, and when he opened his mouth to speak, Seamus saw what teeth he had left were dingy stumps.

"May I sit?" the man asked with a coarse manner of speech. While waiting for an answer, his hard gaze moved between Seamus and Broccan.

Seamus nodded and the man turned, seemed to snarl, and a youth cowered, relinquishing his stool. The man grabbed it and sat without another word, still studying Seamus, Broccan, Donal, Ercc and Maiu.

"I've seen them," the man said, "the ones you want."

Seamus sat up, eager to hear more.

"And who would that be?" Broccan asked in a challenging tone.

"More importantly, who would you be?" Seamus asked, following Broccan's cautious manner.

The man smirked, but lowered his eyes, probably in an attempt to show some modicum of respect.

"I'm Torcan," he dipped his head briefly. "I too want the man and boy."

Torcan, the wild boar, Seamus thought. Fitting name, had his parents recognised such as a swaddling? The man had hard lined grey eyes that never seemed to blink. His expression hovered between a smirk and a glower.

"What claim do you have on them?" Broccan asked, amusing Seamus with his ability to mimic the man's cruel expression. They were two of a kind, he thought: coarse, dangerous and invaluable when the killing began.

"I maybe ask you the same," Torcan said, glancing at each of the men. "You're strangers here. Well-armed strangers. But you're chasing two murderers."

Seamus inhaled. This was interesting to hear. Broccan sat back, crossing his arms.

"Murder?" Broccan murmured. "They slaughtered a band of marauders. We saw the evidence of that. What, ten men? Was that the tally?" he asked Seamus and the other men.

"Eight men. Some say unbelievable," Maiu added, speaking for the first time.

"Murder," Torcan sneered, cocking his head, turning his gaze to Seamus, then Broccan. "Isn't that how you describe it?"

That was exactly how he described it in his effort to win support and run these two messengers - murderers - down. He and Broccan had recruited three additional men from U'Neill's forces at Ashbury. They were poor horsemen, armed but reliable poachers and capable fighters.

"What is your interest in all this?" Seamus asked.

"To steal our glory when we bring these traitors to justice?" Broccan said. "Eh, boys?" he asked the group, before turning his scrutinising gaze back on Torcan.

"Traitors, is it? And murderers. Next you'll be claiming to do God's work," Torcan said, again smirking.

"We are!" Broccan boomed with a wry smile. "God's work, keeping those foul bastards from Leinster."

"What do you want, Torcan?" Seamus asked, recognising this man was different from the other men, who were easily recruited, eager to align with a new power source with the promise of reward.

"I think we can help each other," Torcan said.

"Help each other how?" Seamus asked, intrigued.

"First, I want to know who you are, who you serve, and why it's five of you chasing these two? Second," Torcan paused to glance from Seamus to Broccan, his grey eyes gleaming as he appeared to take the measure of each of them, "I want the boy."

PART THREE

VILLAGE, 13th of JUNE

Noise from the dawning village startled Eloise awake. Unfamiliar voices shouted and cursed. Stools were banged, she heard scraping, as if something was being dragged across a stone floor. These were not the familiar sounds she stirred to every day and the strangeness unsettled her. The pain in her ankle pounded and her cheek throbbed. The unfamiliar voices brought an ache to her heart. Then she heard purring. The orange cat sitting on the overturned manger rubbed against her head.

"Bleeding fuck," Roland muttered, rubbing his face then scratching his scalp before glancing at Eloise. "Beg your pardon." He tried to rotate his head and shoulders. "My neck," he moaned, rubbing it with his hand. "Could have used your cat for a pillow," he added, stretching and sighing. "It's still raining."

Bleeding hmm indeed, she agreed. Eloise could barely move with the pain and stiffness. She held her two hands before her in the dim stable light. The fingers on her left hand were like sausages compared with the right hand. She pushed her sleeve up examining her wrist and arm, swollen as if by a hundred bee stings. Her left leg and knee were swollen to her boot top and she wondered if she could bend her knee. Her left side was hard and stiff from the beating she suffered under the club of the marauder.

"And, nothing like the reek of horse piss in the morning," he lamented, "but I suppose you can't smell that?"

The single door leading to the inn opened. At the other end the workers opened the double doors, revealing the downpour.

"Oh, I say," a man uttered, surprise on his face as he shook the water off his oil skin. "Well, guards." He nodded as he continued for his horse and gear.

"Guards?" Roland muttered, looking about.

"Quite the service," the man said. "I must remember to thank the inn keeper. And you, sir," he added nodding to Roland.

Two other merchants entered. They too were wet.

"Have you ever?" the first man asked, "armed guards for our mounts and gear. Most impressive. I shall return to this inn next market day."

"Eh?" one of the men questioned, looking from Roland to Eloise and back at the first man. "The Dragon Slayer, is it?"

"So I'm called" Roland acknowledged, remembering his moniker from the day before. "And a rough night's labor it was. Look at my apprentice." He pointed at Eloise and she shrank back from the attention, for surely she appeared a swollen toad.

"Rough work, but the lad was poorly last night," one of the merchants added.

"Fought the bandits as if they were dragons. Poor lad, I hardly recognise him myself," Roland glanced at her and winked.

"Good morrow to you all," Roland said with a hint of a nod. "And is there any food left this fine morning?"

"I'm not sure, if the inn keeper hasn't brought your due, I'd hurry," the first man said as he rubbed down his horse.

"So I will. If you'll excuse me, sirs, El," he said to all. "I shall extract some meagre fee from our gracious inn keeper for our services."

"Take a cape," one of the men called.

"Dragon's ate it."

Eloise pulled herself up and limped to Garth, who was foraging upon the barn floor. She was aware of the merchants tacking up their mounts, and she wondered how in God's mercy she would be able to lift a saddle over Garth's back.

As the merchants exited with their mounts, Roland returned to the barn with some stale bread, dry cheese and wine to break fast.

"Saint Alexis be praised, may you have goodness for helping us poor beggars," Eloise said, forcing her split lips to form the words with dignity.

"Beggars?" Roland questioned, dropping his shoulders and hanging his head for a moment. "Even as a humble page," he said taking a deep breath, "I never existed at such a level of poverty. Poaching, tavern entertainment, now begging," he said, shaking his drooping head.

"May you be blessed, my Lord, I have grievous appreciation upon me," Eloise said. What more could she say or do at this bleak hour?

"Me too, appreciation," he said moving close before her. "Let's have your cross," Roland said, reaching for the leather thong at her neck.

Eloise tensed, drawing a deep breath as she stood tall, drawing her shoulders back. Whether as defensive posturing or vanity, Eloise tilted her head to hide her battered left side.

With delicate fingers he eased her wooden cross up from under her surcoat then held it in his palm, studying it, caressing it with his thumb.

Eloise let her breath out, easing into him, the leather thong loose at her unblemished throat.

Wooden cross still in his hand, Roland placed his thumb at the base of her throat, tracing the curve of her neck, until his thumb rested on her pulse. She swallowed. Once again, Roland's thumb followed along her jaw line, as he did when first they met. Thumb hooked in the soft spot under her chin, he turned her face.

She heard his intake of breath and felt the tremor in his thumb. A mirror wasn't necessary; his reaction validated her disfigurement. She sucked in her swollen bottom lip with a mighty gasp.

"I have such shame upon me," he whispered. "So much sorrow." He shook, and muttered something. She felt his hand rest against her face, the wooden cross on her cheek, his fingertips extending into her hairline.

"Heavenly Father, another day, another journey. I beseech the healing Saints and your benevolent kindness to ease my companion's suffering. The lesson is well taken. I shall not be so careless. In the name of the Father, the Son and Saint Alexis, bless and keep us safe. Amen," Roland said completing the fastest mass of this journey.

Roland broke the stale bread in half and handed her a piece. She waited for him to divide the cheese before she tried to nibble at it. Discomfort masked her hunger and pain prevented her opening her mouth or chewing. She must eat. Retrieving the cup from the saddle bags she broke her bread into pieces, put them in the cup and poured some wine over it. A piece of cheese rested between cheek and gum. Roland savored each small bite, with a sip of wine between. It didn't last long and he got up to attend his horse.

"Artoch," Roland muttered. "Why, in the name of Epona." Roland put Artoch's right fore hoof down. Standing, he sighed and put his hand on the crest of Artoch's neck. He wriggled it back and forth, loosening the horse's muscles, then ran his hand down Artoch's neck over the wither, making a few circular strokes on his horse's rump and finishing with some gentle scratching at the tail.

"He is losing a shoe," Roland said to her inquisitive look. Again he stroked his black horse. "It was good last night. The shoe, not us," he said to Eloise. "You catch it on something?" he asked the horse. They both shook their heads. "Damn," Roland said to the horse. "Let's see the rest." Sighing, he continued cleaning Artoch's hooves. "Would you-" he paused, and then looked up at her. "You can't walk, can you?"

It didn't feel like a question.

"I can," she said, limping to him. Waiting for him to speak, Eloise leaned against Garth. He lifted his head and turned an ear to her.

"I need...first..." he sighed then closed his eyes. "I need to curse. Kick something. Drink 'til my mind is numb. And-" He rubbed his neck then stretched and she heard a drum beat of cracking. Dark circles of fatigue blackened his eyes as surely as a fight would. "Drink your wine and bread," he said. "While I make inquiries about a smith, you can assess what we have left." He handed her his leather pouch with the few remaining coins.

Eloise took inventory. Roland had a few coins of large value. They had two grand horses they wouldn't part with, two saddles and pads, saddle bags, a blanket, cup one skin bag, sewing kit, chamois, Reggie's shield, Roland's sword, they each had daggers, his eating knife, the clothes on their backs. *Cara* and her arrows. Roland said they were a day from High

Lord FitzGilbert's castle. They could part with the blanket, the cup, and she didn't need the saddle or pad.

Roland returned wet and gloomy.

"The inn keeper, Master Bryan, like the Lord of New Pembrokeshire, wouldn't take the coin. Said it was too large and he didn't need a Dragon Slayer as a partner."

This had been his dilemma across Ireland, once the small coins were spent: he was rich and poor at once.

"It's pissing down rain. I begged Master Bryan to let you, Garth and our gear stay in the barn."

"That isn't necessary," she protested. "I'll come with you. We've been rained on before."

"You're injured, broken. I don't want sickness upon you," he said, putting Artoch's headstall on.

She didn't need reminding, and the pain in her face kept her from disputing the obvious.

"You can see the farrier from outside the stable. Call or wave for me." He led Artoch to the double doors, then turned. "Wrap up in the blanket. Rest. Don't move unless you need me. We'll leave as soon as I finish with Artoch." He stroked Artoch's neck, opened one of the stable doors and they walked into the rain, closing the door behind them.

Garth looked up. He snorted and bellowed once to his departing friend, Artoch. Eloise called his name and rubbed his withers. He looked to her, then touched her with his nose and returned to the abundance of food still on the floor.

Artoch needed his shoe repaired. She wouldn't dissent. She stroked Garth, examining the abrasion on his face. Better she be crippled than Garth or Artoch. Fortuna's Wheel had blessed them on this travail, they had survived so much. Eloise crossed herself and gave a prayer of thanks to Fortuna and Epona. Once more she ran her hands down each of Garth's legs, reassuring herself he was sound and strong. *Your legs are my legs. We move as one.*

Impatience nagged at her as she wrapped the blanket around herself and pulled Reggie's shield against her to hold in the warmth, then tried to find comfort leaning against their gear. They needed to leave this village and be at FitzGilbert's castle - only one day away. The doors rattled with a rainy gust. Neither of them had oil cloth cloaks to protect them on the road. What fate dictated that this singular, wet morning she would be trapped, safe and dry in a stable? Rest. Wait for the weather: Then all the faster to FitzGilbert's. The orange cat returned and purred her to sleep.

She woke to stable doors banging open. The cat fled.

Two workers brought in three wet, muddy horses. Garth studied them, head up, ears pricked forward. I am the stallion, his posture said. Two soggy men followed the horses, complaining about the miserable riding and the flooding.

Head pounding, Eloise watched and listened as the men untacked the horses and placed the wet gear on racks. Hay was thrown in for the horses. Eloise shrieked as rats scurried around; two ran up her blanket, across her chest, to her shoulder and then up her neck and into her cap. Heart pounding, flush with the heat of terror, she felt them clawing, heard the squealing growls, the pounding surf and salt and the ravenous, demonic rats tearing her apart. This wasn't the beach. She gripped the writhing cap from her head. *Mother of God, now what?* She shook the cap and a rat stuck fast like a rock in a sling. The dreaded thing would surely crawl up her arm and into her clothing to chew her heart out. She flung the cap against the wall once, and again. Turning the cap inside out with trembling fingers she took the twitching rat by the tail and threw it to the center of the stable. The men cursed and lamented, unaware of her presence. With a whimper, she pulled the offensive cap back on her head then patted under the blanket to flush any hiding rats. From over the stall panels, she sought calm watching the thin clouds of steam rising off the warm horses. *Roland, I told you rats put fear upon me.* She clutched the blanket to her, wishing he was there.

"More coming," someone shouted from outside.

"I agree, best get out of the way, one of the men said to his travel partner.

"And lay claim to our bread and board," said the other. The two men left.

Two more muddy horses were lead in, followed by a torrent of curses as the workers labored at their chores, becoming as wet and muddy as the horses and gear.

Where is Roland? Shouldn't he be back by now? She couldn't be sure the time of day in the dim stable. Warm and awake from the rat attack, Eloise contemplated her next move. Pain kept her wrapped in the blanket as she was. How rainy was it, had she heard the word flood? The inn was full of voices, clattering and laughter and curses. She thought of a blazing hearth, a boisterous kitchen, cauldrons bubbling, spits rotating - would such an inn have spits? Would there be pies and pasties? Warm, soft bread to- Hunger stabbed her. There would be a banquet for the wet, weary, paying travelers. *Not for you, not this day. Foolish to dwell on it. There will be food with High Lord FitzGilbert.* But the ache of hunger wasn't listening.

"Stupid girl," a woman screeched. "Pay attention."

Eloise heard heavy footsteps, then crying.

"Get to work and stay out of sight," a man commanded.

Eloise tried to listen, to glean what was happening. So many voices, so much noise and none of it made sense - and worse, Roland's voice wasn't among them.

The stable doors burst open. Eloise roused. She had fallen asleep again.

"El," Roland called, his voice clipped and short.

"I'm coming," she said, thinking how lazy and ill prepared she was. She should have been watching for him and had Garth ready to go.

"Stay," he said, hand up. Artoch and Garth exchanged greetings as Roland put his black horse in the stall next to Garth.

Wet hair stuck to his face and neck. He was probably soaked clear through to his braises once more. The unbidden image of Roland naked at their first fire caused her cheeks to flush. He squatted down next to her. She couldn't read his expression. Once again, he was the impassive warrior as he assessed her head to boots, warm and dry under the blanket, while he labored in the rain. Shame washed over her.

"My Lord," she said.

He tilted his head and raised a finger. She was silent as he scanned the stable, closed doors at both ends. The five new horses ate the food before them, while Garth and Artoch, without fresh food, pawed the floor and shifted their weight from side to side, then tossed their heads demanding a portion. Her heart ached for their hunger and Roland's. Apology postponed, her mind raced with questions. Shouldn't they be tacking up? The day was near spent. His silence wore on her as heavily as his absence had. He didn't reveal discomfort, alarm or emotion, but he couldn't mask the lines and pigment of fatigue.

He inhaled, preparing to speak.

"We have much to consider." He looked about the stable again. More voices shouted outside and in. Roland closed his eyes, grimaced. "Blasted rain, damn road closed, this day lost. Not an inch closer to FitzGilbert." He paused; lips pursed. "Hunger." A large drop of water hung, then dripped from his nose. "First things first," he said, looking at her. "Did you miss me?"

What? His stoic expression softened into a hopeful smirk. Eloise wasn't sure she heard him correctly. His black eyes gleamed, demanding the answer from her. *What about the rain? The flood, the lost time?*

You're drenched and can't travel like that. Of all the silly questions. But she knew the answer.

"Speechless in your humility?" he murmured.

She was, searching for words that didn't exist.

"It would please me to hear you say it."

Her mouth fell open. There was so much more to say. *I missed you*, of course she did, but it went beyond that. The question evoked such emotions.

"El, it's an easy question – you missed me, or you didn't," he said with a snort. "You can write a song about it later."

She let the blanket fall back, and reached out to stroke his wet, bristly cheek, the one she had shaved but a day, two days ago. Emboldened by her action, the words came, "I was inconsolable."

He caught her hand, warm and dry, his cold and wet.

The stable doors burst open to more voices and horses. Roland pulled away, rising before she could touch his face.

"Wait here," Roland said.

"I will not," she said, clambering to her feet. "We have much to consider, remember?" She slipped *Cara* over her shoulder.

Roland gave her a wary look. "Who takes a bow indoors?" he asked.

Eloise continued fastening her girdle and quiver before answering. "Would you leave your sword?"

"Of course not."

The tone of his voice revealed it was not the answer of the impassive warrior.

"We'll hobble the mares outside!" one of the muddy workers shouted over the noise, as the mares squealed, and their two stallions pranced in their stalls.

"More prayers to Saint Alexis," Roland said, squeezing her a bit too hard, then supporting her as she limped beside him. "As we beg once more for a roof over our heads."

"Is there a flood? What happened? Artoch's shoe?" the questions tumbled from her as she limped to the inn with him.

LEINSTER, 13th of June

"I must piss and more," Broccan said, rain pouring down. "Let's pull off here, with the cover of trees. Water and grazing for the horses. Seamus?" he added, though Seamus knew it was rhetorical. The knight and boy could be minutes away, just around the bend. Piss first, then kill.

All the riders dismounted to relieve themselves while the horses took a needed rest. Once relieved, Seamus and Broccan stood with Torcan. Seamus yawned and rubbed his shoulder. Had he slept at all since the siege began? Now this rain.

"Seamus, what say I tow you along? Get some sleep," Broccan said, yawning as well.

They rode day and night chasing the knight and boy, taking turns tying themselves to their horses, attempting to sleep while being towed by the others. God fuck, he was tired and miserable. Torcan was talking.

"You want them dead?" Torcan confirmed.

Seamus and Broccan both nodded.

"I want the boy - alive," Torcan said, "to pay a debt. He won't trouble you, sirs. Not trouble. I'll dispose of him," he paused, "in my own way for the pains he caused." Torcan watched, waiting for a hint of the men's feelings, Seamus thought. The man had a thick, protruding brow that shadowed his deep-set eyes, armored like a battle-aged boar still in his killing prime. "I work. I steal and provide all you need. All of it. I've earned the boy and more."

"You'll never take the boy yourself," Seamus reminded him.

"Nor will you."

Torcan waited. Seamus nodded.

"These outlaws we pursue," Seamus started, "must never reach High Lord FitzGilbert. Never. They must be silenced."

Torcan exhaled through his nose, a snort and sigh combined. Seamus watched as Torcan's expression altered just slightly. His glower reflected his concentration, if only for a moment.

"Two things I tell you," Torcan said, "and mayhap we agree."

Seamus nodded.

"First, the knight. He fights hard to protect the lad. Don't know if they be father and son, brothers or what. He is relentless. You saw his work, the slaughter on the road." Torcan waved his arm in the direction they had come. In the short time Torcan had been with them, Seamus knew Torcan was capable of greater cruelty. "Give me the boy," Torcan continued, his glowering gaze never leaving Seamus, "I promise the boy will never be seen or heard from again. He will vanish. By my hand. That's all I ask," Torcan said, lowering his eyes, a gesture Seamus couldn't remember receiving from him.

"That slaughter," Seamus said, "who were they? Why do you care?"

Torcan kept his eyes down. Torcan's unwashed hair bristled from his skull to his neck. The rain pouring down the back of his cloak resembled raised hackles.

Seamus waited.

"My family," Torcan growled. "Butchered."

Broccan snorted. "Butchered, while attempting a robbery, I think."

"Robbery pleases you now, my Lord," Torcan answered. Seamus could hear the contempt and imagine the sneer.

"The boy dead," Broccan confirmed.

"The boy dead," Torcan agreed, raising his eyes to glower at Broccan. "After he pays the debt owed."

Broccan licked his bottom lip, his grin turning to a sneer to match Torcan's.

"After he pays the debt owed," Seamus said.

"There is such fucking weariness upon me, chasing these two bastards - you can't butcher them fast enough for my revenge," Broccan said. "Better still, tie them to a great turning wheel and let them die of exhaustion. Fucking cow turds."

"I'll work it out of him, he'll naught be seen again." Torcan raised a clenched fist, embedded with dirt and grime to match the lines and scars on his face. "*That* I promise," Torcan said, a cruel grin severing his face. "You kill the knight. I kill the boy."

This wasn't the first time Seamus had made a bargain with the Devil. But Torcan - could he be the last?

Back in the saddle, Torcan reviewed his conversation and his circumstance.

Torcan took risks. He was a marauder, a thief and murderer. It was his family trade. He labored, fought and prayed for success. He lived it all. But he lived on the outskirts. His band was unwelcomed in all but the most savage of places. It was all he knew - until now.

Torcan had taken a risk. He sensed opportunity. Without a sure plan he threw in with these travelling mercenaries. Never had he ventured from Meath. Never had he ridden a horse. Often, he allowed himself to speculate.

Travelling with these men gave Torcan access to greater wealth to rob with more frequency. These well-armed men were not turned away, not shunned from village to village. While they were welcomed in to transact business, Torcan stole to the back, robbing what he could and remembering what he might return for later. He identified easy prey upon the road and with the five, armed men it was all the easier to strip travelers bare. Robbery by cover of honor: the thought made him laugh.

Torcan saw his simple plan to take the bitch was very complicated. He wasn't in familiar territory. He didn't know where he was, from a strategic outlook. He was a piss-poor rider. Even now, his arse ached, and he resented the nag below him. He scratched at his itchy neck. How would he transport the bitch? How would he contact her people for a ransom? For a sale? She still had value in bartered flesh, for as long as she lasted. Family or comrades were not here--yet. He took risks. Without family. Without partners.

Faces, a voice, a mighty laugh clouded his mind. Good moments had existed, when Torcan belonged. That knight and his bitch had slaughtered them. There wasn't need to mourn. Grief was weakness. Risk was his trade. Hatred made Torcan strong. He was planning again.

And why just the bitch? Why hadn't he thought of this before? Because he thought small. In dirt floor taverns and caves. The knight might be of equal value to the cunt. Who were they and why should they be killed when they had value as hostages or ransom?

He felt a flush. Intoxication. Boldness. This time he couldn't keep the edges of his mouth from lifting. He must capture the girl. That was his privilege. Then, with the contract settled between Seamus and Broccan, he might well barter the girl to them. There was enough reward between them, plus the spoils of the kill. First, capture the girl.

VILLAGE, 13th of June

She staggered with the import of Roland's news: they were trapped in this village for another night. The eastern road to FitzGilbert was impassable. Travel in any direction was hazardous with the rain and mud.

"Grim tidings," he said. "I don't like any of our choices." His voice was deep and rigid. "If we stay here, we risk Tiomu's men catching us." His eyes narrowed on her, her injuries, her weakness. "I don't favor our chances. We can risk riding north or south. It's out of our way, adding time and miles to our journey. The streams may still be swollen, and we would be worse off, mayhap sleeping in the rain. Not a way of knowing if Tiomu's men pass through, waiting to ambush us."

Eloise trembled with that prospect. It was scary enough looking over her shoulder day and night without the dread of never knowing where an attack might spring. Another trap, another beating, death.

"You have a say. Have I overlooked anything? Another option? What do you think? Ride or wait?"

They had discussed the options, all grim. Ride or wait?

"Wait," she agreed.

"If Master Bryan will let us stay."

The public room was crowded and boisterous as she and Roland entered. Unlike the gaiety of market day, these travelers hadn't planned on staying, their travels disrupted by rain, sloggy roads and a wagon that got caught in the river, then overturned, causing the blockage and flooding. Many in the room recounted their exaggerated stories of the massive flood to anyone who would listen, and Eloise noted the inn workers were the most attentive, overhearing two of them: "Last night the Dragon Slayer, tonight Noah." All this validated Roland's account.

She and Roland approached the harried inn keeper, holding court as it were, at a board pouring cups of ale.

"Dragon Slayer," he said, "we're beyond full. The village is swamped."

"Your village is in crisis, as are we. My fortune remains the same," Roland said. "I'm capable of guarding your stable again. Same as last night, all we ask is floor space."

"I can work the kitchen," Eloise offered, remembering the noise of food preparation.

"A cripple?" the inn keeper scoffed.

"No," Roland said, gripping her arm, his slip to English revealing tension.

"I'm not crippled. I just can't walk. But I can chop, skin, peel. By your will, my Lord," she implored Roland. "By your will, Master Bryan. My Lord is wet and must dry by your fire. I will work hard. You need help."

"I said not." Roland gave her a shake, glaring down at her.

"It will be warm in the kitchen," she said in a soft voice, ignoring the rude shake.

"Can you skin a hare as well as you gut?" asked a woman, stepping next to the inn keeper, a small child on her hip.

"Indeed I can. Skin it, clean it, bone it, stew it," she answered, nodding to the stern inn keeper. "My Lord and his horse have hunger and will not sleep in the rain," she said, turning to face Roland. "I must," she whispered, "By your will."

"Blathin," the inn keeper called. A girl ran to them, head bowed. "Take this boy to the back, for skinning and gutting," he said, shaking his head.

Roland still gripped her arm.

"Then back to the tally," the woman said.

The girl, Blathin, cringed then nodded her head.

Tally, like a *ledger*, it was a dreaded word and Eloise cringed too. *Stupid girl.*

"I can help with that too," she heard herself say. "I can read." That she could, though arithmetic plagued her. The foul, miscreant numbers changing shape and places, sometimes springing off the tablet entirely to float around before her eyes, taunting her to tears as her parents, Uncle Reggie and the Seanascal scolded and pleaded for her to pay attention and not let her mind wander. But it was the numbers that wandered. "I will help." Roland's grip loosened on her arm.

"What a day, a stupid girl and a cripple." The inn keeper shook his head. "Hares first, off with you."

"I'll gut the hares," Roland said. "They can attend the numbers."

"You may not, by your goodness, Dragon Slayer."

Roland gave the inn keeper a wry smile. "And why not? You think I can't wield a blade?"

The inn keeper returned the wry smile. "I've assurance you can, but you're too big. Two hands to their four. Sit by the fire and dry, mayhap I need your blade later. Foul weather makes for foul tempers. Can I count on you, Dragon Slayer?"

Eloise and Blathin were not in a warm kitchen, but under a leaking oil cloth. Beneath another oil cloth was a large metal cooking rack supporting two large cauldrons and two smaller ones. Two boys kept the fires burning low and steady. In the rain was a wooden crate packed tight with live, frightened hares, some already dead from injury or suffocation. Eloise was gripped by pain and panic. *Were she and Roland trapped in such a cage? Garth and Artoch? Not*, she commanded. *Remember who you are. Dahlquin.*

"This suffering must end, the spirit of these humble hares must be honored," Eloise said, kneeling down and placing her hand upon the tortuous crate. *Blessed Saint Mary and Mother Goddess of us all, goodness upon You, the lives and flesh of Your beloved hares. We honor Your charity and will show mercy.* Time was wasting.

Blathin was not a stupid girl in this venture, and they were soon partners in slaughter, finding unspoken rhythm as they extracted each fighting hare one by one, wrung the necks and proceeded until a stack of lifeless hares lay before them.

That done, they hung one hare at a time from the posts provided for such work.

"Blathin, do you save the hides for tanning?" Eloise asked, before tearing into the skin.

"Tanner boys." Blathin pointed with her knife to a hook on the back wall of the inn.

Eloise sliced down each leg, tugging the fur hide away from the scant little hare. It was still warm, life so recently departed. May you have goodness, blessed hare, she prayed once again. It's God's Plan and the Great Mother's. Blathin was near done with her hare, and Eloise rose to the challenge.

"Blathin, you have hardly spoken," Eloise prompted, starting the third hare, trying once again to engage the girl in conversation. the girl mostly nodded and when she did speak it was only to agree. Roland would like her. Her face bore the blemished complexion of a girl near bleeding age, and she confirmed she was thirteen. She was neither unattractive nor deformed, but was cowed and sullen.

They gutted and skinned the creatures, their cold, wet fingers becoming as red as the flesh. Blathin was fast, already two hares ahead of Eloise.

"Blathin, you're a smart girl."

Blathin stopped, her knife still. She glared up at Eloise. She had one puffy eye, and Eloise knew she had been struck fair hard.

"Are you mocking me?" she asked, not returning to her work, the blade still poised, though Eloise noted the tremor in her hand.

"I am not, you are a smart girl. I've just met you yet look how well we work together. By your will, believe me, you're a smart girl."

Blathin sniffed, Eloise smiled and they both returned to the carcasses hanging before them.

The oil cloth flap covering the doorway to the back of the inn opened.

Blathin's mother, the mistress of the inn stepped out. She looked at the empty crate, saw the hanging carcasses and finished ones on the table.

"You aren't done yet?" she said, scowling.

Blathin shuddered but said nothing, working all the harder.

"Blathin is a smart girl," Eloise, said. "She is a hard worker, and I'm racing to match her," Eloise added.

The woman stared at Eloise, then her daughter and back at Eloise. The child on her hip fussed in the damp air. "Chop them fine and add them to the stew," she said laying down two cleavers.

"This is fast work, Mistress," Eloise said. "I have labored in my father's service, and that of Lord Roland," she added. "We're near done, and I pray you goodness for the opportunity. I bless you and your house for this chance. Blathin serves you well."

The woman nodded, then returned indoors.

"It's true," Eloise said whether Blathin was listening or not. "This work distracts me from my pain and worry. It's not so grand as riding a horse," Eloise fought back the sniffles, thinking of her noble Garth and how much work was left to do. "It's good to help," she said, as she sliced and eased the fur coat away from another hare.

"Mayhap you'd be faster without that bow and quiver in your way." Blathin spoke the longest complete sentence Eloise could recall. "What happened, your face?"

Eloise paused, thinking the best way to avoid discussing the roadside attack.

"Hmm, let's say, this is what comes from not minding my father's ledger. Tally," she corrected.

The oil cloth flap flew open again.

"El," Roland called. He scrutinised the covered workspace and peered into the rain beyond. "This isn't the kitchen and it isn't warm."

"It is not, Lord. But it's warm work. Pleasure upon me to see you drying your clothes," she said, seeing he had removed the surcoat, padded gambeson and hauberk, wearing only his linen tunic and boots, and girdle with sword and dagger.

He snorted. "You're incorrigible."

Eloise sniffed. She had expected, hoped he would say *May you have goodness*. Incorrigible, impertinent, impudent. Inconsolable. She glanced at Blathin. They were smart girls, not rude ones.

"May you have goodness, my Lord, I will add that to the list. I have the finest teacher in all Ireland."

There was a long pause. Roland would like Blathin very much, Eloise reflected. *Damn it, Roland.*

"It pleasures me to hear you say that," he said. "Goodness upon you. Hurry up."

Eloise and Blathin finished the last hares, seventeen all total. That would stretch out a mighty banquet stew for the paying inn patrons.

Roland paced the crowded interior of the inn, humid with anxious, naked men, all their garments strung across the room in an attempt to dry them for the next day's full labor. Some laughed, all cursed, so it was in rainy Ireland. Wet. The women, partially clothed, huddled in the corner beyond the three lines of clothing. Eloise was a problem. A big, fucking, unrelenting problem. She wasn't welcome with the women, and he didn't want her on this side of the curtain. How could something so small cause such disorder? He needed to check on her again, huddled in the blanket in the stable with the village scum. That was wrong. They were laborers displaced from their dwellings by the swollen stream. Still, Eloise didn't belong with them. God damned, Satan's piss rain. He pounded the wall with a clenched fist as he passed. "Roland, you look like a caged animal," she had said earlier, "where are we to go if not here? You said the road east to FitzGilbert was blocked. We agreed it was too dangerous to risk a venture north or south. Best to stay put. Have you come to a different conclusion?" He suppressed a snarl. Foolish girl, she didn't grasp the danger. Even after yesterday's crippling beating--he shuddered with the foul memory, near blind and lame--she didn't show the modicum of fear he expected she should. Mayhap the pain damaged her humors and caused this foolish thinking. Believing she could climb on the roof and shoot Tiomu's men if they appeared. "I can shoot," she had said, "you've seen me." Aye, a heron and hares, not men. Not armed men hunting you down. "I sleep with my bow and arrows." You do that, he had said in angry resentment, sounding more sarcastic than he meant. The day had started bad and become untenable.

Blessed Savior, this inn was indefensible. What if? No, he would find a way to protect her.

Eloise was wrapped up in one of the blankets, under Reggie's shield. How could she sleep with all the grumbling and snoring in the stable? He crossed himself, praying to God, Jesus, the Virgin Mother and all the Saints she sleep safely through the night and he deliver her to- He stopped, unable to form High Lord Gerald FitzGilbert's name. He would deliver her to safety. He couldn't think beyond that.

Back in the public room, ale flowed. Cups and bowls were shared with hare stew or spirits. He was a stranger to this village, these people and their way of life. Eloise was probably right, based on his information of course: Tiomu's men could not arrive this impassable night. All was secure. Some of the travelers got drunk, others bragged of whoring, the villagers cursed and hailed life. In these, Roland was no stranger - to drink and whore and curse and beat some strawman to dust. But he was alone in his confusion, isolated on this mission. This night he had no brothers-in-arms, no unit to share the risk and worry. No one whose wise counsel he could seek. For years High Lord Gerald FitzGilbert had been that man. Should be that man. Now he loomed as a rival. Roland was a knight; he did two things. Tonight, he could do neither.

This was all her fault. He was inconsolable.

VILLAGE, 14th of June

Her ankle pained, her nose was running. They rode without speaking. So much time had been lost. A whole day and night in the village, Roland pacing the inn and stable like a caged animal, frustrated the space was so indefensible. Unusually surly, unwilling to listen to anything she might say, unable to look at her, after telling her the bruising had come and she was black and blue as the stormy sky. After an early start, they were within half a day of High Lord FitzGilbert. The sound of his name had taken on a mythical proportion: safety, salvation, resurrection. Trepidation still plagued her soul; Gerald FitzGilbert may be none of those things. Yet, despite all this, Roland had found the resource to make repairs to Uncle Reggie's shield and once again, she wore it on her back. Roland was familiar with the countryside and recognized the villages and estates. There remained long stretches of fields and orchards that were sparsely populated.

Eloise carried her bow in her hand, ready should anything worthy of trade or a meal cross their path. Her hand was swollen, her fingers clumsy. *With one good eye, would she be able to shoot accurately? Cara*, she thought, stroking the riser with her thumb. A familiar shadow moved at her side and she smiled down at one of her hounds, the other couldn't be far behind. She gasped with the emptiness and felt the tears flood her eyes. The hounds were not there. Beast and Dragon were dead, lost to her forever. Yet all she saw through her tears were her beloved, wire-haired hounds, tongues lolling as they joyously trotted at her side. *Beast, Dragon* she sobbed. The vision so vivid beside her.

"Don't cry," Roland said, not looking at her. "With your will."

He was right. It was weak and betrayed her identity. But her grief was not so biddable.

They ambled on, he looking away and she fighting back her tears and the images of those lost. She lifted her bow, aiming, familiarizing herself with her limitations.

Eloise grieved yet again, knowing many of the fields of Dahlquin lay unattended while the siege raged. Bent from the heavy rains, beautiful blue flowers of flax bobbed with the weight of bees. Another field, a later planting was green and calm. Had Tiomu and his men pushed south? What of the women and their families who had fed Roland and herself that first morning? Were they safe, were those lands still productive?

PINGBEE, 14th of June

Eloise couldn't get over all the people coming and going. Roland said this was quiet compared with Dublin or London or any other large city or precinct. And if not the farm upon village upon farm, Eloise had never seen so many postings: Trespass Forbidden, Hunting Forbidden, Poaching Forbidden.

It was a delight to pass through woods and meadows without overzealous postings, revealing a likelihood for hares or birds. As soon as they made the decision to stop and hunt, a fat grouse took wing. Bow drawn, Eloise followed the bird as it circled in closer to them. She waited. With her left eye swollen shut and her injured ankle throwing her balance off, she missed. Before Roland could be disappointed or complain, she released a second arrow. Wounded, the bird descended some distance away.

The air erupted with curses.

"You fool! Bumbling idiot!" came the sharp reprimands. "That's our grouse, don't touch it! How dare you try and steal our kill."

Roland rode next to Eloise and waited for the angered voice to reveal himself. Roland drew his sword, keeping it next to his right leg. Not wanting to be caught off guard again, he didn't wish to be perceived as overly aggressive either. Eloise pulled another arrow from her quiver and nocked.

A youth stood in the meadow, perhaps a squire by his attire. A knight of about thirty-five years rode out from the woods.

"That's our grouse, been stalking for hours," the knight exclaimed, challenge rising in his voice. He wasn't intimidated by the rough, blood-stained appearance of Roland or Eloise.

"Dead by our arrow," replied Roland, not willing to submit too quickly, but not wanting a fight either.

"It's ours. If we hadn't flushed it, you'd have nothing to shoot at," the knight scowled, challenging them as his squire continued searching for the bird.

Fucking discourteous arse. Roland swallowed his pride and fighting spirit.

"Of course, we're happy to have assisted you," Roland replied as honourably as possible.

Angered by the polite dismissal, the grumpy knight persisted.

"Don't need your help, don't try and steal our meal," he said in his harsh voice.

This was beyond fucking discourtesy. This knight was rude. Roland longed to teach him a lesson, but his responsibility to Eloise kept him quiet. He fumed inside. Not good with words, he preferred to let his sword speak for him. *El Muerte Rojo* had amazing eloquence.

Vulgarities ran through Roland's mind as he fought for a way to maintain his honor and get out of a confrontation. Enough time had been lost, good people were dying at the siege. It pressed on him like a weight, only moving forward lessened the burden.

"Take the damn fowl," Roland finally answered. Eloquent?

Cranky and spoiling for a fight to release his frustrations, the knight was relentlessly impolite. Roland, cranky and spoiling to be left alone was relentlessly polite. The tension built, dragon's breath, ready to burst into flame.

"I had it, until this thief came along," the squire chided from the meadow.

"I'm not a thief," Eloise snapped.

"Enough," Roland said looking at Eloise. He turned back to the knight. "With our sincerest apologies, take the bird," he grimaced. "El, let's go."

"If you can find it," Eloise sneered to the squire. Garth followed her energy and pivoted to face the squire.

"El," Roland reprimanded, fighting to keep his calm. But she ignored him. Her attention was on the squire.

"How is it you've come to carry the shield of Sir Reginald?" the knight asked with a sneer. "Too cocky for his own good. Seems fitting a boy should have deprived him of such a banner," he added in a mocking tone.

Spinning Garth around, Eloise took the bait. She would not tolerate insults to her beloved uncle. This was a siege upon Dahlquin honor. Hunger, fatigue, grief and flaming humors gripped her, stripping her of reason. She wanted to lash out, and for something to go her way on this journey. How dare he talk to her that way?

"He was a great man and I bear his shield with pride. You speak ill of a good and noble knight, so much the less for you," she said. Someone had to suffer, someone must be punished, and the slander of these two made them targets of her erupting rage.

"El," Roland warned.

"He was a lap dog of the Dahlquins, nothing more," the knight proclaimed, chest out, lines etched deeply around his hard eyes. "Probably cuckolded his brother," he scoffed. "Bedded the Sorceress of Dahlquin, I hear."

"You lie!" seethed Eloise, tears welling. Her mother was not evil, and never did she lay with Uncle Reggie.

"I lie?" the knight chided, a big smile spreading across his face, accepting her insult as the challenge he had been trying to provoke.

"Pardon my page's exuberance," Roland scowled at Eloise. "He is young and impertinent. I will reprimand him shortly. By your will, enjoy the grouse with our compliments," Roland said through clenched teeth.

"He is often impertinent, I see," sneered the knight. He seemed to study Eloise's beaten countenance. "Impudent knave, just what I'd expect."

"You have insulted a great knight, apologize," Eloise insisted. She sat tall in her saddle, every fiber of her being enraged.

"Be thankful I don't relieve you of the shield," he added.

Eloise lifted *Cara*, pushing the bow forward and drawing the nock of the arrow back, taking dead aim at his face. The knight was in easy range. Garth stood still and solid beneath her. *This is the risk I take.*

The knight stared into her drawn arrow and Eloise marvelled at how interesting a face looked with an arrow where the nose should be. The nose, between the eyes, even the ear or jaw, she could make this shot. Would the entire arrow penetrate his skull and exit the back? Neither she nor the knight moved. *Do it, do it, Dahlquin, Dahlquin,* she heard the voice of the dead grouse within her head, *end his incessant cawing, cawing,* the dead bird pleaded, in rhythm with her pounding blood. She had hurt the grouse with her sloppy shot, but she could end his suffering now. And her suffering from this cawing knight. Plenty of time to reload, should that squire pose a threat to her or Roland. *Dahlquin, Dahlquin,* pumped in her ears.

"Before the Gods, he didn't mean it," called Roland unable to break the gaze between Eloise and this dangerous knight.

The knight opened his mouth to speak, an apology Eloise hoped.

"You, sir, are pathetic, and undeserving of such a page. The lad is possessed of fighting spirit which you lack," the knight said addressing Roland, but still looking down his nose at her arrow.

"El," Roland growled to Eloise.

No one moved.

"I will see him eat his words," she said. The pain of her injured ankle was distant, like a black cloud rising, or a debt yet to be paid. She was rooted to Garth. With his four unbroken fetlocks he was able to pivot and fly should she need. Their breath came slow and steady together. Spirituality filled her. Archer's Grace: that moment of purity when all the elements aligned and the archer became the bow, the arrow and the target. Eloise possessed the knight. He could not escape her.

Roland rode between them. Blocking her shot, grace disrupted. *Damn it, Roland!* Her arrow couldn't bend clear around him. With the slightest shift of her weight, she and Garth side passed right. But again, Roland was blocking her shot, protecting not her but that rude stranger.

"I'm not afraid of you, *England*," she said, growling the last word, wrath possessing her once more. Had Roland forgotten that knight was threatening their mission, and thus her family? Connacht?

"Silence!" Roland roared with an unearthly voice.

Starlings took flight, sparkling black wings *thwumping*. The fury in his face brought Eloise out of her rage and forced her into his. His teeth were bared. His eyes were cold ebony and fastened on her. Was that lightning she smelled? The black cloud was unleashing a storm, and she didn't think she could weather it.

Roland pivoted Artoch, turning his back to her. Artoch's slashing black tail was like a slap in the face. She lowered her bow, releasing the pressure on the string. Her hands started to shake.

"The boy has a stomach for fight," growled the knight. "I admire that," he added, implying Roland was afraid of the challenge.

"The boy is foolish and speaks out of turn," Roland rumbled back, as if on the verge of losing control.

Roland and the knight debated back and forth about avenging the insults between them. Circling each other from horseback, Eloise thought she saw sparks between them. The tension bore down on her like the stone lid of a sarcophagus.

Had she gone too far? Closing her eye she tried to remember who she was. She *had* gone too far, and was nauseous with shame, but she still simmered with anger and hurt. Why couldn't she keep her mouth shut? Impudent knave, isn't that what he called her? Her father called her impudent. *Impudent, impertinent, and an ugly squirrel* tumbled through her mind creating bitter anguish. Breathing hard, she glanced up at the equally impudent, impertinent knight and her defiance was born anew.

"Let us settle it now, while the lads dress the grouse," demanded the knight. He seemed to relish the idea of a fight while lunch was prepared. "Or should we let the lads settle it for us?" he smiled. "Some entertainment while we dine." He rubbed his hands together as if in happy anticipation. "I'd love to see what that feisty little knave is truly made of. You've taken some hard licks and are still outspoken," he addressed Eloise, his green eyes sparkling with delight. "That would be great sport." His mood was improving, she observed. She felt sick, her ankle stabbed at her, the debt come due.

The returning squire looked at her with increasing pleasure. He could take that scrawny page, his expression said. Eloise knew reducing her to further pulp would without doubt elevate him in his master's eyes. What had she done?

Despite the weight of guilt and fear, she still fumed at this surly knight's rude insults towards her beloved uncle, may he rest with the angels. And her mother, he called her Sorceress and insinuated she and Uncle Reggie...who had given his hand and his life to save her. She would not stand by and let someone degrade his memory.

Taking in the squire's contemptuous looks, Eloise pondered her chances with him. He looked like a hungry animal eyeing his next meal. Eloise felt like a frightened rabbit, rather an ugly squirrel. It couldn't be a fair fight. *Fair fights didn't exist when it was life or death*, her father's voice murmured to her. If she could lure him close, she might be able to disable him, a very slim chance: a slim, miraculous chance...in Hell.

Eloise took the arrow in her trembling bow hand. With her shaking right hand, she lifted her wooden cross pendant to her split lips, kissed it then began crossing herself. *God have mercy, what have I done?* She prayed for the safety of Lord Roland, whom she had stupidly embroiled. She begged forgiveness. She prayed for the safety of her family. At seventeen she must accept responsibility for her actions and the consequences. There was nothing glorious or heroic in this, just resignation.

Roland's mind spun. *What was she doing to him? Was she demented?* Roland didn't know this brash knight or how capably he fought, and today - bruised, exhausted - Roland might not win, and then what? The gamble was too great. No, they couldn't fight. Eloise and that squire definitely weren't going to battle it out. *God's Blood! Impudent girl! Why couldn't she keep still? Had she forgotten the dire plight of her parents?*

"You wish to fight and settle a debt of honor. I wish nothing more than to grant you that," Roland said, stretching out the sentences, attempting to rein in the emotions. "However," he lifted his gauntleted hand. "I beg you grant me an extension. I'm duty bound to deliver this page," he emphasized the word *page*, not squire, flicking his thumb in her direction, "to High Lord Gerald FitzGilbert of Leinster. If you would meet me there in a day, we will finish this," Roland offered. He did want to finish it.

"Page, is it? He looks well past ten years of age," the knight glared once more at Eloise. "He is brash and needs to be taught some manners."

Eloise had her head bowed in silent prayer, crossing herself repeatedly, piety surrounding her and her quiet grey stallion.

"What a noble and honorable lad," the knight said, then sighed.

"Will you grant me a day to fulfill my duty?" asked Roland again. "My squire is there, Val, we'll make it a foursome if you wish," he added to enhance his offer.

"Hmmm," the knight said, scratching his chin. "A truly good fight at Lord FitzGilbert's castle is a tempting offer. Now or later?" He shifted his gaze from Roland to Eloise, still deep in prayer, then looked over his shoulder towards Leinster and back to Roland. "What the Hell, there is enough grouse for all," he sighed. "I accept your offer, knight to knight, squire to squire. However, we travel together. To my knowledge the castle is at least two days ride from here, am I mistaken?" asked the knight.

Roland resented the unspoken implication he might not be at the castle as promised. Nor did he relish the idea of enduring this insufferable knight's company for even half a day. Volatile and dangerous, the knight was. And he and Eloise could not be slowed.

"We have been making very good time. Without doubt we can make the castle by nightfall. I'll wait for you there." Let them try and keep up, thought Roland.

"We'll ride together. Now let's call it done and cook this grouse before it decays. I humbly request you join us for a meal," the knight said, looking the jovial host with broad smile and outstretched arms, as if this open space were his great hall.

"I'm Sir Pingbee of Wexford," he said, then he bowed. "This is Alred, my squire, who is from Meath with ties to Connacht." Alred bowed as well, stinging from the disappointment of battle lost.

"Roland, Lord of Ashbury-at-March, Connacht, and El," Roland said feeling neither expansive nor wishing to say any more about his page. His anger unabated, he couldn't bring himself to look at her.

"Ashbury is a long way from *England*, Lord Roland," Pingbee said, growling *England* as Eloise had done.

"Aye," Roland grunted in English, fixing Eloise with a punishing glare before surveying the terrain. "Let them prepare that bird," he said to Pingbee, putting his sword through the scabbard on his girdle before dismounting.

Arrow returned to quiver, Eloise took a deep breath before lifting her injured ankle and easing it over Garth's back. She held herself. Usually she would drop to the ground landing squarely on both feet. She paused, fearing she would cry out when she hit the ground. Gone was the strength and assurance, the Grace that protected her while facing Pingbee. Without guards, arms and her mighty hounds, the glory of Dahlquin was again a secret deep in her heart. Invoking the strength of Cu Chulainn, she eased herself inch by inch to the turf below. *A pony would be handy*, she thought.

Reggie's shield bumped the back of her head. She felt hands grip her waist and steady her to the ground. Roland withdrew without a word.

Eloise and Alred were to work together to prepare the meal.

"El has a broken ankle," Roland announced, "he can't collect kindling or wood for the fire."

"Broken ankle, as well as that beating," Pingbee gasped, gazing from Eloise back to Roland. "By your hand, sir?"

Roland shrugged, but said nothing. "He is capable of singeing and plucking."

Once the fire was ablaze, Eloise was assigned the task of singeing and plucking the grouse. She burned her fingers on the hot feathers.

"Clumsy," Alred said, "let me help."

Eloise glanced at him and he blew a cloud of smoke and ash into her face. She coughed and rubbed her eye. Having been spared a fight once already, Eloise couldn't let him provoke her.

This taunting seemed a fair exchange to the knights for they did nothing to interfere.

Because they were in a hurry, she jointed the grouse and sliced the thick breasts and thighs to cook faster on the open fire. She stuffed the liver between the fatty skin and flesh of one of the thighs, and the heart in the other, imagining how tasty it would be if she had some onion, parsley and salt. Exalted salt.

"Sirs, do you have any bread?" she asked Pingbee and Alred.

The men shook their heads.

"We neither," she said. "Ah well." She hesitated. "If we had more time, and bread," she said, "I would stuff onions, parsley and bread in the cavity of this bird along with the heart. And such a paste I would have made with the liver." She closed her eye a moment, thinking on such a feast. Food tasted better in the open, she reflected. "It takes at least two hours to roast a stuffed bird this size. In a fire pit…with river stones…peat or lots of wood, of course," she added at last. When no one said anything, she looked about at their hungry, expectant faces.

"You could do that?" Pingbee asked, his eyes glowing green.

"With more time, I could." she said with a lilt. "We shall have cooked morsels in half the time," she continued, "and, oh, the aroma, when all you smell is the bird and not the wood," she said, inhaling deeply through her congested nose, "then it's done," she almost sighed. Pingbee and Alred inhaled as well, as if they too might enjoy the mythical aroma.

Pingbee smacked his lips in approval. "What a picnic this will be!"

Alred's mouth seemed to water at the thought of such a meal.

"A fine picnic, with cider, Connacht ale and summer wine," she added.

Impudence forgotten, Eloise knew she had earned a place at their figurative table.

But Roland's cold expression reminded her that she was still in exile.

Back on the road, Eloise reflected on Pingbee. Once fed, he enjoyed laughing, storytelling and proved to be a most congenial fellow. Gone was the rude and harsh exterior. Not as tall as Roland, but stout like a bull, Pingbee was a large and imposing man, with auburn hair and sparkling green eyes. Fit and capable, at thirty-seven years of age he exceeded the average life span of the typical younger, unlanded sons who traveled the world as knights-errant. *If only he would apologize for his dishonorable words*, Eloise thought.

Alred shoved her, pitching her forward.

Groaning, she regained her seat and glared at Alred. His sneer angered her, but what could she do? This was the way of it, young men in training, sparring, playing rough. Trying to unseat each other. Poking or jabbing. Relentless taunting and bullying.

His sneer turned to a smirk. He shrugged his shoulders and gave her a wry smile. Eloise let her breath out, a truce perhaps. Then he leaned over, stretched his arm and pinched her neck, twisting the skin hard. She yelped, trying unsuccessfully to shove him off, unwilling to use *Cara* to hit him. Reggie's shield was an awkward weight on her injured left side as she tried to keep the reins light and not pull on Garth's sensitive mouth.

"Leave off, Alred. Enough," Roland said, looking over his shoulder at the riders behind him. It was one thing to assign El all the lowly tasks of plucking feathers and gutting the bird, blowing smoke and ash in her face, making disparaging remarks about her skills and loose tongue. These were accepted behaviours between squire and page. But Roland wouldn't allow contact.

The conversation between Roland and Pingbee was interrupted by more jostling between Eloise and Alred. Believing Roland was still angry, she refused to complain or ask for help. She took the abuse. Pingbee smiled broadly and nodded his head in approval. Her quiet acceptance of the harassment only seemed to increase her esteem in the eyes of Pingbee.

"Roland," Pingbee said, "El has fighting spirit, seems he's learned to keep his place after all." He nodded to her again. "The boy has potential, despite his impertinence. And weren't we all a bit impertinent in our youth," he said, more a declaration than a question. He chuckled.

You still are, Eloise thought to herself. *Impertinence grown to rudeness.* Movement caught her eye: Alred trying to box her ear. She raised her arm to block, taking the bruising blow.

"The impertinence and heat of youth," Pingbee answered to Roland's quizzical look.

Roland reined Artoch around, stopping directly in front of Alred, forcing the squire's horse to a stop. Eloise was gratified to see the younger man shrink back.

"Leave off, boy." Roland turned and rode back to Pingbee, who stared back at Alred with a disapproving look. *Don't provoke him,* Pingbee's look seemed to say. Alred flushed and he looked down, then sideways at Eloise. "I'll get you," he mouthed, but it was his hateful expression that made her nauseous with dread.

"The bow is a lowly weapon," Alred said. "A coward's weapon."

Eloise ignored him.

"A true warrior doesn't kill from a safe distance," he continued ridiculing her. "And that-" he said, pointing to *Cara* in her right hand, "wouldn't stop man nor beast. A coward's weapon."

Cara. Praise be to God, Alred didn't know her name, Eloise thought, for *Cara* would surely stop his beating heart and that of his beast and a hundred more. What was an army without the multitude of archers and crossbowmen? Not the hand-to-hand might of the knight, but what a plague upon life. Hadn't he been cowardly enough to share the bounty of her weapon? Fighter's stance. She dare not glare at Alred.

Eloise reached into her pouch, searching for a willow leaf to chew. The taste was startling in its bitterness, but it did soften her physical pain.

Nothing could soften the pain in her heart. Roland hadn't spoken to her since he commanded her to silence. That word and the memory of his voice chilled her. Would he ever forgive her? Could they yet be friends? She yearned for the close bond they were forging. Unbidden the melody and words of the song ran pure and strong in her mind: *Something has awakened and will not be put to rest.* If he never spoke to her again, she would be lost in the emptiness of it.

Don't dwell on him, her guilt was overpowering. All Dahlquin-Ireland depended on them. The time elapsed so quickly, yet the miles passed so slowly. She clutched her stomach and fought back tears. So empty, what was wrong with her? Was Dahlquin dying, was that the emptiness she felt, her parents and kinsmen, perishing even as she and Roland rode for help? *It was not! Don't dwell on that either.* Be a smart girl - how easy it was to give advice to Blathin. Garth flinched. His ears were back and he turned his teeth towards Alred and his mount.

Garth didn't want to follow. His dominant role in this 'herd' had been challenged with Pingbee and his mount in front. Now Garth was behind with this gelding. Eloise stroked his neck, reassuring him, commiserating. She hated it too. Usually sure and confident, today her weight was off, she gave weak cues. She sat up, straightening her posture.

Roland and Pingbee were watching her.

"That stallion is too much for the boy," Pingbee commented.

"He's a grand horse," Roland answered.

"Needs to learn who's in charge." Pingbee looked thoughtful a moment, then smiled. "Like the boy," he laughed. "You should take a strap to that bastard, like the master has done to you," he instructed Eloise.

Eloise blanched. *Take a strap to Garth. Surely this man had to be a Scragmuir. Or English. None but Scragmuir could be so foul and offensive.* She gave him a look of hatred. Didn't she have enough to plague her waking thoughts without this unendurable man? Again, Garth pinned his ears, and she felt his back tense. She let her breath out and tried to concentrate on Garth. Eloise looked past the knights before her and envisioned High Lord FitzGilbert's castle looming on the horizon, sanctuary for them and salvation for her imperiled kin.

"Ride here where I can watch," Pingbee said to Eloise, "take a lesson."

Roland genially fell back, making room for Eloise to ride beside Pingbee. Frustrated, she wouldn't look at Roland as she cued Garth forward to ride next to the most insufferable knight in all Ireland. She had a brief hope that Roland might give Alred a lesson or two in punching and shoving. Garth turned his head to her, bringing her back.

"The reins are too loose," Pingbee said. "Make a fist. Grip those reins," and he demonstrated as his horse pinned its ears momentarily. "If he roots, you'll be ready to strike him," Pingbee claimed, as if this were the way to handle a horse, Eloise lamented to herself hoping his steed would dump him in the mud for his harshness. "And that shield," he continued, "is too big and heavy for you."

Eloise gently tickled the reins and Garth tucked his chin. She touched him lightly with her legs, willing him to understand and perform. She could feel him quiver and expand. He tossed his head and turned an ear to her, seeking her guidance. Pingbee was barking at her, some inane nonsense about spurs and fists and quirts. Ignoring Pingbee, letting her breath out, Eloise focused on the road, envisioning FitzGilbert's castle before her. She didn't think about riding or cueing, just the feel of her Garth, his broad, round back.

"Beautiful," Pingbee said. "See how well that works?"

Despite the injured ankle and poor cueing, Garth executed an elegant right leg yield moving well ahead of Pingbee. At her request, Garth yielded the other way in a collected canter. Listening, playing, mayhap he was as eager as her to do something familiar and correct. Had there ever been such a noble partner as her Garth?

"That's far enough," Roland called.

Hearing the worry in his voice, she clenched, remembering the trap she had ridden into. Garth reacted, halting, jarring her. Stabbing pain radiated from her ankle, up her leg, gripping her gut, making her gasp, opening the split in her lips. Her reaction caused Garth to jig in place, nervously seeking direction. Holding her breath she radiated fear to Garth.

"Too much leg," Pingbee scolded. "Not the horse's fault."

"She has a broken ankle," Roland said crossly from behind.

Eloise gulped, sneaking a sideways look. Then stroking Garth, reassuring him.

"Who?" Pingbee asked, glancing back at Roland.

Alred laughed. "A cockless waste, I knew it," he chided Eloise.

"El," Roland tried to correct.

"I thought you said-"

"He has a broken ankle, remember?" Roland interrupted.

"Hmmm, At-March, in Connacht," Pingbee said, studying Roland. "Reginald's shield," Pingbee murmured. "That's a grand horse. Royal White," Pingbee added, more to himself than as a compliment to Eloise, she thought. "Dahlquin."

His last utterance hung in the air. Eloise couldn't help herself. She stared at Pingbee, wondering if he had concluded her identity. Broken, isolated, with only an angry, surly Englishman to protect her? Or give her up, she wondered. *Roland would not.*

"Dahlquin," Pingbee shouted, slapping his knee. "You're a bastard son, you are." Pingbee looked back to Roland to confirm his deduction.

Eloise turned to Roland as well, silently trying to communicate whether to go with this declaration, freeing them both from further scrutiny, or was it too close to the truth? This knight, friendly now, could still be the enemy and a threat to them.

Having come to a conclusion, Roland gave Pingbee a wry smile, his brown eyes hard and lined.

"Sir, it could be that you're too smart for us," Roland said.

"I knew it!" Pingbee beamed. "Damn, now which one of those bloody, murdering brothers is the father, eh?" He studied El for any telltale resemblance. "Hubert or Reginald?"

This debate turned her stomach. How dare he? To accuse either of them. Someday, she promised herself, someday, before God and the spirits, he would eat his words.

"A bastard knave," Alred joked, obviously thrilled to have found more fault with the puny page. "A cunt from Connacht. Cunt-achtmen," he continued his joke.

"I'm from Connacht," Roland said, the wry smile replaced with the impassive warrior's expression. "If you insult my neighbors again," Roland said, giving Eloise what could only be described as a courteous nod, "I'll peel the skin from your hairless balls and fillet the rest for Ashbury's hogs."

Eloise felt her heart sing as she watched the color drain from Alred's face with Roland's borrowed threat. She and Garth fell in behind Roland and Pingbee, again beside the dastardly Alred, as they continued riding.

"Sir," Pingbee hailed Roland, "you ride as if pursued by Satan himself!"

Pingbee's voice had a familiar, irritable edge. He was succumbing to the grueling pace and getting hungry, Eloise noted.

Roland looked over his shoulder, and again scanned the horizon for just that.

"We are." Roland crossed himself. Pingbee, Eloise and Alred followed.

"Lord Roland, by your gracious will," Pingbee started. "El is plagued by vast injuries, surely we could offer him a chance to rest?"

Clever, Eloise thought, begging rest for her sake.

Roland glanced at Eloise and tilted his head, questioning. Did she wish to rest?

"You're a slave driver, sir," Pingbee interjected before Eloise could respond. "Look at our horses."

"The next water we come to, the Langston stream is close. A good suggestion Sir, to rest for the sake of El and the horses," Roland bowed his head. "But briefly. Satan does not rest."

The promise of stopping for rest and water seemed to make everyone acutely aware of how thirsty and tired they were.

After attending the horses, Eloise found the willow leaves in her saddle bag. The chamois cloth dropped to the ground. Garth stepped away for better grazing and she retrieved the chamois and tucked it in her girdle. With a willow leaf between her cheek and gum, Eloise sat against the trunk of an oak tree, eyes closed. She was tired of Pingbee and his insufferable squire, Alred. Couldn't he find anything better to do than torment her? And torment he did, even now, kicking her.

"Move!"

Lumbering to her feet, she limped to where Roland sat leaning against a yew tree. She clutched her wooden pendant and prayed to Saint Monica and the Goddess Brigid for patience. Safely at Roland's side, she laid Reggie's shield and her bow within hand's reach and offered to polish his dagger while he rested. She could be close to him, without appearing to have sought his protection.

He grunted. Eyes still closed. He removed the dagger from its scabbard. "You aren't going to gut me, are you?" he asked, one eye peering at her as she reached for the offered handle.

"My Lord?" she asked, confused, "of course not."

"I thought you might shoot me, when you called me *England*," he said, loosening his grip on the blade as she took the handle.

"Alred!" Pingbee shouted and Eloise almost dropped the dagger. "Take a lesson from young El, a moment to clean my dagger," and Pingbee thrust his dagger out toward the disgusted Alred.

Eloise looked up to catch Alred's dagger-sharp glance aimed at her.

"Just you wait," he mouthed.

Just *you* wait, she thought as well.

Eloise felt Roland's gaze upon her. After his borrowed threat to Alred, she thought, hoped, he was getting over his anger. She was repentant. Pingbee and Alred pushed her to the limits of tolerance, but she understood the danger and wouldn't allow herself to be provoked again.

Roland sighed.

She looked up, wondering, questioning, not speaking.

"Your father," Roland said, shaking his head, "has his hands full." He gave her a crooked smile that spoke exasperation, consternation and resignation.

Eloise sighed herself, letting the words form, her apology, the explanation - for surely Roland wouldn't suffer such foul insults to his mother's honor - as well as her appreciation for his friendship, his presence next to her. She inhaled, opened her mouth to speak.

"Roland," Pingbee said, cutting her off. As Roland turned his attention, she hated Pingbee all the more for again intruding on her time with Roland.

"Three days, sir, three days to FitzGilbert," Pingbee said.

Roland closed his eyes and folded his hands in his lap as Pingbee continued his argument that the road to High Lord FitzGilbert's castle was at least three days riding, again questioning the unreasonable demands. She snorted, immediately regretting the indiscretion, hoping Roland didn't hear it. His eyes remained closed as he leaned against the sturdy yew. *Will I never learn to be still?*

"Villages with lodging and drink, Roland! Are you listening to me?"

Thankful she hadn't returned the chamois to the saddlebag, Eloise used it as she spit and polished Roland's dagger. Like most fighting daggers it was easily three mens' hand lengths. She laid it across her finger and noted the heft and balance. Like her father's dagger, it was without ornamentation, but sheer elegance of purpose. The wood handle was aged and the leather grip well-used. Picturing his hand gripping the dagger, she shuddered, longing to feel his fingers wrap around her. Fingers he had nearly broken fighting with the marauders.

"Despite the name, the Soggy Bog has the finest beer and spirits." Pingbee smacked his lips.

"You buying?" Roland asked, eyes still closed.

"With the Lord of At-March present?"

Roland shook his head.

"Cheap bastard," Pingbee grumbled.

"Don't forget it," Roland answered.

Eloise returned the dagger to Roland's scabbard, and awkwardly squeezed herself next to him. "Let me have your hand," she murmured, taking it up and removing his studded gauntlet. "Such fatigue upon you," she crooned, turning his exposed hand palm up, examining the bruises and callouses. His hand was huge. She ran her hand flat along his, easing his fingers open. Working up an excess of saliva, she swished it about her mouth with the willow leaf she had tucked between her lip and gum. Once more, she caressed his warm palm with her own. "This will help," she whispered, spitting the willow saliva into his meaty palm. Before he could lodge a complaint, she was massaging the warm concoction into his flesh. She hummed. As Roland relaxed, she increased the pressure and widened the circular motion, gradually palpating and stretching the tissue.

She moved to his thumb crotch, gently pulling then massaging the webbed skin. She started humming a tune about the thumb, the mighty Dwarf King of the hand. Taking his thumb in her grip she playfully wriggled it, loosening it, letting the weight of his hand pop his joints. His nails were stained, and she tried to dislodge some of the dirt.

All his fingers had little pelts of black hair on their backs. Succumbing to desire, she balled her left hand, then placed it inside Roland's. With her right hand she stroked his fingers, urging them to curl around her fist. He engulfed it. Squeezing once, he then pressed with one finger at a time, from baby finger to thumb and back down again.

Next she embraced his hand in both of hers; taking his pointing finger between her thumb and first two fingers she entwined her remaining fingers with his, then slowly caressed and tugged on his finger, listening as well as feeling for the ping of the joints.

What she heard was something between a sigh and a growl. Although his eyes were closed, he bore the shadow of a smile on his sleepy countenance.

Each finger received the same treatment.

"The road to FitzGilbert is three days riding," Pingbee complained anew. Eloise realized how inadequately she had appreciated the quiet, once Pingbee resumed whining. "You are unreasonable, sir."

Roland yawned then said, "Satisfy yourself," in a patronizing voice, still not opening his eyes.

"Think of the horses," Pingbee countered, hands outstretched. Think of poor, broken El." Now he pointed at her. Ignoring him she continued massaging Roland's fingers.

"You are not under obligation, sir. But I'm bound to deliver poor, broken El to FitzGilbert before he kills one or all of us," Roland added, with a grin on his sleepy face.

Pingbee guffawed.

"You'll want to be well rested when next we meet," Roland said.

"Sounds like you wish to escape us, sir," Pingbee goaded, inciting the underlying tension and threat of their strange association.

"I'll wait for you at the castle or return to this very spot, sir," Roland offered, eyes open, "if your slothful arses are still here," Roland said with a snarling smirk.

Eloise held her breath as the postponed fight resurrected before her, the air vibrating, consuming all thought and energy, Roland and Pingbee eyeing each other like two starving beasts sated only by a banquet of violence. Neither man blinked. Eloise quickly turned her glance to Alred, poised but not moving. Disciplined. Eloise allowed herself to breath, but nothing more. Watching, waiting. Wishing she had *Cara* in hand.

Then as if by mutual arrangement, Pingbee sniffed, Roland snorted, both knights relented. How did they know, what had she missed?

"Let's go," Roland said, standing. "May you have goodness," he said to Eloise. "Ready?" he asked, extending a hand to pull her up, the hint of a smile.

Eloise took a deep breath and exhaled loudly before taking his hand. Pulling herself up, she felt the tremor in his warm hand. Then he slipped his massaged hand in his gauntlet.

With more grumbling from Pingbee about the unreasonableness of the pace and the duration of the trip, they all saddled up.

VILLAGE, 14th of June

Seamus, Broccan, Torcan, Ercc, Donal and Maiu entered the village, drawing stares and enquiries. This village was muddier than the rest, the horses sinking near to their knees. Who lives in such a swamp, Seamus wondered?

"Is hunger upon you, sirs?" a merchant asked. "Space to tie and water your horses, right here."

"Hungry for information," Seamus acknowledged, watching the merchant's expression pale. "We're pursuing a knight and boy, black and grey horses. Did they pass this way?"

"Two days ago was Market Day. Then the flood. So many people. I don't recall the two, then or today," the merchant answered, looking defeated as Seamus and his men moved on.

They continued into the village, questioning and searching, hearing about the flood and Noah, until someone claimed to remember the two and directed them to an inn.

"Dragon Slayer is it?" Broccan commented, a sly grin spreading on his face as he questioned the innkeeper. "He tell you about that, did he?" Broccan queried, distracting the innkeeper and his assistants as Torcan snuck around the back to pilfer the storage chamber.

"His page," one of the wide-eyed assistants started, shaking his head, "looked like dragon bait."

"Face battered. One eye swelled over completely. Couldn't walk."

"Or talk," the other assistant added.

The innkeeper shook his head with the exaggerations.

"Both covered in blood," the first assistant said.

"Bad lot, them two," Broccan agreed.

"They were quiet and kept to themselves," the innkeeper said. "We're a peaceable village, and they didn't bring trouble upon us. Dragons, bah," the innkeeper said, "back to work," he added with a wave of his hand at his assistants.

"By your will, if your lads might," Seamus called to the innkeeper's back. Torcan was, presumably, still robbing the inn and Seamus needed to keep all the men engaged. "If they might draw some water for the horses after all." When the innkeeper turned to face him, he made a show of pulling out his worn, leather money pouch and searching the near empty bag of his remaining treasure. "I can pay," Seamus said, bringing out some coins. The innkeeper studied him and his travel mates before turning his attention to his assistants. Both lads looked to their employer and Seamus thought they were willing to help, and more eager to share their views on the Dragon Slayer and boy.

"Fuck the beasts," Broccan shouted, "if you're paying for drink, I should be allowed. Eh?" he said as he dismounted. All the riders dismounted.

"Horses first," Seamus said, as the lads rushed over to take the horses to the cistern. "Covered in blood, you say?" he asked as he walked with the lads and horses.

Back on the road, Seamus rode with renewed urgency. Riding the previous night had paid off. The rain held their prey over another day.

"Just this very morning, Broccan," Seamus said again, savoring the knowledge.

"We could be riding in their very hoof prints," Broccan said. "The wounded bastards should be easy to take down now. Torcan, your family did some damage after all."

"Breathe deep, Torcan," Seamus called back to him. "Smells like your revenge is at hand."

"Revenge? Smells like death," Broccan shouted.

"They will hear us coming," Seamus said, signaling with his hand for Broccan to lower his voice.

"Bah," Broccan scoffed. "The two of them, blind and crippled, to ambush us."

"None should hear us. You provoke trouble with such boasts."

Torcan spoke up. He was finally riding his horse without being towed.

"You want them dead." Torcan confirmed, not for the first time on this grueling journey.

Seamus and Broccan both nodded.

"As we have discussed, endlessly," Broccan added.

Torcan grimaced but said nothing.

Seamus's horse alerted him to something. *People, horses, livestock?* He raised a hand, drawing the riders' attention, then sliced the air. Silence.

"Good morrow to you, fair brothers," Broccan said before Seamus could utter a salutation.

"And to you as well," said a tall man leading the procession.

The five religious men before him walked in two rows of two and three. They were dressed in homespun grey robes with simple rope belts. Seamus couldn't believe his eyes when Broccan side passed his horse off the road, indicating to the other riders they do the same. The other riders didn't have the skills of Broccan, and their horses went everywhere but off the road. Broccan gave a pious nod to the brothers. Torcan's horse stood passively.

"Pray you have continued safe travels, brothers," Broccan said, "you may have passed dangerous marauders on your journey."

"Blessings upon you. Our travel has been safe," said the lead man. The others remained quiet, observant.

"Indeed. By chance did you pass two travelers on this road? A knight and boy, black horse and grey?" Broccan asked.

The lead man looked back at his fellow brothers. Each one shrugged or shook his head.

"We didn't pass any such travelers."

"Fortuna's favor is upon you. How long have you traveled this road?" Broccan asked.

"Good fortune, you say," the lead man repeated. "Mayhap God is protecting us."

"And how long have you been on this road?" Broccan asked again.

The lead man paused. He was tall, gaunt, with intent yet kindly eyes. He looked at each of the riders; it seemed to Seamus he was assessing their intent anew. "So long as God wills it," he answered.

There was a pause. Once again Seamus was amazed at Broccan's restraint. Just when he had formed his own response to this towering elusive, Broccan spoke:

"Of course, forgive my ignorance in the ways of our Lord, God. We're after two murderous rebels to God and crown. If they're not on this road, we must change our course."

Again, the lead man pondered the request before answering.

"Fucking murder, you say?" said one of the young men in line. "You're well-armed for a man and boy."

This outburst brought chuckles and gasps from the young men in line as well as his riders.

The lead man blanched then admonished:

"Somhairle, shame upon you."

"I haven't taken a vow a silence," the young man said to his leader, his cheeks red with agitation. Then to Seamus and Broccan, "We joined this road a mile back. "Savior Jesus, protect us and these soldiers," Somhairle said and crossed himself.

"And other travelers as well," added the leader, head bowed, crossing himself. The rest of his young men followed his example, including Somhairle.

"May you have goodness, for the blessing," Broccan said, "we should all be on our way. After you," he said, extending his arm, indicating they proceed. Despite Broccan's cordial display, his expression revealed disdain and malice. Torcan appeared a white-eyed boar, poised and ready to gore as he glared at the religious order.

The leader took a deep breath, stood to his full height and with boney shoulders thrust back he warily led his young acolytes through the valley of the shadow of death.

"Young Somhairle," Broccan called after the procession, "find a horse and join us, if you feel the urge."

Seamus watched Somhairle raise a hand in acknowledgement, but the youth didn't look back. *What internal struggle did Somhairle wage? We all struggle.* Seamus glanced at Broccan then back at Torcan. *Most of us struggle.*

"Seamus, you aren't thinking of joining them, are you?" Broccan said, pointing back at the religious parade behind them. "On with us - we've an execution to perform. Then back to New Ulster," he said with a harsh laugh.

New Ulster, with High King Tiomoid U'Neill. This is why we came, Seamus remembered as he and his riders cantered on. *A new kingdom built upon the bones of the usurpers.*

ON THE ROAD, 14ᵗʰ of June

Eloise heard snatches of conversation and laughter between Roland and Pingbee. Fellowship, if not friendship, was forming between these two warriors, the fraternity of fighters. Yet this comradery only existed to keep them together until they could kill each other. Then they would start over and mayhap be friends. She thought about warriors. It was the core of their existence - fighting, protection. Eloise was indoctrinated from the cradle with legends and songs of such heroes. For the good of the ancient tribe, men would obediently risk their lives. Accepting knighthood and swearing an oath of fealty, a new life began, the life a warrior. All the men in her family, from great, great grand sires to her youngest cousins trained for this purpose. Anything less would bring shame.

As Eloise loved the oneness with Garth, and her bow, *Cara*, a good knight loved the feeling of oneness with his steed and sword, the extension of his own flesh and bone giving way to hard metal, without distinction where one left off and the other started. Roland and Pingbee understood this unspoken bond between them and relished the fraternity that bound them together, validating them both in the ancient way of the warrior, the ancient way of men.

"Pussy, pussy, pussy," Alred sneered, his brown eyes boring into her, as if seeing her for what she was.

Such a bond did not exist between Eloise and Alred.

Had he guessed her true sex? A Dahlquin female? Had her whole disguise been undone? What then?

"Little cock sucking bastard," he said, thrusting his tongue against the inside of his cheek.

Her cheeks burned and she tried not to listen. It was the ritualistic tormenting between pages, squires and knights.

Roland and Pingbee didn't seem to hear his taunts. Eloise tried not to pout, letting her breath out, focusing on the road ahead. This was what some squires did. Bullies.

"Ow," she yelped, her hand going to the sting in her cheek.

Alred chuckled. He was throwing rocks at her. He patted the bulging leather pouch on his girdle, leering at her. Apparently, he had spent the rest-time collecting sharp stones to throw.

"That how you got the horse? Taking it in the arse?" Alred chuckled. "And that shield too," he added. "Dahlquin's bastard, Reginald's bitch."

Although she had never met Roland's squire, Val, she wished with all her aching heart that this heroic squire of mystery was here, for surely he would...what? Defeat Alred? Val owed her nothing. And she certainly didn't wish to incur any more debt. Her list of encumbrances was much too long. So many lives already lost. Valuable, Dahlquin lives. Not like the useless turd riding next to her.

He threw rocks at her, at Garth. They stung and she and her horse flinched in discomfort. Again a yelp escaped her.

Roland glanced back, but she didn't indicate her distress.

"Cock sucking, arse fucking," Alred taunted, once Roland returned his attention to the road.

Eloise tried to ignore his words, but she kept a watchful eye on Alred, ducking and dodging the rocks as best she could.

"Arse sucking, cock fucking," he said, sniffing the air, making a disgusted face. "Shit breath, that's what stinks around here."

Alred pulled up sharply on his horse's reins, swinging in behind Eloise and Garth, riding up on her left side, her blind side. Now she rode behind Pingbee with Alred directly behind Roland. The knights said nothing about the change of position.

"Like stinking Scragmuir," he sneered, low as a whisper.

Scragmuir. Eloise turned sharply returning his glare. "I hate Scragmuir," she let out, the miles of suppressed anger and resentment spilling out in the generations-ingrained bitterness at the mere mention of her ancestral enemy.

Roland turned around, fixing his stern gaze on her.

She met and held it, studying his expression.

"My neighbors," he said, giving the slightest tip of his head.

Eloise knew she should lower her gaze, at least her head. She told herself to do it, yet she glared at Roland a moment longer, as if the pent-up frustration forced her posture against reason. What was she doing, inviting violence? Fighter's stance - again.

"Forgive me," she said, concentrating all effort on a humble, penitent voice, since her head seemed beyond her control. Hearing her own congested voice, her shoulders slumped allowing her chin to drop, but her eyes remained on Roland until he nodded his acceptance of her apology and returned his attention to Pingbee.

"You're not just impudent?" Alred said, eyes wide. "You're fucking crazed."

Pingbee said to Roland, "Seems both lads met with a dirty deed, or two."

"Mayhap," Roland, said shrugging his shoulders, not looking back.

They rode on, without a rock or taunt. Eloise didn't want to turn her head, validating that Alred had her worried, annoyed, angry. But what was he doing? Why the cessation of harassment? Slowly she lowered the shield and craned her neck until she could glance at Alred with her open eye.

His head was nodding, eyes half closed. He is falling asleep, she thought with relief, letting her breath out. He was not, she told herself. He is faking. She glanced again to see his head dip, and jerk back up, blinking. Anticipating a rock or cruel word, Eloise concentrated on the road ahead. Waiting. Nothing. Maybe he really was falling asleep. Quiet. Finally.

My enemy's enemy is my friend, Eloise heard her father counsel. She wondered what heinous deed Alred had suffered at the hands of Scragmuir? Was he past redemption? Couldn't Roland see how damaged this squire was, by his *neighbors*? And Pingbee? He claimed he was of Wexford, but surely someone so ill-tempered must have ties with Scragmuir.

Keep your friends close…and your enemies closer. It jolted her, then she smiled, because this time is was her mother giving counsel, Aine's melodic voice, soft and strong, both at once.

Life was full of contradictions. Mayhap Alred was a contradiction. Their mutual hatred of Scragmuir must surely outweigh whatever grievances had developed between them on the road. Stupid, surly, inept. But his burning hatred for Scragmuir was a virtue unto itself.

Then her neck. She was choking. Her hand went to her throat as she fell back, out of the saddle. In a flash she saw the sky, patches of grey and black clouds.

Startled, Garth swung around to see where Eloise went.

The fall jarred her, pain stabbed like a knife, bold as thunder. She couldn't contain the groan that emanated from deep in her gut as she tried to stifle the tears.

"Hmm Hmmm Hmmmmmmmmhhhhmmm," he chortled. *Don't cry*, she kept telling herself, *you'll sound like a girl.*

She saw Roland turn to see Garth, riderless. Alred watched her in unrestrained glee.

Roland drew his sword.

Alred turned, shrugging his shoulders. His mouth fell open when Roland sidled up next to him. Artoch forced the gelding to step away. Eloise saw one forceful stroke and graceful sweep. Roland narrowed his eyes in menace, staring into the terrified eyes of Alred, taunting and intimidating the youth, *El Muerte Rojo* bloodied.

With slow, deliberate movements, Roland wiped his bloody sword across Alred's thigh, one side then the other, leaving a swipe of blood on the squire's wool hose.

Roland leaned over. With the tip of his sword he stabbed something in the dirt and flung it up into Alred's anguished face.

"Yours," Roland said with disdain, dropping the useless flap of ear in Alred's lap.

It was during this frightening movement that pain and realization must have caught up with Alred. He howled. Lifting a hand to the wound, he clutched a fistful of blood.

Garth returned to Eloise and lowered his head, sniffing at her then blowing out his warm breath. She put a hand up to his large head and stroked it uneasily. "Looby," she said, voice cracking.

Roland dismounted; squatting next to her he placed his hand on her neck.

She looked up. His mouth twitched. His eyes were dark and focused. She was thinking, hoping, he longed to comfort her as much as longed to be held. That was out of the question with Alred and Pingbee looking on.

Pingbee appeared so startled by the event he just stared from Alred to her and Roland, speechless for once.

Stifling her burning sobs, she sighed.

Alred howled again. "He cut my fucking ear off! Bleeding Saints! He cut my ear off! Oh shit!" he wailed.

No one addressed his ranting.

"Can you ride?" Roland asked her.

Eloise nodded. Thinking only if he lifted her, placed her in the saddle and...she moaned as he did just that.

She bit her cut lips and rode on, blind with pain.

Hearing her muffled sobs, Pingbee looked back.

"You all right, *son*?" Pingbee asked her, his trepidation palpable.

"El?" Roland asked.

"Lord," she answered, wiping her nose, "My Lord," she added.

Eloise turned to Alred, stupid, cruel, fecund excuse for a Christian. He was bleeding profusely. Some plantain and a few stitches would stop the flow of blood and increase his chances of recovering. Had to keep him alive, she remembered, so Val could kill him; perverse as it seemed, this was the way of it.

They ambled on. To distract herself from the pain, Eloise turned her attention to the traffic on the road: merchants, families, sheep or cattle being driven to castle or market. The upheavals of these past few days crashed on her mind like the pain of her injuries. Dahlquin. Her birthright. Yet what had she done to earn it? Born female. And was she any closer to relief or salvation for her kin? Would High Lord FitzGilbert even receive her? Beaten beyond recognition, wrath and hatred in her wake. Is that what it took? And Roland's petulance, was it a warrior's wrath and hatred? Eloise felt the rhythm of Garth's amble, moving forward, connecting her to her purpose. She could think in the saddle. Was that the relentless message her father and uncle tried to impart? With her so incapable of understanding? Because of her sex? *It was not*, she answered her own question. Unchecked wrath and hatred were synonymous with weakness and easily exploited, as Pingbee had done with her, she remembered. Wrath and hatred were not the answer, but the fuel. Anger and avarice were more fuel. Fuel she too might still learn to exploit, if...she had-

Alred was weaving in his saddle, his tunic covered in blood.

"He's falling," Eloise called. "I need to stop the bleeding, by your will."

"Alred, straighten up," Pingbee commanded. Alred continue to spiral, as if drunk.

"Ho!" she called to Alred's horse as well as Garth. "By your will," Eloise tried again, as the tired horses came to a rough halt. Alred was sallow, his eyelids fluttered. "He's bleeding to death."

"We need to keep moving, El," Roland reminded her. "Pingbee and Alred can wait here."

"Boil some water, plantain, I'll stitch it up. Then we'll be on our way," she said, confused by her own words.

Pingbee was staring at her. *What now*, she wondered, turning her attention back to Alred.

Alred tilted dangerously towards her and she cued Garth to side pass next to Alred's gelding.

"Help!" she shrieked as Alred collapsed against her. "Side, side, side" she barked at Garth, desperate to keep him pressed against Alred's gelding. Pushing against Alred's weight, with the sharp, pounding pain in her ankle, Eloise was unable to give leg or rein cues to Garth. She and Alred were going to fall. She couldn't bear the pain of falling again.

"Alred!" Pingbee growled.

Eloise sank back, planting her butt as if no saddle existed, taking root in Garth's back. Eloise and Garth were one, free of the squire.

"Up," Pingbee grunted.

Eloise realized Pingbee had pulled Alred back and attempted to steady his squire. Gratefully she stroked Garth's stout neck.

"Let's find a quiet place off this busy road," Roland said, bringing her attention back to the heavy traffic.

"Take my excuse, you!" Roland hailed to a passing farmer, driving five cows and steers. "Is there a stream or perhaps a glade for our horses to drink and graze?" he asked. "Out of the way of all the travelers?"

Though the farmer kept his eyes down, he tried to study the group.

"Closest is back the way you came, just a way," the farmer pointed. "There's plenty of water ahead, but not so much grazing."

"I remember," Pingbee said.

Eloise nodded at the farmer.

"May you have goodness," Roland said to the retreating farmer, nodding at Eloise in acknowledgement as they circled back.

Roland helped Eloise down from the saddle.

Pingbee barked at Alred to collect firewood, but the squire tumbled out of the saddle. Shaking his head, Pingbee looked to Roland, "Give us a hand."

Roland and Pingbee each took an arm and helped Alred to the base of a sapling yew, while Eloise retrieved the skin bag with water for Alred.

"We'll attend the fire," Roland said, taking Eloise by the elbow, tossing the skin bag to Pingbee. "You see to the horses."

Though Roland held her elbow, supporting her as best he could, she would not walk. Her injured ankle gripped her with stabbing then throbbing pain.

"Inhale," Roland said, inhaling as an example. "Now blow." He exhaled. "Master your pain."

"Wish we had another grouse, or a pheasant to roast," Pingbee muttered, as he took all four horses to the water.

After a few deep breaths, Eloise was not closer to taking another painful step. She could picture the firewood they needed, the plantain, web. So much more was necessary.

"Nothing to be done for it," Roland said. I'll carry you, as you're spurless," he added, turning his back to her then kneeling down. "Climb on."

What a silly solution, Eloise thought as she reached for his shoulders. When was the last time she was carried thus? Childs play to be sure. She hopped off her right, unbroken side, wrapping both legs around Roland's waist. Roland hooked his arms under her knees, his arms squeezing her thighs tight to him, lifting her as he stood. She gasped and clutched her arms round his neck as she was propelled skyward. With her arms wrapped around Roland's chest, it felt like an embrace. Eyes closed, she let her cheek rest against his wavy hair, not quite cheek-to-cheek as she desired.

"Before Christ, man," Pingbee said. "You have crippled both our servants and reduced us to beasts of burden."

Roland kept walking, ignoring Pingbee's complaint.

"After you kill him," she muttered, her mouth so near his ear, "surely my father will go to Hell and dispatch him again."

"Your family visit Hell often?" Roland asked, squeezing her legs closer round him. Four layers of linen tunic, padded gambeson, hauberk and wool surcoat didn't detract from the sensation of her spread legs upon his back. Her linen chemise and surcoat felt thin and insignificant, and she clung tighter.

"What?" Eloise asked, puzzled. "What do you mean?"

"I'll explain while we collect some *dry* wood," he said, sounding sarcastic, as he loosened his grip on her legs, easing her down to the ground, ending the embrace. Eloise sighed with regret, then groaned with discomfort.

Roland savored the sensation of Eloise sliding down his back, regretting she wasn't before him. Impossible, here and now. Wood, vegetation, then FitzGilbert's castle, he reminded himself.

"You just said your father would go to Hell and kill Pingbee," he continued, stooping to gather some small branches, twigs really, left from previous pilferers. "Your Uncle Reggie told me if I let anything happen to you, he'd haunt me from the gates of Hell." The familiar cold shiver ran down his back as he said it. "Did you feel that?" he asked her. "Damn! I hate it," he complained, crossing himself, brushing his hair down.

"Feel what?" she asked.

"Your Uncle sends his greetings," he said, believing indeed she didn't feel the chill, nor was her hair standing out.

"What are you talking about, you make little sense?" Eloise said. "And my family is not in the habit of visiting Hell."

"Just checking," Roland said with mock relief. He had heard the rumours about heresy. Eloise certainly had a strange way with animals, the wolves, orange cat and a most unnatural connection with that horse. Thoughts of a succubus nagged at his mind. He had only to stare deep within her innocent, wide eyes. Yet...how could she be an animal demon in the form of a beautiful woman? Not a very good one anyway, he considered, as he looked at her disheveled, broken appearance. He smiled, shook his head he put those futile thoughts away.

"When did Uncle Reggie say that?" she asked, taking a deep, tearful breath.

Roland guessed from the tone in her voice she felt like hearing from Reginald. He placed the twigs in her arms before continuing the scavenging and story.

"Eloise, while you were braiding your hair or binding up," he said, moving his hand briskly, "Sir Reginald came to me, with the strength of ten men with all their hands."

She nodded and he continued.

"He grabbed me by the throat," Roland imitated a man choking-bulging eyes, tongue out, "put his face nose-to-nose with mine. He had the most grotesque, terrifying expression, a gargoyle from Hell to be sure," and Roland tried to scrunch his face as miserably as possible.

Eloise smiled, then winced and her fingers went to the laceration on her lips.

"If you let any harm come to her, I will haunt you from the very gates of Hell!" Roland said trying to capture the deep rumble of Reggie's voice, shaking a clenched fist as if Reginald still held his throat. Again, the icy chill ran down Roland's spine, making his hair stand out. "There it is again, didn't you feel that cold breeze, look at my hair."

Eloise did look. Lifting her hand towards his hair, stopping before she touched him. She wanted to reach up and stroke it down, longed to run her fingers through those thick, dark locks, and massage his scalp with her fingertips. A few twigs dropped from her other arm.

Feeling the embarrassment of their closeness while face-to-face, she ducked her eyes and bent to gather plantain. And once again, she regretted disengaging. *Why do I do that*, she asked herself? She didn't have an answer. At seventeen, there weren't answers, it seemed. Arms full of wood, Roland strode back to Pingbee and Alred. *This was wrong*, she told herself. People were dying at home while she admired a man's hair. She sighed with the guilt.

"Am I to start a fire as well?" she heard Pingbee wail. "You go too far, Lord of Abuse."

She bent, plenty of plantain within easy reach.

"Enough plantain?" he asked upon his return. She had quite a handful of sword-shaped leaves.

"And spider web," Eloise reminded Roland.

He grimaced.

She tried to smile. Guilt forgotten; she was back in the present with Roland.

He exaggerated the expression, his mouth contorting, his eyes crossing.

She snorted, hurting her lips, but it touched her that he would make her laugh despite the ceaseless anxiety enshrouding them both. It was hard to remember in this moment they had been mad at each other.

"Shush." He put a finger to his lips to quiet her, then touched his finger to her lips.

Eloise balanced, immobile, his gloved finger pressed to her lips, silencing her, as she tried to decipher the message in his eyes. For once, he didn't turn away but held her gaze.

"What goes on here?"

Roland spun to face Pingbee.

With a look bordering on rage Pingbee pulled Roland by the arm and seethed. "Who is that really?" he growled, pointing at Eloise in a low, menacing voice not heard since before lunch.

Roland stared at Pingbee, also noting the change of mood.

"All will be answered when I've delivered the page to High Lord FitzGilbert," Roland replied.

"I will not wait," Pingbee growled. "Tell me now what *that* is, lest I believe you to be lewd and unholy sodomites," he said with stern conviction.

Roland stared at him in confusion. It was an earful to decipher. He understood the words but couldn't find the context. *That*? She wasn't a *that*.

"Well?" Pingbee almost shouted at him. "What's it between you?"

Roland stared from Pingbee to Eloise.

"That's what I mean," scowled Pingbee, his face pinched with disgust. "What's between you cock suckers? Tell me, or I'll slay you both here and now in the name of all that's holy."

Roland looked up from Eloise to Pingbee; Pingbee nudged his head in the direction of Eloise and back toward Roland. Roland looked back and forth between Eloise and Pingbee. So much at stake, every minute passing, to be held up by such foolishness.

Roland threw his head back, laughing at the absurdity of it all. He bent forward again and slapped both hands on his thighs. Pingbee and Eloise stared in disbelief, for there was nothing funny in any of this.

"What happened? Lord Roland are you all right?" she sounded concerned. "Sir Pingbee, what happened? Maladies rising in Leinster?"

"What the fuck are you?" Pingbee snarled to her.

"What?" she asked.

Furious, Pingbee drew his sword.

Roland stepped in front of Eloise, trying to regain his composure. The plantain leaves dropped to the ground. Tears of laughter collected at the edges of his eyes. He wiped them away with the back of his left hand. He took a few deep breaths and tried to look at Pingbee. The wide-eyed look on Pingbee's face started him laughing again. Such a fretful, irritable man.

"Not the fitting demise of legend or story, such an ignoble death, mistaken as male lovers after all we've endured. Five impossible days. Shame upon me," he gasped. "Just a moment, I promise, slay us not!" and he started laughing again, until his emotional release ebbed.

None spoke, waiting on Roland.

With lightning reflexes Roland drew *El Muerte Rojo* and laughter ceased.

"Sir Pingbee, forgive me," Roland dipped his head, without taking his eyes off Pingbee. "My Maiden, I fear we're discovered, I can't keep your secret any longer," he said, stepping back. He extended his left fist.

Eloise couldn't believe her ears. Roland gave her a curt nod, toward his extended fist. There was nothing to do now but follow his lead. Eloise did as she was told, though every fiber of her body said do not. She placed her hand upon his.

"Maiden Eloise," Roland paused, as if searching, "the Maid Eloise Aine Echna of Dahlquin, daughter of the Lord Hubert of Dahlquin, Faithful Marcher Lord to High Lord FitzGilbert, Lord Hubert De Burgh and King Henry, and his Lady Aine of Dahlquin, daughter of the U'Brien's and our own Viking Slayer, Brian Boru," again Roland paused, glancing at the toes of Eloise's boots, then up her legs, her girdle, to *Cara* slung over her shoulder before resuming his introduction, "niece of the late Sir Reginald of Dahlquin, and neighbor and ally of Ashbury, Ireland, England and God, may I present to you Sir Pingbee of Wexford."

Eloise had imagined a reunion with Pingbee, with just such a formal introduction. In these imaginings her status was restored, she was wearing a surcoat in blue and gold, with the might of Dahlquin behind her. Wrath and hatred set aside for the moment, she swallowed her pride and attempted to curtsy with as much grace and elegance as she could muster on one leg and in such shock.

"Sir Pingbee, of Wexford," Roland continued, "I present you the Maid Eloise Aine Echna of Dahlquin. We travel in disguise, Sir, and again I apologize for the deception, but it's mandatory."

After a long, thoughtful pause, Pingbee appearing suitably impressed bowed, almost touching his forehead to his knees. He took Eloise's right hand and lightly touched his forehead to the back of her hand, saying "Acute surprise is upon me, my Maiden, but equal honor as well."

Eloise nodded, unable to think of an appropriate thing to say to this troublesome knight before her. She withdrew her hand slowly, as her mother would have.

"Let's build a fire, and I'll explain," Roland said.

"Maiden?" Roland said, dropping to a knee, indicating she hop on his back again. Eloise accepted, but found the comfort diminished with Pingbee in attendance.

"Young Alred," Roland said, rousing the squire. Eloise watched Alred lift his bloody head, squinting eyes glaring up at them. "Awake and meet your Angel of Mercy."

Again, Eloise slid down Roland's back, to have both Roland and Pingbee take her elbows, steadying her.

"Maid Eloise Aine Echna of Dahlquin," Roland started continuing with her long familial title, "this is Squire Alred, of Meath and Connacht, did I hear, and this is all I know of the youth?" After a moment of silence, Roland continued. "Squire Alred, Maid Eloise is a healer of some renown, and by a miraculous twist of fortune, she desires to tend to your well-deserved wound."

"Shut up and cooperate," Pingbee admonished his squire.

In bits and pieces Roland explained the whole story to Pingbee as they built the fire, added rocks, and dug a small pit that Eloise could use to boil water, emphasizing in great details their urgency, while Eloise tended to Alred. It was quite a good tale, beyond belief, Pingbee said on several occasions, but maybe it was so implausible as to be true after all. Who could fabricate such a tale?

Eloise studied Alred's wound. What was she thinking, to take on such a wound without her mother's guidance? Eloise was a healer-in-training. Her mother was a renowned healer or conjurer, depending on your source. Eloise suffered the same accusations. Exalted as a saintly healer and server of God or lambasted as the spawn of Satan with unnatural powers over life and death: a realm better left to God. Even male physicians were at risk if their patients were jealous or unhappy. As much as Eloise studied, she couldn't remember everything, and without her knowledgeable mother to guide her, Eloise usually fell back on the two things that stuck with her: whiskey or boil it. They had not a drop of whiskey, and unless she knew absolutely that it must be used fresh, when in doubt, render it down by boiling.

Eloise was flustered by the events of the day and Pingbee's inclusion in the secret to her true identity and their mission. Her body hurt, her mind raced, and her ankle throbbed. With the back of her hand she wiped away a tear and left another smear of road grime and ash. *Mathair*, she called in her heart, *Mathair*. Concentrating on healing brought her close to her mother in spirit. Eloise closed her eyes and tried to hear her mother's soothing, confident voice. *Healers are chosen, you can't turn away,* her mother told her. *Compassion is stronger than hatred. It sets us above the animals.* Eloise longed for her own mother to comfort and heal her wounds. Mayhap her mother needed healing... her mother persevered; Eloise must believe this. *We can do this*; her mother would say. *Help me, Mathair*, Eloise called in her heart, *by your will, help me.* Lifting her hands, she set to work.

With vision from one eye, Eloise snorted and started. Alred moaned and grunted, but sat still, never grabbing her hand or pushing her away.

Yet again, Eloise found she recalled the procedures and medicinals by singing the familiar chants and melodies. Words in verse came readily. How was it she could remember a lesson set to music so easily? Weren't histories set to music for the illiterate? Singing to the sick and ailing was soothing for the healer as well as the patient, entwining prayers and blessings to encourage recovery.

"Flesh can tear, and burn and peel,
It blisters, festers and all manner of color be,
For you dear doctor, use all your senses and feel"

Well, these didn't apply, so she quickly sang through until she came to the verse about stitching a tender wound.

"Attends to the wound with bone needle well rounded,
Close and tight the stitches must singly fall,
To tamper with God's own creation the surgeon is bound,
Greater mending and miniscule scaring are the hope for all "

Alred proved a braver patient than the bullying, hated coward of hours before.

"El, time is wasting," Roland barked at her. "The wood burns down."

Carefully she lined a hole with Tuath's leather cooking pouch. Hot rocks from the fire pit were added to the water-filled leather basin. With more prayers, she dipped the tail hair from Alred's own horse into the boiling liquid, softening it. Despite their earlier differences, Alred was a cooperative patient. His temperament had benefitted from the bloodletting.

"These small, neat stitches are necessary for better healing," she explained. It was a challenge to make the delicate stitches, not pulling so hard as to break the tail hair. Her ankle bit at her, her left side was swollen and both hands seemed unwilling to do the detailed work. Memories of her mother's counsel guided her. "It's not magic nor mystery here. This medicine kit belonged to a squire, like you," Eloise told Alred.

Stitches complete, she placed the poultice of plantain and spider web upon the stitches, still attempting to sing:

"Fresh and green, that's a start
Mash it to pulp, and pray from your heart
Gently the poultice upon the wound lay
When the good is done, take it away"

To bind his head, she sliced away half of his tunic.

"It's all we have," she offered, unhappy with the result, but lacking any proper bindings. "Is this too tight?" she asked, lightly caressing Alred's exposed cheek.

"Well, how is the boy?" Pingbee asked with concern.

Eloise took in a breath, "He needs to rest, you will have to stay here a day or two," she said.

"We ride with you to FitzGilbert. Won't you be staying to help me with him?" Pingbee asked.

"You know we can't stay," she said. "I'll tell you what to do." Too much time had already been expended here.

"We ride with you, we have an argument to settle," said Pingbee

"If you want him to recover, so Val can kill him," she added, "he'll need to rest at least a day or two, certainly until the fever is gone and then only if his ear doesn't bleed." His head was bound up like a grey sphere, with a puffy face protruding. "Didn't you hear a thing Lord Roland said? Dahlquin is under siege, we're at war, and you-" she left it unfinished.

"Bloody Hell!" Pingbee exclaimed.

"Sir," Roland interjected, "Dahlquin and Ashbury need good men such as yourself and the squire. Rest here," Roland suggested, "FitzGilbert's men and I will pass this way on our return to Dahlquin and Ashbury. After each is secured, or before, if you wish, we'll settle the breach between us," Roland said.

"Surely you received such training as a squire," Eloise asked, when Pingbee feigned ignorance to tending wounds, "survival skills in the field, sir."

Eloise went over some basic medical instructions with Pingbee. She showed him how to brew willow bark tea and attempted to show him how to change the bandage if the sutures ruptured and started bleeding again. Pingbee assured her it wouldn't be necessary. Eloise knew from the pale look on Pingbee's face, he couldn't do it. *Unbelievable*, she thought, *up to his knees in gore and he's happy, show him a clean wound and he vomits.*

"At least smell for malady," she suggested.

"I smell rain," he answered, looking up mournfully.

Eloise glanced up at the clouding sky. The long overdue summer rain had arrived.

"Alred, did you hear any of my instructions?" He'd have to take care of himself, Sir "Puke-up" would be of little help.

Alred roused, slowly opening his eyes, looking up at her. Eloise had her right side to him, close to his dry lips for his own voice was weak. "Alred?" she asked. "Alred, if you can't speak, shake your arm or leg for me. Alred?" she pressed.

He extended a hand, his gloved fingers tentatively touching her unswollen cheek. "Are you an angel?" he asked.

"I'm not an angel," Eloise said softly.

"Where am I?" he asked.

"Here by the stream, don't you remember?" she asked.

Stream?" he said, as if trying to think. Eloise could barely hear him. She leaned over to fetch the skin bag.

"Alred," she called softly. "Al-red," she sang, her voice rising and falling in a soothing, though nasal manner, "time to drink." His fingers flinched, and she placed the skin bag in his hands, pressing his fingers around it. "Open up, drink this."

Roland tugged at her shoulder to hurry, so she helped Alred lift the skin bag to his lips and drink.

"You are not-" Alred started. "Where is-" again he halted, obviously confused. "Who are you?" Alred asked, lowering the skin bag.

"Ellie," Roland called.

Eloise stared up. *Ellie,* had he ever called her by her familiar name? His voice was soft, but his extended hand shook impatiently at her. She took his offered hand.

Roland boosted her up into the saddle. She winced with the pain in her ankle and the tears started. Sir Pingbee came over to bid them farewell. She swiped at her tears with the back of her hand.

Roland stood with Reggie's shield in his hands. Saints preserve her, how could she have forgotten that? "It would be an honor," Roland said, "I have-" he didn't finish, but waited for her reply.

"I would have honor as well," she said, relief overwhelming any betrayal she might have felt. "By your gracious will and may blessing and goodness be upon you."

Roland slipped the shield on his arm.

"It's been an extraordinary delight to finally meet the young Maid of Dahlquin," Pingbee said. "Pleasure upon me to meet you again someday. Until then, I will give your greetings to your father," and he extended his hand to her courteously.

"It was extraordinary," she said sarcastically, taking his offered hand with equal courtesy. "However, it's unlikely I'll ever see you again," and she returned his hand to him. "Lord Roland will kill you, and my father will go to Hell and kill you anew," she said with a smile. "Until then, God be with you." She had not forgotten his earlier accusations. Bastard indeed. And rain coming.

Garth's head turned. Alred's gelding whinnied.

"Shit," Pingbee sighed contemplatively, rubbing his chin. He returned to Alred and kicked his foot. "Stupid, fucking thing to do."

Alred groaned and pulled his feet in, close to his body.

Roland reined his horse around, Eloise turned Garth and they headed to the road.

"Cheer up," Roland shouted, looking over his shoulder, intending to bolster Pingbee with the prospect of something exciting to do. "We're being followed by U'Neill's men."

"Eh? How many?" Pingbee asked with mock amusement, raising his fists before his face, ready for a fight, something between a scowl and a grin on his face. "Alred will make a stand, eh?" he said kicking Alred's foot again.

"Who knows," Roland answered, "cover our-" His voice faded, "backs," he said flatly.

Eloise turned, scanning behind them. Not a black raincloud. But just as unmistakable. The speed, the urgency.

"Riders!" she called. But she couldn't hear her own words.

"Tiomu's men," Roland barked. Artoch pawed the ground.

"Here?" Pingbee asked, but he was already running for his horse.

Alred's gelding whinnied again and all four horses responded with agitation.

Stroking Garth's neck, massaging his withers, Eloise counted, *three, five, how many more*, she wondered, her unspoken words catching in her constricted throat? *One more.*

Pingbee tightened his saddle girth, put on his shield and swung into the saddle.

"I count six," she said, "swords and staffs drawn," she added, taking *Cara* from her shoulder. Eloise drew three arrows and gripped them securely in her bow hand. Nocking one she cued Garth forward, bow slanted even with his neck. Tiomu's men were almost upon them. Soldiers, not knights, not all had chain mail, helms, or armor. The two men with staffs were charging in first, the remaining four, already four abreast, filled the roadway.

"Eloise," Roland said, his voice low, growling. "If it comes to a fight," he said, his dark eyes raking over her, "ride."

Before she could nod or answer, he continued, "Southeast. You can do it."

Ride, alone? True, she would rather out-ride danger than confront it. But alone? To the castle?

"Stay close, but be ready," he hissed as the six riders slowed.

"Greetings," Roland hailed, as the men rode up. "Seems a belligerent tiding, armed as you are," he said as the men surrounded them. Eloise wondered if anyone else detected the hesitation in his voice. It seemed Garth did, as he moved closer to Artoch, or had she cued him?

"What business?" Pingbee boomed, surprising Eloise with his calm, almost friendly tone. "Do I know you?"

"You do not," one of the soldiers said harshly to Pingbee, as he glared from Roland to her. He rode a brown horse, and had his sword drawn. "It's the black and grey we seek, the man and boy."

"Them? Why?" Pingbee asked. "Again, who are you to trouble us so?"

The six soldiers seemed to study the three people before them. Eloise noted three brown horses, one grey, one dun and one bay, and all were drenched with sweat, as well as the tethered, unridden horses already grazing. The riders of the grey, dun, bay and one brown had swords. The other two riders had stout wooden staffs. None wore discernible colors or identification. All six studied her and her companions. The malice in their travel-filthy faces scared her bone deep, and she had to look away.

"We've tracked these killers from Connacht," the soldier on a brown horse answered. "Murder in Connacht, trespass in New Pembrokeshire, slaughtered innocent men upon the road. Its troublesome company you keep, sir, I warn you."

Roland flinched. Eloise heard gasps from the people assembling on the road to watch this confrontation. Merchants, families, travelers like themselves.

"Eh, now you've done it," Pingbee grumbled to the soldiers. He glanced back briefly at Eloise with a reassuring smile. "You've got the whelps pissing themselves." He gave Roland a curt nod. "I traded those horses," Pingbee continued. "The boy you seek is there," and Pingbee pointed to Alred, who had somehow managed to stand, a long dagger in his hand. "And I'm your man."

Eloise couldn't believe her ears. Pingbee was assuming her and Roland's identities.

"I think not," the soldier said. "Black hair, black horse," and the soldier pointed at Roland. "Too many days I've heard tales of his murderous trek. And the one-eyed whelp." He pointed at her.

Pingbee shrugged. "One-eyed, one-eared. You were misled."

Roland sat immobile, and Eloise could only imagine the scorching stare Roland laid on this false accuser, one of Tiomu's minions. For it was the same burning hatred she radiated to Garth, who pawed the ground and bobbed his head.

"Find the sheriff," one of the travelers said, seated on a cart, his ducks, chickens and geese quacking, clucking and honking from their crates.

"Call the warden," another man said, standing just off the road.

The crowd had grown, Eloise noted: so many people, mothers and children. Two youths waved sticks, shouting to hurry their small flock of sheep from the congestion on the roadway.

"The warden could settle this," Pingbee agreed. "Go, summon him." The man turned on a heel and started to leave.

"But my quarrel isn't with you, good sir," the soldier said to Pingbee, his eyes wide with concern. "I bid you fair travel," he said, nodding his head awkwardly, probably trying to appear cordial.

"We travel together," Pingbee said, his voice turning harsh. "Don't presume to dictate to me."

The soldier grimaced, glancing at his companions, then back to Pingbee.

"I don't presume, sir," the soldier said. "Yet you travel with unlawful characters. Fugitives."

"We'll let the warden decide. El," Pingbee called to Eloise, "go with him," and Pingbee pointed after the retreating man. "Surrender yourself as a fugitive," Pingbee chuckled.

Eloise looked to Roland. All color had drained from his face, his lips were dry, his eyes glowed black with tension. He nodded his head in the direction of the retreating man. Eloise hesitated a moment before spinning Garth to amble after the man in pursuit of the warden. The men didn't move their horses quick enough to block her path. Was she to seek the warden and return, or make her escape to FitzGilbert? She glanced back, unsure, hoping Roland would give some clue. Instead she followed Roland's gaze to a man on a brown horse, his hard-eyed grimace fixed on her. "I want the boy," she read on the man's lips, feeling him move forward.

"I don't suppose you have a skin bag to share while we wait?" Pingbee asked of the soldiers. "You don't," he answered his own question. "Is there a wine merchant or alewife among you?" she heard him call out to the travelers at large.

The last word was barely out of Pingbee's mouth when the lead soldier stabbed the air with his sword. "Stop them!" he shouted.

Eloise spun Garth around to see the soldiers close in on Roland and Pingbee. The crowd erupted with noise, some running, others frozen in stunned silence. The grimacing man and another soldier broke off, cantering towards her.

She spun Garth again. Riding broken, with vision in her right eye only, Eloise leaned forward, "Go," cueing Garth, who leaped forward like a bolt from a crossbow. But what happened to the man she had been following? He was nowhere to be seen. *Southeast to Leinster.* That's what Roland said. *But...which way was that?*

Quang. The familiar sound of sword on shield. Her family was under siege again.

FitzGilbert and the security of his castle forsaken, Eloise swung Garth around. Arrow still nocked, she galloped toward her pursuers. Full draw. Loose.

She missed the rider, instead snipping the brown horse in the muzzle. The horse tossed his head in shock and pain, spinning and retreating to the circle of fighting men and horses. The result was unexpected but satisfactory as the rider, staff in hand tumbled to the ground. Eloise rounded back for another shot.

The fallen rider came up swinging the staff much faster than anticipated. Eloise sat deep on Garth as her horse tried to veer away from the staff. Artoch was there and Roland intercepted the waning blow of the staff with the shield, deflecting it. Then Artoch swung his hip over, pushing the man to the ground. But the man didn't fall. He slipped under Artoch, wrestling the staff to impale the horse in his round belly.

Eloise nocked another arrow and turning saw the bay horse and soldier upon her. Helm, chain mail, gloves. Her attacker was lifting his sword to strike. She drew, loosed. *Thwang*. Her arrow stuck in the soldier's shield. When she drew, he changed his mind about striking and defensively raised his shield. Eloise didn't have time to cross herself in heavenly gratitude. With her third arrow she shot the soldier in the thigh - a stinging inconvenience as she fled out of range of his sword - into another.

Seeing the sword so close, the hard, bone-splitting edge, she screamed, ear piercing and primal in its terror. She kicked Garth forward, away from the killing blades of her two attackers. She leaned forward, out of the saddle, as Garth leaped from between the converging soldiers. The bay horse shied and spun, making the rider's thrust ineffective. These soldiers were not riding seasoned destriers. The other soldier swung and his sword lodged deep into her saddle. Garth grunted, the force causing the horse to hollow his back and shorten his stride.

"Do not!" Eloise screamed, fearing her magnificent Garth might have been severed, urging him forward despite his potential injuries, for death was surely behind them. She felt the sword pull free, ready to strike again. Garth lunged away, putting some distance between them.

With Garth steadied, she nocked a fourth arrow, aiming for her attacker's sword hand. Draw. Roland, moving, was in the line of shot: he and a soldier, their hair flying, swords and shields banging.

She turned for another target, a man on the ground. Draw. Release. Nock. Draw. Release. Two arrows in his chest, yet he kept approaching.

She dodged, evading a mounted opponent, repositioning herself for another shot. Draw, not knowing where Pingbee or the other soldiers were, fearing at any moment she could be stabbed from behind. Loose. Miss. *Focus!* She commanded. *Don't think about anything but the shot.*

She and Garth again fled the attacking soldier while she nocked another arrow then turned to face her pursuer. Draw. Breath out. Loose. The soldier's sword hand jolted nearly over his head when the arrow struck, his feet jutted forward as his horse slid to a stop. Still holding his sword, he clutched his injured hand to his chest as Eloise reached for another arrow. She had seven arrows left. Grabbing a handful, she transferred five arrows to her bow hand.

Roland was in her line of shot again. *Damn it, Roland!* And his opponent: swords banging, faces grim, their horses pushing, claiming the very ground in a show of dominance. The vision in her right eye was so vivid, as if she saw with the clarity of an oracle. Faces. Like Roland, the soldier on the dun horse didn't have a helm.

"Go," she said, cueing Garth toward the men, nocking an arrow, a soldier in pursuit. Draw. Aim. His face, teeth bared, nostrils flaring. Steady. Just as she was ready to let her breath out and release, the man on the ground resurrected, staff pulling back as if to impale Roland, to drive him from the saddle. Her mind registered with the rhythm of a drumbeat, one arrow, one shot, make a decision. She couldn't stop the momentum of the attack, but having the power to do one thing, one significant action to help Roland spurred her.

Aim. Breath out. Loose. She hit the soldier in his arm, but the staff continued to pull back.

Nock. Draw. Loose. She hit him in the shoulder, as the staff started to plunge forward, towards Roland's exposed back, kidneys and ribs.

Nock. Draw. Loose. The third arrow stuck in his neck. Eloise watched as the staff continued up with diminished energy, glancing off Roland, who only leaned forward as the staff continued scraping up his back. With Roland out of the way, she had a clear shot at his mounted attacker. Nock. Draw. Loose. The attacker turned his head, her arrow tip penetrated his ear, and he toppled from his horse.

Reaching for another arrow, Eloise sensed the soldier behind her. Arrow in hand, she nocked and turned to shoot. Instead of shooting, she collided with a dark mass as the soldier bashed her with his shield. Eloise heard the arrow crack, felt the snapping of the shaft from her fingertips, *Cara* screaming in her hand as she fell back. Garth pivoted and lurched, working to keep her seated.

"Go!" she shouted, her legs out of position to cue her horse forward as she clung to the bow, still vibrating painfully in her hand from the percussion. "Go, go!" she shrieked, righting herself as the soldier shifted his own momentum, bringing his sword about.

Fear buried all pain, but her left leg hummed, like bees trapped in a hive, a steady reminder that she was vulnerable. Even so, Eloise cued Garth, believing her legs to be correctly placed. Garth jostled, struggled but didn't move forward.

Looking out, Eloise saw Pingbee's horse and one of the browns with a rider and staff, blocking Garth, crowding them back at her attacker. Glancing back, she saw her attacker, heard a roar of defiance, his sword coming at her, rather - two swords. She was paralyzed, death was certain. Her mind in some perverse cruelty conjured an image of an artistic red heart, painted on her chest, a bold target for the sword tips, heart, lungs, and ribs pierced and torn. Yet both blades went astray, missing her entirely.

Behind the attacker was Roland, head bleeding, cheeks puffing with exertion, his own sword buried to the hilt through the attacker's armpit and protruding out the chest. Both men were struggling and heaving as Roland tried to extricate his sword. Again Roland was out of sight, behind Reginald's familiar shield as he pushed against the groaning, foamy-breathed soldier, leaving a scarlet swath of blood across Garth's dappled coat.

Eloise and Garth were still trapped in a vicious vortex between the horses of Pingbee and his opponent before them, and the dying man and Roland behind. Hands trembling, nocking another arrow, she tried to place it on the spine of the soldier before her and loosed it. Another arrow, loose.

Pingbee's horse backed, then reared as the attacker swung his staff.

Grabbing another arrow, Eloise sucked in her gut as the soldier jabbed back and the end of his staff thrust past her before she could grasp the arrow. She felt the impact and heard the blunt *thud* as the staff smacked Garth on the head.

"Not Garth!" she howled, drawing another arrow, trying to rise up to place the arrow tip at the base of the soldier's hairy neck, severing his wicked, horse-abusing spine for all time. The man swerved and dodged. Following the line of his hauberk, down his torso, his thigh…unprotected by chain mail, chausses - Eloise aimed, breathed out, loose. He hissed and flinched; his staff useless against her arrow embedded in his knee.

"Eloise!" Roland shouted. "Get down!"

His voice, the words, the urgency. Eloise felt frozen in time trying to respond. It was as if she watched herself bend, lean forward, her right ear resting on Garth's taut neck. She heard the *shoosh* as the deadly staff passed above her, slicing the air instead of her skull. She felt Garth move, saw the tufts of brown hair, where Garth had bitten the soldier's horse. Next the fletch of her arrow then the soldier's boot passed before her eyes as he tipped back, his brown horse scooting forward, Garth right behind him.

Sitting up, Eloise scanned the road, reaching to draw another arrow. She found nothing. She looked down. Empty.

Roland battled the tenacious man on the ground, the staff bludgeoning and striking. Pingbee continued his battle with the soldier on the brown horse, her arrow still in his knee. Motion caught her attention: the grey horse and rider with his sword drawn. Before him on the ground, armed only with a long dagger and one ear, stood Alred.

Eloise and Garth moved in behind the mounted soldier. Alred was her charge. She had stitched his wound and he was her responsibility now. But she was out of arrows.

Her bow made a suitable staff, unstrung, but she couldn't unstring it from horseback.

Leaning forward she took the limb of her bow with both hands and slammed *Cara* over the soldier's head. She yanked back, pulling the soldier, hearing his choking cough, as his hand went to the bow digging into his neck.

"Back, back, back," she said to Garth, her seat cueing, willing her horse to help pull the soldier from his saddle as the soldier tried to right himself, his horse rocking back with the rider's weight. Eloise wanted to grab the other end of the bow, twist around then rotate the limbs so the string cut into his throat. But the end of the bow was lodged too tightly, choking the soldier all the same, with far less effort from her. As he slid from his horse, Eloise kept the bow tight on his throat, until he grabbed it with his free hand. Eloise was forced to release *Cara* lest the soldier use it to pull her from her saddle or hit with his swinging sword.

"Alred," she yelled as the soldier stood, sword ready, "grab *Cara*."

Eloise swung Garth's hip into the soldier, knocking him to his knee.

"Alred!" she shrieked, as Garth continued to step over the soldier. "Grab the bow. The bow!"

Garth sprang up, humping his back, the saddle spun, and Eloise saw the ground come up on her--grass, mud. For a moment she existed in a world of blackness and pain. Sound invaded, grunts, shouting. Forcing her head up, rubbing dirt from her good eye, she saw she was still in the saddle. Where was Garth? Alred had his boot planted in the soldier's back, her bow, the weapon of a coward, twisted around the helpless soldier's neck. *Cara* prevailed.

She heard hoof beats behind her. This wasn't over. Fear and shame gripped her with equal and indistinguishable force, crushing her into the dirt where she lay. She was broken and beaten, a crippled freak, a cunt not a cock. Far from home, in this hostile land of Leinster. *Never,* she shuddered. *Dahlquin will not die faceless.* With naught but the dagger in her calf sheath and the saddle as a shield Eloise forced herself to rise for what must surely be her last fighter's stance.

"Alred," she gasped in warning as the ground shook and she turned to face her attacker.

Before her a black destrier and Roland, sword and shield poised.

She felt herself try to smile as she lifted her chin and heard an unladylike snort. The saddle dropped from her trembling hand.

Unsmiling, Roland surveyed the scene around her. Satisfied it must be safe he dismounted and stood before her, his deep breathing the only sound between them. *Why so much anger upon him,* she wondered? *He was always mad at her, wasn't he?*

"Fucking, Holy, Saints on a Cross," Pingbee said. "Alred, brilliant idea."

Alred was still choking or attempting to decapitate the limp soldier. He tugged and twisted the bow once more before letting it drop with the lifeless torso.

"It was," Alred said, looking around until his gaze fell on Eloise, "her idea," he said, pointing a shaky finger at her, still panting with his efforts.

"Run out of arrows, did you?" Pingbee shouted, as he rode among the bodies examining the wounds as did some of the bravest onlookers from the roadside.

Eloise tried for another smile, or nod of acknowledgment. Still she couldn't speak. The words came too fast, too many and so inaccurate for the torrent of thoughts. After days of anxiety with Roland constantly looking over his shoulder, Tiomu's men had finally run them down, culminating in this bloody siege on a public roadway. Her memory could barely register the images of soldiers, sword blades, the sound of staffs and impacts and screams, and the crush of her helplessness to intervene, to end it. And now her only, utterly useless response was to stand mute.

"Satan's horns," Pingbee called. "Three arrows here. Three more. Ow, painful that," he made a squeamish face. "Is three your lucky number, El?"

She shook her head, then wondered if mayhap it was.

"Roland," Pingbee called, "we may live by the sword," Pingbee said as he swung his sword in a slow, round arc above his head, "but they died by her arrow."

Eloise found her tongue at last, "Book of Maitiu."

"This one's still alive, God have mercy," someone groaned, for the man was contorting upon the ground, unable to remove the arrow embedded in his ear.

"An avenging *Arch* Angel, you are," Pingbee said, chuckling then laughing.

Roland stared mutely from Pingbee to Eloise and back briefly to the strange faces of the stunned onlookers.

"Arch," Pingbee said, emphasizing the hard '*ch*' sound, and laughing some more. "Archery," he snapped when Roland and Alred didn't laugh with him. "Arch Angel. Were you struck in the head? Ah, you were, bloody fuck."

Eloise could hear people gasping and imagined the gore laid out before them. Instead of words, salivation flooded her mouth. She glanced at Roland and thought he looked as peaked as she felt. She and Roland bent over, hands on their knees, side by side, puking and coughing in companionable spasms.

"Aw, that's a foul victory celebration," Pingbee mocked.

Roland put his shield arm across Eloise, pulling her close. She felt the weight of Reginald's cracked shield and Roland's arm on her back, sheltering her. She leaned against Roland as they continued retching.

"The whelps are still pissing themselves," Pingbee grumbled.

DAHLQUIN CASTLE, DAY SEVEN OF THE SIEGE, 14th of June

"Hubert," Tiomu called over the gatehouse. "Let us talk, man."

"Wish to surrender?" Hubert answered back. His ranks laughed and jeered.

"I would offer you the same. Your cause is lost. Save your women and children at least."

"You have shown yourself a coward, and unchristian," Hubert shouted down. "Already my messengers take word of your treachery to Gerald FitzGilbert. You think to fool me with your own two stooges there," Hubert pointed to the staked bodies.

The day after Eloise, Roland and Reginald escaped the castle, Tiomu had three bodies prominently displayed upon tripods in full view of the castle. Reginald's body was easily identified by his garments, his leather girdle hung around his neck and his sword and scabbard lay down his chest. The other two were in braises and tunics only, their features unrecognizable. That was two days ago. Honor dictated that a knight of Reginald's rank deserved a burial, but instead Tiomu left him, a stinking, bloated corpse covered in crows and vultures and flies, like the other two men. As a sign that Tiomoid U'Neill was, like Hubert, a barbarian.

"Meath and Ulster will be warned, even your blood U'Neills will not stand with you against Connacht and Leinster."

"My stooges," Tiomu faked, "look again Dahlquin. It's your own men found dead under the falls, as you see them here."

"Oh," Hubert chuckled, "over the falls, was it?" She had escaped, and Roland, too. God's Blood, he was proud of her. He waved his arm and turned his back. "Let fly," he ordered.

A mighty crack split the air as the "Asp," Dahlquin's trebuchet launched another projectile. The huge stone whistled as it passed over the ramparts. "Again!" ordered Hubert before the stone hit. The men scrambled to reload.

Wood splintered, men shouted and ran. Tiomoid U'Neill looked on in horror as his mangonel lay in broken pieces.

"Here it comes again!" all eyes looked up to see a flaming ball descend upon the broken mangonel. The oil-soaked material exploded on impact and the rest burst into flames. Dahlquin cheered in defiance of the attackers. Crossbowmen and archers picked off as many attackers as they could, before order was regained.

Hubert hugged the trebuchet engineer, lifting him clear off the ground. Diligently had the man measured and calculated to take out the assaulting siege engine. Singing, dancing and more cheers filled the bailey, ramparts and every tower. Aine came out of the infirmary to see for herself. Hubert found her and hugged her. He fought to keep his own tears in check.

After a brief exchange of victory and celebration, Hubert directed everyone back to their posts.

"We must be vigilant. They will be enraged now. Don't get cocky. Back to your stations."

Tiomoid U'Neill also fought to bring his men back to order and position. One of his captains was already drawing orders for the carpenters and woodcutters to return to Hubert's forests for lumber. They would build another mangonel, as well as more siege towers. Resources were on their side of the barricade. Resources, but not time. Tiomoid U'Neill's plan depended on a speedy take-over. That had been his real gamble. He had, mayhap, been too confident in his traitors and his own might. How had Scragmuir been alerted so fast? His men had blocked all the roadways. Yet his messengers told him Scragmuir rode to the aid of their neighbors, Ashbury. He should have been on the way south in three days' time, but he wasn't victorious here.

The Danes and Norse Hebrides were vicious and capable fighters. All had gone as planned, yet Dahlquin stood. Where were the showers that drenched Connacht daily? Five days of clear weather allowed Dahlquin to rain fire upon him and his men. It was unheard of. Did the Heretic of Dahlquin and her spawn control the weather? Were the two ladies to blame for his misfortune? And that Welsh Devil, Hubert.

"Hubert!" he screamed up at the ramparts, hoping to draw his nemesis back. "Hubert!" he demanded. Furious at being ignored, desperate to strike back, to inflict injury and humiliation, Tiomu ran to Reginald's body, waving his arms, dispersing the black birds still feasting upon the remains. Tiomu removed the leather girdle and scabbard, releasing a swarm of flies. Fury upon him, he was oblivious to the rotten stench and putrid decay. "A thousand curses upon Dahlquin!" he shouted, stabbing Reginald's groin repeatedly, but the carrion eaters had already mutilated Reginald's manhood. "Satan's curse upon you, as your flesh blisters away," he wailed, frustrated again, as his men tried to pull him away. "Hubert," he growled, thrusting the sword into what might have been Sir Reginald's mouth. One last, foul act of desecration, but impotent without Hubert to witness it.

An hour later in his tent, Tiomoid U'Neill held council.

"All is not lost," Tiomoid said with force. He had been rethinking his strategy. He glared at each of his assembled officers.

"We have the resources," one acknowledged.

"Scragmuir might still be persuaded, for the hatred of Dahlquin, to side with us," offered another officer, his bloody right arm in a filthy sling.

"Once Ashbury is secure. A show of Irish faith for FitzGilbert, but Dahlquin defeated in the bargain. And three allies for you, Lord," said the first.

"The tide might yet be turned," said another.

"Connacht united," Tiomu said, a wry smile slipping across his battle-stained face. All he needed was one castle, one stronghold to negotiate from. He was U'Neill, he had ties with Scotland as well as Ireland. Louis needed brave men for his crusade. Tiomu would have many soldiers to offer, once he was instated. Just one castle.

Tiomu lifted his wooden cup in toast. His officers joined him, drinking down the watered wine in noisy gulps.

ON THE ROAD, LEINSTER

Eloise watched the large drops make little craters in the dirt at her feet. As Pingbee had observed, rain arrived, in slow, large drops. She stood slowly, her arm still touching Roland's.

"Alred!" Pingbee shouted. "Fetch El's arrows."

Alred looked up, tottered and collapsed. The binding on his ear was saturated with blood.

"Fucking Hell," Pingbee muttered, scanning the faces of the encroaching travelers. "I need a good lad to retrieve the arrows," he called out, "and a bottle or skin bag. I can pay. And where is that damnable warden?"

A young, barefooted boy ran up to Pingbee, "I'll get your arrows, sir."

Pingbee looked the boy over, small, with a snaggle-toothed smile.

"May you have goodness," Pingbee said.

Another shoeless boy ran up and they both nodded their heads, eager to help the victors, it seemed.

"Step lively. Clean them good, and I'll find some token of appreciation," Pingbee smiled at the boys, waving a hand to send them off. "Aqua vitae!" Pingbee bellowed. "We've six, I correct, twelve horses, tack and armor to barter. But I'm a cheap bastard the thirstier I get."

Roland stroked her hair, but with his studded glove, all he managed to do was pull the loose ends. Eloise hadn't notice until now her cap was lost, and her ill-kept braids had come undone in an unraveling mess.

"Can you brush it at all?" Roland asked, as she ran her fingers through the bramble of her once glorious tresses. "Just get the knots out and let it hang, aye? We're in Leinster now, close enough to end this disguise." His right cheek twitched in an attempted smile. Or was it a grimace? Was he still furious with her? Why had he held her so? He was so moody and unpredictable. Even so, she put her arms around him and let herself fall against his chest, taking the weight off her injured ankle. She fought back the tears as his shield arm squeezed her close, hiding her from view.

"Roland!" Pingbee called.

Pushing the shield away, Eloise and Roland both looked up at the knight on horseback. "Ah, may you have goodness, bless you sir," Pingbee said to a man passing him a half empty skin bag. Pingbee took a long drink from the spout, and Eloise was amazed he didn't dribble a single drop. Then he tossed the bag to Roland.

"Tell me that isn't the best fucking drink you ever guzzled, Roland," Pingbee said wiping his mouth with his sleeve. "Grand as a big thumbed whore."

After a long drink, Roland held the skin bag to her, but she shook her head.

"That will put fletch on your shaft, El," Pingbee laughed. "Well, fletch," he corrected, looking away. "Take my excuse, such shame upon me, Maiden."

Was he blushing she wondered?

"At least rinse your mouth," Roland encouraged, holding the skin bag to her.

She lifted the spout to her lips and let the drink pass into her parched mouth. The liquid burned her split lips and she feared she would breathe fire like a dragon as she swirled the distilled whiskey, not ale, about her mouth quivering with pain. Unable to bear the spirit touching her lips again. she swallowed hard as warm tears coursed down her cheeks.

"Roland, you and El- Eloise, need to go, too risky here," Pingbee said, recovered from his impropriety. "Warn FitzGilbert. I'll take care of this mess, the warden. Hand that bag back," he asked, reaching for it.

Eloise was relieved to see Garth and Artoch grazing together on the tall grass just off the roadway. Alred's horse wasn't far off. She whistled and Garth popped his head up, green strands hanging from both sides of his busy mouth. She whistled again, and patted her leg, another cue for him to come to her. He chewed a bit more, his side heaved, and he returned to grazing. He ignored her. Given all she had put him through these five long days, she could understand his reluctance. Eloise limped towards him, two steps before the pain upon her ankle nearly dropped her to her knees. He looked up, waiting, and she called it even.

"Wait, I'll help you," Roland called to her and she sat to wait, massaging her aching leg, willing the pain to subside.

"May you have goodness, the blessings of a thousand saints," Roland said back to Pingbee. "I agree, safest for us to keep moving."

"Twelve horses, tack and weapons," Pingbee said, his voice gone soft as he glanced at the scene around him.

Eloise realized that was probably greater wealth than he had ever possessed. And so it was a fortune, to her and Roland as well.

"I'll have an accounting for you when next we meet. Either here along this very road, or in FitzGilbert's Castle."

The eager boys returned, clutching eight and five arrows between them, and two broken pieces.

"El, how many arrows did you have?" Pingbee asked, but Eloise couldn't register his question.

Garth walked over and dropped his large, dappled face into her hands, but something was wrong. He was so…submissive, defeated.

"Ellie, we have to go. Can you ride?" Now it was Roland intruding on her, tugging at her. "Bleeding Saints," he said, stroking Garth's side, looking at the horse's belly.

She followed his gaze and saw the slash on Garth's girth line. Of course, when the soldier lashed out with his sword, he sliced the girth on the saddle.

"It's not too deep," Roland said, pushing the hair back with his fingers so she could see the wound. "Truly, it's not so deep. But fucking Satan's horns."

"And his eye matches yours, El," Pingbee called out, having ridden over to them. "Here," he held out her bow.

Eloise looked again at her magnificent stallion's face. Almighty, Pingbee was right, Garth's left eye was swelling shut as her own. Curse that damn staff, curse Tiomu and all his foul, unholy, treacherous mercenaries. Not now, she commanded herself, curses and oaths of revenge could wait. Garth. What could she do for him?

Eloise turned her attention from Garth's eye and reached for her bow. *Cara.*

"May you have goodness," she said looking up at Pingbee, then remembered, "fifteen. I had fifteen arrows." She took them from the boys, "May you have goodness, and blessings."

Holding the bow, she lifted an edge from her tunic and squeezed down the length of the string, removing the blood and flesh. She repeated the cleaning, then slipped *Cara* over her shoulder.

"Take one of the other horses," Pingbee was saying. She would not ride another horse. She would not abandon Garth.

"Nay," she heard Roland answer, before she could decline herself. It was like she was suspended outside this scene, Roland and Pingbee talking while she tried to calculate what to do.

"Maiden of Dahlquin," Roland was saying, taking her hand, pulling her attention away from Garth again.

She turned to him, ready to snap, to scream, to lash out herself. She tried to pull her hand away, but Roland tightened his grip. Wrath and hatred reared and kicked, like two unbiddable horses dancing on a precipice. The heat was spreading, embracing, promising to end her suffering...it was a false promise, wrath was weakness. She wouldn't succumb. She looked from Roland to Pingbee, and found they were looking to her. Pingbee's expression, once so loathsome, had transformed. She saw concern and loyalty, the same feelings that had brought her back to the fight. Her fight. She inhaled and felt power inflate her lungs.

"You would do me great honor if you wished to ride with me. Artoch's rump and my waist are at your service, Maiden," Roland said.

She felt the power growing in her hands as she stroked Garth with one, while Roland held the other. Dahlquin was strong.

"Your choice," Roland said. Eloise felt the strength in his gentle tone. "But we must ride."

"Hurry up," Pingbee ordered. "This lot is already pilfering our loot. Make haste, maiden."

"May you have goodness, Lord," she said to Roland as she turned, facing Garth, waiting for a leg up.

"If you have a change of heart, my offer stands," Roland said taking her ankle and lifting her up to Garth's broad, bare back.

"Go, go, go," Pingbee said, as Roland mounted up. "In a few days' time," he called to them as they rode southeast, once again on the road to High Lord FitzGilbert's Castle.

The rain was brief and passed quickly. They had ridden for miles, and only now was her mind beginning to put together the pieces from the horrendous battle with Tiomu's men back on the road. She had done nothing for Garth, there was little to be done. She shuddered, remembering Alred.

"Change of heart?" Roland asked, looking hopeful.

"I have not, may you have goodness for your concern, Roland," she added.

"Cold upon you?" he asked. "Get very wet in that shower?"

"It is not, but again I wish goodness upon you kindly."

"Well, I did, and it would be much warmer for me, if you share my saddle," he said.

"Do you think Pingbee will locate a healer for Alred?" Eloise asked. She didn't know if Alred's stitches had ruptured or if the blood was merely seepage. "He was unconscious when we left," she added. "And I didn't take time-" Guilt threatened to seep over her like the squire's blood.

"Fuck Alred!" Roland snapped. "A few hours ago you wanted him dead. Cold and misery are upon me and you drone on about Alred."

"Sorrow upon me," she started, stung by his foul language, and misuse. She paused a moment, waiting, hoping he would apologize.

"Fucking waste of time. Stitching him up. When we should have been riding." He glared at her. His expression black as a rain cloud.

Eloise tucked her chin and glared back at him. How dare he speak to her in that tone?

"You cut his ear off, remember? He was bleeding to death."

"As you wished. Damned wastrel. When did you lose your heart to him?"

"I never," Eloise paused. "I told you. I don't know why. I couldn't turn my back. Healers-" she didn't finish.

"Healers... Black mag-" Roland stopped himself. "And if you hadn't attacked Pingbee."

"I didn't attack Pingbee."

"You drew upon him, threatened to murder him," Roland growled, startling her with his anger. "And no fighter's stance," he barked, raising a finger in warning, blunt English blurring his speech.

Eloise turned her head. She knew she had been wrong, but still she fumed at the unfairness of it. She felt helpless and angry. Her family name had been grossly insulted, and she was unable to do anything about it. There was no one to stand up for her, or her family. What happened to their friendship, their camaraderie after the battle? She trembled, remembering the feel of his hands, his lips…now Roland insisted on making her acutely aware of that over and over again. She had no one. She was displaced. If something - not something, precisely - if her parents were killed, would she retain Dahlquin? Would the High Lord FitzGilbert or the king reinstate her, unmarried, seventeen? Would she find herself utterly dispossessed, without even her good name? Was life without Dahlquin worth living? Now she was, what? Convent fodder? Convents only took wealthy women. Would FitzGilbert or the king stake her? *None of those*, her parents would survive. She would seek help, and they would send for her. The name would not die here, with her.

"You were fighting over a grouse," she retorted, keeping her chin neutral. "Was that worth dying for?"

"Of course not. You understand nothing."

"I understand when my family-" she started but he cut her off.

"If you had kept your place and been still-"

"I would never tolerate such insults to your mother," she said, her voice becoming shrill.

"Be quiet," Roland said. After a long pause, he added, "By your will."

Eloise flared at this. Her one open eye squinted with anger and her features pinched up on her right side. She pursed her lips together, then exhaled hard through her teeth, and pursed her lips again. Roland could read the vulgarities in her expression. Eloise was fighting hard to behave, and it tempered his anger. He suppressed a grin. It would be discourteous to make sport of her now. Damn, that girl could talk. Not just impertinently, or out of turn. Her perspective could be so different from his, yet she presented such reasonable arguments. A pious blasphemer, devoted seditionist, and the most fascinating and provocative woman he had ever crossed paths with. And the visage in her eyes.

Roland took a deep breath, recovering from his own volatile upheaval. Of course, he was angry, furious. Couldn't she see what she was doing to him? He had never been so fucking, heart piercingly scared. Not in his life, nor for his life. His breath quickened with the memory of that intense, blood-pounding fear. And even before he had a chance to explore this new realm of Eloise-induced terror, she was prattling on about Alred. With nary a word to his own suffering on her behalf. Fucking, God damned, cockless Alred! Roland felt a roar building. Gone was the suppressed smile of moments passed.

Unconvinced that Maiden Eloise wasn't a heretic or succubus, Roland was perplexed by her, drawn to her as a siren's call. Was it death he would find with her, or life? Life. She was life, and to deny that would be death. Who or what she was, he may never know, but he was destined to love and protect her. He had seen in it her eyes when first they met.

The remaining miles to the castle were, as Roland had said, even more populated. She and Roland were never alone. Village upon village, towns or estates, they all blended together. One walled city extended to another, as if Hadrian's Wall had miraculously been completed in Ireland. Less open space and wilderness, more contained, with cultivated woods and parks. And so many people. Eloise was amazed at how many people made up this land. Oh, of course, she had heard stories. But to see them, nameless and faceless in their multitude, it wasn't as she had expected. The wilderness of Dahlquin called to her heart, and she felt the wildness within herself.

For miles they rode without talking, in the summer twilight.

Poor Garth. He was hurt too, his left eye swelling shut from the blow of the staff, just as hers was swollen shut from the mercenary's club. And that sword wound to his girth. Lord be merciful, that may take weeks to heal properly, assuming bad humors didn't infest his proud hide.

"Good boy," she cooed, stroking his wet neck. She hugged him with her legs, hoping he wouldn't take it as a cue, but as the loving gesture she meant it to be. His broad, sweaty back was comforting and familiar underneath her. "You magnificent beast."

Hurting inside and out, Eloise found solace in riding yet again, the rhythm and pulse of the horse unclogging her spirit, opening her mind rather than her eyes. She remembered Sir Pingbee. Belligerent, rude, caustic, yet he was willing to trade his life: for Dahlquin. Even Alred had taken a stand with her.

"We can still make it." Roland said, interrupting her meditative state. "At this pace, I think we can get there in the earliest hours. Shall we push on?" he asked.

Shall we push on? He was asking her, why should he ask her? Didn't she displease him? Who was he? Where did he stand? All these thoughts flooded her mind as she returned to the present. Eloise looked up at him. Roland sat before her on his horse. His handsome dark face looked at her with anticipation in the dim summer twilight. *Anticipation. Happy or sad?* She stared at him, studying him, looking for clues to something just beyond her understanding.

And it was all gone. Her mind cleared of all the philosophy and prayer and turned to FitzGilbert's castle. Hope for her parents' relief, salvation for her kinsmen. Eloise had her immediate destiny before her. Tonight.

"With your blessing and will," she answered without further hesitation, riding on with Roland. *He is a magnificent beast*, she thought to herself.

The darkness brought Eloise in closer to Roland, seeking protection. Crickets chirped. The occasional frog added his love call to the chorus of the night. A few hours ago, she would have been angry for the weakness and betrayal to herself. But those thoughts were behind her now. Eloise cued Garth to Roland's right side as they rode on.

In their silent closeness, Eloise sensed an increasing feeling of dread as they drew closer to the castle of the High Lord FitzGilbert. Five days they had relentlessly pushed forward, completing a two-week journey in that time. There were some who had spanned the distance in six days changing mounts, but she and Roland made the journey in five days, despite many miseries and one day in the village. With their mission nearly completed, she felt a different anxiety and thought Roland did too. Eloise had strived for this hour since fleeing from her home. Now, she couldn't understand her feelings.

Roland felt distress. The cause rode next to him. In less than an hour, he would turn over the Maiden Eloise to the guardianship of High Lord FitzGilbert. This mission complete, he and FitzGilbert's men would devise and implement a plan to liberate Dahlquin and Ashbury, thus defending Ireland from U'Neill and his northern mercenaries. Roland would give her up, submit her to another man's care. It was High Lord FitzGilbert of Leinster. Who better to protect her, but Roland was loath to surrender her. The dereliction of duty stung at his sense of honor, but his heart and body spoke with a greater urgency. His Dahlquin headache had become a Dahlquin heartache.

The travelers made their way through the darkness. This close to home, Artoch was a steady mount, and Roland gave him his head. The tired, hungry horse was anxious to return to familiar territory. Garth followed his companion; the miles had brought these two stallions into a state of mutual companionship based on fatigue. Then Eloise felt Garth's back tense and his head jerked up. Heads bobbing side to side, both horses moved with a stilted step.

Wolves howled.

The wolf song was so close.

"Fuck," Roland muttered, hand on his sword handle.

"Melodious," Eloise whispered, wondering why he was so distressed. "It's like a Gregorian chant," she said, feeling her heart lift, as if the wolves were welcoming her, forgiving her the deaths. For wolves understand.

Then another yodel, farther off, but just as melodic.

"Beautiful," Eloise said, feeling the song resonate within her.

Roland said nothing but gave her a hard, wary glance, intensified by the dim light, as if he thought she might throw her head back and answer them.

Roland didn't hear it, but the wolves told her: Dahlquin stood.

The horses softened and Roland and Eloise continued riding in silence on towards the security of FitzGilbert's castle.

Roland pulled to a stop on a small rise to share with Eloise one of his favorite views of the castle, pointing through some oaks, stunted by the rough conditions on the hillside. There was little to see in the dim twilight, but some fires and torches illuminated the parapets. They were here. Once the home of Roland, and now the sanctuary of Eloise, the castle lay before the homeless pair. Roland never saw his estate in Ashbury. Eloise was displaced while the siege of Dahlquin raged. Not sure where they would find their homes in the next few months, they sat on their horses in silence.

"Wait," Roland said, pivoting Artoch so he and Eloise faced each other, side by side, faces dim in the evening light.

Eloise could barely draw breath as her heart pounded with the closeness of Roland. Darkness made his presence less threatening and she didn't move away.

Removing his glove, he caressed a strand of her mussed hair with his fingertips, until his hand came to her shoulder. He took her arm and pulled them together, kissing her on the lips.

Her heart seemed to stop. Although bruised and cracked, her lips tingled with new sensation.

Roland sat back, placing his thumb on her chin and resting his pointing finger under her chin. Her head tipped back, and her lips parted. Kissing her again, his tongue eased into her mouth. He held her chin so she couldn't retreat.

Frozen in her first kiss, Eloise was alight, captivated by the smooth sensuality as his tongue explored her mouth. Her throat constricted with anticipation, as her shoulders went slack with submission. Unfamiliar tingles ignited within her nipples, and she arched with the sensation, seeking more, almost pulling away from Roland's grasp.

He held her chin firmly, yet so gently. The strength of his hand spread warm currents through her body, the dawning rays of sunlight upon the cold, dark horizon of her new life. Eloise melted into his touch, sinking into the depth of him, being swallowed up. For the first time in five days she felt safe. For the first time in ages, she felt as if she belonged.

He withdrew his tongue, his lips, and his grip on her chin. It was over. Eloise was bereft. A flood of emotions washed over her, she thought she might fall from her horse. He had kissed her. She felt as if a piece of her maidenhood had been taken, it was so intimate. *Had she kissed him back? What should she have done? Had he enjoyed it?* She didn't know how to kiss. Ecstatic and worried, she wondered: *Had she sinned? Did she want more?* Her mouth was still open, and she closed it, savoring the memory. His name formed in her mind, his taste and strength so real, but she was unable to form the word.

"I will speak with your father when I return to Dahlquin," Roland said, moving away and directing them both toward the castle below.

His voice sounded raw but sure. Eloise knew he meant their marriage. Willingly she, *Cara* and Garth followed him.

THE END

ABOUT THE AUTHOR

Born with the horse gene, my first spoken word was "worsey" for horsey. I was drawing, painting and spinning tales of my imaginary equines for years. My Medieval Fetish is nearly as long. I am still married to my high school sweetheart and while raising our daughter and son, I researched the Middle Ages into Middle Age and beyond. I now live the horse dream and we run a boarding ranch in Santa Cruz County. 'Riting, riding, reading and sometimes 'rchery make up my four "R's". The journey continues to find a voice, discover the inner hero and help others find theirs.

For more information on Anne or my books, please visit my website: https://annembeggs.com/ or email: ambeggs@hotmail.com

UPCOMING BOOKS

Archer's Grace is Book One in the Dahlquin Series

Please look for more books coming soon

ABOUT THE ARTIST

Matthew Ryan is both an Historical Illustrator and a Fine Artist. Matthew's work has appeared in Osprey Publishing, Medieval Warfare Magazine, Desperta Ferro Magazine, and Channel 4's "Walking Through History with Tony Robinson" (in the UK). His prints are popular with collectors and history enthusiasts worldwide.

His work combines detailed and painstakingly researched elements along with a painting and drawing style that is both naturalistic and descriptive. His work gives the viewer both an impression of the times and the humanity of his pieces combined with an eye for capturing the landscape, thus putting the viewer in the action. After graduating with a BA Hons Degree in Illustration, Matthew worked for over ten years as a designer before combining his passions of history and art and deciding to work as an historical artist/illustrator. He believes that drawing and painting what he loves and understands has given his work an extra degree of credibility and his passion for what he does can be seen with each image.

The depth and quality of his work builds with each new piece. Matthew looks forward to some exciting new commissions in the future. Matthew is a keen archer and for many years has enjoyed shooting what is now known as the English Warbow. He is also a fletcher, making his own Medieval type arrows similar to those found and excavated from the sunken Mary Rose warship.

Please find more information and view Matthew's artwork on his webpage:

http://matthewryanhistoricalillustrator.com/

Anne M. Beggs